Two Roads Home

Two
Roads
Home

DANIEL GRIFFIN

Published with the generous assistance of the Canada Council for the Arts and the Alberta Media Fund.

 Canada Council   Conseil des Arts   Alberta
for the Arts   du Canada   Government

Freehand Books
515 – 815 1st Street SW   Calgary, Alberta   T2P 1N3
www.freehand-books.com

Book orders: LitDistCo
8300 Lawson Road   Milton, Ontario   L9T 0A4
Telephone: 1-800-591-6250   Fax: 1-800-591-6251
orders@litdistco.ca   www.litdistco.ca

Library and Archives Canada Cataloguing in Publication

Griffin, Daniel, 1971–, author
Two roads home : a novel / Daniel Griffin.

Issued in print and electronic formats.
ISBN 978-1-988298-21-4 (softcover).
ISBN 978-1-988298-22-1 (epub).
ISBN 978-1-988298-23-8 (pdf)

I. Title.

PS8613.R5355T86 2017   C813'.6   C2017-903724-2   C2017-903725-0

Edited by Barb Howard
Book design by Natalie Olsen, Kisscut Design
Cover photo by Carey Haider
Author photo by Kim Longenecker
Printed on FSC® recycled paper and bound in Canada by Friesens

For my parents,
Sharon Thompson
and Malcolm Griffin,
in thanks for their
everlasting faith,
love and support

There is a crack in everything.
That's how the light gets in.

LEONARD COHEN

APRIL
1993
Vancouver Island

PROLOGUE

The five of them, four men and one woman, left their van in a dirt pullout below Bedwell Pass on a Sunday morning in early April. They walked a torn twist of logging road into a clear-cut, little piles of dead wood stacked here and there among the stumps. The slope rose and the logging road started into a belt of cedar and fir only to end abruptly at a churned-up mound of earth — bulldozer, backhoe and dump truck idle at the road head.

Across the cut and into the undergrowth, no trail here: the five just followed the logging road's trajectory. Last night's rain had given the earth a rich, damp scent, ferns and salal, the tangled greenery of the forest floor left beaded and glittering. Trees clung to the slopes, trunks dressed in lichen and moss, knotted roots rammed together. Where the land ran level some of the fir trees stood as thick across as a small car.

Up to the crest of the pass and the five set camp and staked their two tents — bright nylon domes tucked under the arched boughs of a pair of Douglas firs. Bird calls cut the air: larks,

/ / / / /

thrushes, warblers. Wind rustled the treetops and set the old wood creaking. Sunday afternoon and the land around them held an angelic ease.

Pete Osborne shimmied a spindly tree trunk and tied an anchor rope a good twenty feet off the ground, did the same with a second rope on a tree ten yards off, then hoisted a hammock between them, pulled it high enough that it would be hard to cut down. He did the same with their second hammock then climbed into it and gave a yodelling call through the forest. Further along the ridge, Art Kosky hoisted a bedsheet, tied it between two cedars, the words "The Road Stops Here" painted across it, black letters stark in the unruly greenery.

Late afternoon by now, but the light was still good and so Pete called the others around, had them stand in front of the banner and set his camera on a nearby rock. Timer set, he hopped back, stood with the group, pushed the red bandana up on his forehead and smiled as the shutter snapped: the five of them in their twenties huddled at the peak of Bedwell Pass — Pete Osborne, Art Kosky, Fay Anderson, Jeremy Dunn and Derek Newfeld.

Pete gathered wood that evening, worked his way along the ridge for anything dry, and they built a small fire in front of the larger of the dome tents. They ate baked beans, bread and cheese. Before darkness settled, Fay set the remaining food into a single pack, looped rope through its straps and hoisted it to keep bears from their supplies. Walking away she did a little pirouette. The others had turned in and so Pete was the only one to see it — a single turn on the forest floor that made her bobbed hair flare as she neared the tent she shared with Art.

/ / / / /

Daybreak Monday morning and the sound of chainsaws rose from the valley below. The five ate breakfast looking down into the forest, listening to the shrill call of two-stroke motors broken every few minutes by the creak of a falling tree. The backhoe's bucket clanged down against bedrock, the road crew at work. Later in the morning, a blast charge shook the hillside and loosed drops of rain from the branches overhead.

Midway into the day, a man from the company building the logging road hiked up the ridge. He wore a hard hat and a reflective yellow jacket. He asked about their intentions. Art stepped forward and pointed to the words painted on the bedsheet. A faint wind billowed the fabric. The man asked how long they planned to stay. No one answered. Art folded his arms. He had a fiery stare, his gaze steady, his mouth pinched and tight. The five had agreed: no words, no negotiations, and in the end the man turned and walked back down the ridge.

On the morning of the third day, they awoke to rain. Low clouds hemmed the world close and the steady patter dulled the buzz of chainsaws from the valley below. The five waited out the day seated in their tents. Come evening, the sky cleared and Pete shouldered his camera and set out along the ridge. The air was cool and damp. The moon stood high in the sky, a slip of a crescent. He balanced his camera on a branch, set a two-second exposure and held it steady.

On the morning of the fourth day, three students appeared on the ridge, a woman in a bright yellow parka, two men with her; one had a shaved head that showed a fine dark stubble when he removed his wool cap. They'd heard an interview on campus radio: Fay and Art talking about their plan, inviting others to join. They'd hitchhiked up-island and had asked around to try to find the place. No one they'd talked to seemed to know, and they'd spent a night in a clear-cut two miles further north. In the morning they'd followed the sounds of the road crew, the occasional dynamite blast.

The students set a pair of pup tents on an open stretch of dirt. They were eight now. This is how protests grew, how movements swelled into a force to be reckoned with. It buoyed the five, these three new faces.

Late on the fifth day, when the man with the soft voice and the reflective yellow jacket climbed back up the ridge, all eight stood silent across from him. The man raised a sheet of paper, read from the injunction and said the police were going to come clear them out and make arrests. The road crew was closer now. The rusty yellow cab of the backhoe stood partially visible through the low branches, a single dump truck behind it.

The eight managed a fire that night using wood they'd kept dry. Jeremy broke open a cigarette, formed a small plug of tobacco and burned it, an offering to the trees.

Next morning the chainsaws and backhoe fell silent and the singsong whistle of a lark rose through the still air. Wind coursed the ridge, tipped the spires of the ancient trees and carried with it voices from the valley below and then the sound of bodies blundering through undergrowth: feet on the dead branches and broken wood scattered across the forest floor.

Pete had been in one of the hammocks since daybreak, Jeremy in the other. Jeremy had shaved. He sat with his back straight, ready, poised. He was the first to spot the uniformed figures. He called out, said they were coming, his voice brisk, authoritative. Pete raised his camera, set his eye to the view-finder. The nearest of the men was breathing hard. Behind him, a second officer dragged a stepladder through the undergrowth. The shutter release snapped. Pete rolled the film on, returned his eye to the viewfinder.

Fay zipped one of the tents closed and stepped onto the nurse log behind the blue nylon dome. As the first officers neared the top of the pass, she turned towards Pete and Jeremy. The shutter release snapped. "We're not leaving," Fay shouted and Pete took another picture, Fay in profile, leaning forward, chin thrust out, defiant, her dark hair just long enough she could tuck it behind her ears. He took a picture of one of the students. The three had decided they wouldn't get arrested, and they stepped aside, one after another, as the officer with stripes on his arm raised a bullhorn and began reading the injunction.

"You'll have to drag us out of here," Art called, but the man with the bullhorn carried on.

Fay stretched out on the nurse log and let her body go slack as the officers began to move through the woods. Two took hold of Derek and hoisted him. The camera's shutter snapped again, caught Derek's face, angular and sharp, all bone structure, wire-rimmed glasses slipped down to the tip of his nose.

The students had helped Art loop a chain around himself. They'd locked his body to a tree, but the police had bolt cutters with them. They'd come prepared. Pete watched Art through his viewfinder, jaw set, face flushed, body straining against the chains as an officer clamped the bolt cutters down and broke a link with a ping.

The man with stripes on his arm approached Fay. She lay still. She wouldn't walk. She refused to even stand. One man bent to take hold of her legs. Another grabbed her arms. Pete leaned over the edge of his hammock to snap a picture of her body slumped between the two men.

The top rung of a ladder thumped against the cedar tree at Pete's feet and an officer began to climb up out of the under-brush. The man's face drew level, deep-set eyes, red cheeks, a dime-sized mole on his neck. "You mind if I put my camera away," Pete said. "Just so nothing gets broken?"

/////

Art was the last to be pulled in, the last to be carried down-hill once the police had cut the chains he'd wrapped around his torso. Three officers hauled him along a churned-up path, muddy now from so many feet. Halfway down, the man holding his left leg slipped and Art's backside hit rock.

At the head of the new logging road, a man with a TV camera stood on a mound of torn-up dirt. Art raised his head and looked directly into the lens. A few men in work clothes stood by watching. One or two cheered. Farther along the road, a cop had Jeremy by the arm and a single reporter walked alongside, Dictaphone out. Jeremy talked as he walked, hands confined by cuffs, unable to gesture, unable to animate his words. He leaned towards the reporter though, angled his towering body.

This was early spring, before the protests further up at Clayoquot Sound got really heavy, before the RCMP was overwhelmed. On this day, they took the time they needed, held the five for twenty-four hours, then released them to await trial on their own recognizance.

/////

Jeremy walked four miles up the logging road to get the van from below the cut. Twenty-four hours since they'd laid their bodies out across that ridge and already the backhoe had carved its way up into the trees. Two of the ropes that had supported the hammocks still hung visible twenty feet or more off the ground.

The van waited on a dead end logging road. A scrawl of graffiti across the back said "Hippies go home." A few more steps and he realized the windows were gone. Cubes of shattered glass lay scattered across the ground. Jeremy stepped on a shotgun shell as he walked around to the driver's side. The tents, sleeping bags and hammocks formed a jumbled pile beside the van. The students must have done that, gathered their belongings. Jeremy fished the key from his pocket and picked the broken glass from the driver's seat as best he could. The engine started no problem. He dug around in the gear box, found reverse and turned the van downhill.

A blast charge went off as he descended, a rumbling explosion that sent a dull impact through the valley.

That same day, the five started for home, east back over the island's spine and then south. They stopped at a gas station outside Ladysmith, and Fay bought an afternoon paper. She called for everyone's attention as she returned to the van and held the paper out in front of her. The front page showed two men in suits. Jeremy had to squint to make out the headline at a distance: "Committee: 74% of Old Growth to Open."

Time stretched, elastic and slippery, until finally Pete said, "The fuckers."

**JULY
1993**

The ferry's lower vehicle deck smelled of diesel and salt air. Rain had splashed in through oval portals and now lay in pools around the tires of semi-trucks and delivery vans. As he made his way out to the ship's wall, Pete Osborne passed a squat motorhome and then a car with a U-Haul trailer. The air held a chill here where portals gave a view over the straits to low-lying islands. He zipped up his jacket and set his hands in his pockets.

They'd parked the station wagon midship and close to the rail. Fay Anderson sat on the passenger side, head down, hands in her lap, one cupped over the other.

Pete watched her as he stepped around to the driver's side. She'd pulled her knit cap low over her brow. Head bent, it was hard to make out the expression on her face. She seemed to be concentrating, intent on whatever she had in her hands. As he opened the door and settled into the bucket seat, she looked over at him. Both her hands were empty.

"You want to go up on deck for some air?" he said. "Maybe get a coffee."

"I don't need another coffee. It'll give me the jitters."

"A walk might help, a bit of fresh air. I can keep an eye on things here."

"We're nearly there. Not much point now."

Pete squeezed the steering wheel. Even after his walk around the passenger deck, he still felt nervous. He flexed his wrists, turned his hands in and out. A faint bituminous smell laced

/ / / / /

the air. Pete had noticed it the moment he'd pulled the car door closed, a thin scent that caught in his throat, and now he twisted about and looked into the back. A tartan blanket covered most of the crates.

"You notice that smell? Like tar or something."

He started to lower the driver's side window but Fay touched his arm. "It's better we just keep it inside." Her fingers lingered there above his wrist, and as Pete rolled the window up, his whole arm warmed to her touch.

They'd started into a narrow channel and through the nearest of the portals, the rock face of an island came into view, craggy and grey. A little tree grew from the cliff edge. It had a bowed trunk, a thin head of foliage. It seemed remarkably close, like someone might be able to reach through the portal and touch the rock face. The ship's horn sounded with a long deep blast.

"It'll be a relief to get back on the island," Pete said. "To have this part done."

"The end of the beginning."

Pete tried to smile only it felt forced, his face strained. He pinched the bridge of his nose and squeezed his eyes shut. He wanted to say something funny, wanted to make her laugh, wanted to shake off these nerves and return to the sunny mood that had buoyed them last night on the trip out.

Passengers had begun to descend to the vehicle deck. The hold's fluorescent lights fluttered and brightened. A radio played somewhere nearby, a couple of car doors opened and closed. A truck engine roared to life then fell still.

Two vehicles ahead of them, a little girl tried to pull a dog into a camper van, only the dog balked, shifted its weight onto its hindquarters and sat. It was a collie, mostly black with a white streak on its forehead. The girl tugged and the leash strained its neck.

"I used to have a dog like that one," Fay said. "His name was Max. We had him until I was eight or so then my dad took him off the leash when we were in the woods and Max dashed after something in the underbrush. We never found him, but eventually we got another one, Max Two, another collie. He wasn't the same though. Max Two was lazy. He got fat."

"That dog makes me think of this Russian experiment to try and domesticate foxes," Pete said. "It took years, maybe thirty generations, and then the foxes' ears went soft, their fur mottled, their tails pointed up instead of down and they developed a white patch of fur on their foreheads, just like that black and white one."

"How did they do it?"

"Not by being nice, not by acclimatizing the foxes or anything, they just shot the ones that got upset when people came too close. One generation after the other, shoot any that bark or yelp. That's how you turn foxes into dogs in thirty years."

The ramp clattered as they pulled off the ferry and into the light of a grey afternoon. Wind found chinks in the doors and made a breezy whistle as they accelerated.

Over an hour of driving before Pete and Fay were back by open water. The road breached forest for a view of a wide bay, a scoop out of the land, a deep ocean blue. Another half a mile and Fay had them turn inland. She seemed confident about the directions. She pointed, guided them onto a dirt track. "It's called Thurlow Road. There's no sign but that's what it's called."

Shortly after the turnoff, the radio began to cut out. Eventually Fay switched it off and a moment later they found the yellow Pinto in a pullout, parked at the edge of the forest. Pete slowed, eased in behind it. Both the Pinto's front doors swung open at the same time. Derek Newfeld stepped out of the passenger side, his black hair tousled, unruly, wire-rimmed glasses perched high on his nose. Art Kosky emerged from the driver's side, his leather jacket unzipped, arms spread wide, a gesture of welcome.

All the way up Thurlow Road Pete had wanted to say something in this, his last moment alone with Fay, but she now had the passenger door open. Pete unlatched the driver's side. Outside the air was cool and damp, and he could feel it in his chest, as if there was a weight to the air.

On the other side of the station wagon, Art slipped an arm around Fay's waist, pulled her close and kissed her. Pete watched without wanting to watch, unable to look away until they broke apart.

"We thought you might have made a wrong turn," Art said. "We were starting to worry."

"It's just a slow car," Fay said.

"Did you get everything?"

Pete walked around back, opened the station wagon's hatch and lifted the tartan blanket. "One hundred and eighty pounds."

They all leaned close then, a moment in wonder. Derek gave a long, low whistle as he edged the lid off the nearest crate.

"We took everything they had," Fay said.

"This is good. This is enough. Plenty. Divide it into three. Esterway Ridge, List Cove, Dutton. Sixty pounds per." Art tapped a hand on the hatchback glass. "Derek, you take lookout at one end of the road, Fay, you take the other. Pete and I will stash the extras. Eight crates. We can do that in two trips, three at most."

Fay backed off a few steps. She folded her arms and pulled her knit cap low. Pete watched her walk away, an easy rhythm to her gait. Up above, wind passed through the trees and set branches rustling. Art laid an arm across Pete's shoulder. "Turn that frown upside down."

"Me?" Pete said.

"Everything's set. Not a thing to worry about."

"I didn't say there was."

Art pulled him close, tightened his arm around Pete's neck, a headlock, a squeeze. Pete coughed, his breath tight until Art released him.

"Jesus, Art." Pete touched his neck, his Adam's apple.

"Quit it with that hangdog look, for Christ's sakes."

Art leaned in and hoisted the first of the crates. He passed it to Pete, set a second on top.

"You and Fay get along okay?"

"Of course. We get along great."

"No, I mean did you have any problems? Did anyone see?"

"No one. We had to cut the chain on the gate. The magazine just had a padlock."

"No one saw?"

"Not a soul."

The trail broke through a stand of fir trees and followed a gentle rise past a rocky outcrop thick with moss and lichen. Art led. The dirt trail was hardpacked, the soil parched. Old footprints showed in the long-dried mud. A startled bird fluttered up through the branches as they passed.

Two switchbacks and the trees thinned, the trail offered a brief view of the river valley. Another hundred yards and Art stepped off the trail completely and waded into a bed of swordferns. Pete followed and when the ground levelled, he spotted the opening — a loose rock formation, a dark gap in among the stones.

Art had to duck to get inside. He carried in the first two crates, stepped deep enough in that he was fully in shadow. A moment later he leaned out and Pete passed him the next two crates. He shook his aching hands, flexed his fingers. "How did you find this place?"

"Helped a buddy move some irrigation equipment up here to grow marijuana."

"Think it's dry enough?"

Art stepped back into the open, raised himself to full height and lifted a pack of cigarettes from his jacket pocket. "We have a tarp. We could bring it on the next trip."

Back at the road, Pete opened the station wagon's trunk and lifted the next two crates just as Fay's voice cut the air. "Car coming."

North of them, the sound of an engine rose, tires on gravel.

Pete set the two crates back in the trunk and slammed the hatchback. A truck rounded the bend. Art was already on the ground but it was too late for Pete. The truck driver passed with two fingers raised, a lazy wave, the rest of his hand still on the wheel. He had a beard, glasses, the passenger beside him wore a baseball cap. The truck was there and then gone around the next bend and Pete released a long, slow breath.

"That wasn't much of a frigging warning." Art stood, dusted himself off. "The whole point of standing watch is some advance warning."

"Should we move it, should we go somewhere else with all this?"

"Three actions and it'll be gone. Six weeks, eight at most."

"The guy looked right at me."

"You should have gotten down."

"I was closing the hatchback. You think it would have been better if he got a look in there?"

Pete reopened the trunk. The crates felt heavier this time and as they walked, the trail seemed longer. Partway up, Pete propped the crates between his knee and a tree trunk and rested, shook out his hands and arms. Below him, the road cut a pale streak into the side of the hill.

/ / / / /

Once the eight crates were stacked and wrapped in the poly tarp, Art and Pete returned to the dusty shoulder of Thurlow Road. Pete leaned against the station wagon's hood. Art set his fingers in his mouth and gave a sharp whistle.

Fay rounded the bend to the north of them, head back, hands in her jacket pockets. "You find that little cave okay?"

"We could have done with a bit more warning, Fay."

"The moment I heard the truck I called —"

"By the time you called, I could hear it, and I was standing way over here."

She stopped then. Ten yards off she stood in the centre of the gravel road. "I warned you the moment I heard, Art."

"You should have been further along the road then."

"She shouted," Pete said. "We heard her call out. I heard her call out."

"I heard her too." Derek was behind them now, car key in hand. "We going to head out or what?"

"The point I'm trying to make is that lookout is a serious job. Fay didn't take it seriously and this is what happened."

Fay stepped past Pete, past the Pinto and opened the station wagon's passenger door. "You had a good few seconds warning and if you couldn't cover up in that time, it's your own damn fault."

"I got down in time. Pete was the one still standing there."

It was times like this, when knots of tension bound the group, that Pete most missed Jeremy — level-headed, rational, a calming influence.

Fay pulled the passenger's door closed and Pete raised his hands. "We can't be arguing about this just now."

Art stooped and looked in through the station wagon's windshield. "I guess she's travelling with you, Pete."

Derek unlocked the Pinto and opened the driver's door with a low creak. "You know how to get to the quarry, or do you want to follow us?"

"Fay knows the way," Art said. "Better you guys wait here a bit, keep some distance between the stolen car and the one with the dynamite."

Fingers gripped around the door handle, Pete looked in at Fay, watched her through the glass while behind him the Pinto's engine turned and started.

Pete settled into the driver's seat next to Fay. Her knit cap lay in her lap. It had left her hair dishevelled and wild, and a matted clump stuck up above her forehead.

"Art thinks we should cool it here a while," Pete said. "Keep a distance between vehicles."

The Pinto's tires cut gravel with a low crunch. Pete watched the car turn down Thurlow Road. The sound of it passed into the distance. "Art's being an ass," Pete said.

"I don't want to talk about Art."

"I need to talk about something. I need distraction." He held up his hand. The fingers trembled, his whole hand shook. "All day I've had these creeping worries only they're worse now."

"What worries?"

"Worries about what might happen. Worries this could be a mistake."

"That's called nerves. Everyone's got nerves."

"It's more than nerves. I'm frazzled," Pete said. "I'm panicked, I need to —"

"Feel how cold my hand is." She reached for his hand and squeezed it. "My whole body's chilled."

"Are we making a mistake here, Fay?"

"It's all going to work out. Tickety-boo, just like Tammery Mill, just like Westlake."

"This isn't just like Tammery Mill or Westlake. This is different. This is —"

/ / / / /

"I'm nervous too, Pete. Okay? Look at me. I'm keyed up. I'm all . . ." She stopped then and he turned towards her.

"You look fine," Pete said. "I mean, you look great."

"Art is being an ass."

"I was nervous back at Tammery Mill and at Westlake too, but this is worse, that's all I'm trying to say."

"It'll get worse until it's over and then you'll feel better. Tickety-boo," she said.

"My mother used to say tickety-boo. It meant put on your pyjamas and get off to bed."

Pete shifted so he could see into the back as he said that. The tartan blanket lay twisted among the remaining four crates. "We could actually make up a bed." A glance at Fay and he said, "I mean, there's a blanket back there, if you're cold. Or if you want a nap." He turned towards the crates again just as Fay leaned between the seats. It brought them face to face and for a moment she was close enough he could feel her breath, a tremor against his skin. A wild, long heartbeat and then finally he looked up to find her wide brown eyes focused on him. An inch between them and then nothing at all and their lips touched and he wasn't sure if he'd kissed her or she'd kissed him, but her lips parted, soft and generous, and the double thud of his heartbeat rose above all other sounds. She pulled away, but only slightly. Her forehead touched his, and it seemed to him a question. "Is this . . ." he said. "I mean are you —"

She pushed forward before he could say more, kissed him again and cut off his words, pressed herself to him. This time his arms circled around her. She smelled of pine needles and damp air, but above that, the car still held that acrid bituminous scent from the wooden crates.

Fay slumped back into her seat and began unbuttoning her jacket. She pulled it off, lifted her sweater.

Pete unbuttoned his own shirt, tugged at it, extracted himself, and then she was on him, her body across the seats, their limbs tangled as they kissed. He pulled her against him, her bare skin on his, her breasts against his chest, only her foot caught on the gearshift. "Wait," she said. "I'm caught. Hold on." She started laughing and he tried to roll the seat further back, felt for the controls along the side and finally reclined it. She bit him then, teeth sharp on his shoulder.

"We could put the seats down in the back," he said. "Or spread the blanket across the grass."

Hands down, she began to work her jeans. Even as she kissed him, she pushed at them, and he did the same, squirming about, inching his pants down.

Four wooden crates of dynamite sat just above the crown of Pete's head, sixty pounds of it, and he couldn't stop thinking about that. Even as Fay moved on top of him, above all else, he was aware of the explosives stacked inches from his head, the damage it could do, the insanity of it all, the two of them in this car, the rest of the stolen dynamite in that cave, the possibility another car might roll around the bend.

Afterwards, Fay lay on top of him, but only for a moment. As his own breathing settled, Pete leaned forward to kiss her only she pulled away before his lips touched, rolled off him and into her own seat. She groped about for her clothes and in the end, they both stepped out of the car to dress. Fay didn't wear a bra, just an undershirt, a long-sleeved shirt, a cotton sweater, her army jacket. Pete watched as she dressed. He wasn't sure what to say, wasn't sure what this meant, but he didn't want to ask. Maybe he was just supposed to know: quick, impulsive, dangerous, meaningless. A distraction.

Fay stepped into her underwear, her jeans, shimmied her hips before she did up the button and fly. Dusk had settled, light slipping from the land. "Is my hat somewhere here?" Her words were so soft she might have been speaking to herself as she bent to look under the car. They both walked around it twice, looked through the grass at the side of the road. "It must be in there somewhere."

They groped under the seats, felt about on his side and hers. Eventually Fay settled in the passenger seat. "Maybe we should just get going," she said.

Ten minutes to the highway and they were on sealed road. "You think Art might have left any cigarettes in this thing?"

"We have sixty pounds of dynamite back there, Pete."

"I'm kidding. A joke." He reached out to take Fay's hand, but she raised it just then and scratched her ear.

They listened to the radio for a good while, one song after another until they reached the West Coast Road and reception weakened again. As darkness fell, it took the warmth of the summer afternoon with it. They drove with the windows rolled up and the heater on. The road was all dips and turns out here, pavement laid along the contours of the land and then no pavement at all, just dirt and gravel.

They rolled westward along the coastline until Fay pointed to a logging road that rose into lumpy hills. "Here," she said. "This is it." Pete turned and soon Fay had him turn again, onto a secondary road. Dust billowed behind them and their tail lights lit it pink as they travelled into the Kludahk, through dense beds of second-growth trees, up across clear-cut stretches of land.

Pete was lost, his sense of north and south, his instinct for where water lay, it was all jumbled, but Fay guided them, turn after turn through a warren of roads. Art was right. She knew exactly where it was. "One more turn."

"Last chance to back out," Pete said.

Fay didn't answer. It had been a joke. Mostly a joke. They both knew Fay wasn't the one chased by doubt.

She shifted a little in her seat, turned partway to face him. "Straight ahead now. We're almost there. It's on this road."

The station wagon's headlights fell across Art and Derek side by side behind the stolen Pinto. Derek turned his head away. Art raised a hand and sheltered his eyes from the glare, and then

Pete said, "I know what you see in Art, but I sometimes wonder if you're happy with him."

She opened her door. "Now isn't a good time to talk about this."

Art dropped his cigarette and stepped on the butt as Fay emerged from the car. "This is it," she said. "If anything goes wrong, this is where we meet."

The station wagon's headlights still shone and as Fay stepped out towards the quarry pit, they lit the side of her body, her leg, the hem of her jacket, her bare head. Art followed, footsteps noisy across the bed of gravel while Pete sat still, wishing he'd walked after her himself.

/ / / / /

They got back in the cars just after two in the morning. Fay stepped over to the Pinto where Art held the driver's side door partway open. She glanced Pete's way as she got in the passenger's seat. Pete stood still in the open air, fist formed around the station wagon's door handle. A few yards off, Derek bent and unlaced one of his boots. "I got a pebble or something stuck in here." He shook the boot. "It's been bugging me all day."

"I think you're coming with me, Derek."

Pete turned the ignition with a heavy foot on the gas. Derek slid in beside him, sat where Fay had been. Ahead of them the Pinto's tail lights brightened. Pete tried not to think about Art and Fay. He needed a clear mind. He had to focus on the task at hand, but that thought just brought all the day's worries back: a cinch across his chest that shortened his breath and made his heart tremble.

Derek was restless. He couldn't stop fidgeting and he chattered as they drove — about the breathable microfibre in his boots which he untied, took off and retied while Pete drove. He talked about water treatment and desalination programs, about irrigation and selling water to Mexico, distracting them both, or trying to, his voice fluttering through the night.

Pete kept his attention fixed on the road, on the pool of light in front of them. At the last curve before they reached the Greer-Braden warehouse, the Pinto pulled over and Pete stopped behind it. The road widened here, where another secondary road joined it to form the trunk line, a direct shot down to Port Thorvald and to the logging camp there. Derek swung his door open.

"You're going to stand watch here?" Pete asked.

"It seems the right place."

"You think you've got a good enough view along both branches of the road?"

"It should be alright."

Pete rolled on downhill. Another hundred yards, the trees ended and a chain-link fence came into view. A single floodlight illuminated part of the gravel lot and the warehouse's concrete wall. The Greer-Braden sign stood on the periphery of their headlights. It said "Esterway Ridge Warehouse" and had the company logo — a red and grey swirl.

He was here now. It was underway.

CHAPTER
3

The St. Stephen's choir sang into the empty cathedral, their voices rising from the stalls. Through the transept and into the great hall, the music held a life of its own above the pews. The words were Latin and unfamiliar to Tab Harper, but the rest of the choir knew "Magnificat Mysterium" and they carried her along, their voices woven tight, Tab's soprano notes squeezed in among them. She kept glancing down at the sheet music, and guessed at the right places to breath. She did her best at pronunciation. In front of them Mr. Novak hunched over the lectern, hands dancing at shoulder height like his fingers were on strings, each pulling some thread of the tune. He pointed now towards the bass section and his fingers drew them in. The men thundered across the score, voices heavy and reverent. The treble line returned above it, light and airy, carrying the bass singers higher. They were like a dancing couple now, hand in hand and moving together but battling over the lead. Novak straightened. He stepped to the side, palms raised. Voices trailed off. The music faltered and stopped, silence in the cavernous church, a cough. Someone near Tab cleared her throat.

"You're singing like turkeys. Gobble gobble." Novak was Slovakian and his accent made it sound like "hobble, hobble." "This is a song of hope and joy. It's not a lazy drone of boredom. Bass and tenor, what kind of an entrance was that? You sound like hippos rising from the swamp."

/////

The woman to the right pressed an elbow against Tab's arm. Tab gave a quick glance and then shifted a little to give space, but it was tight. There wasn't room. "Staccato bites," Novak said. "Quick, sharp. Excitement." He sang a few lines, lowered his voice for the introduction of the bass line. As he sang, Tab realized the stout woman next to her didn't want space. She'd wanted Tab's attention. Tab glanced over now, ready to smile, but the woman was looking down at her sheet music. She was about Tab's age, but already wearing reading glasses. Novak had made a few introductions last week before Tab's first rehearsal, but she'd never been good with names.

"See," Mr. Novak said. "Easy enough." His hands rose. Open palms turned the statement into a question.

A murmur or two, a couple of nodding heads in the body of the choir. Tab shifted her weight, one foot to the other.

"No." Novak touched a finger to his ear. "You don't see, you hear." There were laughs then. One of the tenors had a particularly theatrical laugh, bulbous and deep. Novak tapped the lectern and raised one hand. "Again from the top."

/ / / / /

After rehearsal, they had coffee in the reception hall. Tab poured herself a cup, black and bitter. The fluorescent lights of the hall made a crescent moon arc on its surface. Tab raised the cup to her lips and looked about. The only name she was sure of was Novak's. A loose knot of men had formed on the other side of the room. It was a squat-looking bearded man who had the outrageous laugh, only now it didn't sound quite real. Maybe because it was so loud. And who could find so many things so funny?

The woman who'd been next to Tab at practice stepped to the urn. Her reading glasses hung by a chain around her neck. An accent of gold lamé shimmered through her sweater. It had a geometric pattern to it. She extended a hand. "Tabitha, right? I'm Alice. Wasn't Novak in fine form today?"

"I've only just started. This is my second —"

"Of course. But you must have heard."

"He does seem a little, I don't know, eccentric."

"That's an understatement, my dear. June Balfour was in his house for tea once. He has a whole wall filled with plates and platters, all of them with pictures of Elvis Presley. Have you sung in a lot of choirs?"

"One. And that was just a two-bit choir compared to this. Then we moved. It's been a year and I thought it was time to do something."

Tab had auditioned in this room almost a month ago. Five or six others had also tried out, and they'd all lined up on the little stage. Only she and a younger man with a bass voice had been added to the choir. That man was standing in the corner now speaking to Novak. He was about Tab's son's age. His hands had trembled something fierce. At the time she'd thought nervousness the cause, but even now they were quivering. His face too reminded her of Peter — narrow cheeks, low chin, even the slope of his shoulders and his loose curls.

Tab was starting to think maybe she should leave when the door at the far end of the room swung open and a priest stepped in. His belly strained his black shirt. He had a well-groomed beard above his clerical collar. "I could hear you lighting up the cathedral all the way from the rectory. Glorious," he said to everyone and to no one. "Absolutely glorious."

At the table, he lifted a coffee cup and Alice reached over, depressed the urn's lever while the priest held the cup. "You're just here for the coffee, not the singing." Alice spoke in a low voice, a gentle poke between friends.

"You do brew a better cup than the ladies in the rectory." The priest spoke quietly too, and Tab turned as though to leave, but Alice touched her elbow.

"Reverend Simms, this is Tabitha. She's new in town and just joined the choir."

"If you were one of the voices I heard this afternoon, we are lucky indeed." He extended his hand. He had an intent gaze, and for a moment, Tab felt like she was being studied. "Will your family be coming to the service on Sunday?"

"My husband will, but not my son. He's away from home." She stopped herself.

"Whereabouts does your son live?"

"He's out west. He's a student."

An embarrassed warmth hit her face as she spoke. Simms's eyebrows rose, and she was sure he knew this was a lie. Simms rocked heel to toe. His bulk swayed. Tab had never been a good liar. And she hadn't needed to say anything just now. He'd only asked where Peter was. Probably just being polite. Tab wasn't sure what Peter was doing these days, but he certainly wasn't at university.

Simms set his cup on a saucer. "I look forward to meeting your husband, Tabitha."

He turned and as he walked away, Alice whispered, "Some people say Simms is a communist."

Tab laughed. A priest, a communist. It was like announcing he was a nudist.

"They even say he went to Russia."

"Oh Lord."

Alice gathered the dirty coffee cups and took a tray of them through a nearby set of double doors into a kitchen. Tab picked up the remaining cups and followed.

"Is he really?" Tab said.

"What?"

"A communist and a priest."

"It's a rumour."

"If I told my husband there was a communist priest here, he might not even step inside. Should we wash these dishes?"

Alice looked down at the empty sink then batted her hand. "Nah."

A sound cut through the night, a creak, a metallic sigh like the opening of a gate. Pete leaned around the corner of the warehouse, held still a moment and looked out into the pitch. Behind him, on the other side of the fence, Art was revving the station wagon's engine. Fay called, shouted to hurry, and Pete started across the lot, but another sound caught his attention — footsteps this time, feet on the hardpacked gravel. Pete turned. There was someone on the north side of the warehouse. Art blared the station wagon's horn but Pete stood waiting in front of the warehouse, in front of that single storey block of a building, the yellow Pinto with sixty pounds of dynamite parked alongside it.

A man stepped from the darkness into the floodlight's beam, a man in uniform, a security guard, thick moustache, glasses perched on his nose. For a moment he stood still, taking it all in — the cut chain-link fence, the yellow Pinto parked against the warehouse wall.

The station wagon's horn had fallen silent. Fay stopped yelling. The world seemed to slow except for the timer in the back of the Pinto, its low buzz held faint in the air. Set to two minutes but not long left now. "Stop," Pete yelled. "Go back. Get away." The night watchman stepped forward though. He stepped in the wrong direction and the floodlight picked up silver threads from his uniform, stitches along pockets and epaulettes. Pete waved, shouted again and just then a concussive

/ / / / /

roar shook the ground. Pete's eyes went white with the burn and he was off his feet. He fell to the ground. Debris rained down: pebbles, dirt, bits of concrete, the shell of the Pinto lit bright with flame. The floodlight blinked out and a great shock of electricity lit the world. Torn wires flipped about, they sparked and hissed. A massive hole gaped in the wall. Papers fluttered through the air. A low-toned drone had taken hold of Pete's head, and his breath was gone. He propped himself up and tried to inhale. The timer must have been off. That wasn't two minutes. One at most.

Pete made it to his knees then dizziness seized him, and he had to focus his mind just to keep from collapsing. A bright glare of white lay over the centre point of his vision, but somehow, through the burn spots, when Pete raised his head, he was looking right at the night watchman, at his body on the gravel near the foot of a fallen electricity pole. "Hey," Pete croaked. "You."

The air was acrid, harsh and chemical. Pete's chest heaved and he began to cough. He looked over his shoulder. All three were yelling at him only their voices seemed distant. "There's a man here," Pete shouted, but his voice sounded odd in his head, muted. "There's somebody here."

Art, Fay and Derek must have already seen the night watchman though. Of course they'd seen him. Pete made it to his feet and stumbled forward. "Can you hear me?" Pete's right leg gave way and he stopped to shake it out. Sparks popped from where power lines lay across the fence and its string of wooden posts. It might be electrified. There might be current running through the whole thing. Derek hammered on the flank of the station wagon. Fay waved, beckoned. All three were still hollering, but Pete shifted his attention to the night watchman, stepped past the Pinto's flames, jagged and wild. A burning heat radiated from the wreck. Chunks of concrete lay strewn across the gravel. Beyond, in the darkness of the warehouse, industrial equipment stood twisted and tangled, metal torn and bent out of shape. From this corner of the compound, he could see out to the far side where a pickup stood with its door open, a light on in the cab. The man had been here all along. In a truck, in a parking lot behind the warehouse.

No blood showed on the night watchman's body, at least not so far as Pete could tell, but the way he lay was unnatural, his body oddly twisted, his right arm tucked beneath him.

"Can you hear me? Can you speak?" Pete bent, fell to his knees and lifted the man's wrist, dug his fingers in. A few feet away, the torn end of an electric cable hissed and flashed. No pulse. What was he going to do now? What in God's name could he do now? Pete loosened the clasp on the man's watch, held his fingers lower down, and there it was, a faint tick, a sign of life. Pete concentrated, waited until he was sure then shouted, "He's alive. I think he's alive."

Art now stood at the gap they'd cut in the fence, waving and hollering, but the cut-away piece had fallen back into place and a spark leapt from one of the cut links. He touched the fence, a single hand on it, then he stumbled back shaking his hand, bent over. The fence had a current running through it. Chain-link fence and wooden posts around the compound and it was all electrified.

Hard to make out what the others were shouting at him now, all three hollering over each other and the ringing in Pete's ears blanketed it all.

That blast would certainly have been audible in Port Thorvald. If the night watchman had called this in, someone would be here soon enough, police and firemen. Pete bent over the night watchman again. Dangerous to try to move him, but he touched the man's chest, set his hand there. "Help is coming. You just have to hold on." The fires provided a flickering light. Wind lifted a sheet of paper and turned it about.

A whole parking lot out there, empty save that one truck.

The night watchman might have been dozing in there, unaware while they cut the fence and drove the Pinto right to the side of the building. Everything had gone wrong. Everything had gone so terribly wrong.

A flash on the periphery of Pete's vision. Lights in the distance, trembling against the night sky. "They're coming," he said. "Someone's on their way."

He lifted the man's wrist again and the pulse felt steady.

Vehicles headed this way meant that if Pete was going to go, now was the time. Beyond the chain-link fence, the station wagon had its headlights cast up the road. Go now and he'd be leaving the night watchman, leaving a man clinging to life. He turned his head, bent close and felt the faint play of air across his own cheek. The man was breathing steadily now. Something bright and metallic winked at Pete: the guard's watch. He picked it up. The watch had some weight to it, a nice timepiece. He fumbled with the uniform's breast pocket only it was sewn shut. The uniform didn't even have a real pocket, the button on it just a decoration. He slipped the watch into the man's pants pocket and felt a folded sheet of paper and a set of keys in there.

Pete could hear the sirens now, even over the ringing in his ears, and he turned his attention out to the road. No sign of the station wagon. A moment of panic, a lurch in his chest. They'd gone. They'd driven on, up the road or back to the quarry. "I'm coming." Pete stood as he shouted. He tried to focus on the flashing lights: two vehicles, bright lights swooping through the night. The others must be waiting for him up the road. They'd just needed to get out of sight. He had the night watchman's keys now. Maybe he could wait until whoever was on their way up hill figured out how to cut the electricity running through the fence and then he could slip out the back. Dark enough Pete might be able to dash off unnoticed.

He walked to the fence line and touched a link, just a tap, then he touched it again, took hold of it this time. The metal felt warm but it carried no current. He turned towards the road and the cut section of fence. Charge out through there and he might find himself standing in the headlights of a cop car. He backed deeper into shadow, walked to the gate. Keys in hand, he had to concentrate to get one in the door latch. Second try and the lock turned. Flashing lights on the road below, vehicles a hundred yards away. Less. Pete waited. He held the door open until a fire truck pulled up on the far side, lights turning in the cab's deck, men calling out as they looked over the wreckage. That's when Pete bolted into the under-brush — once he'd seen people, once he knew they'd take care of the night watchman. He stepped from the side gate into the salal and waded through swordferns, worked a broad circle in the darkness until he figured he'd reached the top of the hill and then he stepped onto open logging road and began to run. Fay, Art and Derek were probably waiting for him just beyond the bend where Derek had stood, away from the compound and out of sight.

By the time he reached the Y-junction, Pete's breath was short. No car, no sign of a car. A logging track rose to the right, a narrow trail that twisted off into the woods. That wasn't the way out. At least Pete didn't think it was. Too many roads back here, too many possibilities. He wiped sweat from his brow and pressed his fingers against his ears, then started along the track to the left.

The quarry was their meeting place. Fifteen minutes at a fast run, if he could find his way in this mess of dirt tracks. If this was the right road, he should reach a turnoff soon enough, and then take the next left.

He still held the night watchman's keys and a folded sheet of paper. Pete dropped them into his pocket just as a car rounded the bend behind him, a sudden blare of headlights. He bolted for the trees. Three quick steps across the muddy culvert and he was at the edge of the forest. He grabbed for a sapling, heaved his body up into the thin woods and started to run. The car's wheels cut gravel with a heavy brake. Pete's feet hammered the dry ground. He glanced back. Light glinted off the car's hood: a cop car — sirens off, vehicle at a halt in the middle of the road. Arms protecting his face, Pete dashed through the undergrowth. Vines whipped him. His lungs strained. He leaped a fallen log, took a quick look back through the forest. The sky was getting light — a curtain inching up across the land, but it was hard to tell if the car was still there. He leaned forward for a better view through the trees. A movement flashed on the periphery of his damaged vision, a figure in the woods. Pete ducked under the low arm of a tree, knocked away branches and kept running. His lungs were desperate for air and his legs burned with strain. He broke through a spider's web, coughed, spat and pulled the silky strands from his face.

The woods opened into a small glade, a bed of ferns. Pete extended his stride as he ran. A cloud of tiny insects rushed towards him. A bug caught in his gaping mouth and then the land dropped off. He was running and the earth simply fell away. Pete stumbled, lost his footing on the slope and went down feet first. He tried to dig his heels in to slow himself, but the world tumbled. Off the edge of a cliff with an awful moment of free fall, then his body hit loose dirt, and it took the wind out of him. He rolled until a fallen tree trunk stopped him. A fork of pain leapt across his ribs.

Looking back, it wasn't hard to see where he'd skidded down the hill, but his tracks didn't start until halfway, and the drop-off that followed was a good fifteen feet. It wasn't somewhere you'd come down if you didn't have to. There on the sheltered side of the fallen log, he caught his breath. His heart began to settle. A river gurgled behind him.

No cop would jump down that cliff. Not without first trying to find an easier way. Which meant he had some time. Which meant he might be able to get across the river.

Pete looked up. Around the blind spot left from the flash of the blast he could see the first hints of sunlight falling through trees and shrubs across the thick bed of forest floor. He inched up and scanned the crest of the ridge: empty — a long rise of tangled green woods. Morning now with blue sky glinting through the treetops' jigsaw shapes.

Soon enough they'd be combing this place. Every inch of it: dogs, teams of cops, helicopters even. He needed to cross the river before anyone else came or he'd be stuck trying to hide in this slice of woods between logging road and river. It meant giving up on reaching the quarry, but what he needed most just now was some distance between himself and this patch of land. He needed to get moving. Pete unlaced his boots and rolled down both socks.

Property destruction is what they'd agreed on. Sabotage, trashing things, destroying the machinery that's destroying the world. Just two weeks ago they'd driven the station wagon all the way to the warehouse and had found no sign of any security guards. Dead quiet every inch of the place. Tonight not only was there a night watchman, but he must have been sleeping or something — dozing on the job, unaware as Art drove the Pinto through a cut in the fence to the side of the warehouse. This was the fear that had gripped Pete all through last night's drive — catastrophe, the possibility it might all go wrong.

And now he stood alone in the Kludahk, in some corner of the vast Elliot Muir logging tract. This was the place Art had said they'd make their mark: their precious second front, an obscure forest no one would expect, no one would be watching, a strike far from Clayoquot, far from Kennedy Lake and the Black Hole with its steady stream of weekend protestors.

Boots and socks in his arms, Pete hoisted his pants and waded in. The cold water numbed his feet. He was in open space now, and visible for a good hundred yards in either direction. Step by step he turned and headed down river. This had to be the Sawyer. Frigid water, but if there were going to be search dogs, he had to break the scent. Two hundred yards then three hundred. Halfway across he felt the keys in his pocket, lifted them and dropped them in the river as the water lapped at his waist, westbound current pressing hard, swift water that had already passed through the hydro dam now bound for open ocean. Step by step until he reached the other side, four or even five hundred yards down river from where he'd started.

Barefoot, Pete stepped across pebbles still cold from the night before. He worked his way up into forest until he was out of sight of the river. If he was going to stop somewhere and leave his scent lingering on underbrush, it had to be a good distance from the water. At a boulder, he sat and began to wipe dirt from his feet.

A white mark still dominated the centre of his vision and his ears still rang, but when he threw a small stone, the clatter of it registered.

A steep hillside rose above this bank of the river. Pete picked a zigzag route along the path of least resistance, skirting dense bush and fallen trees, sopping wet pants chafing his legs. He knocked back fallen branches and vines as he went, pushed his way through. Filtered sunlight spread across the undergrowth, diamond bright spots on ferns and dark soil, until finally the woods parted to form a narrow clearing, a small space eerily clear, except for a recently fallen tree. What looked like a walking stick lay against it. Pete peeled a bit of bark off the stick and exposed the smooth wood underneath. That's when he heard a movement in the forest, a body passing. He crouched. Head cocked, he held his breath. Movement again, and then a doe stepped from behind a fir tree. She walked into the clearing, bent her head and tugged at nearby dogwood leaves. Pete slumped. He wiped sweat from his forehead and lay still.

That moment of relief turned his thoughts full circle back to Fay, the memory of her so close that his mind could almost return him to their moment in the station wagon, pulled over on the side of Thurlow Road, her body on top of him, her pale skin, her lips against his. He wanted nothing more than to go back to that time, back to Thurlow Road to end it all before it had even started. Back out. Stop the others. All of this could have been avoided. Should have been avoided.

That thought brought a realization: it could have been Fay, Art and Derek in the station wagon and not a cop car that skidded to a halt and sent him fleeing for the woods. Maybe it hadn't been the police. Maybe he'd missed his chance.

CHAPTER

5

Three months earlier, travelling down from Bedwell Pass in that graffiti-marked van with the windows shot out, the blast of cold air had kept Pete slouched low in the rear seat, toque pulled down over his ears. Art and Fay sat directly in front of him, Jeremy was at the wheel, Derek right down on the van's floor to stay out of the wind.

The shock of the new land use announcement lay like dead weight across them all. Just months ago, the government had bought half of Greer-Braden's stock and now here that same government was announcing the company could log seventy-four percent of remaining old growth. All of this on the same day loggers had shot the windows out of their van.

As they pulled off the highway, the roar of cold air eased, and Pete sat up again. It had rained at this end of the island and the damp smell of spring held in the air. Street lights set the tarmac glistening. Jeremy pulled over in front of the Bee Street apartment and killed the engine. They piled their equipment and what was left of the supplies on their kitchen lino, tents not even in the stuff sacks, guy lines wrapped around wet and muddy nylon, bundled hammocks a pathetic-looking pile. Art leaned against the door frame as Pete and Jeremy carried in the last of the backpacks. "That whole drive home, I was thinking of all the machinery, all the trucks, all the equipment Greer-Braden needs to operate." Art let those words hang in the air a moment. "What if they were the ones who lost the glass on every vehicle they own?"

/ / / / /

"They'd fix them." Jeremy dropped the backpack he held, turned and sat on it. "They'd get it all replaced."

"It would cost them though. Just like this is going to cost us. Derek figures it'll be more than the van's even worth. If it happened to Greer-Braden often enough, they couldn't afford to carry on business as usual."

"This isn't the time for a knee-jerk reaction," Jeremy said. "This is the time for strategy and patience. So if you're talking about sabotage again, monkeywrenching or whatever, if this is your violent action campaign, it's a mistake."

"A few of us could get it started. Fay agrees it's time to do something that has a bigger impact. Derek too, I think. It wouldn't take much."

"This is nuts," Jeremy said. "This is crazy."

Only the three of them were in the kitchen just then — Fay had walked through to the back bedroom, Derek was in the washroom. Art raised both hands, palms out. "You know what's crazy? Doing the same thing over and over and expecting different results. That's what's crazy. Another peaceful protest that gets us nowhere, gets us arrested."

"You're understating what we accomplished," Jeremy said. "We picked an unknown pass in an obscure forest and almost doubled the number of protestors in five days. The press covered the arrests."

"Congratulations. Now they're over the pass and getting ready to log Spooston Valley. Pristine old —"

"This land use policy could be their big mistake, Art. Industry and government so obviously in bed together. We can't respond by doing something stupid back. Go off half-cocked and God knows what might happen. You don't know the first thing about blowing things up, or burning things down, or whatever you're planning. Not you, not Derek, not Fay, Pete or me."

"If you're fundamentally on board with this," Art said, "we can work through whatever objections —"

"I'm not fundamentally on board with this. Are you listening to what I'm saying? I'm not even close to on board."

They'd argued like this in the past, tug-of-war debates in which Pete almost always sided with Jeremy. Today though, when he interrupted and held up his hands to quiet them, he said, "What if Art's right? We could do something small that would make it difficult for them to carry on, make it more expensive at least. Shift the economics. If we do it carefully."

"These things can't be done carefully," Jeremy said. "You can't blow something up or burn something down carefully. It's not possible."

/ / / / /

Pete used a chunk of his next welfare cheque to develop the pictures from their camp at Bedwell Pass. Seventy-six shots, all of it on slide film. He flipped through the first few at the photo-finishing counter then walked to a narrow strip of a park where he sat on a bench and began again, held each slide to the sky. The shots took him back into the woods above Spooston Valley. This was one of the pleasures of photography — the return to a captured moment, the surprises hidden there.

A shot of a drop of water rolling down a leaf made Pete pause. The next picture was a self-portrait: Pete cross-legged in one of the hammocks. Rain had wetted his hair, darkened it, straightened the curls, his thin lips drawn into the faintest of smiles. He had shots of the canopy, treetop spires backed by speckled sky, shots of mossy trunks. One slide had the man from the road crew who'd walked up the slope to try to talk them down. He had a picture of an officer holding Jeremy by the lapels, another of the churned earth dug away for the logging road. A few pictures caught the clear-cut that sprawled across the slopes below. At least a dozen of the photos showed Fay. The one he liked best was a close-up — her head slightly turned, attention focused on something distant. She'd been leaning against the van, looking away and yet paying attention to him all the same. That summed up Fay in some fundamental way: there and yet not there, with him but not with him.

Seventy-six frames and only two showed Derek — both were from the arrests, both caught him bellowing, mouth wide as he shouted at the officers, a moment captured: Derek's volcanic fury. There were photos Pete skimmed over, out of focus, shutter snapped early or late, a couple underexposed, a couple over-exposed. The problem with most, the reason he flipped past so many: they simply weren't able to capture what he'd seen.

The best of the shots were of people: portraits and close-ups, but what he'd wanted to capture, what he'd turned his camera to most often — the grand trees, the vast cathedral forest stand-ing on the edge of sprawling clear-cuts — his pictures didn't come close to doing these justice. None even touched the heart of the matter. Cameras were such focused and specific tools. Sometimes the world out there just seemed too vast for such a narrow instrument.

A shot of Jeremy caught Pete's attention — in the van with the windows blown out, the top of the steering wheel visible, his body hunched, worn-looking and tired. He'd taken that picture the day they'd been released from jail and in that photo Jeremy looked defeated, drained, harried, so unlike himself — this man who always seemed poised and controlled.

Maybe Art was right. Maybe it was time to do something. In the week since their return, Art, Fay and Derek had been a whirl-wind of energy in the Bee Street apartment — a stark contrast to this picture Pete held — their talk raucous about the need to take action, a change of course, firebombs, targeted arson.

Pete had held himself back. Until then he hadn't said whether he would help or not, but these photos were part of what finally made up his mind: the stabbing disappointment at how little the slides captured, how little he had to show — the gap between ambition and what he actually held.

The last slide in the stack showed Fay, a golden smile, bright blue eyes directed into the lens, a perfect symmetry to her face, a natural balance that seemed the base of her beauty.

Fay too was part of his decision.

/ / / / /

That evening Fay looked through the slides, paused at the pictures of herself, but spent more time with the photos of Art. He had an intent gaze in every frame, eyes focused on the camera. In one he squatted at the base of a fir tree loosening knots in a line of rope. In another he smoked idly, resting on the van's bumper, a third showed him sprawled on the forest floor, body against dirt, dark eyes turned out to the world, his goatee neatly trimmed.

"These are good," Fay said. "Really good."

"Maybe, but it's not like they're going to be printed in *Time*, not in *Maclean's*. They're good enough for mementos, good enough for a scrapbook, if I'd thought to use print film, but they're not going to appear in living rooms across the country."

"You're being too hard on yourself."

"You can take pictures or you can take part, that's what I've been thinking."

"You can do both."

"No, photography is a passive act."

"It doesn't have to be."

"I've packed my camera away."

He watched her working through what he was trying to tell her. She blinked, formed a hesitant smile and finally Pete came out with it: "I'm in," he said. "With you and Art, with Derek. It's time to do something."

Her hand reached out, touched down on his knee. No words, just that moment of contact.

"Has Jeremy been by?"

Her hand slipped away and he regretted speaking. "This morning," she said. "He and Art sat there talking. Arguing actually."

"Is he going to join?"

"He might come around. Or maybe he's not committed enough."

There it was, that vital measurement: everyone held up against this gold standard twinning idealism and commitment. Until that moment, no one would ever have talked about Jeremy as uncommitted. Jeremy was the one who'd gotten Pete involved. Jeremy bound them together. This felt like a family breaking up.

Three weeks later they set off firebombs under trucks at the Westlake parking lot, and they did it without Jeremy: three tubs filled with gasoline and a bit of tar, all of them linked by a hose that ensured they went off in succession. Pete was lookout that day, and even then he'd been so nervous he'd thrown up in the roadside culvert opposite the parking lot. For days afterwards he'd wondered if that would enable police to somehow trace him — DNA in the gastric juices he'd vomited.

CHAPTER

6

Art Kosky sat on the pale orange carpet in the basement suite on Bee Street. Fay lay across from him, knees tucked up, hands folded under her head. Her eyes were closed, but she was awake. They were all awake, Derek on the far side of the room in a rattan chair that creaked as he shifted about trying different radio stations. When the nine o'clock news ended and the announcer started on the stock report, Derek lowered the volume again.

Art lifted a cigarette from the pack in his lap and lit it from the butt of his last.

"Jesus, Art, you're going to smoke us all to death."

Fay opened her eyes and sat up. "Oh God," she said. "Oh please." Both hands covered her face.

"Pete said the man was alive. Let's not panic until —"

"And Pete? What about him? We should have stayed. We should have waited." Her voice creaked, a warbled edge to her words. "At the very least we should have gone back."

"We did go back. I went back. He was gone."

A hundred yards up the logging road they'd stopped the car, then Art got out, walked until he could see a corner of the fence, the fire truck, the pickup parked in the lot, driver's door still open. A pair of men carried the security guard out on a stretcher. A cop car stood behind the fire truck but nothing in the way the men in the compound moved suggested they had Pete.

If Pete had made it out, he'd have gone to the quarry, and so they drove back. Fay waited there. Derek got out and stood

/ / / / /

at the nearest intersection while Art drove back towards the site. Logging roads knitted the land, a jumbled mess, easy to get lost. At the Y-junction he'd turned and tried the other arm of the arterial road. Just after the second bend, he'd spotted Pete. A sharp turn and there he was, only Pete dashed off into the forest. Art went after him, he even started into the woods, but he couldn't do much more with the station wagon stopped in the middle of the logging road and the flash of emergency lights still playing off the dawn sky.

He'd done all he could. He just wasn't sure the others would see it that way.

A series of chimes sounded on the radio, a short musical turn that cut off the weather report. Derek leaned forward and raised the volume. A coil of ash fell from Art's cigarette onto the carpet.

"The radio newsroom has received reports this morning of a bomb blast at a logging station in the Kludahk forest on southern Vancouver Island. Reports indicate that sometime early this morning a single car bomb exploded at an equipment compound owned by Greer-Braden Limited. RCMP report that one man remains in critical condition."

Art released a single deep breath. The next was slow coming.

"No one has claimed responsibility, but this attack follows two similar cases, suspected arsons attributed to the group Earth Action Now. Police are appealing to the public for help and ask anyone with information to contact local authorities. A news conference is scheduled for ten a.m. Pacific time. CBC will bring you further —"

Derek rose from the rattan chair. A single kick and the radio hit the wall then fell onto the carpeted floor. A trembling silence filled the room. Art stubbed out his cigarette. Behind him, Derek paced on the carpet, shoulders hunched, head down. "So much for striking where no one's watching."

Fay stood. "If the police don't have Pete, where is he?"

Outside a truck rumbled past. Art lifted his ashtray with its mess of bent cigarette butts and set it on the end table. "When you got the dynamite, Fay, did anything happen that could link us to all of this?"

"Nothing. No CCTV cameras, no witnesses. It was in the middle of nowhere. There's not much that could connect us."

"Pete could connect us," Derek said. "If they catch him, that's it, we're screwed."

"Or if someone notices that he's missing."

"If anyone you know asks, say he went east to see his mother. Start spreading that story around. A family emergency."

"And if a week from now they find his body?" Derek said.

"His body? Jesus Christ, Derek."

"It's a possibility. We need to consider these things."

"Dead?" Fay said. "You think he's dead."

"Look at it this way, would you rather he's dead or he's ratting us out as we speak?"

"Derek, he's not dead and he's not ratting us out. We say he went camping. Anyone asks, he went back-country camping. Should he walk out of the woods, no problem. It's consistent."

Derek nodded. "It's also consistent if a body turns up."

Fay started towards the door. "I need some fresh air."

"Wait." Art went after her. One hand on her shoulder, he tried to pull her around, tried to get her to face him. "We all have to stay calm here, Fay."

"Derek's talking like Pete's dead. And the other man. The night watchman."

"He's not dead. He's going to turn up. Trust me." He put his arms around her but she'd gone rigid, her body tense, her own arms bunched at her chest. "We just need to cool it a while, lie low." He leaned close. "We did everything we could for him. We tried."

"Are you talking about Pete or are you talking about the security guard?"

Art stepped back. "When I walked down there was no sign of Pete. I drove all over, got as close as anyone could possibly get."

"And you saw no sign of him then?"

Confusion and chaos had clouded everything last night. Art might have been able to stop Pete if he'd gotten out of the car quicker, if he'd leapt out immediately and chased him down. He couldn't say this to Fay though. He couldn't tell her he'd seen Osborne without getting blamed for not following him all the way into the woods.

"I'm not going to pretend this isn't bad, but let's keep our minds on where the true fault lies. We know who is to blame for all this. Next step is to make sure the public knows. Everyone can see this is a tragedy, now we need to issue a communique to point out that Greer-Braden put the man in harm's way after we issued our declaration."

"So it's their fault?"

"What we did last night will have good consequences." Art took a step away from Fay. "What happened was terrible, but good will come of it. People will start paying attention. We're now a force they have to deal with." He raised his voice. He wanted Derek to hear this too.

"What's important here is that we stay focused. We write a communique, part apology, part explanation. No one likes that a man's in hospital, but good things will come of this. Pete will be back. We hold the course. Eight crates of dynamite are waiting for us above Thurlow Road. List Cove and Dutton next. Everyone is listening now. We have their attention, and it's the threat of further action that will institute real change."

CHAPTER
7

When Pete came to, the sun had shifted. Late afternoon and his head hurt — a tight ache across his temples. It took a moment to stand and even then he had to put a hand out to steady himself. Too long since he'd eaten, and his body felt weak, his legs stiff, his steps tentative. He turned his face up to enjoy a moment of the summer sun's warmth, pulled a leaf from an alder tree, chewed and managed to swallow, but green leaves weren't going to fill him up. They might even make him sick. A dragonfly buzzed past, turned, rose and disappeared. Judging by the sun, Pete figured it around five or six.

It was almost dark by the time the woods opened to reveal a dirt road, a narrow strip cut through forest. It had a slight downhill slope. In the distance, the track curved and disappeared. Pete looked one way then the other, trying to decide which direction to take.

There'd be somewhere to find food once he reached the coast, and that's what made his decision: the possibility of food and water. Port Thorvald couldn't be far, and they'd have a pay phone there. He dug change from his pocket as he walked, unfolded the bills, spread coins across his palm: four dollars and sixty cents.

Pete spotted a stand of mushrooms at the ragged edge of the logging road, a whole cluster lit by the moon. He crouched and plucked the largest of them, sniffed it, wiped dirt away, then put it in his mouth. The flesh was soft. It tasted safe, it looked

/ / / / /

safe. He'd picked mushrooms just like these with Bev Norman when they used to camp at Long Beach, and so he ate another and then a third, cleaning them as he went, wiping away soil. His first food since the ferry, and he ate every last one, then stood and walked again.

In time, the air began to cool. The dirt road widened, spread into an intersection, a T-junction with a wide green sign, white letters listing distances to Port Thorvald and Port Renfrew. It was amazing just to see a sign: a reminder of the world waiting beyond the forest. The West Coast Road meant a route home.

On the opposite side of the road, woods rose on a low slope. Light steps and Pete was in the forest. Up a slight rise, he found a broad tree with a thick bed of fallen needles at its base. He needed to sleep. After that he could figure out a plan. He'd made it this far and in a little more time he'd find Fay, Derek and Art — as long as they weren't in jail, as long as they hadn't fled altogether. Although in truth, they could be a twenty-four hour drive east of here by now, in hiding, gone underground. Every policeman, every newspaper, every politician would be after them. If he couldn't find the others, he could surely find Jeremy. That would be a start. Track Jeremy down, ask for help.

CHAPTER
8

Sunday morning and Tab was late. Most of the choir was already dressed and the cloakroom hummed with a low chatter. Tab pulled her robe over her head, and as she adjusted it, a short flutter of nervousness rose. Some of the others were beginning quiet warm-ups. Tab opened her sheaf of music and looked over the opening bars of "Magnificat Mysterium," moved her mouth around the words, practised quietly, her voice muffled.

Novak arrived and the room settled. He led them through warm-ups. Five minutes before the service began, they filed down the corridor and into the choir stalls. Novak stood facing them. He'd trimmed his beard, a close cut, neat and tidy.

Midway into the service they sang "Magnificat Mysterium." Their voices roared through the cathedral, a great boom of an opening, a trilling chord. The sopranos led the tune, a sharp point rising high across the transept. Novak swayed. His hands leapt above him, body captured by the music, fingers leading it. Tab had her feet planted shoulder-width apart, her diaphragm lightly tensed. She'd been practising the song, working on the words at home, the breathing, the short, clipped pace.

Three minutes of singing, point and counterpoint, tenor and treble lines interwoven and then diving apart. After the briefest moment of silence, the bass line thundered in.

They neared the end. Novak pulled his hand down into a fist, drew them quiet, and the last phrase hummed free, rising to the rafters with a life of its own. Silence in the cathedral.

/ / / /

During communion, Tab spotted Frank filing up towards the altar. He had more white in his hair than she'd noticed before. Maybe it was the dim light of the church. Maybe the angle. A red carnation hung from his buttonhole. Their garden was at its peak, a bright blooming that had carried on since June.

After the service, Frank waited for her in the parking lot, engine idling to keep the AC on. The drive home was a good two miles past brick houses, hedgerows and cheerful gardens, block after block of tidy properties. The AC made Tab's eyes dry and she found herself blinking as they turned onto Chestnut. From under the hood came a faint whistle — a rubbing fan belt or an alignment problem as the car turned right. She was about to ask if Frank should take it in for a tune-up when she noticed the police car parked in front of their house.

"Strange," Frank said. Tab kept blinking. She squeezed her eyes shut, opened them again. Another faint whistle as they turned into the driveway. Two officers stood on the porch peering in the window. "Do you think someone broke in?" Tab said, but that wasn't it. She already knew that wasn't it. They were waiting to talk to her about Peter. A great emptiness opened up in her stomach as she gripped the door handle. She squeezed it until her nails bit into her palm then she pushed the door open.

"Mr. and Mrs. Harper?" The policemen were on their way across the grass, striding out to meet them. The taller officer removed his cap. He had a shallow face, almost flat.

"How can we help you?" Frank said.

"It's about Peter Osborne. I understand you're his mother, Mrs. Harper."

"What's wrong? He's okay, isn't he?"

"When was the last time you heard from him?"

"Just tell me he's okay."

Tab glanced at one officer then the other. The nearer man had a narrow face and a neatly trimmed moustache. He cleared his throat. "The RCMP want to talk to him in connection with a bombing out west."

"Peter? A bombing?"

"At that logging company's warehouse?" Frank said. "It was on the news yesterday."

"There's a group calls itself Earth Action Now already wanted in connection with two arson cases. They're what we call people of interest."

"Have you heard that name?" the second officer said. "Earth Action Now. We're told there's reason to believe your son's involved."

Tab stepped closer to the oak tree. She touched its rough bark. The others were still talking, but they sounded muffled as though she was on the other side of a wall or underwater. Manhunt. Terrorism. Greer-Braden. Night watchman. The words were out of order, a tangle she couldn't quite unravel. A nail poked from the tree, rusty and buried deep. Her little finger looped around it while the voices of the three men came and went. It felt like her bones had gone soft. She needed to sit down. She needed a glass of water.

"Do you know of friends he might try to contact? Do you have any names or numbers?"

"We haven't heard from him in a good while. Since Christmas. My wife tried to track him down after we lost contact."

"He left university," Tab said. Somehow in her mind it all came down to that, the moment his life veered off course. "He abandoned —"

"They kicked him out," Frank said. "He's been at those protests, on the barricades, marching through logging camps, all that stuff out on the West Coast."

The shorter officer reached out and offered Frank a card. "If he is involved, this is a whole heap of trouble. It's best he comes in to talk."

Frank took the card without looking at it and started up

the gentle slope of the grass. He didn't look back at Tab, he didn't take her arm. His feet sounded on the wood steps while Tab stood stranded on the lawn. She wasn't sure she'd be able to walk, but she pushed herself from the tree and somehow managed it: one step and then the next.

The shorter officer held out another card. Tab forced her fingers steady as she took it. She climbed the three steps up to their wraparound porch. It was the feature she'd liked most when they bought the house — the old-fashioned veranda, wide, as though from a southern mansion. Only just now she hated it, this big open space: ostentatious and exposed.

Inside, Tab leaned against the door and pushed until the latch clicked. Her body was still but she felt dizzy all the same — the unreality of it all spinning through her head.

Frank breathed deeply. He looked drawn and pale. Tab fingered a section of the newspaper that lay on the armchair. Patches gave a soft mew and brushed against her leg. "Oh God," Tab said, but she had no other words. She crossed to the secretary and pulled out one of Frank's cigarettes. The cat trotted after her.

The police could be wrong. Everyone made mistakes, police included. And even if it were true, it didn't make him guilty. Maybe questions were all the police had in mind. Or maybe these people had coerced Peter into helping them set that bomb, these Earth Action people. Peter was too trusting. Naive. She'd often said that. They could have easily tricked him.

Or maybe the phone would ring. She glanced down at the black box and handset. The police might call to apologize for having made some kind of mix-up. Peter might call. She struggled with these threads of hope trying to assemble something to steady herself. She should have looked harder after their Christmas row, after Peter stopped calling home. She should have actually gone out there, talked to people face to face. It would have been better than just phoning. She could have tracked him down. She could have visited campus, met with professors. She could have posted signs.

And she shouldn't have lied to Reverend Simms on Friday. She'd lied to a priest about her only son and now look. There were so many things like this: should haves and shouldn't haves. When Peter had come home last Christmas, there were times it had felt like she hardly knew him. That was the truth of it. The unkempt hair, those baggy clothes he said were made of hemp. She'd thought hemp was rope and had wondered about clothes made of rope. Turned out it was marijuana. And he had this animosity — a bile that seemed directed their way. They drove too much. He'd insisted on walking the night they went to The Keg. Two miles in the snow. And he wouldn't eat steak. He'd told Frank that Christmas was a holiday of consumption and waste. Christmas of all things.

Once or twice Tab had caught flashes of the old Peter, the Peter from before he'd travelled west. One night the two of them stayed up late playing cribbage, talking across the table, and Peter told her about his life out west, his friends, his interest in photography. Another day Peter made her lunch, served Caesar salad and sandwiches. He didn't want to talk about school though; he avoided questions about his classes and about campus life until Boxing Day when he finally confessed that he'd been expelled. He wasn't getting ready to graduate, he wasn't even in school. Eighteen months with Frank still sending him money for tuition, rent and whatnot.

She told Frank that same day. It wasn't right not to. He'd been the one paying. Frank of course blew his lid, and that same night Peter collected his odds and ends, a few books, his camera, a handful of clothes.

/ / / / /

Just after six that evening, the phone rang and awoke Tab. A woman spoke on the other end. "It's Alice," she said in a high-pitched, energetic voice. "From choir." It all thundered back. She'd been waiting for the police. Or for Peter. Sitting in this chair, waiting for someone to call and explain how it had all been a mistake, a terrible misunderstanding.

Tab heard her own grunt, a guttural response.

"I had a thought after I got home," Alice said. "Would you and your husband like to join Dick and me for brunch next Sunday?"

Curled in the armchair, Tab could feel her body giving way. This is what it's like to melt. The world simply wears you into nothing. Even as Alice spoke, it felt like the phone was slipping from Tab's hand.

"There's a great place on Ridings Road called Sunshine. We could even invite the good Reverend Simms. He's taken a liking to you."

"Next Sunday," Tab said and she heard herself as though from a distance, an echo. "Alright then." She tried to force life into her voice. She needed to maintain herself. She'd wanted to meet people — she'd joined the choir to try to get out more. She couldn't simply fall apart out of fear of what Peter might or might not have done.

"I'll call Reverend Simms and make sure he's free. He always is though. For bacon and eggs at least."

Alice talked on for a minute but the moment she paused, Tab cut in, voice as upbeat as she could make it: "So we'll see you for practice on Friday?"

"Yes, of course, practice," Alice said.

That evening Tab and Frank ate quietly, a simple meal served in a corner of their vast house. Cutlery scraped porcelain plates. Ice tinkled in their glasses, unusually bright and loud. From the hallway, the grandfather clock ticked. Across the table, Tab could hear Frank chewing his food, slowly, methodically, the same way he did everything.

"You should call Martin," he said after a while.

"What good would that do?"

"Tell him what you know. The boy's dad should —"

"I don't want to talk to Martin. I don't know anything yet."

"Your mother maybe?"

"It might kill her. It might finish her off, this." She moved a potato around her plate. "I only want to talk to my son."

"You think that's going to happen now that the police are after him? All these months spent God knows where and now that the police are searching for him, you think he's going to call?"

Frank took his plate to the sink. "You have to consider reality here, Tab."

"There's no need to be mean about it."

He left the kitchen. In the living room, the TV snapped on.

Sitting alone at the table, Tab realized she hadn't even cried yet, not really. Years ago she'd cry at the drop of a hat. Now she sat at the dining room table and concentrated, let her face go soft and made her eyes narrow until she finally raised tears. At first they simply welled in her eyes, but after one rolled down her cheek, she truly let go. Heaving sobs wracked her body. She reached for a dinner napkin. Her lip quivered. Her body felt weak.

CHAPTER
9

Pete awoke, body gone from cold and damp to hot and sweaty. His clothes clung to him. At first he thought it had rained, but it was his own sweat. His stomach felt swollen. Images from Esterway Ridge had tangled his dreams — the night watchman on his back, body still, Pete bent above him. In this dream Pete couldn't move, couldn't say a word, but the night watchman spoke. He said, "Please," over and over again while Pete stared down at him.

Woodland noises rose. Pete shifted onto his side to try to get comfortable, only moving sharpened the pain in his belly. His mind was still there on Esterway Ridge, haunting images close, his body tense, a knot there on the forest floor. If only he could go back. If only he could return to that moment before his finger hit the timer button. If only the night watchman had stepped out earlier. Before the timer had started. If he could, he'd do it all differently. Stop, walk away, leave the stolen Pinto, leave the explosives there against the side of the building.

A vehicle passed in the distance and then Pete heard another sound nearby, maybe a deer, some sort of movement in the sha-dowed forest. He managed to stand. An animal, only his vision was blurry and he couldn't quite make it out: smaller than a deer, a dog maybe, a wild cat. It came into focus for a moment, the dark rough fur of a baby bear. Pete turned and began a brisk walk. He stumbled uphill, hands out seeking something to steady himself. He tried to run. The land flattened. Its mother

/ / / / /

would be nearby. A baby meant a mother, but Pete's muscles ached, his head hurt and his bowels were loose. He shouldn't have eaten those mushrooms. He shouldn't have let his hunger get the better of his judgment.

Pete walked as far as he could before he gave in and lay down at the base of a tree. When he awoke again, the land was fully dark and he was hungry. The fever had passed. At least he thought it had. He didn't feel hot anymore, but his body still ached as he stumbled about, slowly realizing that he didn't know which direction led to the road. The sign last night had said six kilometres to Port Thorvald. He tried to picture a map. Beyond Port Thorvald and the mouth of the Sawyer River, a wide peninsula jutted seaward. That's where he was. Somewhere in the southern corner of that block of land cut on one side by the West Coast Road and bound on the other sides by open ocean.

He lay down to rest. Curled in a ball on the cold ground, he pulled up his knees and slept again, but as he slept, his mind returned to Esterway Ridge, to the smoking compound, the night watchman lying still. A thin and restless sleep until a wracking cough brought Pete upright. He retched and spat a few bitter strings of bile then scratched a bite on his elbow. Another inflamed his collarbone and he scratched there too. He had to get moving. He had to get somewhere. Rolling land, trees for as far as he could see. There wasn't even a trail here.

People died like this: exposed, sick in the woods with no one to even notice they're missing. Human bones lay scattered across this land, but if he could walk, he could find his way. He was on a peninsula bound by a road and by water. Uphill would lead to a road. Downhill to water. If he could find one or the other, he could get home.

Gradually a trail opened in front of him: a slight break in the underbrush, a track so faint it might have been a deer run. It seemed to lead along the side of the slope, but at least it was a path. It was something to follow, a way to keep headed in one direction. Eventually the path turned downhill and although it wasn't what he'd intended, the pull of gravity was seductive. Reach water and that would be enough. Just follow the coastline back. Plus he might find fishermen, or campers, loggers, hunters. People dotted the coast in unexpected places.

CHAPTER 10

Inez Pierce was seated in front of her easel when a movement in the forest caught her attention. She edged forward on her stool just as a man stumbled from the woods near the trail that led to Seeley's Bay. He took a few more steps. Mud caked his clothes. He wiped his eyes, looked about, then spotted the two rough-cut statues, Ray's twin carvings, and he stood staring at them. Scout was slow to realize a stranger had walked into her territory, but she raised her head and barked. Inez set a hand on the dog's neck. "Hush."

The bark caught the man's attention and he looked towards Inez, hand raised to shelter his eyes. He didn't seem to spot her though. Another moment and he walked on.

Inez set her paintbrush in the easel's tray. On the canvas she'd begun a painting of the cedars she'd once named Fred and Ginger — two trees grown close so that their boughs moved together even in a light wind. The man was now just a few yards from those trees. Three more steps and he could have touched one, but he carried on down the slope. He was tall and pale, his hair curly and light enough in its colouring to show a clump of mud and dead leaves caught in it. Inez walked after him, past blackberry bushes and a pair of old tree stumps on the path that led to the woodpile. The dog trotted beside her.

"Can I help you? Are you lost?"

The man touched a stump of wood. He managed to line up his rear end and sit. Only then did he turn towards her. His

/////

shirt was misbuttoned, and it hung unevenly from his shoulders. He had a wide forehead, steely eyes.

Scout barked. "Don't mind her. She's harmless. I'm Inez."

"I'm thirsty."

"Alright. Okay." Inez turned. The man seemed to be alone. No movement among the trees that skirted this end of the beach, no one behind him. "Just wait here. My son can run to the cabin for some water."

Dennis was nearby. At least she thought he was. He'd been working on his kayak, sanding the most recent coat of shellac. Inez called out and walked down to the rocks where she found Dennis seated with his illustrated guide to kayak building.

"A man's just stumbled in here. Says he's thirsty. Can you get us a cup of water? Maybe something to eat."

Dennis angled his head. "A camper?"

"I don't think so."

Inez walked back to the clearing where the man sat on the stump. "Are you lost?"

He seemed to be preparing words. He licked his lips. He looked pained. "Sick. I've been sick and lost." He squinted as he spoke.

"Is there anyone else? Anyone you were lost with?"

He shook his head. Inez crouched and brought her face level. He had the start of a beard, thin lips, a faint scar below one eye, a short seam of puckered skin.

Dennis arrived with a mug full of water, both hands wrapped around it. The man took a noisy slurp and his Adam's apple bobbed. "This is my son, Dennis," she said. She was still kneeling there and she set her wrist against his forehead where a faint streak of mud marked it. "You're burning up. You want to rest a little?"

The man's chin dipped.

"Maybe my bed?" Dennis said.

Inez turned to her son. Theirs was a little cabin, densely packed even with just the two of them. "Gunter and Maggie's place would be better." She turned back to the man. "There's an empty cabin on the ridge. We could walk you up there, lay you down for a rest."

"I feel sick."

He looked it too. His mouth hung open. Both eyes looked weary and red-rimmed. He stood though, and Inez and Dennis arranged themselves on either side. Arms around his shoulders, they walked with a shuffling step. The man's body had a bony, winnowed feel and even braced by the two of them, his steps came slowly. They paused at the single arbutus tree that marked the start of the path uphill. Inez reached out. She held onto a branch and looked up the muddy track. Gunter had never put any effort into making a proper trail. This was just a track formed by years of tramping boots.

The cabin itself stood in a clearing, a crooked shack leaning hard for the ocean. As they approached, Inez could only imagine what this stranger must be thinking, but this was the best of the four empty cabins, despite its tilt. The windows were intact, it had a cot. A single room, and a man as tall as this one might touch both north and south walls at the same time, but at least the roof didn't leak. He'd be dry.

Inez looped an arm around the stranger, tightened her grip as they stepped onto the porch. Inside, it took Inez's eyes a moment to adjust. The place smelled musty and closed off: winter's mould still hiding in the corners. The cot's springs sighed as the man settled. There were no sheets, no pillow: one mattress and that was it. A dresser stood on the far side of the room. "See if you can't find a blanket in there, Dennis."

"Thank you," the man said, his eyes already closed, his hands folded across his chest.

Inez pulled a crate from under the counter and sat on it. "What's your name?"

That would be good to know. That would be a start, but his eyes were closed now, his breathing slow. His lip had a cut she hadn't noticed before — swollen and marked with dried blood. "Jesus, you're a sight."

Behind her, Dennis was going through the chest of drawers, searching the cabin. The stranger reached out just then, felt for her hand and gave a squeeze. "Thank you." Another squeeze and this time the pressure remained. "For taking me in." She let him hold her hand. He looked peaceful. His breathing softened.

"There're no blankets here," Dennis said.

"You could take the grey one off my bed. And maybe bring a pillow."

"He's going to be okay, right?"

"I think so."

The door opened then banged shut. Inez listened as her son crossed the clearing. Morning light brushed in across the cot and across the man's dirty clothes. She extracted her hand. He didn't have a thing with him, other than his clothes, this dirty-looking jacket tied around his waist. Just wait until she wrote her sister about this.

/ / / / /

Gunter had rigged a gravity-fed spigot and Inez used it to fill a bucket. She found a dishcloth hung under the window, long ago dried and gone stiff. She soaked it and worked it over the man's forehead and nose to clean away the mud. His eyes fluttered. She pulled the dirt and bits of leaf from his hair.

The stranger wasn't bad looking under all the mud. He had a round, soft face. He might have been twenty-four or twenty-five, a good few years younger than her.

Dennis returned with a pillow and a blanket and he brought up the same chipped mug the man had used at the woodpile. Inez raised the stranger's head and slid the pillow under it. "More water?"

His cheek twitched, but he was asleep now and Inez set the mug on the stool by the cot. "We'll leave that for him." She stretched the blanket over his body. "Probably best we leave him in peace." Two steps across Gunter's dusty floorboards and she was at the door.

Back in her own cabin, Inez switched on her weather radio. The speaker had a tinny sound. She adjusted the aerial, shifted the radio's position just an inch or two and listened to the afternoon's marine forecast. The weather report had long ago become a feature of her life here. She checked it once or even twice a day. Northwesterly forty-two knots, seven-foot high tide at 3:15, four-foot low tide at nine.

"Dennis, have you collected the eggs and cleaned the coop?"

"Not yet. Do you think we might have saved that guy's life?"

"Go take care of the chickens, Dennis. You can work on your kayak after that."

"How do you think he got here?"

Lost camper seemed the most likely explanation. Or maybe he'd run his boat aground. Only he wasn't dressed like he'd been on a boat. He wasn't really dressed like a camper either. He was dressed like he'd pulled his car over to the side of the road and wandered into the woods — until he was too dirty to be recognized.

The way he'd staggered in here, he might have been lost a week. Although if he'd been gone that long, search parties would surely have been out by now. She'd joined two searches in the five years she'd lived here. Once for a boy just about Dennis's age. Eventually, they'd found him sitting in the middle of a logging road.

/ / / / /

Inez returned to Gunter and Maggie's old cabin just before dinnertime with a bowl of soup and a mug of tea. She carried them along the switchback trail on top of one of her sketch pads, a wide hardcover book that suited as a tray. On the way up the ridge, she had to hold it one-handed against her hip, free hand reaching for tree trunks and low branches to steady herself.

The door to the cabin had belonged to the interior of some house years ago — it had never fit quite right and the whitewash was peeling.

"Anyone home?" As she knocked, it occurred to her that the stranger might have walked off. Or he might have taken a turn for the worse. Could he have died lying there on that old mattress? This was how Inez's mind worked: momentary lurches to absurd possibilities — absurd because of course, when she opened the door, he was there in bed, still breathing, eyes closed, blanket tangled. The floorboards creaked beneath her feet. She set the book, the soup and the tea on the counter, slipped her bag of pencils into her pocket. "You awake, stranger?" She touched his cheek above the line of his stubbled beard. He was still warm. "I've brought food."

The man's eyelids fluttered then rested closed. The water mug Dennis had brought was still full.

"A little soup and you'll feel better." She set the bowl on the stool, perched herself on the edge of the bed and nestled a hand behind his neck. She raised his head and spooned broth into his mouth. A little dribbled down and caught in the stubble on his chin. His lips smacked. The pressure against her supporting hand said he was finished. He was ready to lie back.

The mud on the man's clothes had spread across the mattress. It had dried and was beginning to crumble. She could bring up some of Ray's old clothes, those she hadn't used as paint rags. The stranger was a similar size only skinnier, his body lean and hungry-looking. She touched his front pockets, right side then left. Both empty. He mumbled something though. She leaned closer. "Don't," he said. It was soft, a sound just above a whisper, but it made her heart quicken with embarrassment. "I was just wondering if you had any ID."

His breathing settled and he released a gentle strum of a snore. Through the afternoon her mind had run over the various possibilities — hiker, camper, berry picker, birder, surveyor of some kind, marijuana farmer, a man somehow connected to the forestry industry, a mountain biker, someone who'd been riding back-country motor-cross even. Dozens of possibilities had passed through her mind, all of them innocent enough. The man had been lost. A rare event but not unheard of. The fact he was so sick was what made this unusual.

Inez reached for her sketch book, chose a pencil and while the stranger slept, she drew. She always started with momentary impressions, quick strokes — pencil and charcoal on paper.

The human face has no lines, it is nothing but surfaces and shades, and on paper Inez's impressions were all shadows and curves. After each, she turned the book so that repeated images lay together at odd angles, a medley of offset drawings. A rare pleasure lay hidden in this kind of rough and short-lived work. The demands of colour had been haunting her paintings. These last few months her work had leaned too heavily on the brighter end of the palette, even while living here in a world void of artificial colours or tropical brightness. Maybe colour itself had been hampering her work. With charcoal, the world was all structure and shades, a flatter and simpler place to be.

Inez flipped the page and started another drawing. There was something irresistible about capturing a face unknown to her and yet intimate as well. She'd send a sketch to her sister along with her account of the story. Whatever the story turned out to be.

Years ago, Ray had shown Inez a book by a German photographer. Each page had two images of a person who was dying, one shot just days before death and another taken just hours after death, all close-ups, and all laid out on facing pages. The left side always had the living face, eyes still open in a pained and sickly gaze.

Some people say the essence of beauty is youth, that to be young is to be beautiful, but in truth, the essence of beauty is life. To be alive is to be beautiful. That's what Inez had seen in those photos. Next semester the art school had arranged permission for her to draw at a hospice. It meant long bus rides across the Lions Gate Bridge. A thumping dread rose in her on every trip. She'd had to force herself to make the journey — although it wasn't the ninety-minute bus ride that distressed her. Waiting on the other end were rooms full of the dying.

She had a talent for it though. She'd known that, but for years after drawing at the hospice, she'd shied from the form, and it was even longer before she again sketched a face. Now here she was once more drawing someone who looked like he was at death's door. She knew he wasn't going to die though. His cheeks already had some colour, less of the wasted and waning look that had been so haunting just this morning.

Soon enough he'd be awake. Soon enough he'd be walking about and then he could tell them how he'd landed here.

Art Kosky closed the apartment door and looked along the footpath towards Bee Street. No one in view. He cut across the gravel parking lot behind the building to an alley that ran down the centre of the block. At Douglass Street, he turned south. It felt good to be out of the apartment, good to be moving. A chill from last night's fog clung to the morning air.

Three blocks on, a bus rolled past, slowed, signalled then pulled over at the next stop. Art ran. He wouldn't have made it except an elderly woman caught the wheels of her shopping cart on the bus's entrance platform. Art bent and lifted the cart, helped her inside.

He was at the library a few minutes before nine. People stood clustered around the entrance waiting for opening time. Art kept walking, lit a cigarette and smoked as he walked. A trip around the block and the main doors stood open.

Three typewriters sat in a row against a wall on the library's second floor. Art took the one in the corner, the same typewriter he'd used with their previous two communiques. He rolled in a blank sheet of paper, set the margins, opened his notebook and began to type out what he'd written there.

Statement Concerning the Greer-Braden Compound Bombing

Earth Action Now takes responsibility for the action at Ester-way Ridge. Our sole target was the machinery stored in the Greer-Braden warehouse, the machinery that clear-cuts forest, destroys our mutual heritage, causes landslides, undermines

/////

biodiversity and reduces our very oxygen supply. We took specific
precautions against hurting people. We posted a lookout and put
ourselves at risk by remaining at the site to ensure we could see
the target at all times.

What the press hasn't said is that the night watchman got out
of his truck only after the two-minute timer was set. He'd been in
his truck out of sight behind the compound. When we saw him,
we tried to warn him of the bomb. We waved him away. After the
blast, one of our members stayed close waiting for help to arrive.

We are all deeply sorry for what he's suffered. This was never
our intention.

— Earth Action Now

It was short and to the point, text he, Derek and Fay had been able to agree upon. Their first draft had included a list of demands: reversal of the government's new land use policy, an end to clear-cutting, conservation guarantees for all remaining old growth. Fay had insisted they cut these words but they were with Art still. For years he'd sent letters, petitions, pamphlets, piles of words like these, years of words, all of them stacked in some office and ignored. That was part of what had brought them here. Years of getting nowhere, shut out, turned away cold, frustration built up and bound to boil over.

It had started last May, just over a year ago. He and Jeremy had brought in two Earth Firsters for a seminar on direct action. One was from Oregon, the other from England. They'd called the session More Effective Protesting. Nothing new in it really, but during the morning break, when Art created a sign-up sheet for a carpool to Bridal Veil Flats, Fay tore a piece of paper from his three-ring binder and posted a second sign-up sheet titled "Direct Action Volunteers" with a note that said, "Put your body where your mouth is."

He and Fay had only been together for a couple of months at that point. They'd met at a party in March then bumped into each other again at a sparsely attended benefit concert for the Leonard Peltier Defence fund. They'd shared a drink. Fay had invited him home. The story she'd told ever since was that Art more or less moved in after that.

At the end of the session with the two Earth Firsters, almost a dozen people had signed up for the carpool to Bridal Veil Flats, but the Direct Action volunteer sheet had only four names: Art Kosky, Fay Anderson, Derek Newfeld and Jeremy Dunn.

Pete joined the group that summer. Jeremy brought him north with a couple of others to protest the expansion of the clear-cut beyond the flats. Pete settled into the group well — he was easy to talk to, clearly committed. Throughout that summer and fall, they'd travelled up-island for a series of disruptive protests, Fay and Art together on every trip, chained to trees, strung up in hammocks, their bodies laid out in front of a bulldozer. Come spring they gave up on Bridal Veil and targeted the new logging road planned across Bedwell Pass. In Art's mind, it wasn't the fact he'd pretty much moved into Fay's apartment after their first night together that cemented their relationship: it was the solidarity of those trips up-island, the two of them a unit, together every day.

And now here he was typing out words to try to justify an explosion that had almost killed a man.

Art used the coin-operated Xerox machine to make copies of the statement. In a stall in the second floor men's room, he pulled on wool gloves and wiped off the paper. He wiped each sheet with gloved hands, wiped both sides against his shirt sleeves and finally against the fabric of his jeans. He did the same with the envelopes then sealed them with a drip of tap water.

Art mailed the letters then walked back to Bee Street. It was a good two miles, but the sun was high, and he smoked as he walked. He turned onto Bee Street just before eleven to find a police cruiser parked directly in front of the building. Two uniformed cops stood on the sidewalk. A flare of panic rose and

Art's feet stopped. The men were talking but it wasn't clear if they were coming or going. He started walking again, but still had no idea what he should do. Derek was in there. Fay was in there. One of the officers started down the footpath that led to the basement suite. The other started up the front steps. Quan's Convenience Store had a pay phone, but it was too late for that. Calling wouldn't help. The cop would just hear the phone ring. He might hear Fay answer it. A bead of sweat trickled down Art's ribs. July, and he was wearing a leather jacket. As he lowered the zipper, he caught a glimpse of the cop knocking at the side door. This wasn't a raid then. Two officers, one squad car. They just wanted to talk. They had questions. Following some kind of lead. Once past the building, Art quickened his pace. He turned at the corner, jogged as far as the alley then turned into the little parking lot. The cop was gone from the side door. Out on Bee Street, the squad car pulled away.

Art slid in his key and knocked gently. "It's me," he said. "It's Art."

Fay stood in the hallway. "Fuck," she said. Her face was white, her voice withered.

"Get your stuff," Art said. "Collect the bare essentials then we get in the car and go."

"They were here. They were just knocking."

"I know. I saw. Where's Derek?"

"Asleep."

"He didn't hear?"

Fay shook her head. "The one knocking stood so close I could hear his radio. He was right there. I could hear the crackle of static on his radio."

"They wanted to talk, Fay. They were sniffing around for something, that's all."

"How do you know?"

"One squad car, an officer upstairs and an officer down. They obviously had no warrant."

"I don't know, Art. I just —"

"It was something routine. I could tell by their body language. They knocked on the door upstairs as well." Art leaned forward, kissed her on the lips. "Let's get some camping gear and go for a few days. Just in case. Grab the basics, any canned food we have."

"And what about Pete?"

"We can come by later and check on the place. We just shouldn't stay here for a while."

Derek stepped into the cramped kitchen. He squeezed the bridge of his nose.

"We think we should leave," Art said. "At least for a while. Lie low somewhere. Get your sleeping bag, your camping gear."

"What's the rush?" Derek's voice was sleepy and stiff, a yawn hidden among the words.

"The cops just knocked," Fay said.

Derek looked from one to the other like they might be joking. Fay slipped past and walked down the hall.

"You serious?" Derek said.

"It's temporary."

"You're telling me the cops were at the door?"

"Consider this a precaution."

Derek raised a fist, punched the drywall. He hit it again as Art stepped past, a heavy thud. By the time Art turned to look back, Derek had split the drywall open.

"Five minutes and we're in the station wagon." Art collected a sleeping mat and a down sleeping bag. He stuffed them into his pack, picked out a few items of clothing, a rain jacket, a pair of jeans, a few shirts, hunting knife, water bottle. "Time to go."

In the hallway, Art touched the broken drywall and a bit of plaster crumbled between his fingers. Derek was tightly wound at the best of times, only it was worse now. Every minute of these past three days he'd seemed taut, ready to snap.

CHAPTER 12

The familiar thump of the newspaper awoke Tab. She was down-stairs on the sofa, bathrobe on, dozing after a restless night. The moment she opened her eyes it was there: the police had come by. They wanted Peter. They wanted to talk to him about a bombing.

Frank was upstairs in the shower. A floor away and she could still hear the spray of it. At the door, she squatted and scanned the paper's front page then flipped through to the national section. "Community Seeking Answers after Blast." The photo below the headline showed a man with a broom of a moustache and a cleft chin, rimless glasses. Owen Tuggs now in intensive care in a Victoria hospital.

Tab carried the newspaper into the kitchen, laid it on the counter and stared at the picture, stared at the name Owen Tuggs, let the black bones of the letters settle on her retina. The article said he had a nine-month-old baby. It quoted his brother Dustin: "The whole family is in shock. Owen's a good man. He was just doing his job, providing for his family. Whoever did this needs to step forward, anyone who knows about who did this needs to step forward."

Upstairs the shower shut off. Tab started in on the article all over again. This time a different name leapt out, Inspector Lawrence Burrell, Integrated Intelligence, RCMP. He said they were following all leads, they had every available officer on the case. He'd held a news conference and the article quoted him twice.

/ / / / /

Of course, none of this meant Peter had been involved. No mention of his name, no suggestion of anything to link him to these Earth Action people.

The stairs creaked, and that pulled Tab's attention away from the paper. She folded it and put it by the stove. She hadn't started breakfast yet, hadn't even put on the coffee. Frank stepped into the kitchen, settled onto one of the stools at the island and switched on the TV.

Tab occupied herself with the coffee. The TV fell silent a moment. On the opposite side of the island Frank fumbled with his lighter, struck his thumb against the wheel. He was wearing a suit, had his tie already done up. He drew on the cigarette and inhaled.

Tab set out cereal and milk. "You're going to work?"

"Have to. Quarterly reports tomorrow."

She pulled his cigarettes closer, lifted one and reached for his lighter. She didn't want to be alone in the house. "I couldn't sleep last night."

"You should take something. You should see Dr. Lambert."

Tab poured two cups of coffee. She drank hers black, smoked while the morning sunlight passed through the back door's window and warmed her legs. On TV, a reporter was talking about traffic holdups, a bad morning commute. God, what did people consider news these days? Things were happening in the world, awful things.

Frank stood and finished his coffee.

"No granola?" she said.

He kissed her on the cheek. His face was lively with the scent of Old Spice. "Better days are coming."

A moment later, the side door closed. The car started. Frank often said better days were coming. He said it when the Maple Leafs lost their division last year, said it when she sprained her ankle and needed crutches. He even said it after their parakeet died. Would he have been so flippant if it were Steven or Jimmy? If it were one of his own sons?

Later that morning, Tab called directory assistance to get the RCMP's Vancouver number. She dialled, spoke to a receptionist then waited on hold. Guitar music tinkled in the background. It was still early, not yet eight out west. She ran her thumb down the side of the cork board that stood propped behind the phone. On the other end of the line, Burrell answered, his voice shorn and quick. "Larry Burrell speaking."

"My name is Tab Harper. I'm Peter Osborne's mother. I don't know if you —"

"Mrs. Harper," he said. "Thank you for calling."

"You know who I am?"

"I know who Peter Osborne is."

"I hope it's okay that I called. I saw your name in the paper. The police came by my house." She stopped there. She hadn't planned out her question. "I'm wondering, I mean, this may seem like an odd question, but is it possible there's been a mix-up?"

"A mix-up?"

"With my son, I mean. It is possible you have the wrong person."

"Mrs. Harper, your son and the people we believe he's with are the target in one of the largest police operations this province has ever seen."

"Oh." Her voice was faint, barely a sigh. She'd had hopes. Even this morning in the clear light of day she'd clung to a secret hope for some kind of mistake.

On the other end of the line Burrell was still talking: "At this moment, it would be impossible to overstate how important it is that your son get in touch with us."

"I was looking for him before, you know. We'd lost touch and so I called everyone out there, people he knew, his friends. I called the university, even the police."

"Do you have any notes from that search? Any kind of records?"

"I've been thinking I should start looking again."

"I'm not sure that's a good idea, Mrs. Harper."

"If I could find him, I think I could help him clear his name."

"Mrs. Harper, your son will get due process, but you have to understand, we believe this group set a bomb that almost killed a man."

"My son isn't dangerous, Inspector."

"Your son is wanted for questioning, and the best way for you to help him, and to help us, is by telling us all you know."

"If I found him I could hire a lawyer. Not that I think he did this, but just in case, I mean, if he was somehow involved then we could at least negotiate a plea bargain or something."

"Mrs. Harper, why are you calling if not to help the investigation?"

She wasn't sure how to answer that now. She'd seen his name in the paper. He was the man in charge. "I want to find my son," she said.

"Believe me, I understand."

"I don't think you do though. I don't even think you could. Until you're a mother, you couldn't."

Handset back in the cradle, Tab reached for her address book, flipped through until she found the number for Bev Norman, an old girlfriend of Peter's — a woman she'd talked to earlier in the year after losing touch with Peter. Tab pressed the receiver tight against her ear until a message cut in to say it wasn't a valid number. She tried again then phoned directory assistance. They had four listings for B. Norman and she went through them one by one. On the third, Bev answered.

"It's Tab Harper, Peter Osborne's mother." She waited for a response. "Are you there?"

"This isn't a good time. I'm running late as it is."

"I just wanted to know, I just had one question."

"I don't know anything about this stuff, if that's what you're calling about."

"After all that looking back in the spring, I never found him, you know, never got in touch at all."

"I don't know where he is."

"Do you think he could have done this, Bev? That bombing on the island. Could he be involved?"

Tab waited. The woman's breath travelled down the line in faint trembles. "I guess I do," Bev said. "If I'm being honest. Not that I have any evidence. I mean, I wasn't trying to cause trouble."

"What do you mean?"

"It was in the paper and all over TV and ever since those two firebombings, I've had this awful feeling, this anxiety. I called the tip line just in case."

"What did you say on the tip line?"

"I was just trying to help. You have to understand —"

"Please just tell me what you said."

"I told them Peter's name and then I remembered there was this other guy. I remember his name because it's my brother's name. Arthur. Only I think this one goes by Art."

That wasn't a name she'd heard before. Art.

"What did you say about Art? I mean, who —"

"I'm late for work, Mrs. Harper."

"If I came west," Tab said. "Could I see you? Could you maybe help me?"

CHAPTER
13

Inez tied the blinds above the sink and moved the breakfast dishes from the counter into the basin. She added the empty bowl and spoon from the tray she'd taken to the stranger then switched on the weather radio and waited for the southern coast report to repeat itself. Fourteen knot winds increasing, chance of afternoon showers, high of twenty-one, low of twelve.

"I should go swimming." She said that to herself as much as to Dennis. He had his head down, book in hand, lips pursed.

"Are you staring?" Dennis said without looking up.

"Request permission to stare, sir." She gave a mock salute.

"Permission denied."

"What are you reading?"

Dennis tilted the book to show its cover. Some kind of murder mystery.

"Andy give you that?"

"Loaned it." The boy marked his place and closed the book. "What do you think the stranger's doing here?"

"Could be a lot of things. Perhaps he was a tourist, wandered out to see the coast then fell ill. Maybe his boat crashed against the rocks somewhere nearby. For all we know his rental car is out there waiting for him."

"You say murder mysteries are boring, but if you'd read a few yourself then you might know."

"Know what?"

/ / / / /

"The mud and leaves in his hair means he's been sleeping or lying on the ground, so he's been lost for some time. He's also sick. And yet no search party."

"You're quite the sleuth."

"Which means no one else knows he's missing. Based on his clothes, some kind of day tripper or weekend camper maybe."

"When he's feeling better, we can ask." She set the remaining breakfast dishes into the empty basin. "It's going to be a nice day. Why don't you take care of the dishes then go do something."

"I'm going to work on my kayak." He opened his book and returned to reading.

/ / / / /

Inez's wetsuit hung on the clothesline strung between the corner of her cabin and the spruce tree's trunk. She pulled it from the line and stripped standing on the steps of her porch, tugged the neoprene over her legs and hips. She'd inherited the wetsuit from Leo Savoi, a kid who'd pitched a tent here and surfed for a few months back in '88. He'd been an odd one: plenty of money and all the latest camping gear. Two months or more he stayed then he started telling people his father had died and he had to return to Switzerland. It was never clear how he'd known his father had died. He just upped and left, gave Andy his longboard, gave Inez his wetsuit. It was loose at the shoulders, which made it easier to swim in, but the neoprene squeezed tight across her hips and chest.

Inez stuffed strands of her hair into the sides of the hood as she walked across the sand and into the icy Pacific. Ocean water passed through the neoprene and touched her skin. Her legs tingled with a cold burn. A few more steps and a churning wave lifted the water level. Her breath caught, and then she pushed off, threw her arms forward and began to swim directly out towards open ocean. Her cheeks and lips touched water, ice against exposed skin as she ducked under the curling wave, and swam past the break to where the swell was calmer. She turned there, took a deep breath and cast out in a line parallel to the beach.

Twenty-four hours the stranger had been here and Inez still hadn't told anyone. Not Christian, not Oscar, not Andy. Some protective instinct perhaps, or maybe it was the desire to hoard a secret, a little thrill all her own, the fact that this stranger had landed in their laps carrying with him a bundle of unanswered questions. Although Dennis might have told someone, Andy at least. Andy occupied the cabin nearest theirs, and had a collection of books Dennis liked to pore through.

The swell rolled under Inez's body. She cast out an arm and took in air. Almost every day, spring, summer and deep into the fall, Inez swam the length of the beach, down to the rocky spit of land that stood between Baker Beach and Paulson Bay, then she turned and headed home. Today the swell was unseasonably rough and by the time she neared the rocks, her breathing was ragged and strained. The flutter of her kick had weakened. Her arms felt weighted. Feet down, she touched sand. A couple of wheezy breaths and she turned and started back towards her end of the beach.

When he'd given her the wetsuit, Leo had said that if you swim every day you never get sick, no colds, no sore throats. It was a warm fall day and he held it up to measure against her. This was before Ray left, and he swore she'd never use it, a flat out declaration. Although, if he hadn't said that, maybe she never would have — there'd always been that combative element between them.

Memories like this often surfaced while Inez swam — her mind groping for distraction from the physical strain. Arms raised, stroke after stroke, and as she worked her way back along Baker Beach, Inez was transported to those dark days after Ray left in the autumn of '88.

They'd only been at the Point four months, and yet with Ray, decisions were often sudden and ferocious. The day he announced he was leaving, Inez wasn't sure if Ray was leaving her, leaving the Point or leaving both. She'd had to ask him outright.

After he was gone, darkness took her down, a steady tug that grew into an engulfing pull. At times the weight on her chest was so heavy she could hardly breathe. She'd lain under the covers and told Dennis she needed rest. She said she wasn't feeling well. He was eight. What was she supposed to say? At least Dennis had never started calling Ray *dad*.

On one of those first mornings after Ray left, Dennis and Gunter caught a coho from the rocky edge off the Point. Standing in the doorway, Dennis held it high, but the best Inez could do was a grunt. Her son's grin slipped and Inez hated herself all the more. She didn't feed the chickens, didn't water or weed the winter vegetables. When people stopped by, Inez found nothing to say. The cabin seemed big all of a sudden. Four hundred square feet but somehow big and empty without Ray.

For almost a week, Inez didn't get out of bed and when she did rise, it wasn't because of Dennis: Leo's wetsuit sat folded on the dresser and she remembered Ray's insistence that she'd never use it. That afternoon, she undressed and pulled the neoprene over herself. The searing shock of cold water felt good, and for a while she just submerged herself. Waves knocked her back, and she went under then rose again, mouth filled with water. She heaved, coughed and spat, and it occurred to her she might have some subconscious wish to drown herself.

That thought took hold as currents carried her. She tried to lie still, let her body travel, and in the end, she crawled onto the rocks at the edge of the Point. The studio stood there, the one Ray had built for them at the base of the Point. All his canvases and paintings were still in there. Standing in her wetsuit dripping water, she unfurled the paintings, lay one unframed canvas over another and looked across the dark cityscapes, minutely detailed, brick and broken curb stones, garbage cans and hooded figures, shopping carts, faces at dusk. He hadn't painted anything since coming out here. She hadn't either. They'd built a cabin and this studio. Ray had done a few wood carvings, but all these paintings were from the city and looking at them now, it struck her that Ray had been painting the periphery, avoiding what really mattered. None of these paintings came even close to any fundamental truths.

The next day, Inez returned to the studio. She mixed dark, earthbound colours, what she came to call a coastal palette, and for the first time since they'd moved here, she painted.

Rebirth powered those first few brush strokes, and spite too — a defiance and pleasure in painting over his work. Beyond all that though, an overwhelming feeling of relief enveloped her. This thing she'd come here to do, this art, this painting, it was waiting for her. It had been here all along, ready and willing. All summer they'd been building, preparing, setting themselves up and here this was lying in wait. She looked out the window to where the woods were shaded to blue — a million uncut Christmas trees, dark and shadowed and she remembered how she'd wanted to paint this place, how excited she'd once been at the thought.

That night, Dennis said, "Are we going now that you're better?"

"No," she'd said. "We're not going anywhere."

/ / / / /

Inez let the surf carry her in earlier than she usually would have. She wasn't halfway back across the bay, but she paddled in with the waves then crawled up onto the sand. She spread herself on the sharp slope just above the reach of the swell and hauled in air. It was turning into a beautiful day, already warm if you could get out of the wind.

As Inez crossed the stream's delta on the way to her cabin, she passed a "No Trespassing" sign she hadn't noticed before, nailed a few feet above her head. She stopped in front of it. Christian mustn't have spotted it on his last search. Unless they'd been back. She looked up and down the beach. The logging company had turned vicious these past weeks: a wild dog marking its territory, pissing on every tree it could find. Inez pressed her feet hard into the sand. Walking the last hundred yards to her cabin she forced her mind still and refused to let it travel into the dark thoughts surrounding the threat of eviction.

At her cabin, Inez peeled off her wetsuit. Scout trotted over and sat nearby as Inez hosed herself off with a brief blast of the stream water she piped down from the hill. She patted the dog, wrapped a towel around herself, hung her wetsuit and went inside to get dressed. The dishes were washed and stacked, Dennis gone. Inez gave the Coleman stove a few short pumps and sparked a lighter above the burner.

All this past month, whenever someone walked down towards this end of the beach, Inez's first thought was of lawyers and of logging company agents, police even. Although of course, she hadn't thought that when the stranger arrived. He'd walked from the woods, clothes streaked in mud, stumbling along a path that dead-ended at Seeley's Bay.

Inez made tea and carried her mug outside, enjoying the porcelain's warmth and aware of the weightless exhaustion of her body.

A cup of tea might do the stranger good, wake him up enough for a conversation. She was as curious as Dennis as to how he'd gotten here. She took another gulp then spotted Christian crossing the clearing below the garden fence.

He had one strap of his overalls undone. It made them hang a little looser but his belly still stretched the denim. He appeared to be chewing something, moving a wad around his mouth.

"I hear you're harbouring a fugitive," he called from a few yards off.

"Fugitive's a stretch," Inez said. "Some guy stumbled in here yesterday, on death's doorstep."

"What's he doing here?"

"Recovering."

"What are the details though? What did the man say?"

"He mumbled a bit."

"You didn't consider introducing us? Taking care of the formalities?"

"For crying out loud, Christian, he's asleep. He's half in a coma." Inez's fingers tightened against the smooth sides of her mug. Christian's bluster always made her a little defensive, his king-of-the-hill approach to conversations.

"Inez, you can't be half in a coma."

"There's a 'No Trespassing' sign by where the stream meets the beach."

"A what?"

"A sign."

"Fuck."

"I figured you'd want to know as apparently I'm to report to you every time something happens around here."

"Oh come on, Inez, don't blow this out of proportion. I'm trying to say there are social norms. Niceties. It ever occur to you these two events are connected?"

"The sign and the stranger?"

"Maybe he's with Greer-Braden, maybe he's a lawyer, maybe he's the guy going to make us an offer."

"That's funny. That's in fact hilarious. He's in Gunter's cabin. Take a look at your supposed company lawyer. Take a look at the man about to make us an offer."

"I'm just saying for an example, Inez. A for instance."

"He's pretty out of it. It'll be a one-way conversation, but go ahead and ask how much money he's going to offer us."

"I think you're overreacting a little, Inez."

"Maybe he's even got it on him. You could pat him down."

She watched him go, a lumbering walk, like his body had grown too big for its frame. She wondered if maybe he'd been drinking.

"The 'No Trespassing' sign is that way," Inez called. "Down the beach not up the ridge."

Christian passed through the fruit trees without acknowledging her comment. Even the shortest of the trees now stood taller than Christian. Both the apple and pear trees showed some small hard fruits.

Inez flexed her toes and pressed the rocker back and forth. To follow Christian would somehow reveal too much. Her thumb pressed against the rim of the mug. Why was she being so possessive? A slow count to one hundred, and then she pushed herself from the rocker and walked after him.

Of all the people still at Baker Beach, Christian had been here longest. He claimed to have been here so long he didn't remember why he'd first come out. There'd been people before him, of course, a man trying to work a copper claim at the far end of the bay, a couple of draft dodgers. The only draft dodger left was old Ernie, and he'd arrived a year or two after Christian. The numbers had dropped in the wake of the eviction notices. Maggie and Gunter left over two months ago, Inez now the only woman left at the Point.

By the time Inez reached the top of the ridge, Christian was already leaving the cabin. He closed the door gently and made sure it latched.

"So?"

Christian turned. "He's asleep."

"I guess you did most of the talking then?"

"Every story that starts with a stranger arriving in town ends in trouble, Inez."

"You still think he's with the logging company?"

"That doesn't look so likely."

"What's the problem then?"

He held a finger in the air. "Trouble with a capital T. Think of Shane, Music Man, Pale Rider, all those things."

"Christian, I have no idea what you're talking about."

"You say he came here without anything more than the clothes he was wearing?"

"That's right."

"No ID, no wallet?"

"When he's awake, we can just ask him."

She wanted to step inside and check on the stranger herself, but Christian's bulk occupied the little porch with a proprietorial stance, so she turned and started down the trail, retraced her own footsteps. A bit of tea still sloshed about in her mug. When she reached the sand, she tilted her head back and drank it.

CHAPTER
14

Tab flew west on an early morning flight, arrived before noon and took a bus to the RCMP building, a four-storey structure: grey, concrete and lined with narrow windows. She gave her name and appointment time to the clerk and a few minutes later, Inspector Burrell strode out. He touched her elbow as they shook hands. "Mrs. Harper," he said. He had a ramrod posture and square shoulders. It made Tab think about how close his name was to the word *barrel*. "Come on in and we can find a spot to talk."

Tab signed a guest register. The clerk slid a visitor pass across the counter, and Burrell led her through a set of double doors to a short flight of stairs. They passed clustered desks and office doors. Tab read the name plates: Sergeants and Staff Sergeants, one other Inspector. Burrell stopped at the final door and held it open. The office beyond was spacious and tidy. A baseball trophy occupied the corner of his desk along with a coffee mug. Three cushioned chairs stood opposite. Tab took the middle one.

"Care for a coffee?"

"Already had one on the plane. Two in fact." She held her purse to her chest, gripped it in both hands.

"I do appreciate you travelling all this way, Mrs. Harper. I've arranged for Sergeant Reynard to go through your notes and address book with you."

"Where do you think Peter might be? I mean, you must have

/ / / / /

your suspicions." She had spent most of her morning flight preparing this question. Now she tried to make it sound as casual as she could.

Burrell leaned forward. "We've followed up on all my suspicions, but if you've got any I'd love to hear them."

"I haven't. He still hasn't called me, in case you're wondering. I'm ready to look though. I'm ready to start in where I left off."

"Mrs. Harper, I hope that's not why you're here. I realize you want to help, but at this point you need to let us do the investigative work."

"The last time I saw him was Christmas. He was back for the holidays. It didn't go well, not from the start. My husband and my son, they argued. Frank's my second husband, Peter's stepfather. When I learned Peter had been expelled, I told Frank, which I maybe shouldn't have. He'd been paying tuition, paying for what we thought was tuition. Peter's father isn't really able to do that kind of thing, financially speaking. Frank had a fit. It was a big chunk of money."

"If you find him and don't report him, you could be considered an accessory after the fact."

"I want him to clear his name."

Burrell leaned back, and the springs of his chair creaked. "Mrs. Harper, the press is on us, politicians are on us. This morning I got an earful from a man on city council who is getting pressure because Greer-Braden's stock price has fallen. Their stock price, for God's sakes."

"I've got to at least try to find him."

"Greer-Braden is going to announce a twenty thousand dollar reward, and we're hoping that will loosen some lips. The best thing you can do is tell us everything you know. The names of his friends, his contacts, people you remember him talking about. Anything."

"I know. I will, but I've already talked to everyone I could think of. I mean, earlier in the year I did."

"Let me call Reynard. Did you bring the notes from your search?"

"Will this count? I mean if it somehow did come to laying charges, will this help my son?"

"I'm not the crown prosecutor, but I report all cooperation. If it should lead somewhere, if this helps locate him or any of the others we're seeking —"

"I have another idea. It sounds like there are others in this group. The mothers would tell me what they knew, before they'd tell you. Is there someone named Arthur or maybe Art?"

Burrell had the phone in his hand, but the name got his attention. He dropped the receiver into its cradle. "Arthur Kosky. Do you know him?"

"It's a name that turned up in a conversation. Could you put me in touch with him, or maybe his mother?"

"His mother lives in Sidney, over on the island."

"Kosky. Sidney," Tab said. "I guess her number would be in the phone book?"

"Look, I probably shouldn't have said even that much, but if she tells you anything, I want to know. And I want you to share everything you can, no matter how minor, with Sergeant Reynard. Even if it's just names and phone numbers, that's still helpful."

Tab didn't leave the RCMP building until almost four. Outside, the sun had ducked behind thick clouds. A taxi took her to the Howard Johnson she'd booked. From her room, Tab called directory assistance and spelled Kosky for the operator. There was an N.P. Kosky in Sidney. She wrote down the number and address. It took a moment for her call to go through, but eventually a woman picked up and said hello in a muffled voice.

"My name is Tab Harper and I'm phoning with a strange question. Mrs. Kosky, do you have a son named Arthur?"

There was a tick on the line, the faintest repeated click.

"It's about Esterway Ridge," Tab said.

"I don't think I want to talk to you."

"Mrs. Kosky, could I come and see you?"

The line was already dead. That had been a stupid way to start the conversation. She should have planned out what to say, should have introduced herself as Peter Osborne's mother. She dialled again. The phone rang and rang. A minute or more she waited then let the receiver slip from her hand into the cradle.

That evening, Tab walked to a nearby mall. It had rained since she was last outside, and the evening air still held the scent of it. In the food court, a Rod Stewart song played over the sound system. No words, just a piano, but Tab knew the song and sang snatches to herself as she ate from a box of noodles. There wasn't much chicken in the dish. It didn't even have many vegetables.

A woman passed pushing a double stroller. Near the middle of the food court stood a group of teenage girls. A young couple passed on the other side of Tab, and then a family of five. All of these people were in their own worlds, a bubble stretched tight around each of them. Just a week ago, Tab had been like that — absorbed in her own solitary world.

She'd helped Peter come out here. He'd wanted to come west and Tab had convinced Frank to pay for it as long as Peter got into a good university. It had hurt that her son wanted to go so far away, but she'd also hoped it would help heal the rift between him and Frank, somehow reset the relationship.

Peter always used to say Tab took Frank's side in things. He'd accuse her of choosing her new husband over her son. And maybe he'd been right. At least some of the time he'd been right. Helping Peter come west was partially atonement.

In the end, he got into three universities, every one of them over two thousand miles away.

/ / / / /

Back in the hotel room, Tab opened a bottle of rye from the mini-bar, poured it into a plastic cup and tried Mrs. Kosky again. Two rings and the woman answered. Tab's heart leapt. "Please don't hang up."

She had words prepared. She'd written notes on Howard Johnson stationery. "My name is Tab Harper and my son and yours are both suspects in the Esterway Ridge bombing." That was the first time she'd spoken words that linked Peter and the bombing. The phone line crackled. "I wanted to talk to you, Mrs. Kosky."

"About what?"

"I'm trying to find my son. I flew all this way to talk to anyone with some kind of connection, and I just thought. Because Arthur and Peter. Could we talk?"

"You're out here then? You're on the island?"

"I was planning to take the ferry over tomorrow."

"His name's Art," she said. "It's not Arthur. My son goes by Art."

CHAPTER
15

A noise awoke Pete, a sound from outside. He sat up a little and the bed springs creaked. Sunlight streamed through the window above his feet. Outside someone knocked, a quick rap on the door.

"Come in," he said, his voice thin and raspy from lack of use. A woman leaned her head in. "Welcome back to the living." Her name was Inez. Strange he remembered that. She carried a steaming bowl on a tray. Pete drew his hands from under the blanket. His lips were chapped. He was hungry. "Thank you."

She set her tray on a stump of wood that stood by the cot then reached out and touched his forehead. Her hand felt cold against his skin. She smelled of sawdust, of salt air and open ocean. "Fever's gone," she said.

"Where am I?"

"Gunter and Maggie's old cabin."

"But what is this place?"

"The Point. Baker Beach." Her face brightened in a brief but lively smile. "Just a few quiet people living quietly on the edge of the earth."

Pete's head sank back onto the mattress. "Of course," he said. "The squatters."

"That's not a term I like. We just live here. We're residents. Pretty simple, really." Another smile, punctuation to her words.

/ / / / /

"We're all curious about you. I don't even know your name yet."

"Ash McCabe." That had been his grandfather's name although everyone had called his grandfather Bud.

"Inez Pierce."

"Thanks for taking me in. And for the food."

"Not often a stranger stumbles in here half-dead. We've been laying bets on how you wound up here."

Bets were good. Bets meant no one actually knew what had happened. "Who is we?"

"There's Christian and Andy, Ernie, Oscar. My son, Dennis. There are a few empty cabins like this one." Inez raised her hands, palms up in a gesture that said *that's it.*

"The soup smells good. I could eat a horse right now."

"Broth's about all I've been able to get into you." She passed him the bowl. Pete lifted the spoon, took one sip then another. He let the soup roll through his mouth, salty and warm.

"Did you get lost?" Inez said.

"Me?"

"I mean, is anyone looking for you?"

He had soup in his mouth and the spoon at his lips. He swallowed and set the spoon down. Before he could speak though, she was talking again. "I guess I'm wondering if there's anyone we should notify?"

"No." One solid and definite shake of his head and he raised the soup bowl with both hands. He needed to keep his face calm. He had to keep thoughts from piercing through and giving himself away. They were squatters. They'd have no TV, no newspapers. This was the one place in the country where people might not yet have heard of Esterway Ridge.

"Dennis asked if you were in a coma," she said.

"I guess I was pretty out of it."

"You had a fever. You talked a little."

"What did I say?"

"Nothing too discernible."

"As long as I didn't embarrass myself." He offered a smile, but a nervous tremble made his face feel plastic. Who knows what he might have said while sleeping. Pete raised the bowl again, but there wasn't much left now. He needed to compose a good story, one believable and easy to remember, explain how he'd wound up here, buy himself time until his strength returned. As long as he kept his head and gave nothing away, he might be able to get out of here before any of them had even heard the words *Esterway Ridge*.

"You thanked us for saving you," Inez said. "That's one thing you said when you were still delirious."

"I guess you did save me, didn't you."

"You don't have a car out on the road or anything like that?"

"I hitchhiked." This was it, the start of his story.

"We like people with cars. Nothing like a lift into town. How did you come to be lost?"

"Walked down a logging road, turned off it after a while, went and found a clearing and staked my tent." He'd started in without really having a story planned. The words just flowed from him. "I wanted to be in the wilderness. Alone. Second night I think I ate some bad mushrooms, got sick and spent a day or two wandering, hallucinating maybe. Suppose I could have died." He ended it there. That was enough. "Who won the bet?"

"What?"

"You said you were betting about how I wound up here."

"Oh. Dennis, I suppose. My son. I guess he was closest to what you just described."

A son might mean a husband and a husband might have more questions. She'd only mentioned three or four men. He should have remembered their names.

"Do you want to rest some more? You still look tired."

"I am tired. I feel weak."

"If you're ready for a short walk later, mine's the painted cabin down by the beach."

"Yours?"

"Mine and Dennis's."

Inez rose from the stool, balanced the tray against her hip, and set her free hand on the doorknob. Pete stood to see her off, but on his first step he hit a low rafter with a shock that echoed through his skull. Bright flashes crossed his vision, and he bent, swore and pressed both hands to his forehead.

Inez was there beside him. She set down her things and helped him lie back. He could smell her again — the salt of her sweat, a tinge of woodsmoke. "Rest," she said, and although he was wide awake, and a charge of energy coursed through him, Pete kept his eyes closed. The woman's hand touched his shoulder. A moment of steady pressure then she rose, crossed the room and the door latched behind her.

/ / / / /

How had Pete wound up here? He'd been thinking about this ever since the blast, retracing roads taken, casting about to assemble the jigsaw pieces of his past. He'd first come west four years ago when he was nineteen, moved out here to shed himself, that was the best way to put it — ready to start again. Oddly enough, those were the same words his mother had used before she'd married Frank. She'd been ready to shed herself and start again. She might even have been ready to shed Pete. For years he'd felt like a burden in that new life of hers — the stepchild, the third wheel. Any answer to the question of how he'd wound up here started at least that far back.

In marrying Frank, it was like Mom had somehow switched sides. She started saying the things Frank said: Pete had to be more appreciative, he had to be less selfish, it was time to grow up. She joined Frank's church, started going to meetings of the Ladies' Auxiliary, hosted dinner parties for people at Frank's office. That was her new life and then five years later it was Pete's turn: an escape two thousand miles from Frank and his manicured house, on one of an endless series of tight-laid suburban streets.

Pete couldn't have imagined two more different worlds. Even now he could remember the most minute details from his arrival. The plane had banked just before landing and offered a view over a rolling carpet of the darkest shades of green, a beautiful stretch of land cut by coast and water and on that water, acres of raw logs in booms, an earth-toned blanket that filled the estuaries and waterways around the airport. That image burned his memory. It was like the first time he saw logging trucks: flatbeds packed with tree trunks thick around as Pete was tall, three or four trucks in a row and Pete there on the side of the road watching them pass, caught between horror and wonder. Those two visions were nothing to the first time he saw a clear-cut: the bald hills, the broken land, an entire valley torn up, a wasteland that looked like pictures of no man's land from the First World War.

He read a Garrett Hardin article called "The Tragedy of the Commons" that November, not because it was assigned in class but because Bev Norman said he should. By Christmas he was writing for the Dissenting Voices page of the student paper, articles about the raping of the land — forestry and mining companies, twentieth-century robber barons. He wrote about other things too: autonomous anarchy, wealth redistribution, corporate crime and liability. In September, he'd come west with slacks and button-down shirts, but he flew home that Christmas wearing a checked flannel jacket, Doc Martens and jeans rasped at the knees so the denim showed thin and white.

January he returned on a one-way ticket. Frank hadn't offered a return fare and Pete hadn't asked for one. He was so sure he'd found himself out west, sure he'd landed in the right place at the right time. The cold war was over, the Berlin Wall down, the world at peace, Eastern Europe free and optimistic. Things could be different. Now was the time. The environment was the compelling generational challenge and it was time to do something about it. Pete had talked like that, Bev too, all those people he used to know. Rivers were dying, forests disappearing, wildlife on the brink of extinction. Now was the time to do something, the time to forge change in the world.

Strange to think of where they were now, all those people. Bev would be in her cubicle at the Ministry of Health, owner of a newly built waterfront condo. She'd done exactly what they all used to rail against: students today, suburbs tomorrow, just like the flower children of the sixties who'd voted Conservative a few years later.

Pete knew that somewhere near the heart of his decisions lay a stubborn core — a determination to chart a different course, a determination not to be like everyone else. That was the tap root of any answer to the question of how he'd wound up here. Even as a child he'd been sure he had a purpose. He was meant for something important. All those years living with Frank and still he'd felt it.

Shortly after he was expelled, Pete spent one of Frank's tuition cheques on a camera, took it up-island, into the churned up clear-cuts he'd seen the year before. He'd tried writing for the student paper about what he'd seen and now he thought he might be able to show the crimes committed in the wilderness through pictures.

The trees where Pete grew up had narrow spindly trunks, their lean bodies eking out a life in rocky soil. The wilderness out west was such a contrast — so vast and rich, ancient and mighty trees, graceful giants that had stood here since before Columbus. And yet so many had already been mown down. People here on the coast didn't seem to realize what they had and how unique it was, how important. On that trip up-island, Pete shot roll after roll of film, photographed stumps that were as wide across as a dining room table, and afterwards he tried sending some of these pictures to newspapers, magazines, galleries even, but they all came back, rejection slip enclosed along with the returned slides. A few months later Pete met Jeremy Dunn. They were at the Anarchist Book Fair and they sat together. Jeremy had an enthusiastic smile and a light laugh. He'd looked directly into Pete's eyes, unblinking and steady. Pete told him he was a photographer and Jeremy said they could use a photographer.

A direct line led from that moment to Esterway Ridge and to Pete's presence there. If it weren't for Jeremy he'd probably never have joined the protests at Bridal Veil Flats, he probably wouldn't have gotten involved with Art, Fay and Derek in the first place, wouldn't have been with them at Bedwell Pass, wouldn't have made his home in this knot of activists. It was partially chance that had taken him down a road so distant from the ones Bev and others had followed, partially chance he'd wound up here. Another part though was optimism — a pervasive belief that he could make a difference, that change was possible and he could be part of it. He was meant for something big, something important. He'd been so sure this was his purpose.

CHAPTER 16

Walking the switchback trail down from Gunter's place, Inez found herself thinking of David Milne. The trees here often put her in mind of his Northern Ontario paintings — stark black against canvas deliberately left a dimpled white. She'd admired Milne for years. Part of the attraction was in the courage it took to use black. In a landscape. And more than just a little. One painting she remembered had been etched in black and set against the white of untouched gesso. He'd woven both extremes into his sparsely layered look.

Inez had tried to imitate Milne's way with paint and the modernism he brought to landscapes. This despite the fact Milne was part of the painting establishment that Ray so disliked. Ray had often said The Group of Seven had ruined it for everyone else, and the irony was that not very many even knew their names. He'd said this when he discovered Inez reading Milne's letters, and said it despite the fact Milne hadn't even been one of the Seven. Ray's influence on her was enough that Inez returned the book to the library without finishing it. She'd read his letters since though, and that was how Inez learned about Kathleen Pavey.

Milne had had a little cabin, a rundown spot on the edge of a lake in Northern Ontario. It was 1939 and he'd been painting there, holed up in this cabin, estranged from his wife. Kathleen Pavey had been in a canoe, alone on a camping trip. A squall blew her ashore, and that's how the two of them met, strangers

/ / / / /

in the woods. Kathleen thought him half-crazy. He was pacing, talking to himself, sick and on the edge of madness. She thought he had cabin fever and didn't want to leave the man like this, so she stayed and took care of him. He'd been in his fifties at the time, unbalanced, isolated, struggling in the north, living in his little cabin, painting the land he loved, yearning to capture that world and yet almost driven mad with the effort.

That was the heart of it: the thrill of stumbling upon a stranger in the wilderness, blown ashore by a squall or staggering from the woods on a dead-end trail. Christian might have thought it a problem, but for Inez it was a rare moment of excitement.

Back at her cabin, Inez settled in the rocker, set her feet on the railing made of driftwood and gnarled tree branches. It was a chilly morning and the breeze carried a salty bite. She wanted a cup of tea. She wanted to go and start her work, get into the studio while she could still make something of the day, and yet she was distracted now. It had been odd to hear the stranger's voice. Odd too the way he'd winced as he talked, almost a tic.

In the end, Kathleen Pavey had become Milne's wife. They were married in some Unitarian ceremony, not in any legal way. Milne was always legally married to his first wife, but he and Kathleen had lived out much of their lives in that little cabin on the side of the lake without running water, without electricity. In Inez's mind it had always been Kathleen that kept him going, Kathleen who maintained his sanity and thereby kept him painting.

CHAPTER 17

Art lifted a thin strip of baseboard moulding cap from the pile on the floor. The little basement apartment was still in the finishing phases of construction and a bundle of offcuts occupied the middle of the room. Art bent a piece and the wood snapped as he flexed it.

Fay sat on a sleeping mat beside the only light in the room, legs crossed, tin camping plate in hand, the last corner of a sandwich still on it. The suite was a single big room with no furniture save the folding chairs they'd brought down from the empty house above. They'd also found a desk lamp with a forty watt bulb in it, and the lamp cast a pool of light across Fay's legs.

Art pulled back one of the sheets of cardboard they'd set in front of the windows to hide the light. An opaque film coated the glass but through a thick scratch he could see a single car parked in the cul-de-sac and further along a garage door standing open. The next house down was still just a frame, its wood bones pale in the night. The father of Art's friend, Nathan, had built several houses at this end of Mulberry Crescent only his finances had gone dry and he'd since declared bankruptcy.

No sign of Derek out there, no sign of the station wagon. Not that he was likely to park it on the cul-de-sac.

"Only one place even has its lights on," Art said. "Half the houses in this development aren't even finished, the half that are seem unoccupied."

/////

"You think they might get a warrant, break in and search Bee Street?" Fay said.

He sat beside her on the sleeping mat. "We didn't leave anything incriminating."

Fay plucked at her shirt, dipped her head to check for body odour. "Everything is starting to smell."

He leaned closer, angled his head down.

"What?" she said.

"Let me smell."

She tipped up her shoulder, pushed him away.

"I miss you," he said, voice low then, almost a whisper.

"I'm right here."

"Not really. Not since we started this thing, since we went from us, from me and you, to Earth Action Now." That was the truth, nothing had been quite the same between them since they'd broken away from Jeremy Dunn and started down their own path. It wasn't just the fact they'd been living as a group, it wasn't just having other people around. Even now, with only the two of them, something wasn't quite right. He leaned close, kissed the tendons of her neck, bent his head into the crook of her shoulder.

"Derek will be back," she said.

"Not for a while yet." He kissed the edge of her jaw, the lobe of her ear, her cheek. He reached around, cupped her breasts, but she stood and his hands slipped down across her belly, fell away over her hips and thighs. "Wait," he said, "hold on a second," but she was already halfway across the room, camping plate in hand. She looked good though: even walking away from him she looked good — a flare to her hips, her shoulders set back.

Fay turned on the tap, rinsed her plate in the trickle of cold water that came from the faucet. She planted her palms on the counter, looked straight into the cardboard taped to the window as though she could see through it and into the backyard.

This thing between them, this rupture, it came from Esterway Ridge: Pete's disappearance, the shock of a man so badly injured, a man who might not walk again, might not even live. In the year and a half they'd been together, Art had seen Fay angry, frustrated, worried, excited. He'd seen it all, but underneath she'd always been feisty. He'd never seen her defeated, never despondent, and then overnight she'd become a different person — a distant cousin to her old self.

Seated on her sleeping mat, Art waited, hoping she'd come back, convinced it would mean something if she did. If she came back to him now, if she turned and crossed the room, it would mean all was well. And so he sat still. After a time he said, "Fay," but only in a whisper. He said it a second time, louder, and then finally rose and crossed the room.

He turned her around and kissed her, touched her face and the soft edge of her cheek, desperate for contact now, for the warmth of her body. His fingers ran along the angle of her jaw and he kissed her there, kissed the line of her neck, lips on ribboned tendons, on the hard edge of her collarbone. He began on the buttons of her shirt, slipped it from her shoulders and led her across the room.

He switched off the only lamp and they sat together in darkness. A little pressure and she lay back. Art spread himself across her, kissed her lips, her cheek, her neck and his hands slid down. He worked at her belt buckle, tugged off her jeans, all this while she lay still, body unmoving beneath his until finally Art said, "What is it? What's the matter?"

"I dreamt last night that Pete was here. That he was with us again."

He rolled off her. "Is that what you've been thinking about?"

"You say you're sure he's alive, so where do you think he is?"

"I don't know, Fay. I have no idea."

"He could be dead."

"He's not dead."

"If you knew he was dead, would you tell me?"

"Why would he be dead? And if he were dead, how would I know?"

"You're not telling me everything from when you drove back."

"I promise you I have no reason to believe he's dead." He waited and said nothing more, hopeful this would satisfy her, put an end to this line of questions.

"And so he just disappeared?"

Art let his eyes settle closed. "I know it's crazy, but that's what it seems like."

Fay pulled an unzipped sleeping bag across her body. With neither of them speaking, the house above them felt deeply silent, the whole development quiet tonight.

The door swung open. Fay sat up. Art sat up. He reached for his shirt. They had the light out, but a faint nighttime glow passed in through the open door and after a moment Derek said, "Jesus, you two." He set the grocery bags down.

"We thought it was locked."

"We're on the run, a man is in hospital because of us and you're fucking like rabbits?" The door settled closed behind Derek and it left the room dark until Art switched on the floor light. Beside him Fay's cheeks were red and streaked. She'd been crying while she lay next to him.

"Didn't we have an understanding?" Derek said. "That this wasn't going to happen."

Art tucked in his shirt. He couldn't say it hadn't happened. He couldn't explain that Fay had lain limp below him until he'd rolled off and so he just said, "Sorry."

That wasn't enough though. Derek had his hand raised, finger up. "When I let you talk me into this shit show, we agreed to set aside personal connections." Two big steps towards them, his fury swollen to fill the room. "All equal, all committed, one purpose. You think this isn't hard enough as it is?" Derek said.

"Don't look at me," Fay said. "Look at him." She rolled her shoulders and plucked at her shirt as though to resettle the clothes on her body.

Derek still paced, criss-crossing the room, his steps powered by anger. There'd always been something unpredictable about Derek, a volatility there. He finally stopped, sat in one of the folding chairs. "They printed our communique."

Art stood. "That's good. Excellent in fact. Any edits? Any changes they slipped in?"

"Take a look." Derek tossed the paper over. "There's an article about Owen Tuggs. They say he's still in intensive care."

"Does it sound like he's improving?" Fay asked.

"It's a newspaper article, not a doctor's report."

Art spread the paper on the dusty concrete floor and turned from the picture of a house fire on the front page. They'd printed the communique just below the fold on page two. He started reading it aloud. They'd printed it word for word. After the first paragraph, he slowed, stopped. No point reading their apology aloud. "You can't ask for better publicity than that. This is the kind of attention we've been looking for."

Their words in the paper was a sign of progress. No question that the blast on Esterway Ridge had launched them forward. Tragic, yes, but they'd written two communiques before this and neither had made it into print.

Reporting filled the remainder of the page. A picture showed the hospital where Owen Tuggs remained in intensive care. The article included quotes from his brother, his wife. It said the RCMP had nineteen officers full-time on the case. Art forced himself to set the paper aside. The words printed there would only dilute the relief he felt at seeing their communique in print. It meant progress. It meant their message was getting out there.

"Let's eat something. Let's celebrate. What else have you got in those grocery bags?"

Derek handed out slices of bread. They spread peanut butter and jam with Art's jackknife.

Art wiped his hands on his jeans, helped himself to a second slice. They'd been like family once, tightly knit and bound together, but everything changed once Jeremy left and it was worse now, worse since Esterway Ridge — the bickering, the tension, the sharp-edged tempers, all of it new. He cleared his throat and tried to put some energy into his voice. "While you were gone, I drafted another communique. Fay helped. It has some of the ideas we took out of the last. More political. They printed that one, so they might print this one."

"Does it present our demands?"

"Not demands per se." Across from him Fay held a single slice of bread in her hands. "You want to say anything about it, Fay?"

"No."

Art reached out and twisted the desk lamp so its light spread over his knees. They'd had good news today. Their communique in print was a sign. He had to ignore Fay's mood, he couldn't let it spread, couldn't let it get him down. He turned the page of the notebook. "It starts, 'Dear People.' Something like that. 'Dear Citizens.' Are you listening?"

"I'm listening," Derek said.

"'Species rise and fall. Societies rise and fall. If either is to endure beyond its own weaknesses, it needs a rare self-awareness: the ability to see when it is wrong and to understand when its path is too steep or leads to abyss. Beyond this heightened self-awareness, societies need individuals willing to act against personal interest, willing to risk their lives to pull their species back from the brink. Even then it may not be enough. Beyond those willing to lay down body and soul, survival may also require some who are willing to take up weapons, risk violence and the possibility of hurting fellow citizens.'" He stopped there. He looked up.

"That's it?" Derek said.

"No, there's a little more. 'Corporate greed and the fiction of continuous growth have cornered too many into the false belief that we can endlessly consume, endlessly pollute, endlessly destroy the life around us, and yet also keep living ourselves. We cannot. The wise among us know this. The righteous among the wise act. The brave among the righteous have taken up arms against the machinery that is destroying our earth and will, if unchecked, destroy our species.'" Art paused before he looked up from the notebook.

"So?" he said.

Derek stepped closer. He knelt and took the notebook from Art's lap, angled it and flipped to the first page. "I like righteous among the wise, brave among the righteous. That has a ring to it, but what about all that stuff we cut from the last one? Demanding a reversal of the land use policy, an end to old-growth logging. When we started, that was the —"

"The goal of this one is to get some attention, some support even. It's the political and philosophical framework. Maybe after List Cove we introduce demands. We're in a strong position now but we'll be in a stronger position then."

"Fay?" Derek said.

She hadn't even taken a bite from her slice of bread. She sat still in her folding chair. "The man could die. Owen Tuggs could. Pete's God knows where. That's all I can think about."

/ / / / /

They lay in a row on the dusty concrete floor that night, three mats, three sleeping bags. Most of the suite was below grade and the place stayed cool day and night, despite the summer heat.

Fay had curled on her side facing away from Art, lamp set just above her head. She had a book there but hadn't turned the page in a good few minutes. Art was sure she'd snap out of this funk. She just needed a bit of time, some distance. A few feet away, Derek lay with his headphones on.

Fay eventually reached over and switched out the light, but a few minutes later, Derek said, "Shit," and a rustle of nylon rose from the corner, the sound of a zipper. "Motherfucker."

"What is it?"

"Unbelievable."

Fay switched on the light and Art had to squint to keep his eyes open in the brightness. Derek still had his headphones on, Walkman held tight in his right hand.

"What is it?"

"Eleven o'clock news." Derek pulled the earphones halfway off, lifted the speaker from his left ear.

"And?"

"Tonight they announced a twenty thousand dollar reward. Greer-Braden's put money on our heads."

Art released a long, slow breath. A hollow sensation rose through his chest, and he could feel Fay looking at him, Derek too. Both had turned to him.

"Is that twenty thousand for each of us," Art said at last. "Or is twenty thousand for all of us combined?"

It was a shock and a surprise, but that's all this really was: a bit of news that didn't need to change anything. "I'd have thought I'd be worth a good twenty thousand dollars alone."

"You're not going to take this seriously?" Derek said.

"It's a shock to hear that kind of thing, but it's essentially good news."

Derek set his head back against the Gyproc wall. "Good news?"

"They're desperate, Derek. This is what I've been telling you. They don't know how to handle us, don't know what to do, and the fact they're desperate is a good sign. If they're desperate now, think of how they'll be after List Cove and Dutton."

He spread his hands, opened his arms, more confident now that the shock of the reward announcement had worn off. It was proof they finally had everyone's attention.

"We should go to Thurlow Road, check on everything there. It might even be worth going into the woods to do a test blast, maybe trying a different ignition system. We need to make sure List Cove goes off without a hitch."

"How the fuck are we going to plan another action with a reward out?" Derek said.

"They're scared," Art said. "They're desperate. They're throwing everything they have at us and it's not working."

They had to stay on track here. Hold the course: List Cove then Dutton Pulp and Paper.

CHAPTER
18

Mrs. Kosky was a slight woman with a long face and a pinched mouth, hair done up in tight curls. She met Tab at the door and led the way down the hall and into her living room. She favoured one leg when she walked, a faint limp until she stood behind an armchair and rested her weight against it.

"Let me put the tea on. I'll be back in a jiffy."

Tab sat. The sofa creaked as she settled into it. Photos hung on the wall opposite — Mrs. Kosky, her husband, two boys with them.

"I take tea black myself," Mrs. Kosky called from the kitchen. "But I'll bring out milk and sugar."

Tab drew a notepad from her purse and set it on the coffee table, pulled out a pen and laid it next to the notepad.

The kettle rose to a whistling pitch, and a moment later porcelain cups clinked against saucers. Mrs. Kosky returned with a teapot and cups on a tray. "This is Chinese tea, not Indian. Art brought me bags of it, all loose-leaf." She looked over at Tab with a flash of a smile. "Art's got his birthday soon."

"That will make for a difficult day. How old will he be?"

"Twenty-eight. I'm sixty-eight myself, you know."

"You don't look a day of it." She did though. She looked every bit of it — her eyes heavy, her face deeply lined. These past few days might have put years on her.

As if Mrs. Kosky were reading Tab's thoughts, she said, "All this stuff, it almost put my husband in his grave. He's

/ / / / /

seventy-seven. He hasn't been taking this well." She lifted her teacup.

"Do you know where our sons are?"

"Why stir the pot, Mrs. Harper?"

"They set a bomb. I mean, someone did. Maybe them. There's a man in hospital."

Across from her, Mrs. Kosky slid her hands down her legs and straightened her dress.

"I've been reading the newspapers compulsively," Tab said. "Trying to figure all this out, trying to understand."

"The police came by my house, knocked on the door. That very same day, Art called. He just said not to tell them anything. Shortly after that his pay phone ran out of money."

"Owen Tuggs has a son and a wife who live on the coast somewhere. She's been on the news. She said he wasn't even supposed to be there. He was just filling in for someone who was sick."

"Greer-Braden only hired security because there'd been talk about this kind of thing. They were the ones who sent him out. You know that, right? They deliberately put the man in harm's way."

"I was hoping you knew something, Mrs. Kosky."

"I know a lot of things."

"Was Art angry? Did he seem angry to you?"

"Angry? Art? No. He loves the outdoor world, the wilderness, animals."

"Has he ever been violent?"

"Mrs. Harper —"

"Please call me Tab."

"You obviously know nothing about my son."

"He'd spend less time in jail if they turned themselves in. I mean, if they did in fact —"

"Whose side are you on, if you don't mind me asking?"

"I didn't think there had to be sides."

"The way you're talking, it makes me wonder."

"Peter's twenty-three. It feels like just days ago he graduated from high school."

In a nearby room, a clock marked the hour with a single cuckoo.

Tab started in again. "The last time he was home, we got in a fight. He and his stepfather never got along. He cut off contact after that. More or less disappeared. I tried to look for him, I called around, talked to people he knew, but I was two thousand miles away and had no real idea. About all this, I mean. Earth Action and whatnot."

"So you want to track them down and try to get them to stop?"

"And turn themselves in."

"Who are you to tell them to turn themselves in? To say stop if they're not saying it?"

"You might not have heard of this out here, but a couple years ago when police raided a drug lab in Orillia, they just burst in and started shooting. They said they'd been fired on, only no guns were ever found. The people inside had been destroying the drug lab and it made a pop like a shot."

"This isn't drugs, Mrs. Harper. My God, they're not doing this to make money."

"You're misunderstanding. That wasn't the comparison I was trying to make."

"They're not doing it to hurt people either. And there's lots that agree with what they're standing up for."

"Including you?"

"Don't believe everything you read in those so-called newspapers. You asked about my son, well, I know he's nothing like what they're making this group out to be."

"I just want to make sure no one else gets hurt. That's why I'm here."

"That man was asleep in his truck then he walked into the blast. That's how it happened."

"Can't we try to stop this before there's another?"

"They deliberately sent that man up there. Even his wife said he didn't normally work a night shift."

"Surely there's something helpful you can tell me."

"I've said all I have to say."

Tab set her teacup down. She'd hardly drunk half of it. A moment later she stood and Mrs. Kosky followed. Standing at the door, Tab noticed an envelope on the hallway sideboard, an unmailed card addressed to Art Kosky, stamp already on it. Mrs. Kosky lifted it away just as Tab's gaze settled on the address. She saw the writing clearly though: 369A Bee Street.

/ / / / /

Bee Street turned out to be a one-block side street parallel to the estuary north of Chinatown. The street sign was bent and Tab passed it twice before slowing to properly read it.

369 stood halfway down the street — a tall, thin building with a flat roof. Tab parked the rental car and looked at the place. Every window had its blinds pulled. The wooden steps looked worn. They needed a coat of paint.

"A" was the basement suite with an entrance around the side of the building. Metal grills stood in front of the glass, the door a solid wood panel, dented and scratched. Someone had written "A" at its centre. Tab knocked. Bits of paint had chipped and the beet-red of the previous coat showed in streaks and splotches. Another knock. "Art?" she called. "Peter?" One more knock, hard this time. Her knuckles smarted. "My name is Tab. I'm Peter Osborne's mother." Ear to the door, she waited and then walked around front. Three letter boxes there, A, B and C, all empty. Up the steps, a brass letter marked the first door. It had once been a number three but had the top half cut away and had been flipped around to look like a "C". Tab knocked and peered through a gap in the blinds. She shifted to the next door over and knocked there. Two in the afternoon. Not likely to find anyone home at this hour.

Tab sat in her car and looked at the box-shaped house, the covered windows. Peter had been a happy boy. When he was little he had been carefree and joyous. Part of the change had been Frank. She'd known this. She'd watched it happen — the two of them tangled, herself caught in between. Peter's move out here was supposed to change that but when he returned it was only worse. She'd seen it on that last visit — a bitterness risen up in him, resentments with a self-righteous air, full of talk about the arrogance of others, of logging companies, oil drillers, mining companies, their political lackeys.

He flew west wanting to start again, but when he came back it was all still there and somehow grown worse — an angry burn to him. She'd thought the tension in the house had been Peter and Frank, but on both trips home Peter had seemed distant in a way he hadn't before — a widening gulf cut between them.

Tab tore a lined sheet of paper from her notebook, raised her pen and started with the date.

"I'm trying to locate my son, Peter Osborne." A simple, plain script, every word as clear as she could make it. "If you read this note, if you know where he is, would you please contact me?" She added her address and phone number and at the bottom wrote her name. Across the street she slid the note into the mailbox marked "A".

CHAPTER
19

Pete awoke with a spasm of pain that lanced his chest and shot into his left arm. His lungs strained, but he couldn't get a full breath. He rolled from under the blanket and slipped off the cot, but his legs and arms didn't react quickly enough and his body hit the floor. One desperate gasp and the pain seemed to ease. Another breath and he shifted onto his side.

He'd had a repeated dream these past few nights: the instant the night watchman stepped around the corner of the Esterway Ridge warehouse and into the floodlight's beam. This was the moment he relived over and over — the two of them standing still and staring at each other.

Bracing himself above the counter and its plastic basin, Pete opened the spigot and splashed cold water across his face, rubbed his right hand over his chest and tried to rid his mind of those images, tried not to think of the night watchman and of what might have happened to him — whether he was conscious, whether he'd lived. He turned his attention out the window. The night sky lay sown with stars. Below that expanse, the tips of trees swayed in the wind, a ragged line of points. Still further down, dark soil, the earth itself.

He had to come to grips with this, find a way to deal with the memories that lurked so close, had to find a way to stop his mind retreating into the could-have-beens, the what-ifs. Every memory from Esterway Ridge carried with it a lead weight wish to travel back, a physical yearning to be there again

/ / / / /

and to do something, anything, differently — stop it all before that timer started ticking.

It was still possible that what happened at Esterway Ridge could change things for the better. Or could at least start that change. The government had negotiated with the FLQ after Pierre Laporte's death. That was a precedent. It could be happening now. They could be discussing terms. One bomb blast enough to scare sense into people. That's what he had to keep at the front of his mind: the larger purpose. They'd taken action on Esterway Ridge for all the right reasons, and now companies like Greer-Braden might just start listening.

They'd left eight more cases of dynamite above Thurlow Road. The plan had been three actions in quick succession and then negotiations. So as long as no one got hurt at List Cove or Dutton, this could still work out. Even if the blast at Esterway Ridge hadn't jolted people off their complacent asses, the next action would.

Standing before the cramped cabin's lone window, all of this seemed possible. More than possible, it seemed probable. Except that he was off on the edge of the continent, miles away from it all. Alone.

He had to find the others. It would be daylight soon. He could spend the day eating and resting and then leave after dark. He'd find a pay phone. He'd call until he got through to someone. Another day or two and he'd see Fay. What had passed between them may have been nervous lust, or the need for distraction, but the thought of seeing her still had a pull.

If he couldn't get through to anyone by phone, he'd just have to start walking. First night he'd make it to Sooke, sleep in the woods during the day and the next night he could make it to the western suburbs. From there he'd slip unnoticed onto a bus packed with commuters. Next stop Bee Street. Jeremy's place if he had to.

Pete had seen Jeremy only once since their return from Bedwell Pass. Just a couple of days after Pete told Fay he was in and ready to join, Pete and Jeremy had met for coffee at John's Diner. The moment they were seated, Jeremy leaned forward and said Art was crazy. Unbalanced. Jeremy said this more than once but all the while insisted he wasn't trying to change the group's decision, he just wanted to make sure Pete didn't get involved.

It took a while for Pete to come out with it. He flattened both hands on the Formica tabletop, looked over his fingers as he spoke: "I told Fay I'd help. I said I was in."

That stopped Jeremy. He pulled his cup a little closer, lifted it by the handle then set it down again. An REM song had started on the stereo. It was half over before Jeremy spoke again: "What happened to documenting the movement? Pictures that would show what's going on out there, the land they're destroying, all those bald clear-cuts."

"I don't think I was ever truly a photographer, Jeremy, just a guy with a camera."

"Hundreds of people work to make this movement peaceful, to ensure mothers and babies can be part of it. What Art's talking about could very well turn people against it all." Jeremy paused as the waitress stepped near. "Think about public reaction. This could set everything back, the protests building in Clayoquot."

"You said you weren't going to try to stop us."

"Us? It's us now, is it? I hope you're not doing this because Fay's somehow talked you into it."

"I'm doing this because I think it's right. I think it could make a difference, could be what we need to do to change things. More of the same isn't going to help. Taking more pictures sure as hell isn't going to help."

"What if you do this and someone gets hurt?"

"No one is going to get hurt."

"The whole plan is insane, Pete."

"It could actually be the smartest move any of us has ever made, only maybe you can't see that because it was Art's idea, not yours."

"You think that's why I'm against this?"

Pete didn't answer that question. Nothing was going to be the same without Jeremy.

"Anyone can start a guerrilla campaign, Pete, but how many people can end one? Better yet, how many people can end one successfully? Before you get involved, ask Art how he's going to stop, how he's going to end this."

That question clung to Pete, barnacle-like over the next few days, but he didn't ask Art, not just then he didn't.

CHAPTER
20

The trail down the ridge was easy to find, an eaten-away stretch of dirt, muddy and thin. Driftwood lay scattered about the beach, logs knocked up to the treeline by storms past. Pete sat on the back of the nearest log. Someone had chainsawed chunks from the end of it, pieces cut away for firewood or some other use.

Inez's cabin stood a hundred yards off, its bright colours ribald in the summer sun, the door an eggshell blue, shingled walls all orange and yellow, windows and door trimmed with purple and green. She was hanging wash, a basket at her feet. She lifted a pair of pants and a shirt then stretched out a sheet. Wind pressed it against her and for a moment outlined her slim body, then she turned back towards the cabin. There was a looseness to her limbs, something watery about the way her joints moved. On the porch, she slipped from her rubber boots, opened the cabin door and was gone.

Further along the beach, a man stood on a low shelf of rocks exposed by the retreating tide. He wore a straw hat and a loose red shirt, had a white flecked beard. He set a length of seaweed into a nearby bucket. Long and green, it looked like kelp or maybe alaria. The beach looked to be littered with the stuff. It would make for a healthy meal. Pete's stomach rumbled. He'd come down here for food. He needed to eat.

Eventually, the man stopped collecting and began to walk down the beach. Pete slid across the driftwood log and walked

/ / / / /

to the sandstone shelf himself, picked a tangled length of laver from the bottom of a tide pool, tore away a strand and jammed it into his mouth. It had a slimy texture, cold and gritty, heavy with the salt of the sea. Pete swallowed though. He took another bite and another. It would settle his stomach. It would keep him from starving. A soft sound on the sand behind him made Pete turn. Inez stood a few yards off. She raised a hand, sheltered her gaze and stared at him.

"Breakfast," he said and he could feel the flush of embarrassment on his cheeks. He'd been crouched like an ape eating seaweed.

"You must be feeling better if you made it down this far."

"Fit as a fiddle." The forced cheer in his voice made his words sound odd and unfamiliar. "You ever eat this stuff?"

"Not if I can help it."

"Did you know there's a special part of the tongue that tastes seaweed? It's one of the five basic tastes, not bitter, not salty, just, you know, seaweed. *Umami,* it's called."

"You might think of rinsing off the sand and the salt. Or you might think of coming over for some porridge. Although we'll have to put an end to the room service now that you're up and about."

"Porridge sounds excellent. I'll bring some alaria or laver or whatever this is."

She smiled and set a hand on her hip, the look of a woman preparing stiff words. "Seaweed doesn't play a very large role in our diet here, Ash."

It was odd hearing that name, and Pete took a moment to pin it to himself. "Someone came by here earlier collecting seaweed. That's how I got the idea."

"Old Ernie. He is the one person here that does actually eat quite a bit of seaweed."

Inez talked as she led the way along the beach. She pointed to where Ernie lived, halfway along the ridge, although Pete couldn't make out the cabin — the trees were dense, a woven curtain across the land. He tried to hide the effort it took to keep pace with Inez, tried to control his laboured breathing. "Ernie once collected twenty pounds of chanterelles," Inez said. "A gold mine of a haul. It could have made him almost a thousand dollars, but he ate them instead. Dried what he couldn't choke down in a week."

A spent wave reached out across the sand and for a few steps, Pete's boots cast up drops of water like glittering chains.

"I call this the Painted Lady. In winter the drab greyness of the world gets to me so after a couple of winters, I decided to brighten the landscape."

"And every can of paint you had to haul in by hand?"

"Hauling paint is the least of it. Sit and I'll check on the cook."

Pete eased himself into the rocking chair that stood halfway down the narrow porch, looked out over its railing of dried tree limbs plucked bare and woven together into a sort of tangled fence. Out on the water, waves set and rolled in, turned and broke, one and then another.

The cabin door opened and slapped shut, and there stood Dennis: curly red hair, tanned cheeks. He raised a hand in greeting.

"I'm Ash," Pete said.

"I'm making porridge."

"Pleased to meet you, Making Porridge."

Either the boy didn't hear or he didn't think it was funny. "How do you like your porridge?"

"I'm hungry enough I'll love it however it comes."

"It comes with goat's milk, no sugar."

"Okay." Milk sounded good, protein.

The boy rapped on the pane of glass overhead. "Inez, he wants milk." He opened a lawn chair. "Do you have an apartment?"

"Me? Well, sort of. I guess you could say I share one."

"We used to live in an apartment, in the city. Except that I can hardly remember it. There were lots of cupboards."

"You don't have cupboards here?"

"We don't have a lot of things. A record player, a toaster, TV, blender, stairs, light switches. We do have lights though." As he talked, his feet tapped against the legs of the folding chair, an offset rhythm to his words.

"Lights?" Pete said.

"Sunlight, lantern light, candle light. Just no switches. Although of course, nobody's got a switch for the sun."

"This is true," Pete said.

"Captain Cook was here in 1778. Everyone thinks he just went to the South Pacific, but he was here too, also Sir Frances Drake and the Spanish. I know a lot of things about this place. The Nootka and Salish are the main tribes here on the coast." Dennis brushed a curl of hair from his forehead. "Ask me anything you want to know."

Pete shifted to face the boy. "Where would you have to go to make a phone call? I mean, there's no phones here, right?"

"That's what you want to know?"

"You said anything."

"There's one at the gas station before Port Thorvald. Four bays over, and you could even get there by boat. Seeley's Bay, then Bodega Bay, Merchant and Buckley."

"What about on foot?"

"A path goes up to a logging road. Take that and turn right at the highway. Do you need to call someone?"

"I was just thinking that if I had needed a doctor, someone would have had to walk all the way out to the road and back to town."

"Inez has a two-way radio for emergencies."

A radio: that could be a problem. There must have been news broadcasts about Esterway Ridge. "Is a two-way the only kind of radio you have here?"

"That plus a weather radio. For getting the forecast."

"What about for news?"

"I don't think the reception's so good."

No radio, but there were other ways to get news. "When was the last time anyone who lives here went into town?"

"These aren't proper questions."

"You said I could ask you anything."

"Port Thorvald, Renfrew or Sooke?"

"Whichever."

"A couple of weeks ago, I guess."

The door behind them swung open and Inez stepped out holding a board with three steaming bowls of porridge balanced on it. She'd taken off her jacket and had tied her hair back into a loose ponytail. A pendant hung from a silver chain around her neck.

Maybe no one here had heard about Esterway Ridge yet. It seemed possible. Tonight he could just walk out, find that pay phone and call for help. Things might have settled a little by now. Hopefully they would have. At least enough that someone could drive out and pick him up.

21

Inez sat in the remaining lawn chair and passed out the bowls of porridge. Across from her, Ash looked comfortable seated in the rocker, this stranger who'd collapsed into her arms. He'd recovered well, more colour in his face now, and he and Dennis seemed to be deep in conversation. "I hope you like porridge," she said.

"It reminds me of my Urban Food League days. Couple of people there insisted porridge was the most environmentally conscientious food and convinced me to stop eating cereal — Cheerios, Rice Krispies, that kind of thing."

"What's the Urban Food League?" Dennis said.

"We wanted to turn all the grass on campus into veggie gardens. The proposal got shot down, but we started digging up the lawn anyway. We posted signs. 'Students Need to Eat Too.' 'Breaking the Chains of the Commercial Food Chain.' Security kicked us off, but a few of us came back at night, made two or three nice gardens, got seeds planted."

"So you're a student?" Inez said.

"They kicked me out."

"For planting gardens?"

"Others accepted a censure offer in order to stay. I took a more principled approach, didn't think we should just turn around and say it was wrong when it wasn't. I take it neither of you wants any of my seaweed as a second course?"

/ / / / /

"The only thing Dennis and I do with seaweed is truck it up to the vegetable garden and dig it in as fertilizer."

Ash's back straightened and his spoon touched down against the rim of the bowl. "I could do that," he said. "I mean, I realize I owe you. It wouldn't take much to collect —"

"Relax. You don't owe us. You're our guest."

"How about he owes us a fishing trip?" Dennis said. "Over in Seeley's Bay the fish practically jump into the boat."

"Seeley's might be a little far until he's rested." Inez scraped together a last spoonful from the oats remaining in her bowl.

"He could help get the kite down." Dennis pointed around the side of the cabin.

Ash leaned past her for a look.

"Last week he lost his kite in the sycamore's branches."

"Tree climbing happens to be a skill of mine."

"Go and get him the ladder then, Dennis."

"He said he could climb."

"It's a good ways up before the first branch."

Dennis carried his empty bowl inside, slipped out a moment later and headed towards Phelps's old cabin where they kept the stepladder. Inez watched as he trotted past the vegetable garden then turned to Ash. He'd been here four days now, a physical presence at the Point, but despite spending hours with him, and feeding him, she had no real idea of who he was.

"You got kicked out of school, you came here to camp, you used to eat porridge, what else can you tell us?"

"There's not really that much to tell."

"It's not often a stranger stumbles in here. We're curious."

"Well, in terms of where I'm from, back east, I guess. That's where my mother is."

"Brothers? Sisters?"

"Two stepbrothers, though both lots older, and now a baby half-brother, but mostly it was just my mother and me. My dad's in Arizona. He's the one with the new baby. That's the basics."

I came west for university, got as far away as I could get without getting wet." He set down his bowl. "Pretty soon I knew this was home."

"How did you know this was home?"

"This is the interrogation, is it?"

"You're like a celebrity in a village of six souls." Surely there was nothing wrong with asking a few questions after all she'd done for him.

"I was fourteen when my mother remarried. The man's name is Frank. The perfect example of a suburbanite, a buyer of useless junk and gadgets, a believer in the real estate market, in markets in general, in capitalism and corporatism, in plastic and petroleum. He buys and sells futures, which is essentially a way to make a mint on things failing. Worldwide drought and everyone's crops die but for him it means money in his pocket. So, we fought. From the start. From the very day we met. Whatever he was for, I was against. Whatever he was against, I was for. My mother used to pull me aside and tell me not to antagonize him. She'd tell me this was his house we were in. It was like she'd married up in the world and didn't want me jeopardizing it."

"What about your father and his new baby? Sounds like there's a story there."

"I haven't actually seen the baby. My father's doing his own thing."

"That's probably the right line for Dennis's father too. Doing his own thing." Dennis had never really met his real father, not since he was a baby, anyway.

Dennis was back now, ladder over his shoulder. Christian walked with him, hands tucked in his overall bib.

"Whoa," Christian called from a few paces off. "There he is, the new face in camp." He stepped onto the weedy grass and approached the porch from Ash's side. "Who the heck are you?"

"Ash McCabe."

"Christian. By name but not by nature." Christian trotted that joke out just about every time he met someone new. "Tell us then, Mr. Ash McCabe, what brings you to our neck of the woods?"

"I was sick and lost. It sounds like I almost died."

"We know that. We all saw that. What is it that brought you into the woods in the first place?"

"This is interrogation number two, Ash."

"Bet you a woman was involved." Christian gave Ash's arm a tap. He was more than a little drunk. "Am I right? Did you need to get away for a spell?"

"I lost my job, I wanted a break."

"Well, welcome to the Point, my friend. We've had some unusual arrivals, but it's fair to say yours tops them all."

Inez spotted Oscar standing by the nearest of the apple trees, shoulders stooped, canvas hat pulled low over his brow. Andy would be here before long, maybe even Ernie. The stranger was drawing everyone out. "Hello Oscar, come meet Ash."

Oscar stepped forward, gave a slight bow, nudged his glasses up on his nose. "Pleased to meet you. Glad you're feeling better."

Ash stood and reached over the rail to offer his hand.

"This is the best economical decision you could have made," Oscar said.

Ash glanced at Inez and his face revealed a moment of confusion. "I hadn't really thought about that angle. The economy of it."

"He's passing through," Christian said. "Crashing in Gunter's cabin. Temporary."

"We're all temporary now," Inez said.

"It's a very accommodating place." Oscar scratched at his beard and rubbed a hand across his face. "Aside from certain fundamental problems with land title and ownership."

"No one wants negative energy around," Christian said. "We need to think positive. We all need to have a figure in mind and visualize it."

"A technique," Oscar said, "for which no one has provided objective evidence."

Christian and Oscar were off and talking over each other as they often did, chattering in parallel lines. Eventually Oscar said, "Head in the sand is what allowed World War II. Head in the sand is what killed six million Jews." He didn't raise his voice. He wasn't even looking at Christian as he spoke. Inez had lost track of how this statement figured into his argument.

"Totally self-sufficient," Christian said. "Summer time's the prep season though. Winter hits hard."

"The trick is realism. If realism could be considered a trick. I'm not a believer in tricks, but I am a believer in realism."

"You applied for pogie?" Christian said. "Inez can tell you how. She's the expert. Free government money."

"I'm not the expert. We get a baby bonus. Andy's the one on welfare."

"Not that it really matters," Christian said. "You're not staying, are you, Ash? Just passing through."

"Is that true?" Dennis said.

"For God's sakes," Inez said. "No one is staying. At this point, do you think any of us are really staying?"

A silence settled. She'd spoken more loudly than she'd intended. All this babble, this flurry of talk, and she'd started shouting.

She turned to Ash. "We're being evicted."

"I'm sorry to hear that."

"It's nothing immediate. I mean, we hope it's nothing immediate." She didn't want to talk about this, didn't want a big argument in front of Ash.

He'd turned away from them though and was facing the water and the far side of the beach. "I can see why you like it here. I mean, if I'd known about this place a few years ago, like after I got expelled, I might have come and stayed. Plenty of times I've been out this way. Not Baker Beach, but the coast,

Port Thorvald, up and down here, quiet time by the ocean, sitting in among the big trees."

"Lots of people talk like that," Christian said. "Back to the land, collective living. Not many mean it. Fewer still last a winter. This place isn't what it seems, Ash. No easy living here."

"I'm not as wimpy as you might think, despite being lost in the woods. I'm good at communal living, I've tried —"

"This place has always been more for loners than for joiners." Christian hooked his thumbs into his overall straps. "People who come out to be part of some movement, they don't last. The ones who last here are the ones who come to get away."

"What's wrong with joiners? With being part of something bigger?" Ash looked about, at Oscar, at Christian, at her. "Movements, collective action, that's what's brought humans up from nothing."

"I'm just saying the people that last are loners not joiners. Refugees from the twentieth century."

Those words hung in the air, and Inez knew they held truth: in one way or another all of them were refugees. Out on the water waves curled in, long rows of whitecaps. Beside her, Ash stood. "I promised Dennis I'd rescue that kite."

He stepped down off the porch, bent and lifted the stepladder, and he and Dennis set off side by side, exchanged a few words as they crossed the scrubby grass at the edge of the beach. Inez waited until they neared the tree. "Are you two so excited to have a new face around that you can't clamp your mouths for more than a few minutes? It sounds like we're all two steps from the nuthouse."

Christian stepped onto the porch and settled in the chair Ash had just left. "Oscar is two steps from the nuthouse."

"I've seen him before," Oscar said. "Very familiar face. Clear as a bell."

"He was watching you this morning, Inez. On the beach."

"Watching me?"

"Set out the wash."

Inez stood and collected the bowls. Ash had the stepladder at the tree now and she watched him lean it against the trunk. Ash was an unusual name. Short for Ashley maybe. Old-fashioned.

"Ever occur to you he might be lying?" Christian said.

"Lying about what?"

"I don't know. Something."

It hadn't occurred to her. At least up until then it hadn't, but now her mind cast back over the few conversations they'd had. She wasn't a naturally suspicious person. She liked to think she took people as they came, as they presented themselves, but she also knew it wasn't words that betrayed a liar so much as the way the words were spoken. Inez remembered that tremor in Ash's cheek. Nothing like that today though — at least not that she'd noticed. He'd recovered. He was like a different person this morning. He was climbing the ladder's first rungs now, reaching up into the low branches.

Inez stepped inside and let the door swing closed behind her.

22

Pete set the stepladder against the tree trunk, climbed to the top rung and reached for the nearest branch, pulled himself onto it. Up three more branches and on his tiptoes he could reach the kite, a homemade affair, thin sticks and a sheet of clear plastic poly. He freed the body easily enough, but the braided tail had caught on a second limb. Straddling the next branch he shimmied out and managed to release the rest of the kite.

Twenty feet off the ground now and he had a good view. Directly below him, Dennis crouched by the fallen kite. Beyond, Pete could see across Inez's moss-covered roof and down the length of the beach. A perfect golden arc of sand hemmed end to end by a low ridge. A gentle slope at this end, the ridge looked more like a cliff at the far side of the beach. Halfway along a stream cut across the sand. Dennis was untangling what remained of the kite string. "You staying up there?"

"I like the view."

A cool breeze set the branches rustling. Inez had already gone inside. Pete watched as Christian and Oscar walked away. Which was fine. He'd faced enough questions already. He needed a little time alone. Arm wrapped around a branch, he shifted his body to face the wind.

In the days after their first action, after they destroyed those three trucks in the Westlake parking lot, Pete had been a bundle of nerves. A tremor seized his heart every time he saw a cop. Every set of flashing lights set off a brief panic. In his

/ / / / /

quiet moments, alone at night, he wondered if joining this group had been a mistake: just because he realized he wasn't a real photographer, just because he realized what he was trying to do with the camera hadn't worked, did it mean he should get involved in this?

Pete didn't doubt they were right, didn't doubt they had to do something, but maybe he wasn't cut out for it. The trembling fear that had him vomiting as he stood watch on Westlake River Road, it still had a grip on him.

That week they sent their first communique — wrote it to correct earlier newspaper reports that the arson had been "Springtime vandalism by local hooligans."

The days wore on. Time melted Pete's doubts. He'd started living at Bee Street by then, and maybe the weeks of tight living helped set him at ease — Art, Derek, Fay and Pete in the two bedrooms of Bee Street, all of them tangled together. In May they started planning the action at Tammery Mill.

Late that month they set firebombs in the mill's main cutting house with the same set-up — plastic tubs filled with gasoline. They mailed a communique to all the major news outlets, which is when they'd first started calling themselves Earth Action Now. Pete and Art worked on this one together. In it they'd declared the southwest of the island the second front in the fight against deforestation, clear-cutting and old-growth destruction.

Pete's doubts, his fears, they all surfaced again in the wake of Tammery Mill, but this time, it wasn't his fear of arrest, it wasn't a worry he didn't belong. He worried they were getting nowhere. No one published their second communique. They'd sweated over it, they'd chosen every word carefully, but what was the point if no one beyond a few editors read it? Their two actions seemed to have done nothing — no talk of policy change, no discussion of land use or clear-cut levels. Law and order, police work and pledges to track down the perpetrators dominated the news coverage.

That's when Art started talking about stepping up their actions — not just arson this time, an explosion, something no one could ignore. Fay was there when Art first said it, Derek too, all four of them seated on the ratty orange carpet in the living room at Bee Street, and into the silence that followed, Pete asked Jeremy's question: "How are we going to end this, Art? It's easy to start, harder to end, successfully at least."

"What we've done so far is just barely annoying. We need to step it up. Then we can negotiate. A couple more actions, but this time they need to be on a different scale — big enough to impact the whole forestry industry. Then we'll be in a position of strength."

"Firebombs in a lumber mill and under a few trucks," Derek said. "Probably not enough to do more than just get their attention." Derek's words almost always felt like an echo of Art's, his opinion in lockstep.

That same night, Fay told them about her summer working on a road crew, holding the stop and go sign, and about the dynamite stored in a magazine outside Squamish. "They have crates of it," she said, and right then, that very night, an uneasiness settled across Pete's shoulders. It wasn't worry, and it wasn't fear, it was a more distant relative — a feeling that came and went over the next few weeks, a feeling like watching your own life from a distance, observing without control. But when Fay suggested the two of them get the dynamite, take the ferry over, drive up to Squamish, Pete said yes.

/ / / / /

Pete lay down on the sway-back mattress in Gunter and Maggie's old cabin that afternoon and tried to sleep. Thoughts of Esterway Ridge crowded close though, bound him up, memories he tried to push aside but couldn't — the night watchman's blackened face, his own finger on the timer button, the faint tick as the seconds counted down.

Pete pushed himself out of bed. The sun had passed its high point. Half the day behind him. He had to stick to his plan, walk to Port Thorvald that night and work the pay phone until he found someone who could help. Another full meal and then he'd go.

The stump nearest the edge of the ridge offered a good view over the bay. Colonies of mussels lined the rocks that flanked the Point. They'd make a good meal. Or he could fish. Dennis had said there were so many they practically jumped into the boat over in Seeley's Bay. Inez would loan him a rod. Worst case there was always seaweed.

Pete ducked into the cabin, collected the plastic bucket that sat in the corner and carried it down the trail and along the beach. In front of the painted cabin he called for Inez, but the curtains were pulled and it looked dark inside. He walked past the swing and carried on along the flank of the Point. The tide was now low and retreating waves exposed seaweed-covered boulders. Mussels clung to their edges, patches of them, shiny and black. This is just what he'd needed. Two more waves broke then Pete followed one out. The boulders were long ago worn smooth, their sides bearded with seaweed. He took a mussel in each hand, twisted them free and tried to hop back across the rocks but water rose and engulfed his feet as he scrambled for dry land. He dropped the mussels in the bucket, turned back.

A new wave crashed in. Pete stepped down across the rocks and grabbed two more mussels before the water rose again. The shells were larger further out, and he followed the next wave down to a thick cluster, took two mussels as icy water swirled around his calves, a chill that shot through his body. He held his balance. The wave retreated then he pulled out shell after shell. They were big, they'd make a real meal. This was exactly what he needed. A wave broke around his legs and he braced himself, waited until the water fell back then stripped still more shells and tossed them onto the bank.

When Pete finally walked from the water, his jeans were stiff and heavy. His toes tingled, every step wet and uncomfortable. The bucket had some weight to it now, a full meal, and he'd need it all if he was leaving tonight.

At a bank of salmonberry bushes, Pete stopped and picked a few of the darker ones. They were hard and sour, but every bit of food counted. He worked his way down the path, ate until his cheeks puckered, then noticed a glass-walled cabin in the clearing beyond the berry bushes. All the windows were mismatched but they combined for a shimmering reflection of the rocks and the dark spread of water beyond. A few more steps and he could actually see into the cabin. A single window on the far side gave a view of the drooping boughs of a spruce tree beyond. Pete's eyes shifted focus. An easel and a painting stood inside. He stepped around to the doorway. Two thick planks of wood formed a rough step, and a loop of string held the door closed.

Pete knocked even though he knew no one was inside. Curiosity about the paintings had a hold on him and he slipped the loop of string from its mooring. Inside, the wall of windows opened up the narrow rectangular room. A still life of flowers and gourds stood on a table, easel propped beside it. Pete removed his wet boots and crossed for another look at the canvas. Flattened onto the painting's surface, everything from the still life looked squished together and slightly distorted.

He set his hand on the narrow workbench that ran beside the easel. Thick globs of paint marked it, splatters of colour dented with brush marks. The space below the counter was packed with paintings, rolled or stretched on frames. Pete pulled out the nearest, a raucous abstract — colours ribboned and roiling across the canvas. He slid out another: a landscape, all earth tones and grey horizon, the coast on an overcast day. The next canvas offered a muted vision of the land, hash marks of water with a sort of quilted look to the trees above it; the fourth a single tree deep in the forest, its sisters standing behind it, wide trunks rising into massive spires.

More paintings followed and though Pete knew he was prying, he couldn't help himself. The landscapes were warm and they were grand, hypnotic in their ability to capture in paint what so many of his own photographs had failed to show on film. He held one painting in both hands, eyes close, shifting his gaze and his focus until he felt like he'd stepped inside it, this brooding portrait of the gentle forest.

The door behind him creaked. Inez stood there with a hand on the doorknob. "I don't normally let people in here."

"I'm sorry. I just . . ." He still had the painting in his hands. "I was wet and cold. I looked in. Is this your studio?"

"Ray built it, but yes, it's my studio."

"Do you have shows and that? Do you sell many of these?"

She laughed, only it sounded forced. "Never sold any, no. Although the restaurant in Port Thorvald hung three of them for a few weeks last summer."

"I'd buy this. If I had money." He turned the painting to show her. "And a place to put it."

"Wait. You've got to watch how you hold them. Your knuckles are pressing into the canvas."

Pete set the painting down. Touching only the edge of the frame, he held it upright, but Inez stood beside him now. She took the painting and slid it into the rack then also turned the easel away, faced it towards the wall. "This is my private place, my workroom."

"I'm sorry, I was just trying to get dry, trying to warm up." That wasn't the truth though. These paintings had drawn him in, they'd entranced him. He'd wanted to look at every one.

"I've been waging war with my own sense of colour."

Pete slid his feet into the sopping leather of his boots. "Who's winning?"

Inez held the door and Pete caught himself staring at her, drawn in by the bright spark in her eyes, the wide smile. He was trying to reassemble his understanding of this woman he'd just met — account for her ability to create paintings like these and just then he realized that she was looking straight back at him.

"Where did you learn to paint like that?"

"I went to art school for a bit. Ray was one of my teachers."

"But those paintings in there aren't his?"

"I painted over all his canvases. My way of getting back at him."

"If he could see what you've done in there he might forgive you."

"Maybe. Maybe not. I think he looked at this land in a different way than I do."

They started walking. The trail led through a dense stand of trees then onto the sand of Baker Beach.

"I used to be a photographer," Pete said.

"Used to be?"

"I never seemed to be able to do what I wanted with the camera. It made me feel like I was at a distance, standing on the sidelines."

"Photographers don't stand on the sidelines. Nor do painters. We bear witness."

For a moment they walked in silence. Pete had tried to bear witness. Those were the words he'd used to explain what he was doing, but it had never been enough. With both photography and before that with the written word, it was like he'd picked the wrong tool. What he'd really wanted was for people to stand up and take notice, for people to see and understand the environmental crimes committed in their names — outrage, horror, anger, that's what he'd wanted, but his pictures drew none of that. The best of his photographs were actually people, faces, close-ups.

The wind had shifted, thatched clouds hid the sun, and Pete switched the bucket from one hand to the other as they walked.

At last he said, "I was trying to shoot landscapes. I wanted to photograph what you paint, but eventually it struck me that the camera might not be the best instrument. Standing in your studio, I was sure of it."

"I'm never sure of anything myself. Least of all in regard to my paintings. Doubt chases my every step."

At the fire ring, charred wood ends stood blackened in cold ash. Pete set down the bucket.

"How about I add some potatoes," Inez said. "Or maybe some bannock. We can make a meal of it."

"I'll get a fire going."

"There's wood piled around the side there. I'd invite you in, I mean, I'd be more hospitable, but our cabin is small. Tiny, really. Socializing's usually an outdoor affair."

Pete tightened his arms around himself and watched Inez hop onto her narrow porch, light on her feet despite the gumboots, a slight and energetic woman. She stepped inside and the door swung closed behind her. He kept his attention turned that way even after she was gone. Inez was attractive, beautiful even. She shimmered out here in the rugged wilderness. Fay had been magnetic, a singular point of attraction, while Inez had a softer pull, less urgent perhaps, but the more endearing for it.

Pete turned to the fire ring. He needed paper, some kind of fire starter. His hand dropped to his back pocket. He had a sheet of paper folded there. It would be a start. He unfolded the sheet and then remembered it had come from the night watchman. He'd pulled this sheet out when hiding the watch in the man's pockets, pulled it out along with the keys just as the flashing lights from emergency vehicles caught his attention.

The sheet of paper crinkled as he spread it. It had the fibrous feel of paper that had been wet and had since dried. Some of the ink had smudged, but most was still legible, a computer printout with four columns: names, places, dates, times. Esterway Ridge caught his eye. It was a security detail roster. Beside Esterway

Ridge on July 9 it said O. Tuggs. He must have been the man at the warehouse that night.

And then Pete noticed another detail. Four other sites on the roster — List Cove, Keats Landing, Hardy, Pincher Valley. Pete's finger hovered over List Cove. The next target. Another stolen car, the next four crates of dynamite. And if they'd had one night watchman a week ago, God knows what would be waiting now if they showed up at Greer-Braden's List Cove office with a carload full of explosives.

CHAPTER 23

When Tab arrived at the Grindstone Café, Bev Norman was already waiting. She rose from a table in the corner as Tab looked about the room. She was slim, no makeup, her hair loose. Tab introduced herself and sat. A moment of small talk and then Bev said, "I hope you didn't come all this way just to see me."

"No, not just you. Other people too."

"Because I'm not sure there's much more I'm going to be able to tell you, Mrs. Harper."

"I know. And that's fine. I understand." She touched the handle of her coffee mug, looped one finger around it. Framed movie posters lined the wall in front of her, all of them from the black and white era. "Could you maybe help me understand the why of all this?"

Bev nodded. She seemed to be thinking about that.

"Did you ever think Peter was an angry person?" Tab asked. "The last time I saw him, he seemed to have all this stored-up animosity. A kind of burn in him. I keep wondering: could anger and bitterness explain all this?"

Bev settled back in her seat. "I'd have said he was frustrated. Maybe a little lost. Certainly tired of people who couldn't see the obvious. What he thought was obvious."

"What was obvious?"

"Waste, consumption, greed." Her hands moved as she spoke, a few quick gestures. "We've cut down ninety percent of the old growth forests on this continent. How much longer do we wait?"

/ / / / /

"You agree with him then? I mean, the protests, the —"

"Our government bought millions of dollars' worth of Greer-Braden shares then three months later opened most of our remaining old growth for clear-cutting by that same company. The government that sets the rules also owns a majority share in the company they're making the rules for."

"So set a bomb?"

"I'm not excusing it and I'm certainly not advocating it, but you asked why so I'm trying to explain. People get tired of marches and demonstrations, picket signs, letter writing. They get impatient, desperate enough to think there's some quick fix. This government was supposed to change things, Mrs. Harper. The Socreds, we knew that party would never do anything, but this government was supposed to be different."

"So that's it? He got upset at the government, got tired of protests and peaceful demonstrations?"

"Have you been to Clayoquot yet? Have you followed the protests there?"

"I've seen it on the news."

"They're the biggest protests we've ever had in this country. It's a lot of people, a lot of attention. I just hope these bombings don't create too much backlash."

"Is there anything at all that you remember, anything that might help?"

"I don't know if anyone told you this, but Peter got kicked out of university mostly because he wouldn't admit he was wrong. We'd been digging up campus to plant veggies and promote urban gardening. Once we were caught, the rest of us accepted the censure, wrote apologies in advance of the disciplinary hearing. He didn't. He said it was wrong and he wouldn't. Ever since, nothing any of us did lived up to his ideals. He seemed lost for a while, and then he met these other people. Professional activists, protesters, anarchists. They had some communal living set-up. There was a knot of them, a group he fell into."

"Do you know any of them, other than the Art guy you mentioned?"

"There was a woman involved."

"In this group?"

"Pete liked her, I think."

"Do you know her name? Anything about her?"

"I was already on the outside of things by then. I had a job, an apartment. Once you can see all that the world is doing wrong, all that government, industry, capitalists and the establishment are doing wrong, it becomes easy to criticize one another. There's a sort of measuring being done all the time. Who is committed and who isn't. He was disappointed in me, thought me unwilling to back up words with action, or at least, not with enough action to satisfy him. Once Pete was committed to a cause, he was fully committed. That's just how he was."

This was true. Tab knew it. This described Peter to a T. "When I first heard about all this, I thought of him being sucked in, brainwashed or something. Like the Russians used to do."

"When I first heard about this, and you're going to think I'm terrible, Mrs. Harper, but I have to admit it, I thought of Peter. Right away this awful feeling rose in me."

"You knew."

"That first arson was on some trucks up-island, the next at a mill. I don't know if you heard about this where you live, but it was all over the news out here and I knew then. Suspected at least. I didn't do anything though, didn't call the police, didn't say anything. It was economic sabotage and no one got hurt. But when I saw this, when I heard it that morning —"

"You called the police?"

"I didn't tell them anything more than I told you. Peter's name, Art's name and that I thought there might be a woman in the group. I mean I didn't have any evidence or anything."

Tab reached out then, laid her hand over Bev's and squeezed. "I met with Art Kosky's mother, you know. He's also wanted.

For questioning at least. Did Peter ever talk about a basement apartment on Bee Street?"

"It's possible. Maybe. They all shared a basement apartment somewhere like that."

/ / / / /

The road back to Bee Street led past the hospital, an imposing brick structure, a central tower with broad wings stretched out on either side. She'd seen the hospital on the news, knew this was where Owen Tuggs was recovering, and now she pulled into the visitor's parking lot. Tab told herself this was impulse, a sudden whim, but she'd felt a pull ever since she'd reached the island, a need to get closer, to see for herself.

Once inside, Tab didn't ask for directions, didn't ask after Owen Tuggs or intensive care for fear she might be turned away. She just followed the signs, walked long corridors, her flats a soft tap on the polished concrete.

The intensive care unit occupied the east wing on the fourth floor. Tab passed a nurses' station and two women bent over a chart. She had no idea where she might find Owen Tuggs, and didn't know what she'd do if she did find him. He wasn't conscious, the papers had said as much, but Tab still might be able to peek inside. She could pass by the room at least.

Through a set of double doors, a cluster of people caught Tab's attention. Two doctors had their backs to Tab. Framed between their white coats stood Linda Tuggs. Tab recognized her from pictures on the news — Owen Tuggs's wife, her angular face, loose blond curls dusting her shoulders. The sight stopped Tab short. She'd imagined a bed, an unconscious man, perhaps a locked door. She hadn't expected to see anybody. Certainly not Linda Tuggs. She had to force herself to carry on walking.

Three people stood near Linda. Owen's brother was one of them. He'd given a statement for the family, had read from a small square of paper while the cameras rolled. The room they stood in front of must be Owen's room. Back there, just out of sight, he lay unconscious, and Tab passed as slowly as she could. A second set of double doors at the end of the corridor stood locked. She pushed on the handle, rattled the doors. Now she'd have to walk past a second time. She turned and looked down the broad corridor with its yellow walls, gurneys, empty wheelchairs and monitoring equipment pushed aside to keep the way clear.

By the time she approached Owen Tuggs's room for the second time, the two doctors had already stepped inside, and Tab stopped a few yards off. Linda looked worn, gravity pulling on her, dark rings under both eyes. An older woman now had her arm around Linda. Her mother perhaps. "I'm very sorry about your husband," Tab said, but she stood too far away and she hadn't spoken loudly enough.

"What?" Linda said.

"I recognized you from the news."

Linda seemed to understand then. She said thank you. Tab glanced to her right, caught a glimpse of the foot of a hospital bed but nothing more. A steady beep sounded from inside the room.

Tab left without another word, hurried past the nurse's station where a woman looked up, and asked if she had an ICU pass. Tab waved, a dismissive flick of her hand as she turned the corner to face the bank of elevators. She pressed the down button, hit it a second time even after it was already lit. The doors opened with a ding. Tab backed into the corner, folded her arms about herself. On the second floor, a nurse wheeled an empty gurney into the elevator and they began to descend again.

/ / / / /

On Bee Street later that afternoon, Tab stood in front of the clapboard house. Peter had been here, days ago or maybe weeks ago, and he might be back, or Art might. It seemed possible, only the sight of Linda Tuggs, and the memory of her reedy voice, had thrown Tab, it had rattled her confidence. Even if she found

Peter, what made her think a few words from his mother would change anything?

It took all Tab had to heave herself from the car and walk the footpath to 369 Bee Street. She knocked on the side door with a heavy hand, waited, listening, and then went up the stairs and tried the next two doors. At the one marked B, the deadbolt scraped back and the door eased open. An old man stood at the threshold, heavy jowls, stooped shoulders.

"My name is Tab Harper." She hadn't expected to find anyone home. "I'm looking for my son." She had a dozen pictures of Peter in her handbag, and she fumbled through them now. "I think he might have lived down in the basement apartment, or at least he had a friend who did."

The man shook his head without taking the photo. "Not here."

"I haven't heard from him for six months now," Tab said. The gap in the doorway narrowed. The man was withdrawing, but Tab set a foot on the threshold and blocked the door. "Would you have a good look and maybe try to think?"

"Not in number C. Mrs. Simms lived over there."

"What about A though?"

"She's gone now. Empty. People come and go."

"He might have been staying with a man named Arthur Kosky. People call him Art. My son's name is Peter Osborne." She raised the photo again.

"It's a girl lives down there. Fay something or other. Are you with the police?"

"I'm looking for my son."

"The police came around, knocked on my door, knocked on all the doors. Used to be this was a neighbourhood. Families used to live here. An empty place is asking for trouble."

"Did the police find anyone? Did they talk to the girl downstairs?"

"A very nice gentleman, just a few days ago. He wanted to know if I'd seen anyone around."

"Could you give me the landlord's number? Maybe he could help."

"He's no good, the landlord doesn't give —"

"But he might know if my son's been around."

"He's never here. My tap's been leaking, the oven door doesn't close."

"I see. Okay." Tab dipped her body in a brief bow and backed off a step. If the police had been by without finding them, she didn't stand much of a chance.

On her way back to the car, Tab noticed a bank of newspaper boxes. Nervous flutters rose inside her every time she looked at a front page, but she fumbled through her purse for change, lifted the top paper from the pile and carried it over to her rental car. An article below the fold discussed the twenty thousand dollar reward. Near the end it quoted an MP named Tierney who'd said the reward terms should be dead or alive. His words were in quotes: "dead or alive" is exactly what he'd said.

Tab rested against the side of the car and read the paragraph again. Just yesterday she'd read a letter on the comments page warning that we would become like London: unable to have public garbage cans for fear of a bomb in one, all because of a few eco-terrorists. That was the term they were using: eco-terrorists.

Tab sat in her car, but couldn't bring herself to start it. She didn't know what she should do next. Coming on top of her encounter with Linda Tuggs, this dead or alive talk had alarmed her. Words from an MP no less. It was like the wild west, something from a lawless frontier.

Tab left the rental car and walked to a pay phone. Broken glass from a beer bottle lay scattered about and she kicked the larger pieces aside as she plugged in a quarter, dialled Inspector Burrell's number. The moment he answered, she started in: "People are talking about dead or alive in the newspaper. A Member of Parliament said this. A price on their heads. Is that what this reward is about?"

"Mrs. Harper?"

"Have you read this morning's paper?"

"I can't read every newspaper, Mrs. Harper."

"This is an MP, a man named Devon Tierney. Is he one of the people telling you what to do?"

"I don't take orders from any MPs, Mrs. Harper."

"I want you to promise me you won't shoot him."

"Mrs. Harper, I appreciate your loyalty to your son, and I appreciate your desire to help."

"Just tell me what to do. I don't know what to do. I don't know where he is. I don't know what —"

"Go home. Wait this out. We're close. Sixteen good leads in the past twenty-four hours. We have a hotline established. Nineteen officers full-time on the case. We're close, Mrs. Harper. Just let us take it from here."

"Take it where though, what —"

"Get on a plane and try not to read the papers."

Tab shifted and a shard of broken glass crunched underfoot. Maybe he was right, maybe it was crazy for her to be out here. "Will you tell me something? Will you tell me why people do things like this?"

"I don't study the why, Mrs. Harper."

"The newspapers call them eco-terrorists."

"Like I said, stop reading the papers. Get on a plane home."

"It's not as though they're the PLO or the IRA or one of those, is it?"

"A man is in hospital. We've got a warehouse blown apart, a group making threats of violence through the media."

"Today I talked to Bev Norman, a girl Peter knew. I believe someone in your department has spoken to her. She says the only reason this happened is that people ignored them when they did peaceful protests. The government and industry ignored them, I guess. When nothing changed, they started setting firebombs and then —"

"Mrs. Harper, this is a democracy. Look on the news and you can see lots of other countries that settle things with bombs, but not here. Bev Norman and whoever else can talk all they want about having a worthy cause, but that doesn't mean she'll agree with the next group of radicals that starts setting off bombs."

"She wasn't trying to make excuses. She was trying to explain."

"It can only end in one way, Mrs. Harper. With arrest, with the court system. In front of a judge."

CHAPTER
24

In the cabin, Inez cleaned four potatoes, set them in a pot and added water. She put on a poncho sweater, ran a brush through her hair and, before stepping outside, checked herself in the mirror. First time in months she'd picked up the hand mirror. She knew what it was: a fresh face in their midst, a man. Life was lonely out here with Ernie, Christian and the like, worse since Maggie had left.

On the beach, Dennis had found Ash. He now sat in the lawn chair with the missing strap, watching while Ash fanned the small fire, worked a lick of orange flames into a peak above the stone ring.

It was nice to see the two of them getting along so well. It had been months since she'd seen Dennis in this kind of sunny mood. Part of that was all this talk of eviction, the uncertainty of it, Gunter's departure, change in the air. No matter how much Dennis had hated it when they'd first arrived, five years later this was home and the possibility of leaving made him anxious and unbalanced. The same applied to her, of course. The same held for all of them.

By the time Inez reached the fire ring, the flames had risen into a cheery blaze. Dennis already had the grill set up. Inez raised the cast iron pot. "Brought potatoes to boil."

"I was just going to cook a few of these mussels then hit the sack," Ash said. "It's been a long day."

That stopped Inez a moment, but in the end, she put the pot

/ / / / /

down, set it square at the centre of the grill. The fire crackled and threw out sparks. When Ash finished cleaning the mussels, he set a handful on the grill. Out on the water, gulls swooped and dived, a flutter over the rising swell. Inez angled her head westward. The sun was getting low. "It's going to be a beautiful sunset." Dennis turned and the two of them looked towards the sinking sun, but Ash seemed distracted, hunched close to the fire and lost in thought. He zipped up his jacket, unzipped it again.

"Before we moved here, back in '88, we camped for a week. It was May, the weather like this, beautiful sunsets every night. Do you remember that, Dennis?"

"We were in a tent."

"Just over five years ago."

The first few mussels cracked open and drops of salt water spilled into the fire and-sizzled. Ash scooped a few onto a plate. He held it out, offered the first plate to Inez. "Have some." He made a plate for Dennis, one for himself. They added more shells from the bucket and ate as the sun sank, the three of them side by side, gazing out past the low fire to a western horizon painted in streaks of orange and pink. Scout sat close. She panted. After a while, Inez tossed her a cooked mussel.

The potatoes reached a steady boil, and when the last round of mussels was ready, Inez lifted the lid. A cloud of steam mushroomed. She spooned potatoes onto plates, white bundles of heat in the chilly evening.

Ash accepted two small potatoes, ate them hot then dumped his shells into the fire and set down his plate. "I'm sorry to eat and run."

"That's alright. Let me walk you up the ridge." Inez stood. "I'll make sure you find your way."

"I'll be fine."

It was hard to read his face in the settling darkness. "There's a warren of paths back there." She popped the last bit of potato into her mouth while Ash lifted his socks and boots from where they'd been drying by the fire. "Dennis, would you take the plates in, bring everything into the cabin?"

Dennis was still chewing but he nodded agreement and Inez followed Ash across the sand, matched his pace. "You were quiet this evening. Are you okay?"

"Distracted, I guess. I've been thinking."

"About what?"

His feet kicked up sand. They neared the driftwood that marked the top of the beach. "It's a tragedy, what they're doing here, kicking you off."

"Well, I don't know. Maybe it's time," she said. "For me at least."

"Time for what?"

"A change." They started along the switchback trail. Inez led. Now and then she reached out to touch trees and branches, feeling her way in the darkest stretches. "I've got a sister in Winnipeg. She lives in a big house in the suburbs, two kids, two cars, a dog, a husband. She has a room free. Dennis could go to a real school instead of having me as his teacher."

"You're saying it's not a tragedy they're kicking you out of your home because you can move to Winnipeg and stay with your sister?"

Inez laughed at that. "It's an option. There are others."

"It's also a crime to kick people off land like this, to kick them out of their homes."

They stepped into the clearing in front of Gunter's place and Inez turned to face Ash. *Crime* was probably the right word, but Inez had been trying not to look at it that way, trying not to let it swallow her up. The possibility of eviction had become all-encompassing these past weeks. "An aunt of mine used to say, 'In the end everything will be alright.' Whenever things went wrong she'd say that and one day I asked, 'What if it isn't alright, what if it doesn't work out?' She said, 'Well then, you haven't reached the end yet.'"

Ash was an arm length away, a shadow in the inky night. Moonlight touched the edge of his cheek. Inez stepped closer. "And so I keep reminding myself, getting evicted isn't the end. It might even be the beginning, and we won't know if it's been good or bad until we truly reach the end. Maybe I'll arrive in Winnipeg and get discovered, and then it will have worked out just as Aunt Beth used to say."

Ash raised an arm. He reached out and set a hand on her shoulder, a silent connection, the start of something. But then he pulled back and turned away. "Maybe you're right," he said. "Maybe it's more beginning than end."

And then he was gone, slipped into Gunter and Maggie's cabin while Inez stood alone, gripped by the feeling of something half finished.

CHAPTER 25

Alone in the cabin, Pete stood in darkness with the words *every-thing will be alright in the end* still rattling inside him. Inez had said that directly to him. She'd looked into his eyes as she spoke and he knew it was true. No matter how badly injured the night watchman was, this wasn't the end. Another chapter waited. Good could come of this, would come of this. It's what followed that mattered. As the wind overhead and the clap of breaking waves swallowed the sound of Inez's retreating footsteps, Pete touched his pocket and the slip of paper folded there. He had to get moving. He had to tell the others List Cove would have a security detail.

Pete stripped the blanket from the bed, rolled it and slung it over his shoulder. Inez and Dennis didn't need it. They wouldn't pass another winter here.

Pete found his way down to the beach. Halfway along it, someone had nailed up a wooden sign that said, "Way Out." A scramble up the trail to a lookout point and he turned. Moonlight cut a wide stripe across the water. Stars furrowed the sky, and he stood still, gazing out and prolonging the goodbye.

Surely the night watchman had survived. The firefighters would have had enough medical training to keep him alive on the way to the hospital. The man had been injured, no question. He may have been badly injured but as long as he survived it meant Pete wasn't a murderer, and that's all Pete wanted: for the night watchman to have lived.

/ / / / /

Almost an hour to get to the highway, the trail hard to follow in the darkness, but once on the logging road, the highway itself was only ten minutes further. Pete continued along the dirt road, pockmarked and rutted with shallow culverts on either side. Up above, telephone lines ran from pole to pole. The West Coast Road: a long thin arm he'd travelled half a dozen times. Pete was tired and moving slowly by the time the gas station appeared. Open water and a few cottages stood behind it, all their windows dark, although one had a car parked out front. Pete folded his arms about his body. This was the place Dennis had talked about: the nearest pay phone.

Pete dug into his pockets, and spread change across his palm as he walked the last few yards. His quarter clinked down into the belly of the box and the receiver bleeped. Pete suppressed the urge to say a silent prayer, beg favour from a higher power he no longer believed in. He pressed zero then started in on the digits for the Bee Street apartment. The operator answered. "I want to make this call collect, but you have to let it ring once, hang up and call again, or no one will answer."

"We don't normally do that."

"I know. I realize. It's just that I'm stranded here. I need help."

"Your name?"

"Just say Pete. They'll know who I am."

He listened for the distant ring. It came once then silence stretched while the operator redialled.

"Thanks," Pete said. "For doing that."

The phone began to ring again, slightly muted on the other end of the line. Behind him crickets called into the night. Wind worked its way through the treetops. They should be there. Someone should. Pete's toes curled, and he realized he was holding his breath, his body tense. He ran his thumbnail around the plastic edge of the phone box.

"No answer."

He gave the operator Jeremy Dunn's number. Pete hadn't talked to Jeremy in three months. He hadn't wanted to see Jeremy after Westlake or Tammery Mill, hadn't wanted to hear Jeremy's opinion. Maybe he'd feared it. He'd avoided John's Diner and a few other places, telling himself he'd wait until it was over, wait until they had something to show. Maybe he'd been afraid of his own wavering resolve. Now he heard a muted ring on the line and finally Jeremy picked up. The call went through.

"Jeremy? It's me. It's Pete."

"Jesus Christ."

"It's okay, I'm alright. I've been lying low."

"Okay? It's not okay, it's —"

"Listen, I'm trying to find the others."

"The others?" Jeremy's voice dropped into a whisper. "Do you have any idea what's going on?"

"I just said I've been lying low."

"After all this, you're calling me now? With a manhunt on, a twenty thousand dollar reward, hotlines open for tips —"

"That's okay. That's alright. We knew this would happen." He tried to put some energy into his voice. "Nothing wrong with some attention." He looked through the booth's glass to the cottages and the pebble beach, the moonlit water beyond. "Do you know where the others are?"

"I don't know. I don't want to know. Art came by. He wanted money. I got the impression they're hiding in the suburbs somewhere."

"Can you get them a message about List Cove? I need you to tell them they have security there."

"Pete," he said.

"Can you find them for me, Jeremy? It sounds like you could maybe get in touch."

"The cops were by too."

"Jesus. When?"

"They came up and knocked —"

"Did you say anything?"

"I probably should have."

"But you didn't?"

A moment of silence on the line. "Part of me wishes I had," Jeremy said.

"What the hell are you talking about?"

"Haven't you heard about the security guard?"

Pete squeezed the handset, pressed it close.

"It was just on the news. He died in hospital."

"No. That can't be. No."

"They said he never regained consciousness. He was on life support this whole time."

Pete had watched the explosion knock the man back into a twisted, unnatural sprawl, and from the moment he left the night watchman's side, a secret fear had nestled in the back of Pete's mind: maybe the night watchman wouldn't make it — somehow in the time it took to get to hospital, the man's breathing might stop, his heart might fail. And here he'd dived into this conversation with Jeremy avoiding the most important question, pushing it away, stopping himself from asking. But it was here now: blood on his hands. Pete's shoulder pressed against the side of the phone booth. He dug his thumbnail into the wide groove at the edge of the booth's plexiglass. Now how could everything work out in the end?

"Pete?" Jeremy said.

"Yeah, I'm here, I'm just . . ."

"Tell me this is over. Tell me there's no more and it won't happen again."

"That wasn't even half of it."

"What wasn't even half of it?"

"A third of it. We stashed the rest above Thurlow Road."

"You mean, you're going to do this again?"

"List Cove then Dutton Pulp and Paper. They're using old growth trees to make phone books for Christ's sakes."

"A man is dead."

"Find Fay, find Art, and just tell them about List Cove. They'll know what to do. They'll change the target. Nobody wants anyone to get hurt."

"I told you Art's unbalanced, I told you it would lead to this. Go off half-cocked, and who knows —"

"I don't need a lecture."

"Pete, do you have any perspective at all on what's going on? You let him talk you into fighting some kind of guerrilla war that killed a man and could very well end up killing the movement."

"It went wrong. It was an accident."

"They're calling you terrorists, and now it will be murderers too. You're tarnishing the biggest peaceful protest —"

"You think more peaceful protests are going to stop a land use policy set in place by a government that owns half the company it's supposed to be regulating? Someone had to stand up, Jeremy. Someone had to take action."

"I should go, Pete."

"Don't hang up though. Wait. Just." Pete's knees touched together. He leaned against the call box, willing himself down the wires, into the phone and out to where Jeremy stood. "You need to find them. Or at least help me find them. To warn them, to tell them."

"You're asking me to become an accomplice."

"No." A tight ball of frustration caught in Pete's throat and he could feel the sting of rising tears. "You wouldn't be," he said. "Not like that. I just need some help."

"I can try to find you a lawyer's number. I'll look that up right now."

"What am I going to do with a lawyer? Who does that help?"

"You could strike a plea bargain. Tell them about the dynamite above Thurlow Road."

"Forget I said anything about that. Just find Fay and Art. I need to get through to them. I need to —"

The line went dead.

Two or three steps across the gas station's dusty concrete and Pete stood in open air. He couldn't walk across the island. It wasn't in him. Whatever energy he'd mustered, whatever determination he'd had, it was gone now. He'd killed a man. He'd been the one. They'd drawn straws to see who would go in and connect the timer. Fay had pulled out the cigarette with the broken end. She was the one who should have gone in, but she'd balked. She'd held the timer out and said she didn't know how to work it. Pete had extended his hand and took the little device from her, an attempt at gallantry — an offer meant to impress her.

A long chain of coincidences like this had led him here, so many points at which his life could have diverted, could have followed some other road. He wouldn't be here if he hadn't met Jeremy at the Anarchist Book Fair. If he hadn't been wearing a T-shirt that said, "Canada: Brazil of the North," they might never have started talking, he might never have met Fay and Art, might not have followed them up-island to disrupt logging in Bridal Veil Flats. They wouldn't have got the windows shot out of their van at Bedwell Pass, and if the government hadn't announced its land use policy the very next day, maybe they'd never have firebombed the Greer-Braden trucks in the Westlake parking lot.

Standing there in the cool ocean breeze, these memories, this weighted chain of events had a physicality to it. Pete could smell the dampness of the apartment on Bee Street where they'd planned Tammery Mill, basement windows dripping condensation. He could hear the hum of the baseboard heaters. He'd crashed there night after night. He'd lived there. These people, they'd become family, or close to it: living together, working together, a shared cause. And now here he was alone, stranded while they lay low, hiding in the suburbs somewhere.

They'd do it again. Pete was sure of this. They'd drive to List Cove with a load of dynamite not even realizing a security guard had been posted there.

If Jeremy wanted to make sure no one got hurt, the best thing to do was to warn Art and the others to choose another target. That's what would prevent a repeat of Esterway Ridge. Pete turned to the phone box. He hit zero then dialled Jeremy's number, reversed the charges. The phone rang and rang, one long bleat after another.

CHAPTER
26

Pete slept restlessly, his mind uneasy, dreams a torment. Bent over Owen Tuggs's body, feeling for a heartbeat, hammering his fist on the night watchman's chest, banging away at flesh that seemed to melt and disappear even as Pete tried to revive the man.

Pete awoke, thrust from the dream, the world around him still dark. In time he drifted back into sleep, back to Esterway Ridge and into punctured dreams. A man was dead. Because of him.

At sun up, Pete rolled onto his side and turned away from the window. He was in Gunter and Maggie's cabin, on that thin mattress under the shelter of a patched up roof, back where no one had heard of Esterway Ridge. He kept his eyes closed and lay still, grey wool blanket tangled about him. He wanted an escape, he wanted a dreamless sleep.

A quick knock and Dennis shouted, "Inez said we could go fishing today."

Pete sat up. "Okay. Alright." Boots on, he glanced in the mirror that hung from the room's centre post and ran a hand down his jaw and across days of stubble. He'd crossed a line last night. He knew his actions had killed a man, and yet he'd returned here — no real thought of turning himself in, no effort to press on, find the others and try to make something good of all this. The man staring back from the mirror had turned tail, retreated to a place where no one knew him, a place he could hide.

/ / / / /

Outside the wind was a brisk slap. Dennis had perched himself on one of the stump end stools. "Want to paddle around to Seeley's Bay and go fishing?"

That sounded good: food, protein. He sat though, took in a lungful of air, breathed deep.

"Packed us lunch." Dennis raised a little cloth sack.

"Lunch is good," Pete said. "Lunch is just what I need." Best way to shake these dark thoughts was to occupy himself. He needed to get moving, stop sitting around dwelling on what he'd learned last night. Activity. Exertion.

Dennis led the way along the edge of the ridge, down a trail Pete hadn't followed before. It twisted through a stand of trees, led to a small clearing and a shed. "We'll need a second rod," Dennis said. "This is Phelps's old cabin. A woman named Bethany-Belle stayed in it before him." It was storage now, its only window stood wide open, no glass in it at all. Pete peered in while Dennis fumbled about inside: a shovel, an axe, a chainsaw, a pair of buckets, crab traps stacked together. In the corner, two plastic tubs sat side by side, lids on each. A coiled hose lay on top. The light was faint, but the buckets seemed to be identical, and the hose that connected them ran from the top of one to the top of the other.

Dennis stepped out carrying a rod, a bucket and a net. "Have you seen my kayak?"

He pointed around the side of the shed. It stood on a pair of sawhorses, about six feet long, white canvas pulled taut around a frame. Pete stepped closer, lifted just the nose of it. The boat was almost weightless; it rose in his hands like there was nothing to it.

"You made it yourself?"

"A book from the library had instructions in it. You glue it for the most part. There's two layers, a hull and a deck, two separate sheets of canvas with no punctures, no nails in the bottom or anything."

"It doesn't leak?"

"Shellac it with some really thick coats and the water can't get in. Soon as it's done, I'm going to take it over to Merchant Bay for some kayak surfing." Dennis lifted the thing and lowered it over his head. "What if you had a kayak for a head?" The boat rested on his shoulders now. "You'd have to live outside. You couldn't fit through any doors. Every time you looked around, you'd bang into something." He turned one way then the other and the kayak's bow swung back and forth.

Pete stepped back and peered in through the empty window a second time. He leaned through for a better view of those plastic tubs. Both were labelled finishing plaster, both still had handles. He'd seen plenty of incendiary devices and that's exactly what these looked like — plastic buckets connected by a length of hose. Light one and at intervals it would ignite any others. It was the foolproof approach to arson, a way of starting a fire at multiple points almost simultaneously. They'd laid buckets just like these filled with gasoline and tar under company trucks in the Greer-Braden parking lot on Westlake River Road. They'd used the same type of devices to set Tammery Mill on fire.

Dennis had the kayak on the sawhorses now. He lifted the rod and bucket. Pete lifted the net and followed the boy down a trail through a bank of scrub and onto the beach. Walking away, Pete told himself that he hadn't gotten close enough to really be sure. The hose might have just lain coiled on the two tubs. Or even if it did connect them, there were other possible uses. The hose could be for some kind of overflow. The tubs might be storing something. For all Pete knew, the hose was just an easier way to pour whatever liquid they kept in the tubs.

Down on the beach, Dennis and Pete dragged the aluminium Gunderson to the water's edge. Pete unlaced his boots and removed his socks. Out on the water, the swell rose, curled white then crashed with a clap. They were substantial waves and it would be work to get past the break.

Pete stepped over one of the pontoons and into the canoe. Ocean water sent a sharp chill into his legs, and he drew air in through clenched teeth. His feet were only wet a moment, but even then it numbed his toes.

Inez stepped from the cabin and came down to the rocks at the base of the Point as Dennis pushed off and the canoe glided into the froth of a spent wave. She waved and called, "Good luck."

A churn of white water hit the bow and the tips of both pontoons, and sent the boat back with a jolt. Pete wiped the spray of salt water from his face and dug his paddle deep, but the next wave was already rising, a glittering ridge just yards away. It crested, curled white and broke with a clap. Pete tried to set aside all thoughts of the two plastic buckets and their connecting hose. He leaned out, dug his paddle down and pulled hard. His right hand dipped into frigid ocean and the blade hit sandy bottom: the water wasn't even waist deep here. Pete glanced over his shoulder. Dennis had his head bowed. They were only four or five canoe lengths from the beach and Pete was already panting, the physical exertion a welcome distraction. He switched his paddle to the port side just before the next wave hit, another cold spray thrown across his chest and face.

Ten minutes of steady work and they were out past the break. Pete set his paddle across the gunwales and heaved in air. A cramp laced his side and both arms trembled, weak from exertion. Inez still stood on shore and she raised her hand in another quick wave. She was slender, even in her baggy clothing a gentle flare to her hips. She looked good standing on the beach waving and Pete found it difficult to look away.

"That was the hard part," Dennis said.

Working their way around the Point and into Seeley's Bay meant a moment in open ocean and for a few heady minutes, they cut the swell at right angles, canoe pointing straight out to sea until Dennis shouted to turn. Settled into a low point between waves, they backpaddled and aimed the bow into the next bay over. Wind on their side now, they made good time. Seeley's spread before them, dark cradle to the choppy ocean water.

Seeley's was endless forest, dark and deep, a tangle right down to the rocky shoreline. No sign of habitation here, no smoke trails, no cabins.

The threat of eviction might explain the firebomb back at the shed. Someone had decided it was better to torch his cabin than have some bulldozer knock it down. And who was Pete to argue with that? And of course, with all the departures lately, it was equally possible whoever had built the firebomb was long gone. Maybe no one around here today actually knew what it was for. Just a couple of buckets sitting in an old shed. That is, if it was a firebomb in the first place.

Dennis slid his paddle along the bottom of the canoe and reached for the tackle box. "Best spot on this stretch of coast. Guaranteed salmon."

Pete tucked his legs up so he could turn fully around. He tried not to think about what he'd seen in the shed, tried also to keep out thoughts of Esterway Ridge and Owen Tuggs. A clear mind is what he needed. The tackle box stood open. Dennis already had a rod in hand, hooks tied to his line. Pete threaded his own hook and added sinkers, tied the knot as best he could.

"Christian's trying to arrange some moving money," Dennis said as he cast. "Maybe he could get you some too. He thinks none of us should go anywhere until they pay our expenses and whatnot."

"Who is it that owns the land here? Who's kicking you off?"

"Greer-Braden."

Pete pursed his lips and released a soft whistle. Inside, his stomach tucked into a spiral dive. Greer-Braden. The very words stilled him. They had their claws dug in everywhere, even in these tangled woods, these ancient trees, moss thick across their backs, row upon row of peaceful giants. "They want to log it."

"Who?"

"Greer-Braden, the people evicting you."

"They didn't even know we were here until a few months ago. At least no one in headquarters knew we were here."

"And what about stopping it? What about fighting to stay?" His mind was racing now, exactly the sort of thoughts he'd been trying to escape.

"Andy's cousin looked into squatter's rights. He works in city planning on the mainland. No one's been here long enough though, not even Christian. Plus we wrote letters, and when it all started, Gunter and Oscar spent some money on a lawyer."

"Lawyers? God, lawyers won't help. Corporations like that can out-lawyer anyone."

"What do you mean?"

"Just trust me, I know Greer-Braden. Writing their lawyers to cajole or plead or whatever. Zero chance. Possession is nine-tenths of the law. Dig a trench, stop the bulldozers. Peaceable occupation. Declare yourselves an independent nation state or something. You need to be creative. The way you talk, it's like nobody here wants to stay, nobody's willing to fight for it."

"Did you just say you know Greer-Braden?"

Pete cast over the bow. "Not personally, I just mean I've tried to stop them doing things before."

"What kind of things?"

"They're part of what's wrong with the world today, Dennis. Seventy-six countries have lost all their frontier forests. You ever heard of a place called Easter Island? Hundreds of years ago the people there cut down all the trees and their society just fell apart. Food grew scarce, people took up cannibalism, civil war broke out, they couldn't even make canoes anymore. You know what they asked for when the first Dutch sailors reached the island? Wood. They wanted their trees back. And now here we are with less than ten percent of our old growth forests left. Knock on Greer-Braden's door to try to say this and they'll close it in your face. Send letters and they're ignored. Picket their offices and they'll get a court injunction. You know who owns half of Greer-Braden? Our own fucking government so getting them to do something is useless. Send all the letters you want, Dennis, the system's stacked."

"There are other things we could do, other ways to pressure them."

Pete immediately thought of the two plastic tubs stored in that cramped shack by the beach. "Like what?"

Dennis was reeling in. He shrugged as he worked the rod. Pete waited. "Do you have any specific plans?"

"I guess not." Dennis set his rod down.

It was absurd to link the plastic tubs to Greer-Braden or to some kind of protest. These were isolated facts, his own mind the only thing connecting them. Pete began to reel in. Time to stop talking about this stuff. Time to catch a fish.

The boat rose and fell with the swell. Cast and recast, but still no fish, not even any bites. Dennis dug his paddle into the water and turned them, swung the boat to face the swell. He was good with the canoe, able to manoeuvre it well, even with the two pontoons. Ocean water slapped against the boat. Dennis lifted the lunch bag. "Hard-boiled eggs. One each." He had carrots in there, cold potatoes and cheese as well. He called it lunch, but it felt more like a snack, just enough to quiet Pete's rumbling stomach.

It started to rain. Light drops at first, scattered and occasional — a ping or two against the aluminium canoe, little drops into the water. Overhead though, clouds stacked up and in time the rain thickened.

"The fish don't seem to be exactly jumping into the boat, Dennis."

"What if one day, you saw a big hook coming down from the sky and on it hung a juicy steak?"

Pete shifted in his seat and angled his head as though it might give him a better look at the boy.

"Or maybe a dollar bill on a hook. If someone up there, like an alien maybe, could do that, he'd catch so many humans."

Pete's reel clicked, a tight metronomic beat. "I think if someone up there was smart enough to dangle a hook from the sky, they'd have better ways of catching us."

"I think a dollar bill on a hook is pretty good." Dennis's grin had gone lopsided. He looked pleased with himself.

"They have a dollar coin now instead of a bill."

"Maybe a ten-dollar bill."

Dennis yelped. He hit the stopper on his reel and the rod dipped low. A good pull then he released line and the fish took it on a long deep run with enough force that the stern of the boat came around — a single fish dragging a twenty-foot aluminium canoe and its two pontoons. Stopper released, Dennis gave some line then fought to take it back. His rod bent, another deep arc. Pete watched. Arms folded, he tried to keep warm. His cotton jacket was soaked, its fabric stiffened and dark. A flash of silver rose to the surface and a moment later the fish passed under the boat. "You want to get the net?" Dennis said.

It broke water, a long silver body splashed into open air, then it dove. Dennis's hands gripped the cork as the rod bent. The fish didn't have much line though. Pete leaned out, sank the net into the water between gunwale and pontoon. He lifted, hauled the fish into the boat while its tail flicked and shook drops from the netting. Dennis clubbed it. Two dull wet thuds and the fish lay still.

A wave lifted the stern and passed under the boat. "Hell of a catch." Even in this dull light, the scales shimmered, white underbelly exposed to light for the first time. "Look at that. Look at the size of that one."

"I'd say twelve pounds."

Pete raised his rod and sent the tackle out into the rain. It hit water, his reel clicked, rose to a whir. Next time he cast his line over the other side of the canoe. That's where Dennis had caught the salmon. At least Pete thought so. He was all turned around now. "If you want," Dennis said. "We could go home now."

"You cold?"

Dennis's teeth had started to chatter. He'd seated himself and had tucked his hands between his knees. "We can all eat this," he said. "There's enough for us to share."

Baker Beach was shrouded, the forest a formless band, a dark blur in a world of grey. Even as the bow of the boat ground sand, it was hard to make out more than a thick belt of woods.

Pete stepped over the gunwale and into the shallows. His legs were cramped from sitting so long and he was wet and cold. His clothes clung to him, chafed his legs and shoulders as he and Dennis dragged the canoe out of reach of the rising tide. The lone fish still sloshed about in the rainwater at the bottom of the boat. Dennis reached in. Two fingers behind one gill, he raised the fish, held it at his side, tail fin just short of touching sand.

"Inez is good at cleaning fish. After that we can fry it." With that, Dennis started back towards the cabin. Through the sheets of rain, the Painted Lady was a muted smudge some hundred yards off.

Rainwater had pooled in Pete's boots. He emptied one then the other, managed to lace them, then followed Dennis across the sand, wet leather weighing down his feet.

Dennis had left the door open a crack. Pete wiped water from his face, raised a fist and knocked — a good, hard rap and at that very moment Inez pulled the door wide. "Look who it is. Come dry off. The fire's blazing."

CHAPTER
27

Inez stepped aside to make space for Ash, aware now of how he might see this cramped one-room space. She pulled a shirt and a pair of Dennis's underwear off the wash line that stretched above the wood stove, collected her knitting from the sofa. She stacked a pair of plates, gathered a few books.

"Come stand over here and you'll be warm before you know it. This coast is an unforgiving place. Weather turns on a dime."

Ash still dripped water as he crossed the room, wet clothes pasted against his skinny body. "You see Dennis's fish?"

"I'm going to put it in the pan in a minute. Dennis, see if you can't find some dry clothes for Ash, something to change into."

"Your paintings look good in here," Ash said. "I've been meaning to ask you about them, about the landscapes in particular, how you created them."

"Practice, I guess. I spend a lot of time doing it." She looked at one then the other, a landscape painted on a wide piece of fence board that had washed onto the beach one day, the second a small square canvas, portrait of a dirt path through shrouded woods. She'd always liked the darkness in that one, the cavernous feel it offered. "To paint a landscape I think you have to live it and not just look at it. You need to step inside, really and truly be there."

Dennis held out a change of clothes for Ash, a shirt, a pair of pants, old clothes of Ray's she'd not yet turned into rags.

"I'll turn away," Inez said. At the counter she lifted her knife.

/ / / / /

"I appreciate this. Food, shelter. You saving my ass again."
Nose to tail Inez cut the salmon's belly and removed the
innards. "We've got crab bait here, Dennis. I'll put it in the
bucket."

She caught Ash's reflection in the window as he dressed,
youthful and muscular without his shirt on. It was flattering
the way he talked about her painting. She hadn't heard talk like
that from anyone. Ever. Inez looked over again — stole a glance
as her knife came down behind the fish's gills. She slid the fish's
head away, flipped the body around. She'd have to throw a meal
together around the fish. They were low on supplies. Half the
mason jars above the sink stood empty. Macaroni elbows were
a possibility. Serve them with a little olive oil. No need to run
out to the garden on a night like this.

Inez filled a pot with water and carried it to the wood stove.
One more body and the cabin felt crowded. She emptied the
jar of macaroni into the water and set the lid on top. She could
feel that Ash was watching. He stood directly behind her, just
a couple of feet away, this man who'd been a stranger just days
ago.

"Either of you two know about the most famous fish in the
world?" he asked.

"Jaws." Dennis sat perched on the edge of his bed. He'd
pulled on his purple sweater and the toque she'd knitted.

A great hiss rose from the fry pan as the first cut of salmon
hit the hot oil, and the smell of it soon filled the room.

"It was a coelacanth," Ash said. "And it was a celebrity
because in the '30s its face was in half the newspapers in the
world. A fisherman caught it off the coast of South Africa, five
feet long, blue, and someone discovered that it matched a fossil
for a fish scientists had thought extinct three hundred million
years ago. A living dinosaur is what newspapers called it."

"Jaws still sounds more famous."

"The crazy thing is, coelacanths now are almost extinct.

Because of overfishing. Trophy fishes, specimen catchers. It's a fish that survived three hundred million years after it was assumed to have died off and now we're wiping it out anyway. Not even to eat. It's inedible. Makes you wonder about us, doesn't it?"

Inez bent for a look at the salmon. She pressed on the nearest fillet. Nearly ready. "What does it make us wonder?"

"About mankind. About humanity. If we can't see the big picture clearly enough to avoid killing off even our living fossils, how are we going to make it ourselves?"

"The three of us are going to make it by eating this salmon. Dennis, can you bring the plates around? I'll drain this pasta."

Their table was a cut-off Formica countertop mounted to the wall near the doorway. Barely two feet wide, it stood before a broad window. Curtains back, it offered one of her favourite views: across the beach and over the water, all of it still hazy in the slanted rain. Three stools there and just enough space for all three plates.

Easing onto the stool beside Ash, Inez's hand brushed against his thigh. Ray's old track pants. "It's good to have you here." Inez poured water, filled the three glasses. "Life can be a little quiet out this way."

Ash raised his glass, clinked hers. "Thank you."

"Me too," Dennis said and held out his tumbler.

They started in on the meal, rain patter percussive against the roof and window while they dug in. Next to her, Ash handled his knife and fork carefully, small bites balanced on the tines of his fork. Fish gone and not much pasta left on his plate, he paused, laid his fork down a moment. "Dennis tells me it's Greer-Braden evicting you. The forestry company."

"They own the land, but no one seemed to know or care until this year."

Two men in suits had walked down on a clear February day. She'd watched them cross the beach. Almost five years she'd lived on this land and throughout that time she'd done her best not to think about who owned it, ignoring the possibility this day might come. Christian had been here fourteen years. Ernie almost as long. Everyone in this neck of the woods knew and no one seemed to care. Until just months ago.

The two men in suits hadn't said much. They went around and collected names, asked questions, took pictures. Eviction notices didn't arrive until April.

"They're bastards," Ash said as he picked up his fork.

"Greer-Braden? That's one word for them."

"And so you're negotiating some moving money?"

"Trying to." She took a gulp of water. It had become an obsession around here. The hope of a bit of money in their pockets.

"Ash knows people at Greer-Braden," Dennis said.

"What?" Inez wasn't sure she'd heard right. "You know people?"

"I wouldn't exactly say I know people."

"He's not friends with them," Dennis said.

"Certainly not friends."

"What's your connection then?"

"It's not like I've got some kind of inside track, I've got no strings to pull. I was just saying to Dennis that I've spent a lot of time trying to stop industrial-scale clear-cutting."

"We don't know anyone there," Inez said. "Not a soul. No one listens to us. We wrote a letter asking Greer-Braden for five thousand dollars each. We broke it all down, explained our moving costs. Christian's actually a pretty good writer, but no one ever replied."

"That's what you care about? That's what you're after?"

"You think we're asking for too much?"

"No, I just wonder why no one is fighting to stay, fighting to make this a permanent squatter community or something?"

"I could use some money, Ash. We could."

"Money's money. This is your home."

"It's not like we didn't try, but I've been a single mother since I was nineteen, and on top of that, I tried to become a painter. God knows why." That was supposed to be a joke. She tried to chuckle, but didn't manage it.

"You are a painter, Inez. A good one."

"Unfortunately, that's not all that matters."

"It's enough. It should be enough."

She leaned back so she could see past Ash's shoulder, a clear view of her son. "Dennis, when was the last time you had a new coat or a new pair of jeans?"

"Brand new?" Dennis said.

Ash twisted on his stool and faced her squarely. "I get it," he said. "I know. My mother mostly raised me by herself."

"We've scratched and saved and gone without too many times to count."

"I'm not against you asking for money. All I meant was that I'm surprised no one's trying to stay. No one's arguing for a perpetual squatters' camp, the kind of place anyone who wants to can come and live off the grid. Wouldn't that be worth fighting for?"

Fork across her plate, Inez straightened her back, shifted in her seat and looked out over the churning white water that crashed against Baker Beach. "I don't know if there's room left for that kind of place, Ash."

Decisions loomed. These last three months she'd been putting things off, but she couldn't do that much longer. Soon enough they'd be down here, soon enough they'd be ready to bulldoze this place, her home, her son's home.

CHAPTER 28

After they'd finished eating, after they'd cleaned up, and after Dennis had crawled into bed, Inez pulled the curtains above the kitchen sink and above the table. Rain still peppered the windows, the roof and the sides of the cabin, audible even above the hiss of the lantern. Pete had perched himself on the narrow sofa. The cabin was warm. It had the cozy feel of home. Behind them Dennis's breathing had softened into a gentle snore.

Inez gave the lantern a few brief strokes, and the mantle rose to a white-hot blaze. She hung it overhead then returned to the centre of the room.

"I know you think it's bad we're asking for money, that you think it's undignified or whatever, but I want you to understand something —"

"You don't need to justify anything, Inez."

"A push would probably do me good."

Both hands up, he tried to wave her back. He'd made too big a deal of this. "Please," he said, keeping his voice low so as not to wake Dennis.

"It's going to get me off my ass and out of my cocoon." Her arms tightened about herself. "I could give you the whole song and dance about there being no place left for artists in society. That's the kind of thing Ray used to say sent him out here."

"I don't disagree. The world we've built, it's constricting, unjust —"

/////

Inez was still talking though. "The truth is, ever since I started painting, I've had this idea, this unshakable conviction that the judgment of others, the crush of people in the so-called art world was what held me back. So I thought I could be free here, I could become a painter with no one looking over my shoulder. Not that they were. It was mostly my own fear of inadequacy. Five years later, my fear, my midnight worry, is that I've been wasting the best years of my life, and my son's life, trying to teach myself to paint. So maybe it's time to go."

"Pick a dealer or a gallery from the phone book, take some of those rolled-up paintings and send them off. That's what you need to do. It's nothing to do with where you live."

"They're not good enough. They're not ready. I still haven't got it right. Not just right. Colour, this land."

"You do have this land just right. Believe me, I know."

"And to be honest, I could do with some money. I could do with a break and Dennis could too. He's here on the coast with no school, no kids his age." She spread her hands, palms open and up. "So that's it, speech over. Everything off my chest, but just so you know, we did try to stay. We wrote all the angry letters we could think of. Now we're just looking for the best way out we can find."

"And as your aunt said, 'In the end everything will be alright.'"

"I say that to myself over and over these days."

Inez settled. The sofa's springs were weak and she was close enough now that their knees touched. She didn't pull away. Nor did he. A pocket of connected warmth, his leg against hers.

"This whole cabin creaks and shifts. Look at it hard and the wood moans."

"In Ancient Japan they used to make the emperor's bedroom floorboards squeak so assassins couldn't sneak up."

"That's exactly the sort of thing Dennis would say. No wonder you two get along so well."

Something had shifted between them now, a lighter tone to her voice, an easiness between them. "He's a good kid," Pete said. "He's smart and interesting. We do get along well."

"That's nice of you to say."

"You're a good pair."

Silence lingered and then Pete noticed her smile — a quiet lift to her face, the sort of smile connected with a passing, happy thought. A moment later, she took his hand in hers. "Anyone ever tell you your fortune?"

"I know my fortune. Four dollars and ten cents. It's in my pocket."

She laughed, a breezy chuckle as she bent his wrist and angled his palm. There it was again: Inez's own private smile while the tip of her finger scored the skin of his hand. She was some strange combination of strength and vulnerability, at once one and also the other, a blend uniquely hers.

"This is your lifeline. It's hard to see just now." Her head dipped as she examined his palm, finger trailing across it, a faint contact, and yet his whole arm could feel it, all of his body brought to attention. And he knew what would happen now, where they went from here. He could feel it. A flutter in his chest, breath quick in his throat. All he had to do was let it happen, let the flow carry him along. And why not?

She was talking now, telling him his fortune, his future, her voice just above a whisper. "These creases mark tragedy. You see the way it intersects with your lifeline?"

"Tragedy, eh? Does it happen around the age of twenty-three?"

That caught her attention. She folded the fingers of his hand closed. "I turned thirty-one in April."

That was a mistake. He shouldn't have said anything about his age.

"I'm a very mature twenty-three."

But they were off on the wrong topic now, and his hand was

back in his lap. He smiled at her, or did his best to smile, except that the muscles in his face had tightened. Overconfidence was the problem. He'd been getting ahead of himself. He'd already had them in bed together.

The lantern above them spluttered and its light began to retreat. Inez stood. "We're on a lantern-light ration."

Pete kept his eyes wide while shadows formed around the shapes in the room, and slowly the world around them returned from the pitch of darkness. Inez found a candle and a lighter. The wick caught, and she cupped her hand around it.

He stood and moved towards her. The candle light cast her buttery and pale, features faintly shadowed. They stood a breath apart, the candle firm in her hands, the only thing between them a wavering lick of light. He lifted it away, set it on the counter and turned. There she was waiting. He kissed her, lips connected but hesitant until her body was against his, the weight of her close. Her arms reached around him. Fingertips digging into his back, she took hold of him, the swell of her breasts soft against his chest. Pete's hands dipped, slid down the small of her back, pressed there, held her close until she rose onto her toes and whispered, "We have to stay quiet. We can't wake Dennis." Another kiss, her lips on his, so full, so nicely formed, her breath a faint whisper and then she took his hand and led him past Dennis's bed, past the wood stove with its door open, the dying embers a dim knot of red.

A low dresser stood alongside Inez's bed giving it a bit of privacy. Standing by it, she turned and pulled him to her. They kissed again, and he tugged at her clothes as they kissed, pulled up her sweater. A brief fumbling and then he started on the buttons of her shirt. It was hard in the dark, moving by touch, fingers in the lead. He pulled his own shirt over his head, and the moment skin touched open air, goosebumps rose and a shiver dropped down his spine. He was against her now, their bodies together, his warmth and hers. She was a slim woman, narrow waist and slight breasts, a shapely body buried under all those layers.

"The candle." She pulled away and stepped across the room, tiptoed on socked feet, milky skin exposed in the wavering light. Candle out, the cabin was truly dark except that the curtains on the window above the bed hung open. Moonlight fell through the glass, a faint streak down the bedspread. Pete bent and slipped under the covers then raised them for her. She slid in close, brought herself up against him, her face near enough that he could feel her breath on his cheek, on his lips. Their noses brushed as they kissed and she reached down and touched him, just her fingertips, just a moment of contact until he rose up, pulled himself onto her, skin on skin, his weight across her slender frame. Blanket fallen down across his back, he pressed his body into hers.

Afterwards they lay together, bodies intertwined, hearts settling into a quieter echo of one another. When Pete's eyes closed, images from Esterway Ridge were waiting for him — the lick of flame from the half destroyed Pinto, the still body lying on gravel. All evening Inez and Dennis had distracted him, kept his darker thoughts at bay, but now that his eyes were closed and his body still, they were back: Pete had taken a life. He was a murderer. Worse still he'd run away, and here he was on the coast doing nothing about it, lying beside a woman who didn't even know his real name.

CHAPTER

29

Inez lay on her side with Ash tucked against her, his knees against hers, hips nuzzled close, Dennis's breathing a gentle strum on the far side of the room. Above them the sycamore groaned, old wood bent by wind, a friendly voice, joyous, celebratory. Beyond that lay the sound of lapping waves, water on sand, one voice in a chorus of sound.

For a moment, Inez wasn't sure if Ash was asleep or awake, but then his body twitched and she whispered, "Good that Dennis slept through it."

She twisted about so she could see him properly, propped herself on an elbow. Who would have thought. The stranger here in her bed. "Can I ask you a question?"

"Anything."

The faintest rays of moonlight touched his face and gave him a statuesque sheen, features carved of stone. Youth always held such beauty. She'd come here young, and maybe even beautiful, but this place had aged her.

"What is it?"

Inez was unsure of her question now. Her thoughts had trailed off, circled around. She'd wanted to say something about him being here in her bed, the random wonder of it, a stranger stumbling in here, a chance encounter. Instead she let herself fall back. Darker thoughts had taken hold. "I'm so unsure of myself these days. All this uncertainty. I've got all these nagging worries."

/ / / / /

"I don't blame you."

She looked over at him again now, profile a shadowed line in the darkness of the cabin. "Have you ever heard of Gwyn John?" This story had haunted Inez since Ray first told her about the woman five or six years ago. "She was a painter in England, sister to Augustus John. He's famous, a portrait artist. You can see his work in galleries. Gwyn was also at the Slade and maybe better than him, but she was a woman. After a while she went to Paris. She met Rodin and fell in love. I don't think she did much art after that. One solo show in all her life. She's famous for being his model, his lover. One of many, I guess. She became a recluse, died penniless, died broke and sick and alone. And that's not a problem, lots of artists did. But she died without having spent her life painting, without having lived up to what she could have done, could have been. Her brother's got books written about him. He did portraits of the most famous people of the time. Gwyn's a footnote. That's what happens to women artists. That's what happens to all kinds of women if we're not careful."

"What about Emily Carr?"

"There's lots of counterexamples, but Emily Carr, she followed Lawren Harris for years, devoted to him. She painted this land, this very land like it was the icebergs and snow out of a Lawren Harris painting. Most of her work, years and years of it had his smooth and still look. And then, I don't know, she was probably sixty or so when she broke free. That's when she soared. Not that they were lovers. It's not like Gwyn John. Carr was always painting, always her own woman in so many ways, but influenced as women can be by men."

"The Emily Carr room is my favourite part of the municipal gallery. I once saw a map that showed where she painted. All over, really: Lillooet, Friendly Cove, Chemainus Valley, Alert Bay and the Queen Charlottes. And I was actually there once, on Moresby Island. I took my camera, walked through a valley where she'd done a series of paintings, old trees, a pale yellow to their bark, the kind of willowy look she gave to tree trunks."

Inez set a hand on his bare chest, a light touch on thin curls of hair. "It's a funny coincidence. We both like Emily Carr."

"Those trees on Moresby were all gone. That valley she'd painted, the one I wanted to photograph, it had been clear-cut down to stubs: a great stretch of stubbled land, nasty broken stumps cut so long ago they were going grey."

"When I first moved here, I brought a small backpack of paints and a portable easel. I'd carry them into the forest, but on the second or third trip, I discovered a wide stretch east of here all cut down to stumps, deadwood stacked, broken trees gathered like piles of garbage. For a week I forced myself to go out and paint what I saw and then I retreated, hid myself here where the great trees are still standing, the old cedars, the soaring firs."

"Now what will happen to all those trees?" he said. "What happens if people don't stand up and stop this kind of thing? Remember what you said about bearing witness?"

"This coast has been my muse, but all I can do is paint what I see, what I feel."

"Have you considered other places off the grid? There must be somewhere else you could go to paint if you had a mind to."

"I guess there are places like Bamfield or Gold River, more remote, further north, but I'm not sure they'll be on my list, Ash."

"What's on your list then?"

"You. You're on my list." She kissed him then, brought her face close to his and her body against him.

CHAPTER 30

Derek drove, up across the Malahat in the still evening light. After Youbou, Art counted the turns to himself and at the fourth, he pointed. "This one. Slow now." Derek signalled and turned onto Thurlow Road. A spray of purple and blue wildflowers twisted across the grassy shoulder. They passed a set of mailboxes then two or three gravel lanes. Beyond, the road narrowed to a track, stretches of it eaten away by potholes and gullies. The cedars grew close here, knitted in the road and left the car in shadow.

They'd gotten the news last night, Derek had heard it on the radio: the night watchman had died in hospital, taken off life support. Derek repeated the news with the relish he saved for setbacks and misfortune. That was Derek: he'd never seen a glass that wasn't half empty.

They all held silent a good long while. Art's first instinct was to issue another communique — get their message out in public, but that wasn't what they needed and so he held his tongue. Action is what they needed. It was time to do something. In the morning Art again raised the possibility of driving to Thurlow Road, getting enough dynamite for a test blast, ensure they could properly set the timer. "At the very least," Art said, "we need to get out of this dingy suite."

"I don't know about using dynamite again," Derek said. "That might be a mistake."

"It would mean some fresh air, some space to think."

/ / / / /

Fay nodded and after a long moment of silence, she said, "Alright." And so here they were, driving up Thurlow Road, and it felt good to be outside, to be getting ready for their next action. Stasis had been part of the problem these past few days: shut up in that suite with nothing but each other and their own thoughts.

Derek applied the brakes at each pullout they passed, slowed to look up over the steep hillside. "I'll tell you when," Art said. "It's not yet."

He leaned forward himself for a better view into the trees. One more bend and Art said, "I think it's the next one."

They rounded a sharp curve, and the road widened here to accommodate the turn. Two police cruisers occupied the pullout beyond.

Derek hit the brakes. The tires cut dirt, a long drawn-out skid. "Fuck." The blue and white cars were parked nose to tail and pulled over on the side of the road.

"You don't need to stop," Art said.

"The cops."

"Back up," Fay said. "Go in reverse."

The tires spun. Derek twisted himself, stretched an arm across the passenger seat and took the turn in reverse. The engine gave a whine, the rubbing of a belt, a low drone from under the hood. A hundred yards and the road was wide enough to turn around properly. Three point turn, back and forth, quick with the gears, the tires noisy on the dirt and gravel track until finally Derek had them on the road again, speeding east and downhill. "Fuck," he said again.

"We could have just driven by them," Art said. "You could have just carried on instead of skidding to a halt."

Derek hit the steering wheel, banged his hand against it again and again. "This is insane."

Fay pulled herself up between the front seats. "Did anyone see? Was anyone in those cars?"

Art touched Derek's arm to steady his own trembling hand. "It's okay. There'd be sirens by now if they'd seen us." The two cruisers had been pulled right over to the side, one car with its wheels on the edge of the rise, its whole body at an angle, nobody in them, at least not as far as Art could tell.

Derek squeezed the steering wheel. "Someone must have ratted."

Fay leaned forward, hovered between the two of them. "Could someone have stumbled across it?"

"It could be Pete," Derek said. "They might have him in custody."

That stilled them all and they reached the T-junction in silence.

"Did either of you ever tell anyone about our spot on Thurlow Road, even before we stashed anything there?"

"Never," Derek said.

"Fay?"

"No. Jesus no."

"Remember the two guys who drove by in a truck when we were unloading?"

"You're saying this is my fault?"

"It's possible is all I'm saying."

"If it was the guys in the truck," Derek said, "there's nothing we can do about it. But what if it was Pete?"

Fay pulled herself up from the back seat, leaned close again. "What actually happened when you drove back to Esterway Ridge? You said the cops didn't have Pete and you seemed so sure of it."

"I didn't think they did."

"Why though? What made you think that? Every time you tell us about driving back it's vague and unclear and yet —"

"It was vague and unclear. Chaos is what it was."

"You can't know the cops have Pete unless you saw them with him. The inverse is that you can't know the cops don't have Pete unless you saw him alone, not with the cops."

"I was guessing, okay? I didn't know for sure. I put two and two together."

"What two and two? What evidence, what reason to conclude —"

"Enough of the grilling, Fay. Maybe they do have Pete. Is that what you want me to say?"

Derek switched on the radio. "If they had him, it would be all over the news."

"Maybe they just took him in. Maybe they didn't have him before but do now."

"So," Fay said. "We go from thinking maybe the cops don't have him to being sure they do."

"I'm not sure of anything."

"As of now, we need to assume they have him. Operate that way until proven wrong." Derek rolled the dial across the AM band. "Would Pete know about the suite?"

"He might guess. He knows Nathan."

"That would be a problem."

"We could spend the night in the car," Art said. "By morning if something has happened it would be in the papers. If it's all clear, we can head to the suite and lay low while we figure out what to do next."

"And if it's not all clear? If they do have him?"

"Speculation doesn't help. The police cars could be there for some totally different reason. They could be there because of the truck that drove by while we were unloading. Let's head to Barrow Arm, spend the night in the parking lot then check the news in the morning."

"This is all going south, Art."

"We just have to stay calm."

"I am calm," Derek said. "The problem isn't with me. The problem isn't whether I'm fucking calm or not, Art."

CHAPTER
31

Tab took a taxi from the airport. On Earle Street, she stood in the shade of her front porch while the driver carried her suitcase up the walkway. As she flipped through her keys, the telephone inside started to ring. She turned back the deadbolt and swung the door wide, but by the time she got to the phone, the caller was gone. Her heart settled while her fingers lingered on the receiver's smooth plastic. Someone might have read her letter by now. Someone might have seen it and called her. She stood by the phone, waited there a few minutes, spotted a note from Frank saying Alice had called to confirm their brunch date.

Late that afternoon, Tab switched on the radio to keep herself company while she unpacked her overnight bag and that's how she heard about Owen Tuggs's death.

Tab had to sit as the news sank in, the meaning of it a physical impact on her. Peter, these Earth Action people, they'd be wanted for murder now. Everything had changed. Owen Tuggs dead. Murdered. Tab watched all the TV news she could find that afternoon. She turned from one channel to the next looking for images from the West Coast, news from the family, shots of the hospital.

Standing in the ICU corridor twenty-four hours earlier, Tab had sensed the grief that lay across Linda Tuggs and her family. She hadn't acknowledged it at the time, but part of her knew that Owen Tuggs wasn't going to make it. She'd seen it in their faces — a family already in mourning.

/////

Tab told Frank the moment he stepped inside. He set down his bag, hung his jacket and hugged her without speaking. She felt so weary now, so worn away. It wasn't a matter of jetting west to find her son. It never had been. None of this was going to be as easy as she'd hoped.

That night as Frank poured drinks, Tab asked what he thought about getting a lawyer for Peter.

Frank set down the rye, stirred the drinks, passed one over. "It's a little early to start getting fleeced by lawyers, isn't it?"

"Please don't make this about money." Tab took a long drink, let the alcohol settle through her. "I called Dick today."

"About this, about Peter?"

"Dick said he could meet with us tomorrow if you want. With all this news, with this man's death —"

"There's jurisdiction here, Tab. Dick's going to what, fly to court? Commute on a plane? Criminal law isn't even his area."

"He's just someone to talk to. He could maybe give us some names, some advice. He knows about these things."

"Remember that book Pete had at Christmas? The red one with the tape on the spine."

"You mean the *Anarchist Cookbook?*"

"That book was about bombs. It was about how to blow things up."

"It was about all sorts of things, Frank. People have these books. It's like having a Che Guevara T-shirt."

"It's not like a Che Guevara T-shirt. A man is dead, Tab."

Tab took another sip from her drink. She could feel a fight building, a frustration she'd tamped down now set free. Owen Tuggs was supposed to walk out of that hospital. He was hurt, yes, but he was supposed to survive. Peter was supposed to be there on the island, living in some communal arrangement or becoming a photographer. He was supposed to be there when she went. And now everything had gone so terribly wrong, everything spinning out of control.

She finished what was left in her glass. The ice cubes tinkled as she set the tumbler down. "Are you saying we shouldn't get a lawyer? Is that it? That my son doesn't deserve the help of the law?"

"Don't make this my son, your son, Tab."

"If this were James or Steven, you would hire the best —"

"Jimmy or Steven wouldn't have done this."

"Oh, I see, so this is his fault."

"Of course it's his fault, are you listening to yourself? Does no one take responsibility anymore?"

"You go on about responsibility, what about your responsibility, Frank?"

"Exactly what responsibility do I have for him that I didn't live up to? Food, shelter, money, tuition, everything."

"The responsibility to get along. The responsibility to make him feel at home. The day we moved into your place on Linden Street, you told him he could bunk in the shed."

"It was a joke."

"Whenever you say something mean, you turn around and say it's a joke."

"It was full of tools. Who could possibly think I literally meant he was supposed to sleep in the shed?"

The phone rang, a single bleat that cut them both short. Tab crossed the room and lifted the handset.

"Mrs. Harper?"

"Yes?"

"James Tide, *Vancouver Sun*. I'm phoning about your son, Peter. I'm working on a story for tomorrow's paper."

In Tab's chest, a dark stone fell earthwards. The press had his name, his name and her name. The man's voice shrank to a distant tremor as the handset slid from her ear. She settled the receiver into the cradle. Pictures would be in the paper soon enough. Everyone would know.

"Who was it?"

"No one." Her fingers drummed the chair back. Both hands looked wrinkled, veiny. Her knuckles were starting to swell. She used to like her hands and their long slender fingers, but now they put her in mind of a cabbage leaf.

"When I was out there, I left a note at a house where they maybe were. Maybe they lived there or maybe it's a house where they come to collect messages. Maybe Peter will call."

"Maybe. Hopefully."

"I lied to the police for him once. He was in grade seven or eight. We'd only just met so I don't think I told you. I was probably embarrassed. These neighbourhood boys used to make smoke bombs and what not, set them off in the alley. One day someone called the police. When the cruiser pulled up, I went and got Peter, told the officer he'd been inside until just a moment ago. I marched him back, but those other boys got taken home in the police car."

"That was a long time ago."

"Maybe I've taken too much responsibility. Overprotective perhaps. It's how you are as a single mother."

"If he sees that note I'm sure he'll call."

"If he does, and if we can convince him to speak to the authorities, we'll need a good lawyer."

"I'll come with you to see Dick then. If it makes you happy, I'll come."

CHAPTER
32

Awake and restless before daylight, Art slipped from the station wagon and set the door closed with a gentle push. He lit a cigarette and checked his watch. Almost five. He hadn't been sleeping well these past few days, awake in the small hours.

They'd know soon enough. If the police had Pete, it would be in the news this morning. The date on his watch said July 18. His birthday. A few more hours and his mother would try to call him. She'd set the phone in the Bee Street apartment ringing over and over again.

Three cigarettes were left in Art's pack and a few loose butts rattled at the bottom. Dawn was coming and the stars were growing faint. Those remaining might actually be planets — Venus or Jupiter. This rock he stood on was a planet just like those — one more pocket-sized ball spinning at a thousand miles an hour. A cog with eight other cogs in a solar system that was slowly bending and spilling away from the centre of a galaxy in the folds of a continually expanding universe.

When they'd first met, he and Pete Osborne had talked about stars, astronomy and deep space. At Bridal Veil Flats clear nights were rare, but when the clouds parted, the stars showed lively and bright and he and Pete had lain under them once or twice, staring skyward, talking.

The idea that Pete might have betrayed them had tilted Art's world and left his mind groping through the past for clues and explanations. Sitting above Barrow Arm, he could picture Pete

/ / / / /

easily enough, and the image that came to him again and again was from Esterway Ridge: the moment Pete took the timer even though Fay had drawn the short straw. Something silent and private had passed between Fay and Pete just then.

On any other night he might have talked himself out of pursuing this line of thinking, doors like that best left closed, but the possibility of Pete's betrayal had a grip on him. At the station wagon, he slid into the back where they'd folded the seats down. He set his arm across Fay's shoulder. "You awake?"

She murmured an inaudible response, a single syllable.

"What were you and Pete talking about just before he went into the Esterway Compound?"

She wiped her eyes. "What?"

"Right after he took the timer, you said something about talking later, something about waiting for him."

"What are you asking me?"

"You two had some conversation there which the rest of us weren't in on."

She shifted from him, pushed herself up a little. In the driver's seat, Derek grunted and shifted about. "I'm trying to sleep here."

"Pete had a thing for you. You know that, right? He always did."

"What do you mean, had?"

"Has, had, whatever."

"Will you two be quiet."

"He took the timer for me, he went in after I drew the short straw. I told him I'd be waiting."

Art leaned close to Fay's ear and whispered, "Derek and I waited almost an hour at the quarry." This was a fact he'd not acknowledged until now, even to himself.

"So?" she said.

"You two pulled up and when you got out of the car your shirt was misbuttoned, your hat gone."

Fay pushed at him. "Get off me."

Art pulled his arm back. "I'm not on you."

She turned away, but it didn't matter. Art already knew. Maybe he'd known before. Maybe he'd known all along, the shadow at the edge of his thoughts, the reason he'd been turning those moments over in his mind: "You fucked him, didn't you?"

Fay didn't answer, but Art's certainty had solidified, and the station wagon felt closed in now, the space tight and stuffy. His breath cut short. He started to sweat as he pushed the door open, slid out head first. He took in the cool morning air, walked a tight circle then lit another cigarette. He drew hard on it, smoked with a quivering ferocity.

Part of him had suspected something between them. That night on Esterway Ridge, driving through that warren of roads headed for the smoking wreck at the compound, whatever had passed between Fay and Pete was niggling at him, his mind circling back to the moment Fay had arrived at the quarry and said she'd lost her hat.

A black column of smoke had marked the morning sky as Art reached the Y-junction two hundred yards from the compound. He'd turned the car and headed along the right-hand branch, and there was Pete, scrambling across a mound of dirt and into the woods. Art could have gone after him. That was the truth. Right then he could have dashed into the woods after Pete, but he sat in the station wagon a few seconds too long, distracted maybe, confused certainly, suspicious, unbalanced.

And now could this same man have gone and betrayed them all? Could he have turned to the police and ratted on them? Art wasn't sure which hurt more, Fay's betrayal or Pete's.

Morning light had begun to spread across Barrow Arm. Birds chattered in the forest, wind rippled the water and a pair of loons emerged around the nearest point. Seated on a cold grey boulder, Art watched as the sun poked up over the horizon and spread its reflection across the dark water. A chipmunk scurried past, paused, looked over at Art.

One of the car doors opened and closed. Footsteps sounded on the bed of gravel. "We just heard a radio broadcast," Fay said. "The police found a stash of dynamite on a tip from an anonymous source not connected to the group. It said the police believe the dynamite belonged to us. They mentioned the reward again."

"It must have been the guy in the truck."

She sat beside him on the boulder. "My fault then."

"We could have moved it. Pete suggested we move it." He looked down to the cigarette pack in his hands and ran his thumbnail along the edge of the cellophane. "This. I mean you and him, it's why he took the timer for you at Esterway Ridge, isn't it?"

"It was stupid. I wasn't myself. I'm still not myself. Ever since that day I've been, I don't know."

"Is it Pete or is it what happened at Esterway?"

"What happened with Pete isn't what you think. At least it's not all what you think."

He waited then, looked over the water and its chevron white-caps to the ragged trees beyond. He waited for her to speak.

"I was revved up with all this nervous energy and he was worried. He was scared, that's the truth of it. He said he wasn't sure we should be doing this. It was distraction."

"That's why you fucked him?"

"You were being an ass. He was talking like he might back out. We were both nervous. I'd have told you, I'd have explained it except everything that happened since has been like this crushing weight."

Wind rustled the long grasses that led down to the shoreline. "By everything that's happened since," he said, "do you mean —"

"A man is dead, Art. We killed —"

"Alright. Okay. I know."

"Half of me is still back there. A man dead, Pete gone and I sent him in there, I got him to take the timer even though I drew short straw."

"Good is coming of this. Look at the effort they're putting in, what it's costing them to try to stop us. You have to look at the positive side of things, Fay. Our tactics are working."

"I agreed to this because I believed in what we're doing, believed someone had to stand up. I still do. Mostly I do. These past few days though some part of me would probably walk away if I could."

"You just have to open your eyes to everything that's going right."

"Last night, wide awake, I found myself wondering if there was some way to extricate myself —"

"Stop talking like this, Fay."

" — but I'm in up to my neck."

"The reward, our communique in print, these are signs. We're getting somewhere here, Fay."

"Where though? Where exactly are —"

"We have everyone's attention. Press, politicians, industry. Look at how hard they're working and they still haven't got us. We're two steps ahead of them and we can stay that way. We just need to agree on our response, on where we go from here."

Footsteps across the gravel and then Derek stood beside them, his shadow cast long across the boulder. "So you've sorted this out then? The two of you —"

"The three of us are going to decide our next move together. It's going to be like you said, all equal. Consensus." Art looked to Fay, looked to Derek, opened his palms. "Does that sound alright?"

Fay's chin dropped, a slow nod. If they were going to carry on, Art would have to swallow his resentment, his anger. He'd have to set it aside and find a way to bury what happened between Pete and Fay.

Derek had started talking: "I've been thinking about what we need to do, about how to respond. We need to start basing our moves on first principles."

"Which means what?" Art said.

"The fundamental problem with the environmental movement was building it on the idea that you can change industry practices and economics with a mass movement that wins people over one by one: it proved impossible, too slow. And so it naturally evolved into disruption, think Bridal Veil Flats, or Bedwell Pass, put your body in the way, make it hard to carry on logging. A slightly more radical approach, but similar results. Or lack of results."

What Derek said was true: the Kennedy Lake protests and the Friends of Clayoquot Sound were a farce in action. 7:00 a.m. every day the protesters were at the barricades then within an hour the RCMP would make a few arrests and the barricades came down so logging trucks could roll, a show for the cameras, pretend opposition by people full of themselves because they thought they were making such a difference. All those protests at Clayoquot Sound and as far as Art could tell they hadn't stopped a single hour of old growth destruction except for the time someone burned down the bridge over Kennedy Lake — that single act of arson evidence of what a group like Earth Action Now could accomplish.

Derek was still talking: "The three of us, the four of us actually, understood what a third wave could do. Change the industry's economics through targeted sabotage. Tilt costs against the forestry industry. A small group can hit them hard in a way that damages their bottom line. This is where we split off from Jeremy."

Art looked over at Fay, tried to gauge her reaction, divine what thoughts passed behind those pale blue eyes as Derek stepped up like he was the one who could lead them out of crisis. A few more seconds and Art cut him off: "What's your point here, Derek?"

"Maybe we've already done that. They've got a reward. You said yourself they were desperate. We could put our demands out there and say we're open to negotiations."

"No. The only way to negotiate successfully is from a position of strength. They think they have us pinned down. They're wrong on that, but we still need to re-establish ourselves, build back to a position of strength."

"If we're doing this by consensus," Fay said, "you can't just say no."

"Alright," Art said. "Tell us what you think."

"I think we need some space, some room to breathe. It's hard to even think about what to do next locked up in that suite, especially if the cops might knock any second."

"Derek?" Art said.

"A cousin of mine has a cabin in the Slocan. We could hole up until winter, but at some point we need to issue demands."

"We said this end of the island would be our second front. Now you two want to leave?"

"They knocked on our door at Bee Street," Fay said. "They found the dynamite. Maybe we have to cool it a while just to survive."

At least she wasn't talking about walking away, turning their backs on everything. "You're okay abandoning Pete?" Art said.

"I'm not even sure he's alive anymore."

"You both think this is the right move? A rebuilding period, a cooling off period."

Fay nodded.

"We could issue that press release you wrote," Derek said. "Keep our message out there. Even after that we could issue the occasional communique from the Slocan. Introduce our demands which could open things for negotiations."

"I just said we're not negotiating."

"But this is supposed to be a collective so you don't decide, Art."

"Being a collective doesn't mean we make mistakes, doesn't mean we do things we shouldn't."

"Fay?" Derek said.

"One thing at a time," Fay said. "Get to the Slocan first."

"This could be the time to make a deal. Pete was the one who took the timer in. He was the one who technically set the explosion."

"What the hell are you talking about?" Fay said.

"It's something to keep in mind, that's all."

"Blaming what went wrong on Pete is not the answer to anything."

Art stood. "Who did what is not a negotiation tactic."

"At some point it could be important," Derek said.

"We agreed we'd go up to your cousin's cabin. That's what we're going to do."

Derek stared at him a moment, held his body still, chin thrust out, but then he turned his back, and his feet crunched down into the gravel as he walked away.

Art knew he should say something now, knew he should call Derek back, but instead he reached for Fay's hand and squeezed it while Derek pulled open the car door and dropped into the driver's seat.

CHAPTER 33

Inez awoke to the first strains of morning light, and there he was, warm in the envelope of her bed: the stranger naked beside her. Beyond the dresser that blocked the rest of the room, Inez could hear Dennis's breathing, the sound of his presence. She sat up and looked over the dresser's back. The boy lay still under the blankets, his head turned away.

Inez settled again. The covers had slipped and exposed Ash's bare shoulder, the top of his arm. Her hand hovered at his forehead above a swoop of matted hair. Nothing wrong with a little pleasure in life as long as she understood that's all it was. The thing was not to get too attached. Not to let her loneliness pull her into something for which she wasn't ready. Over four years since Ray and even now she wasn't sure she could trust enough to start again. And at the end of the day, what did she really know about this man other than that he was twenty-three, son of a single mother, a former student, a former photographer? Although of course, that was probably part of the attraction, the layers teased away rather than revealed.

Snuggled close, she whispered: "Sneak outside. Pretend to arrive for breakfast."

That did it. He wiped his eyes and looked about. She raised a finger to her lips. Half a nod and he reached for his clothes. He'd have to walk by Dennis to get to the front entrance. Tiptoe in socked feet and he could probably make it. As long as he hit

/ / / / /

no loose boards. "Use the front door. That door at the back just goes to the toilet."

He kissed her first. The lightest flutter of a kiss, lips against hers and then he was crossing the room, barefoot past the sink, bundled clothes in his arms. They were like teenagers, tiptoeing around dozing parents.

A floorboard groaned. It sounded a deep note, but Dennis didn't react. Ash was at the door now. He blew a kiss and slipped outside. A moment later the waft of cool air reached her at this side of the cabin.

Inez dressed and crossed the room. Dennis had his eyes open. He smiled.

"I thought you were asleep."

"Just resting."

"Care for pancakes?"

"Really?"

"Why not. Splurge."

"Are you making them for Ash?"

She backed off, bent to look for the flour jar under the counter and left his question unanswered.

The mason jar had enough flour for three or four pancakes. She measured a cup, added baking powder. For the egg, she stepped outside. Ash sat in the rocking chair grinning at her, a lick of hair standing up, curlicue above his head.

"He didn't see?"

She shrugged. "Maybe."

"I'd meant to leave earlier."

"It's okay. It's fine."

Around the side of the building, she propped open the gate and stepped into the chicken run, opened the coop door. "Good morning, ladies." Rhonda slipped out and the others followed, a three hen parade while she reached in and felt about the corners, dug at the straw until she found one egg, and another.

Dennis, Inez and Ash ate the pancakes outside on the porch,

in the warmth of the morning sun. Blackberry jam on lightly browned flapjacks, two each, a small stack, a touch of honey on the side.

Food eaten, Inez set her plate down. The day sprawled in front of her, a wide blank canvas much like every other day — time to paint, time to swim, and yet her mind was topsy-turvy now. Here beside her was this man who'd spent the night in her bed. And on top of that, ever since she'd made those pancakes, she kept thinking about how she'd soon have to go into town for supplies. They were low on just about everything and she'd need to organize herself for the trip, write a list. She'd have to get their baby bonus cheque, collect the mail, return library books, send her sister a letter.

Inez looked over as Ash eased himself back in the rocking chair. He had a handsome profile. He'd look good for years to come, distinguished even once grey touched his hair. Just behind him, her wetsuit lay folded over the washing line, limbs all hanging down. Swim and then paint. Or maybe paint and then swim. She had an energy coursing through her, and she needed to get out to her studio. No need to go into town just yet.

As if he'd read her mind, Dennis said, "Ash and me are going to play chess."

"Ash and I."

"And then maybe he could help me with the kayak?"

"Perfect." Inez clapped her hands. That would work well, the two of them spending the morning together. "I'm going to paint."

CHAPTER 34

Dennis set the hand-painted chess board on a stump in a sunny spot south of the cabin. Pete pulled two lawn chairs across the grass and turned his to face down the length of the beach, a view over sand and water. The ocean looked chipped and dark, but the horizon held clear, just one boat out there, its sail a small triangle of white in the distance.

Dennis slid a pawn two squares forward; Pete did the same. Inez left the cabin as the game got underway, walked along the rocks and disappeared behind the tangled blackberry bushes.

"Why do you call her Inez?" Pete said after a time.

"Because that's her name."

"But you never say *mom* or *ma* or whatever?"

"Unless I'm trying to get my way. Then I say 'Please Mom.'" He gave the words a little singsong twist and took one of Pete's pawns with a piece that was either his castle or his queen. The pieces looked equally tall and both had square tops, whittled bits of wood with carved marks in an attempt to differentiate them.

Pete moved his knight forward. At some point last night, a thought had embedded itself: he might be able to live out here, not Baker Beach of course, but one of those more remote spots Inez had mentioned — Bamfield or Gold River. It was really just another way of going underground. A few years here and he could truly become Ash McCabe. It was an option, one of several roads he could take: turn himself in, try to track down Fay and Art, or try to find a way to live in obscurity some place like this.

Despite Jeremy's advice about getting a lawyer and going to the police, Pete had never given serious thought to turning himself in. This place had a pull on him though — out here on the edge of the world. Inez and the others might never actually put two and two together. It's not like Pete's name was in the paper. At least not yet. And even if his name did come out one day, he could hardly imagine a group of people less interested in helping Greer-Braden Limited.

Pete shifted his castle and lost another pawn. "What would someone need if he wanted a set-up like yours?" Pete asked. "A cabin like you've got here, only somewhere more remote like Gold River or Bamfield."

"Why would you want to go up there?"

"This community, this set-up you've got here, I'm sure there are lots who say it's the way of the past, but it could also be the way of the future. Fossil fuels, oil, power consumption, clear-cutting. Modern society could come to a grinding halt if we're not careful."

Pete shifted his bishop. He should have been paying more attention to the board, but his mind had veered off down this new path: this was the frontier, the place people reinvented themselves. If he had to, he could just become Ash McCabe.

"What would you need to build one of these cabins? Like that Phelps one, just a small place."

"I don't know, tools, equipment."

"What kind of equipment?"

"Building equipment, an Alaska sawmill. The best thing would be to have a boat. You set it mostly on land but somewhat in water and that way no one can ever tell you to leave because you're under maritime law."

"And you can move around."

"You'd still want a garden, a chicken coop, a goat or whatever on land. The boat's just where you sleep."

A boat then. It made sense. It seemed obvious. Only what would it cost to buy a boat?

"Check," Dennis said and Pete looked at his pieces anew.

"I thought this was my king." The wooden king looked too much like his one bishop, same height, same rounded top.

"V is for bishop, X is for king."

"You could have carved in a B for Bishop and K for King."

"V kind of sounds like B and X kind of looks like K."

"I'm distracted," Pete said.

"Are you thinking about building a cabin here?"

"The problem with here is that no one seems to be sure how long it's going to last."

On his turn, Pete again moved his king, but Dennis kept pressing, forcing him further across the board. He said check again. The way he smiled drew his lips thin.

The lawn chair creaked. "It would help if I could figure the pieces, like if I could tell a king from a bishop, a rook from a queen." His king was one square over now, but Pete knew the next move: Dennis would take his castle.

Maybe starting again was the answer. Somewhere remote, quiet and isolated. It didn't have to be forever, just for now, for the foreseeable future. He wasn't going to be able to find the others holed up in some suburb while he himself was trying to keep out of sight. Maybe Jeremy could. Jeremy might be able to find them and warn them away from List Cove. What Pete could do is find a way to survive, to lie low and rebuild his life. If he wasn't going to find the others and he wasn't going to submit himself for prison or rat out his friends, what other options did he have?

/ / / / /

Pete didn't help Dennis sand the kayak in the end. Chess game over, he followed the trail Inez had walked, skirted the edge of the blackberry bushes tracing a gentle rise through a stand of fir trees. Her studio door stood ajar. From the edge of the stepping stone path, he peered through a window. Light spread across the floor, bathed her neck and her shoulders as she bent over a painting.

He rapped on the door, pushed it open with a quiet hand and stepped inside. A pair of paintings he hadn't seen before hung on the far wall, landscapes peaceful and grand: wild ferns tall around the base of trees, a light, open space in a brooding forest. The second painting showed a churning ocean, rocky shore, a stormy moment on the coast. Bearing witness was the right term for these landscapes, portraits of the earth's wild corners.

The floorboards here didn't creak, and Inez carried on painting without seeming to realize how close Pete now stood.

She was working on a still life, the objects in it somehow abstracted on the canvas, flattened onto the painting's surface, a bundle of yellows. "It looks good," he said. "Like the sun touched down here on earth."

That drew her attention and a quick, bright smile. For a moment he stood in the warmth of it.

"Any chance your favourite colour is yellow?" he asked.

"What?"

"Your sweater, that painting. I just noticed how much yellow you have around."

She turned to face him, brush by her side.

"It's the spectrum's brightest colour," he said. "More yellow photons than any other colour. Little bit of trivia there."

"These are my work clothes, and this sweater is ochre not yellow."

He stepped up and touched the sweater. "You look good in yellow. But you'd look better without it on."

"I know maybe why you're here."

He tried to lift it, tried to pull it off. He wanted her close, wanted to hold her, lose himself in her body, but she kept her arms down, held them at her sides.

"I'll be too cold." She leaned close as she spoke and kissed him all the same.

"We could keep our clothes on. At least we could keep most of our clothes on."

"Tonight." She kissed him again and he was intensely aware of her body under all those clothes. "I'm painting now, I'm working, but tonight you can stay over again."

"That's great. I'll look forward to that." He stepped towards the glass. A thin mist of condensation had formed along the bottoms of the windows. Even here in this weighted landscape, flashes of yellow showed in the dense greenery, a tinge in the moss and lichen on the backs of trees and on the sun-touched ferns. He turned to Inez. "When I was a kid, I heard about someone who could taste colours. There's a word for that, a diagnosis."

"Synesthesia."

"I tried it, you know. I might have been ten or so and I went and ate coloured things — yellow, red, whatever. You know how kids associate colours and tastes, pink is bubblegum, purple grape."

"Probably not how synesthesia works."

"I tasted the tip of a red pen, licked the ink. That's how I was as a child, literal about everything. Maybe I still am."

"Art's kind of the opposite of that, don't you think? Everything more than the literal, multiple planes all layered and operating together, a depth beyond the literal. That might even be a definition for art."

"I like the sound of that."

"You have a depth beyond the literal too, Ash. More to you than meets the eye."

"Don't be so sure. I'm the guy who tried to taste red."

"How did it taste?"

"Do you think you could paint a taste?"

"Someone probably could. What about photography, could you photograph a taste?"

That was an odd thought: a photograph of taste.

Inez was still talking. "I've seen pictures that have made me salivate, in food magazines, big coloured photos."

"If I was able to capture something that true on film, the last thing I'd use it for is putting pictures of taste in magazines."

"I saw a picture of lamb and onions on a skewer on the page of a magazine I was using as fire starter. I tore it out, pinned it to my wall. That's how good it looked."

"Lamb and onions. I don't even need the picture to salivate."

"We're not exactly gourmet here." Inez held her brush in the air a moment and her words seemed caught, half formed. Slowly she turned from him. "I've got to get to work here."

"Sure. Of course. I'll see you when you're done."

Inez's brush hovered above the canvas, but didn't touch. "Can I ask you a favour?"

"Anything."

"It's going to sound strange, this request. We're all so caught up in this eviction thing, this attempt to get moving money. I'm not sure we're seeing straight."

Those words brought him back to Baker Beach. For a moment there he'd lost himself, her smile and their shared pleasure at the conversation had carried him off. Now a studied concentration played across her face.

"You'll be lucky to get two hot pennies from Greer-Braden," Pete said.

"That's what worries me."

"What's the favour?"

"Would you go ask Christian about it? Talk to him about what he's doing, how it's going. Fourteen years he's been here, way longer than anyone else, and maybe this is just his way of trying to hold on a little longer. Maybe we're all deluded, sitting around hoping someone will dump five thousand dollars in our laps."

"I'll ask him."

"It's hard to get to the specifics with him, it's like he's retreated into a sort of defensive crouch."

Pete started down the flank of the Point, paused as he passed through a stand of cedars. He needed a minute. He needed to stand here alone and quiet. Thirty feet above, the branches swayed, bent by the onshore wind. Pete stepped further into the trees, reached his arms around the base of the nearest cedar, laid palms across its sinewy bark, alive with moss and lichen, touched his head to the trunk. Ear against it, he could hear the wood, the deep groan of it, the tree's voice.

It had been years since he'd found peace in the wilderness, years since he'd stood among the trees and wondered at these ancient beings and their massive spires. The forest had become a battleground these past few years. Even when he'd been trying to capture it on film he'd been demanding something of it. Even writing about it for the student paper, he'd walked into the woods with expectations. The awe and reverence he'd felt on first seeing trees like these had hardened long ago. It was easy to wrap yourself in fury, and somehow harder to recapture the quiet, peaceful wonder that used to draw him into the woods.

He could do it though. Standing among the ancient cedars, the gentle giants, Pete knew he could live somewhere on this coast, among these trees, or among trees like these. A knot had loosened in him since he'd landed here. Part of that was living on the land, bound to the sea here where the continent ended. Part of it was also Inez — their connection easy and natural.

There at the edge of the forest, it struck Pete that he might one day take up his camera again, bear witness in the way Inez talked about — live it rather than just look at it. Maybe this was his road, his way to start again.

CHAPTER
35

Art let himself in his parents' back door, wiped his shoes on the mat and stepped into the kitchen. A faint sound travelled from the living room, peals of laughter and applause from the TV. Further into the kitchen, Art set a hand on the rickety Formica table. It gave a faint creak. The smell of pipe tobacco laced the air. Overhead, a cuckoo clock ticked. Art's eyes dipped closed, a moment of relief, a quiet recess. And then the TV volume dropped.

"Mom?" he called.

The sound of movement rose from deeper in the house, footsteps, the creak of door hinges, then she stood in the hallway. "Oh Lord. Oh good Lord." Arms out, her whole body seemed to lift as she took him into a long, smothering hug.

"You're okay? You're alright? Let me get a look at you."

"I'm fine," he said, but the sting of new tears touched his eyes.

"All this talk, all this trouble."

He wiped at his nose. He blinked. "I can't stay long, Mom." He had to get control of himself here.

She took his hands, held them in hers and gave a squeeze. "I knew you'd come. I just knew it. I was getting ready to bake you a cake." She looked past him and through the kitchen door which he'd left open. "You haven't got anyone with you?"

"No. I saw Dad leave. Off to the pool for his afternoon swim." He'd told the others he was going to Bee Street for their welfare

/ / / / /

cheques. He'd taken Fay's bank card to get out whatever money he could and then he'd driven here. A birthday indulgence.

"I can't stay long."

"Sit. I'll put the kettle on."

"You might not hear from me so often now, Mom."

"The police came by and a reporter called. I didn't say anything. Of course I didn't. The other day, that woman from —"

"I'll try to give you a call now and then to let you know I'm okay. Just a phone call here and there, but you can't talk about it. Not to anyone. From here on, you just have to say you've never heard from me. Did you get that, Mom? That I'll still try to call."

She smiled at him, face warm and bright.

Some part of him considered this weakness, coming here without the others knowing, caving in to the need for respite. "I brought you something," he said. "It's just little."

"You're the one with the birthday, Arty."

He lifted a plastic figurine from his pocket, a baby chick that wobbled on its platform. It had been on display in the store next to the bank machine he'd used to empty Fay's account. It only cost two dollars, marked down with a handful of leftover Easter displays.

"I'm going to put it right there above the sink." She set it beside the jade plant. "Twenty-eight years old." With that she smiled a brief, pinched smile. "I think I should bake us that cake."

"I need a favour. I'm wondering if you can spare any money to hold me over."

"Sure. Whatever we've got."

Volumes from *Encyclopedia Britannica 1974* dominated the living room bookshelf. The right-most book on the middle shelf had a ragged cloth bound cover, the lettering worn off the spine.

She flipped it open. Charts, plans and numbered diagrams filled the book. Near the middle lay a few twenty dollar bills.

"Will Dad notice?"

She passed them over, six in total, one hundred and twenty dollars. "I'll deal with him."

"Tell him I'm borrowing it."

"How about a cup of tea? How about we sit a moment?"

Art folded the bills into his front pocket. The cuckoo clock said one-thirty. Early still. He had time. "A cup of tea."

Art sat on one of the vinyl kitchen chairs and his mother set out the teapot, put two cups on a tray then leaned on the counter while she waited for the water to boil.

"How's your hip?"

"Pains me at night, and with the bad weather. When the rains come."

"This has been hard on you. Don't think I don't know it."

She stepped towards him then, crossed the narrow room.

"They're slandering the lot of you, in the paper, on the news, saying all sorts of things."

"Don't listen to any of it."

"Of course I don't, but with this kind of publicity —"

"It means we're getting somewhere, Mom. It means we're having an effect, which is more than I can say for the state of things in years past."

"You've got to be careful though, that's what I'm trying to say." She took his hands and held them while silence swelled. Behind her, the kettle began to boil.

Outside a newspaper landed on the front porch. "That'll be the afternoon paper."

Art stood and stepped into the hall. Once the paper boy had passed on to the next house, he leaned out and there it was: four grainy, black and white photos on the front page, their faces in print: "Suspects Named in Esterway Ridge Bombing."

"Fuck." Art said it on a short, faint breath. He backed up against the wall. All four of them, names and photos on the front page, Pete Osborne too. He clearly wasn't in custody, and he certainly hadn't ratted them out. He was still in the woods, lost or maybe dead.

From down the hallway came the soft footsteps of his mother's slippered feet.

"We're in the newspaper. Names. Photos."

"Oh dear," she said. "Oh Lord above."

"I'd better go."

"His mother came by." She angled her head towards the bottom left picture.

"How do you mean, 'came by'?"

"She came to see me because she wants to talk to you. She's trying to find her son."

"She's here? On the island?"

"She was. She flew out. She was upset, desperate even."

"And she wants to talk to me?"

"She left her number if you want it."

CHAPTER 36

Tab stood at her closet door and pulled on the olive dress she'd bought last fall. July now and it had been hot since mid-May, but the tags still hung from the dress. She pulled it down across her body, arranged it on herself, but the dress didn't hang naturally. She caught a glimpse in the mirror. Her face looked puffy, like she was retaining water, no makeup, her hair big and unruly, circles hung under both eyes.

The closet's overhead light flickered. Tab touched a grey pair of slacks with the tags still on and then a chartreuse blouse she couldn't remember buying. She could give half these clothes away without even noticing. Peter had said exactly that. Dressed in his clothes from the Salvation Army, he'd said, "Why do you need all this stuff?"

She'd had an answer for him at the time. She'd said she liked her clothes, said they made her feel good. Now she wasn't so sure. Had she somehow lost her moral bearings these past ten years?

The phone rang with a cheery buzz that carried through the house. The downstairs ring was off by a beat, like an echo from the other end of the building.

Tab walked to the landing. A flutter rose through her stomach as she lifted the handset. On the other end, a woman said, "Collect call from Arthur Spring for Tab Harper."

Tab's mouth went dry. "Accept."

A faint click and then a man said, "I understand you're looking for your son."

/////

Tab's chest flattened and her breath vanished. "I am," she said. "Who is this?"

"Art Kosky."

"Oh God. Oh thank you. I was hoping you could help —"

"I understand you've been looking for me."

"Yes, of course, I wanted —"

"I can't talk on the phone though."

"It's okay. I'm alone. I mean there's no police here or anything. Have you got Peter with you?"

"We need money, Mrs. Harper."

"What?"

"We're broke. We need help."

"You want money?"

"How much can you bring?"

"With me? You mean to see you? I don't know. A couple of hundred dollars. When —"

"No. More than that. A thousand. No, two thousand."

"Two thousand dollars?"

"Three if you can."

"I can't."

"Two then."

"I need to see him. I need to hear his voice."

"I'm going to set a time to meet, okay? Bring two thousand dollars and wait in front of a restaurant called Kettle Top in Glendenning at twelve noon on the nineteenth."

"That's tomorrow. I can't. Not then."

"There's flights. You can do it."

"Make it in the afternoon just to be sure."

"Four o'clock then at the Kettle Top."

In the background, a car raced past, the sound of its engine close for a moment.

"I want to know that Peter's okay."

"There can't be anyone with you. Just you and just me."

"But what about my son?"

The pale hum of a dial tone cut in. Tab looked at the receiver in her hand. She'd promised to tell Burrell if she discovered anything, but she couldn't do that now. If the police got involved it would mean no negotiations, no plea bargain. They'd have Peter in custody.

"Kettle Top," Tab said to herself. "Four p.m." Back in the bedroom, she wrote it on a pad of paper and then from the top of the closet, pulled down her overnight bag and set it on the bed. It was three o'clock. Frank would be on the sixth or seventh hole by now. Before she did anything else, she needed to go to a bank.

CHAPTER 37

Christian and Andy were seated on low benches set in a sunny patch of dirt in front of Christian's cabin. As Pete approached, Christian raised a hand. "God awful good day to you, Ash. Care for a nip of shine?" The words ran into each other, a lazy slur.

Pete had seen Andy once or twice over the past few days. He was a fraction Christian's size, a lean and wiry build with a wild dark beard. Pete offered his hand, introduced himself. Andy raised his cup. "New batch celebration."

"Mind if I sit and talk a bit?"

"Fine with me." Christian held a large mason jar in one hand, a chipped brown mug in the other. "Talking's free."

Pete eased onto a narrow seat made of sun-bleached driftwood. It shifted under his weight. "If you weren't squatting here, where would you guys go?"

"I'm not squatting here," Christian said. "I claim this by right of my Métis blood."

"I didn't know you were Métis."

"Part Métis. On maybe like his grandmother's side."

"You can't be part Métis, Andy. Métis means part."

"Where would you go though, besides here? Gold River maybe? Bamfield?"

"Bella Coola," Christian said.

"Why?"

"Less campers. Less dimwits. Less people asking stupid questions."

/ / / / /

"What about you, Andy?"

"Go mobile. Wheels." Andy thumped his chest as he spoke, a solid hit like he was trying to release a belch. "If we had set this up in a mobile way, we wouldn't have these problems."

"How could a place like this be mobile?" Christian said. "This is the opposite of mobile."

"I know, I said if."

"I'm just looking for ideas here, guys."

"You thinking of setting up a situation?"

"Dennis was telling me a boat would be the best approach. Moor it half on land, half on water. I guess I've been thinking."

"Oscar, the guy you met the other morning, he's always talking about a boat. Good idea until the storms hit."

"Good idea because he can afford a boat."

"You could find a sheltered bay," Pete said.

"You got a boat?" Andy said.

"No."

"You know how to sail, how to operate a boat?"

"It was an idea is all."

Andy crossed his feet then, touched his beard. "Ocean's a beast. Don't mess with the ocean."

"It just seemed easier than building a cabin, getting hold of all the tools and equipment."

"Did you come over for a nip?" Christian raised the mason jar he held.

"I came to talk. Inez wanted me to discuss Greer-Braden with you."

"Discuss what?"

"Who are you talking to there?"

"Lawyers."

"That's it? Lawyers."

"All kinds of people in legal. They got a whole department."

"Hold on a second, do you not even know who you're negotiating with?"

"Lawyers. I just fucking said that." A twist to his face then, disapproval, disbelief, almost a snarl.

"Talking to lawyers isn't going to get you anywhere. Especially if you don't even know their names."

"I got their names. I can find out their names. We've been writing them letters."

"You need to go after the people actually in charge of the company. The president or the board. Those are the kind of people who can do something. Lawyers are just —"

"And you're an expert?"

"I've had some dealings with Greer-Braden in the past, and Inez asked for my opinion, that's all this is."

"And your opinion is we should talk to the president of the board."

"The president and the board. The president's name is Hollingsworth. The chairman of the board is Fred Long."

That caught Christian's attention, the fact Pete knew the names. Andy started to speak, stopped himself.

"You know these people?"

"Not personally."

Christian set out a third mug and poured drink from a mason jar. "Have a hooch."

The moonshine lit Pete's tongue, a burn that triggered his gag reflex. He managed to force it down though, and a trail of fire rolled through his chest. One deep breath, a cough and his tongue felt scrubbed.

"Good, n'est-ce pas?"

Pete couldn't answer at first. He coughed and shook his head. "Rocket fuel," he said at last.

"So that's it? Walk up and talk to those two guys? Hollingsworth and Fred whatever?"

Pete settled in his seat. "You've got a better chance with them than with their lawyers."

Andy held out the jug, but Pete pulled his cup away before Andy could refill it. He finished what remained and the blaze scorched his throat and chest. His ears tingled.

"You could start a civil disobedience campaign. You could try for press attention. Maybe some of each. Civil disobedience might include barricading logging roads, disruption, chaining yourselves here. There's more militant options of course."

"Militant like what?" Christian shifted back, head angled Andy's way as though to confirm something with the man beside him. Pete thought again of the two plastic tubs stashed a hundred yards away, the firebombs, but just then, Christian took hold of Pete's mug, spilled more liquid into it. Moonshine already padded the sides of his brain. A warm ease had settled across his body. He lifted the mug though, drank from it. Christian stood. He'd spotted something along the beach. Pete turned. A handful of people had gathered high up on the sand. One of them shouted, a low holler. It might have been Ernie, the man Pete had seen gathering seaweed his first morning down on the beach. He was waving, green wool cap in hand. A squat man stood beside him and a third person trailed a little further down. Christian stepped past the fire ring to the edge of the ridge.

At this distance it was hard to make out the figures, but the two men with Ernie looked to be wearing hard hats.

"Maybe it's the sign posters."

"Who are the sign posters?" Pete asked.

Christian had already started down the trail though. He broke into a jog and disappeared from sight. Andy followed.

The trail wove down the wooded slope and switched back once as it descended. Pete had to concentrate to walk straight. Andy and Christian were already out of sight. A goat stood tethered to a stake in the dirt. Pete paused. "A goat," he said. Both its horns were crooked. Pete looked around, waited and listened. Ernie was still out there, and still shouting. Christian yelled back. Pete could hear his boots on the soil. Or maybe it was the soil he could hear under his boots.

The sign posters might have cops with them. Or they might actually be cops and not sign posters. Not that he was sure exactly what sign posters were, other than the obvious, other than the fact they might be here to post signs.

CHAPTER 38

Inez ran high on the beach and the toes of her boots kicked up sand as she went. Christian ran ahead of her. Further on, Ernie seemed to have quit trying to stop either of the two men, just walked alongside them now, talking as he went, his voice still raised. The nearer man had something slung over his shoulder, equipment of some kind.

Christian reached them first, both hands up, his body a blocker.

"They say they're here for documentation." Ernie's voice had gone shrill.

"What the hell kind of documentation?"

Inez closed the last few yards at a walk. The nearer of the two men set down the tripod that had been across his shoulder and tilted back his hard hat. His beard was flecked white. "We need to take some levels. And we need an idea of configuration. How many of you are still here?"

"None of your fucking business."

"Christian," Inez said.

The bearded man raised a hand, palm out. A snake tattoo stretched across his sunburnt forearm, green and a little faded. "We've got a job to do here, that's all this is." The tripod had a sighting tool on the top and some kind of surveying device. The younger man stood behind it, arms folded.

"Are you going to give us the moving money?"

/ / / / /

"Moving money?"

"Fuck you. Get out." Christian kicked sand against the bearded man's legs. He reached over and pushed the tripod to the ground.

"What the fuck was that for?" The younger man bent as he spoke and set the tripod upright. Inez touched Christian's elbow. She tried to take hold of his arm, but he was still talking. Peaceable living, reasonable accommodation, court jurisdiction. These were the things he was saying only he was bellowing, a flush to his face, his features contorted. The bearded man stepped in front of Christian, slipped his body into place. "You going to let us do our job?"

Inez tugged the sleeve of Christian's jacket. "Just let's calm down here."

Christian wasn't listening though. He stood face to face with the bearded man, body tense. Another pull on his coat but Christian shook her off. "Did I not make myself clear?"

"We're just doing our jobs, mister."

"Your job is to get the fuck out of Dodge."

The bearded man sidestepped Christian. "You going to let the drunk one do the talking?"

"We're reasonable people," Inez said.

"From the very start, all we've been trying to do is negotiate," Andy said.

"How about we just begin at the beginning. My name is Sid. This is Teffy." The bearded man offered his hand to Inez, but Christian spoke before she could take it.

"If your employer wants us to move, he needs to pay moving expenses." He turned to Andy. "What are those guys' names? Chairman of the board and that?"

"We know Fred Long," Andy said. "And the president of Greer-Braden, Mr. Hollingsworth."

"Where the fuck is Ash? That's who needs to come over here and talk to these guys. Mister full-of-advice."

Inez looked back. Where was Ash? She sheltered her eyes. She couldn't see Dennis either.

"Listen, we're here for three quick things: survey measurements, pictures and a list of how many shacks are still occupied."

"Shacks?" Inez said.

"Houses, okay? Buildings."

"Survey them so you can flatten them?"

"Listen," the bearded man said again, but Christian stepped forward, reached for the tripod and took hold of one leg. The younger man tried to intervene. He grabbed Christian's arm and the two were at each other in a sudden flurry — bodies close and tangled. The bearded man said to stop, he said to hold on, but they were hitting each other now, fists and elbows. A few quick grunts and they fell to the ground and landed with a heavy impact, Christian on top of Teffy, only they rolled, turned over once in the sand. Inez stepped closer. She reached out but didn't touch. A piece of clothing ripped, a loud tear and then Teffy was up. He was standing. His eye looked puffy. Two steps away and he adjusted his shirt, tried to set himself right. He kept blinking as he touched the sighting tool on top of the tripod.

"You'd better go," Inez said.

"Okay, let's all just calm down here before things get out of hand."

"Things already are out of hand," Andy said. "You guys need to leave."

"At least let us take some photographs." The bearded man had a small camera in his hand.

"Alright," Inez said. "One."

Behind her, Christian still lay on his side. He groaned, a deflated wheeze, the release of pain.

"And then also an elevation of the land. We'll set the sighting tool then take one simple —"

"Forget it. Just get out." Inez stepped forward, aimed a finger into the hills. "Both of you." Teffy turned with the tripod slung over his shoulder, and it swung as he turned, hit Inez square on the chest. Christian still lay on the ground. One step and Inez fell back over him and hit the sand with an impact that took her breath away. "I'm okay," she said, only she could barely form the words. Her temples throbbed. The bearded man knelt. "Go," she said. "Get out."

"Okay. Alright."

The bearded man lifted the survey tripod from Teffy's shoulder. "This could have been avoided. This got way out of hand." A few steps down the beach and the two men exchanged words. Teffy turned, camera raised. Christian said to fuck off, but Teffy kept snapping pictures. One and then another. Scout had come down from the woods and she barked at the two men, chased after them. Inez didn't call her off. She stood and dusted the sand from her pants.

"You shouldn't have tackled him, Christian."

"He tackled me."

"They'll be back with a police escort and a court order."

"You could report him. Assault charges. Taffety or whatever his name was."

"Teffy, Christian. His name was Teffy. I sometimes wonder what planet you're on."

"He knocked you over. Unprovoked."

Inez felt around the back of her neck. "Unprovoked by me. Very fucking provoked by you." Her neck felt knotted. She twisted her head.

"Go to the doctor and get diagnosed. Greer-Braden might finally pay attention to that. A whiplash lawsuit."

"It's not whiplash. Your head has to go forward and then back like a whip." Andy dipped his head, threw it back to demonstrate. "A concussion maybe." He held up his hand. "How many fingers?"

"Two and a half."

Andy wiggled the little stump of his index finger. "Right on."

"At least go talk to the police and get our side of things on record."

"You're always ready to tell people what to do, Christian. Boss man of the squatters. Boss man of the soon-to-be-homeless squatters."

One hand massaging her own neck, Inez started to walk. "Maybe it's time to move on."

He trotted to catch up. "What the hell are you talking about? We can't have everyone leaving. We need to stick together."

"You don't have a clue what we need, Christian."

"The threat of a lawsuit is perfect. You're telling me that won't get attention?"

"It's time to be realistic. Moving money is a fantasy."

"This is real, Inez. You've got whiplash or a concussion or whatever."

Inez worked her hand down the taut muscles of her neck, turned a little and headed off towards her cabin.

CHAPTER
39

Pete watched from a distance, forearm pressed against the trunk of a fir tree, resting there while that cluster of people came together halfway down the beach. Their voices reached him, shouts and sharp words, brief trails of conversation, and then two bodies tangled. Christian fell to the ground along with one of the men who'd been wearing a hard hat. Inez yelled at them and reached out as though to try to pull them apart. The two men hadn't come for him. Whoever they were, this wasn't about Esterway Ridge. One of the figures was up again and standing and just then, Pete spotted Dennis hesitant on the rocks at the edge of the beach, arms by his sides while he stared out at the mess of adult bodies high on the sand. Pete called to him but Dennis started running, broke onto the sand in a sprint. Inez now lay on the ground, flat on her back and the men with hard hats had turned. Both began backing off.

Pete stood a little longer, stock still and self-conscious. In time the others turned this way, and headed south towards him, Inez and Dennis arm in arm. Christian had shifted his trajectory. He headed into the woods at a steady rumble of a pace. Andy and Ernie stood together by a tangle of hawthorn. Pete stepped out to greet Inez and Dennis. "I was just coming down," he called. "I tripped and fell."

"We were wondering where you were."

"I was talking to Andy and Christian and they just took off. Who were those people?"

/ / / / /

"Surveyors. Something to do with the eviction. Christian tackled the younger one then the guy pushed me over. He knocked me back and I hit my head."

"You okay?"

"My head hurts. I need an aspirin."

They crossed the loose sand together, Dennis and Pete on either side of Inez.

"Christian said I should sue Greer-Braden for personal injury."

At the cabin, Dennis held the door. Inez removed her boots and stepped inside. Dennis followed and then Pete. "You must think we're all crazy."

"It does seem to be getting out of hand," Pete said.

"Things have changed here. It's not like it used to be." Inez crossed the room, stood on tiptoe by the shelves, took down a pair of jars, shifted things about. "Dennis, would you go see if Oscar has any aspirin? My temples are throbbing."

The boy slipped outside without a word, and the door settled closed.

"Why don't you sit down for a bit, rest and take a load off."

She set both mason jars back on the shelf, stepped across the room and collapsed onto the sofa.

Pete had to leave. The surveyors would be back soon enough and next time they might come with a police escort or court officials — people with questions, people trying to figure exactly who was on this land. But Inez and Dennis also had to leave, and sooner rather than later it seemed.

Seated on the sofa's arm, Pete leaned close. "Part of me wishes I could stay, move out here, live on the coast with you and Dennis, make a life."

This was the truth. Whatever Inez said about life here having changed, for him, Baker Beach had been a refuge both physically and mentally — a shelter, an escape, one he wished he could just carry on living, hidden in this little community, bound up with these people on the coast. "I was thinking this morning of how lucky I was to walk into your life, to stumble upon this community and upon you in particular. It just kind of feels like it was meant to be, and by this point, I think it's pretty clear you're not going to get any moving money."

"I've been starting to think that way myself."

He stood on the cusp of this new life which had presented itself, a door flung open and he had to at least try to invite her. They were a good pair. He'd felt the spark between them from the moment he saw Inez leaning over him up in Gunter's cabin. Even the way she looked at him now warmed him — everything with Inez so different than it had been with Fay, their bond a full circle, not the crooked tines that he and Fay could never fully connect.

He had a choice, more than one path forward: he could go off on his own up the coast, or he could try to do it with Inez and Dennis, and who knows, maybe part of Inez actually wanted to carry on living this way but was afraid to do it alone.

"What about another spot on the coast?" he said at last. "You, me, Dennis. Some place more remote and not on industry land. We could live just like this. You could paint. We could be free."

"Ash," she said, but he raised his hands, cut her off before she could say any more. She wasn't even using his real name, but he couldn't think about that now. Even if he'd known how to explain it all, this wasn't the time.

"There's not going to be any moving money, Inez. It's getting crazy and it's only going to get worse." He knelt and brought his face level with hers. She'd been respite these past few days, an escape from his own tormenting thoughts. Together they'd started in on what felt like a new life. "Would you consider beginning again some other place?"

"Remember the cocoon, and needing to get back to the world."

He took her hands and held them in his. Maybe he'd broached this the wrong way, started in on the wrong side of things. "You, me, Dennis. The three of us. We make a pretty good team."

"Ash, I'm not even sure of what you're saying, and I need to understand. Are you saying you want to start a life with me and Dennis, or are you saying you want to live in a cabin off the grid?"

"Both. Together."

Her hands slid back into her lap. "I've done this. I've lived this life. Five years now —"

"But this is your inspiration, your influence, this coast, these trees, this wild land. You don't need to leave here to paint, you need to stay."

"This life isn't what you think it is. Our first winter here was hard. It was awful. Thinking about it now, it's a wonder we stayed. It was probably just too cold to leave."

"Summer would be the time to go then, right? Get everything set before winter. If you're willing to do this, I mean. Given what just happened, you're not going to be around here much longer and you're not getting a penny to move."

"Ash, I appreciate your impulsiveness, I admire it even, but we hardly know each other. I've got Dennis to think about. This just isn't the sort of thing —"

"I know. Of course."

"Six days you've been here. Half of those you were asleep."

"Think about it, that's all I'm saying." Pete walked to the counter and filled a cup from the drinking water jug, carried it across the room to her. "See if the idea grows on you."

Once Dennis was back with the aspirin, Pete stepped outside, settled in the rocking chair and folded his arms around himself. The wind was high, a buffeting onshore breeze. A flock of gulls passed low over the waves, rose as a group then fell into a single file above a white-edged breaking wave. He could easily live out here, happily leave everything behind and start again. Earth

Action Now was over, at least for him it was. A new life loomed close enough he could almost touch it — a peaceful and quiet life, somewhere like this among the mighty trees at the continent's edge.

And maybe this was a way to atone: live a good and simple life, in this corner of the world. Inez might still come around. The idea might grow on her. She might join him. If not he could do it on his own, or find another community like this farther along the coast.

Off to the left, Christian emerged from the woods and skirted the banked driftwood, walked high on the loose sand at a loping gate. Pete squinted. Christian had two plastic tubs in his arms. The incendiary devices.

Pete immediately turned away. His whole body shifted and he looked back out over the water. Two tubs, a green garden hose connecting them. Christian with a firebomb. He wished he hadn't seen it. He wished he'd never come across those things. That moment of relief he'd felt, the satisfaction of a decision made, that was gone now.

Pete returned his attention to the treeline, back to the ridge, Christian's cabin a smudge against the apron of greenery. He tried again to convince himself they weren't firebombs. They could be part of Christian's still. That seemed possible. More than possible, but he was already up and headed across the sand. He needed to know. He didn't have to get involved, but he did need to know.

The trail wound past Inez's fenced-off garden and travelled between rows of squat apple trees. Muddy for a stretch and then the path cut uphill, switched back on itself. Half buried stones formed steps here and there. He just had to make sure Christian wasn't going to do anything too stupid. That's all this was. He'd ask. He'd put it out there and see what the man had to say.

From a few yards off, Pete raised a hand and called out.

Christian sat on the same wooden bench he'd occupied that afternoon, wide boards, cedar grey with age, sunlight pasted across it.

"Out of the woodwork at last," Christian said. "Mister full of advice."

Pete brushed his hands down across his jeans. Best to get it all out in one breath, a single straight question. He poured himself a couple of inches of moonshine and downed it in a single fiery swallow. A moment to catch his breath and he said, "Have you got any particular plan for those firebombs you were carrying a minute ago?"

"What firebombs?"

The two tubs stood side by side against the wall of his cabin. Pete pointed.

"That's nothing. That's none of your business."

"I'm thinking Greer-Braden," Pete said. "If I had to guess, I'd say this was some sort of plan B you might have been toying with, something the others might not necessarily know about."

"You just know everything, don't you."

"They're going to know who did it, Christian. Anything you do anywhere even near here and they'll know in a heartbeat. You'll never get a penny of moving money if you set off one of these things."

"I'm not getting moving money anyway, am I?"

"So what is this, revenge? Don't get what you're looking for so you strike back?"

"How about this, how about I don't know what the fuck you're talking about, and you scamper off to wherever you came from."

"Suspicion's going to land on everyone, Christian. They'll be combing every inch of the place. And what if they suspect Inez? What if social services sweeps down and takes Dennis? Worse, what if they suspect Dennis and he ends up in juvenile? What if a wildfire razes the coast and someone gets hurt, killed even."

"No one's going to get killed."

"Because you're an expert at this? How many arsons have you set, Christian? How many firebombs have you tested? I take it you got the recipe for that from the *Anarchist Cookbook* or somewhere? Gasoline with a little tar mixed in to help the fire spread."

"It wasn't even me who built it."

"Who built it?"

"The junior engineer."

"Who?"

"Your man Dennis."

"Dennis? You got Dennis to build this?"

"I didn't get him to build it. He just did it."

Pete released himself onto one of the makeshift wooden seats.

"He came over one day and showed me."

"What are you doing getting a twelve-year-old involved in this kind of shit? He's a kid, Christian. Does he know what you're doing?"

"I don't know, does he? You seem to have all the answers."

Pete raised his hands, both palms out, but he sat there still, held on a rough-cut plank in front of Christian's cabin. Down on the beach, the Painted Lady stood half obscured by the branches of the giant sycamore. Moss had formed over the red paint on the roof shingles.

Dennis of all people.

/ / / / /

Pete took his time walking back. The sun hung low in the sky, getting on towards evening. A thread of smoke rose from the Painted Lady, a trickle bent by the onshore wind. He stood by Dennis's kayak, lifted it, turned it over then set it down. Amazing that he could put a thing like this together with so few tools, a twelve-year-old boy with instructions from the library. Pete peered into the little shack, the place where Phelps had lived. Wheelbarrow, axe, toolbox, crab traps, a metal frame that might have been Christian's Alaska sawmill.

The muddy switchback trail took him down to Baker Beach. Standing on Inez's porch, Pete peered in through the window. Dennis sat reading. Inez lay on the sofa, body still, eyes closed. One tap on the glass and Dennis looked up. Pete beckoned then stepped down off the porch. He wanted to be out of earshot, beyond any chance of Inez's hearing.

Christian could do what he wanted. It wasn't Pete's business to intervene, to stop Greer-Braden from getting a bit of what they deserved. He had obligations though, to Dennis, to Inez. Pete tried to think it all through, tried to gather the right words as Dennis stepped out. The boy pulled a wool hat down over his head and started towards the edge of the beach.

"You guys planning to firebomb Greer-Braden?" Pete said at last.

"What?"

"I talked to Christian."

"About what?"

"In the future, if you're ever going to do something illegal, Dennis, if you're going to do something stupid, don't do it with people who can't keep their mouths shut."

"What did he say?"

"That he's going to firebomb some piece of company property."

"Now?"

"He said you built them."

"But only to see if they'd work, only to try it."

"He said it was your idea, Dennis."

"It wasn't my idea. I mean, I wasn't serious. I was mostly joking. It wasn't like —"

"What if he sets one off and it kills a man?"

"How is it going to kill a man? It's just two trailers in Port Thorvald. No one lives in them. They're offices."

"Unintended consequences, Dennis. If you go off half-cocked like this, things are bound to get out of hand."

Pete had never imagined the damage sixty pounds of dynamite could do: a gaping hole in a concrete wall, the stolen Pinto a twisted wreck. The blast had knocked the night watchman back ten feet or more, his body had hung airborne. Those images were with Pete still, burned into every part of him.

"I just showed him what I made," Dennis said. "It wasn't something we decided. It wasn't supposed to be like what you're saying."

"You don't understand the kind of things that can happen once you start down this road."

Back at Esterway Ridge debris had rained down, stones, pebbles, a spray of dirt as the floodlight went out. The air turned sour, acrid and chemical, and it had set Pete coughing, his lungs strained for oxygen as he stumbled across the gravel to the night watchman's twisted body.

"We weren't even sure we were going to do it," Dennis said. "We were talking, that's all. We were going to be careful."

"You think this is careful, Dennis? This is the opposite of careful: fumbling for a quick fix to a problem for which a quick fix doesn't exist. I used to be involved in this kind of thing."

He had to take care here, he had to pick his words. Anything he said to Dennis would eventually reach Inez. But he also needed to convince the boy. He needed to make sure Dennis stayed out of this.

"I've set bombs like that myself. I was part of a violent protest group."

A pair of ships hung on the horizon, grey and ghostly outlines. Beyond them lay vast open ocean.

"You were?" Dennis said.

"We used the very same type of incendiary device."

"Did they work?"

"They set fires, they destroyed things." Pete kept looking

out towards the misty horizon, Dennis a presence beside him. "I know where this is headed, Dennis. People here are concerned about something important that no one else seems to care about. No one is listening, and so at some point, it feels like you've reached the end of all your options. I know what that's like: screaming so loud without anyone listening. Eventually you lash out."

"It's not that. I just wanted to see if I could make one, if it would really work."

"This kind of thing feeds itself, Dennis. It starts when Christian decides to use your device to burn a building, or a trailer or whatever. People will get upset for sure, people will get angry, but that's it. And then . . ." He stopped himself. Along the rocks at the edge of the Point, a sea otter scrambled down to the water's edge, long sleek body, there and then gone, slipped into the water.

"And then what?" Dennis said.

Pete watched the otter go and it took a moment to regain his train of thought. "Nothing changes," he said, and that was the truth of the matter. "The world carries on almost like it didn't happen, and so you do it again, bigger this time. After all, you've come this far, you're already looking at jail, you've committed to this path, and you've convinced yourself this is the way forward. Plus you tell yourself the problem is your actions haven't been big enough, not high enough impact. So you make the next one bigger."

This was the truth of how they'd escalated to the use of dynamite and the plan for Esterway Ridge, List Cove, Dutton Pulp and Paper. Maybe it was also the truth about why it would never work. What do you do next if nothing changes? He sounded like Jeremy now and he knew it: impossible to use destruction to stop destruction.

"Before you know it something really bad has happened. Something you didn't expect or want."

"You're making this out like some big plot." Dennis wiped at his nose, he sniffled. "It was an idea, that's all. I just built it to see if it would work and then I showed Christian."

"Does Inez know? Is she part of this?"

He shook his head. He looked on the edge of tears.

"It's going to be okay. It's going to be fine. I'm just trying to help you not make a mistake. Is there anyone else involved?"

"Andy."

"That's it?"

Dennis nodded again, wiped his eyes.

"I was telling your mother I think we should go away together, the three of us. Start again somewhere more remote, Bella Coola or Gold River."

"With you?"

"If you want."

"What did she say?"

"That she'd think it over."

"That's what she always says." He seemed to be recovering himself. He managed something of a smile.

"Things are going to get out of hand here, Dennis. There's no moving money coming. Not even Christian thinks so. It's going to get ugly and it's best we're gone."

"Are you going to tell Inez?"

"She should know. About the possibility, I mean. She doesn't need to know you built them."

Pete set an arm across Dennis's shoulder as they walked towards the cabin. "If Christian talks to you about any of this stuff, come and tell me."

He could feel a turn in his life, a warm certainty to the road ahead: Gold River, Bamfield, Bella Coola, somewhere like that. The rugged corners of the land had always been the place where people reinvented themselves. Plenty were still living underground from the '60s — people from the Weathermen and the SLA. There were FLQ members who had quit, gone underground or adopted new lives, slipped back into society.

A little luck and he might convince Inez to come with him. Say the right words about what Christian was planning and she'd surely come around. If she didn't, so be it, he could go it alone.

CHAPTER
40

Inez lay still on the narrow sofa, awake now but drowsy. Ash was working in the kitchen. His movements showed a confidence, an easy familiarity. He tapped a wooden spoon against their cast iron pot, a brief rhythm. A moment later he turned and caught her watching. "Feeling better?"

She sat up, gathered her bearings. The headache was gone, but the shock of the encounter still numbed her, the violence of it. She turned her head and a dull pain spread through her neck.

"No concussion?"

"I don't think so. Sore neck though." With that she remembered Christian's new plan: a lawsuit, a claim against Greer-Braden for personal injury. Some new attempt to squeeze money from them.

"Is it okay if I collect some eggs for dinner?"

"If there are any there, please do."

The door stood open a crack as Ash walked around to the coop. Seated on one of the stools, Dennis had his book out, the pages of it angled to catch the last of the light through the broad front windows. Inez shifted for a better view of her son. And then she remembered the afternoon's other event: Ash's invitation. Big choices in life often came when least expected, when least convenient. She'd said she wanted options. Problem was she'd never been impulsive. Even before having Dennis, Inez had been careful by nature — maybe that's what drew her to impulsive men. Ray had been like that. To a fault. And here was Ash.

/////

There was something thrilling about being pulled into these easy decisions, and the ferocious determination that carried them forward, only it already felt like she had more than she could handle.

Ash returned with two eggs in hand and cracked them over the skillet. "Sit tight. Five more minutes." As the eggs sizzled, he backed away from the wood stove. "I have to tell you that Christian has some kind of crazy plan up his sleeve. He's talking about firebombs and revenge. Did you know this?"

"Christian is always talking."

"Things are going to get ugly here, Inez. One way or another it's time to leave, and I think the three of us should leave together."

She glanced over. Dennis still had his book raised. "I know. You said that already."

"Inez, just so I'm clear: Christian is talking about setting two Greer-Braden trailers on fire in Port Thorvald."

"Oh God. Should I talk to him?"

"No, it's fine. Not now. What happened with those surveyors is only the start of it though. They'll be back tomorrow except there will be more of them, a police escort even. Or maybe they'll decide to airlift a bulldozer in. All of these things are possible. And who knows what Christian will do then."

She lifted her hand and touched her forehead. "Can we not talk about this now? Can we just . . ." It was all happening too quickly. That was the problem. All of these things a sudden crush. She needed time. She needed space. Her headache had begun to resurface.

Pete waited until after Dennis was asleep, waited until after Inez had taken him to bed, waited until they were together, naked, bodies spent, the two of them warm and close. A comfortable ease had settled, and he set his head close beside hers. "Have you thought about it? About leaving together, starting again somewhere further along the coast?"

"I'm flattered and all, but this is crazy talk, you know that, right?"

"Because you've got Dennis to think about?"

"For sure. I mean, that's part of it."

"Dennis is going to be fine. Don't worry about Dennis. You need to trust yourself, your gut, your instinct."

"It took me years to get over Ray, to get over him leaving us here. And Dennis's father before that. I trust too easily, Ash."

He kissed her, the softest of contact, a loving kiss.

"I've just never been this impulsive."

"You tell me then. You decide where to go and if you'll let me, I'll come."

Inez propped herself on an elbow. "Are you serious about this, or are we just talking?"

"I'm serious."

"It all seems so fast." She fell back onto her pillow. "Maybe rent a place in Port Thorvald or Renfrew? Maybe stay with my sister?"

"All three of us?"

/ / / / /

"I could write to her and ask."

The sounds of the night rose, the turn and clap of waves, the gentle sigh of an onshore wind. Get halfway across the country and he could hide in plain sight. Maybe people they met would just assume he was Dennis's father. He didn't have to set up in a new squatters' camp. There were other possibilities. He let them roll around in his mind a while then shifted close and spoke in Inez's ear. "Your decision. Your sister's place, or a cabin further north. Or somewhere else entirely. My dad lives in Tucson, we could try there. Warm weather."

"What about you and your life? You must have an apartment, a place, friends."

"I guess I'd get my camera, a few other things. Clothes." He might be able to slip into the place on Bee Street if he had to. Maybe he could convince Jeremy to help.

Part of Pete wanted to let it all out then and there, his real name, his true story, and he tried to think of the right words to get started. Even if it was just a partial confession, he had to share something, if they were actually going to leave together — words that at least hinted at the truth. But Inez's breathing slowly settled into the softness of sleep and although Pete thought of waking her, eventually he rolled onto his back, too attached to the possibility of this new life together to put it at risk with a confession so soon. He needed time. He needed to build trust.

He would come clean with Inez, of course. And soon. In the fullness of time he'd square up with everyone else too — Inez first, but at some point he'd call his mother, his father, he'd let all of them know he was alive and well. Until then they might go through hell, but he couldn't help that. Not just now he couldn't.

/ / / / /

Up above, a tree creaked, an old-wood groan, a sound that brought Pete from sleep. He shifted about, raised himself. Moonlight scalloped the branches of a nearby fir tree. A branch snapped. Pete moved close enough to the window that his breath fogged the pane. He angled his head one way then the other, and that's when he saw it: a bear at the edge of the beach, only the bear was white. Pete wiped the fogged glass. What looked like a polar bear stood outside the cabin. Wind tickled the branch of a sycamore just above the bear's head. Pete closed his eyes and reopened them, sure moonlight was playing a trick or the glass was distorting his view. It moved though, the bear lumbered forward. Pete nudged Inez. She made a noise, but by then Pete was out of bed. "A white bear," he said. "A spirit bear." Pants on, shirt in his hands, he stumbled to the door. The wind was a cold slap in the face, and he was wide awake. Goosebumps rose along his arms and shoulders. The bear was in the woods now and standing still, looking back as though waiting, great white form motionless in the shadowed woods as Pete walked through the skirt of forest. Two body-lengths away, Pete slowed. A spirit bear on the island. It didn't seem possible. He raised an arm without any sense of danger. Another few feet and he could have touched its clumped and matted fur, but then the bear grunted. Pete's heart jumped. The bear's head dropped and turned. Its muscles rippled, and the great animal laboured on. Pete glanced over his shoulder. The cabin was dark and quiet. Inez hadn't followed.

Pete ducked under a low branch, stepped around a boulder and waded through a bed of swordferns, attention still fixed on the animal in front of him. Twigs and dead leaves cracked underfoot.

The bear stopped. Pete tried to steady his breathing. His right hand gripped his chest, and he took a few quick steps to close the gap. Branches reached out, vines tangled his legs. The bear was moving again. It broke into a trot and Pete had to run to keep pace. He tripped on a fallen branch and sprawled where the soil was loose and damp. Mouth full of dirt, he spat and coughed, brushed off his shirt. The bear was half-hidden by tree trunks now. Its pale fur picked up the few shards of light that reached the forest floor. Pete stepped forward. A cramp laced his side. Moonlight played through the swaying trees. The bear was in the distance, briefly visible and then gone.

He turned fully around. No path here, nothing but the marks of his own feet. Pete rubbed the dirt off his hands. He could have imagined it. He could be going crazy. He thought again of Christian's hooch. Could it have been an after-effect of the moonshine?

As he turned he noticed a clearing, a break in the woods. He was standing within sight of Christian's cabin. Moonlight lit his path. The two plastic tubs still sat against the wall, the hose curled on top. The white bear had led him here to within yards of Christian's cabin. Pete stepped forward, crouched and lifted each tub. Both empty.

Back in April, standing in the Westlake parking lot, before Art set off those first incendiary devices, before their first major act of property destruction, Pete had been standing lookout. A paralysing nervousness held him there, and at that moment, he'd have backed out if he'd had the chance. Maybe all of them would have. If for some reason their incendiary devices hadn't worked, that might have been the end of things. Maybe. And maybe Christian didn't really want to do this, not truly, despite his anger, despite the vitriol.

Pete stood and followed the dark trail over to where Phelps had lived. Inside he felt about until he found a rusty chisel. At Christian's cabin, he knelt again and forced the blade down into the bottom of the first tub, leaned his weight on it, cut one wide gash then did the same to the second tub.

CHAPTER
42

Inez awoke early, the cabin still dark and the spot on the bed beside her empty. She ran a hand across the mattress. The sheets had gone cold. Last night she'd forgotten to draw the curtains and pre-dawn light pasted the windows with a faint glow.

The surveyors had come yesterday. That thought brought Inez fully awake and all that had happened yesterday tumbled back. Maybe Christian was out of control, especially if this talk of firebombs and revenge was true. And maybe it was all but over at this point. One way or another, she wouldn't be here much longer: quietly without a struggle or pulled kicking and screaming, with Ash or on their own. Decisions loomed.

Inez pulled a shawl around her shoulders and stepped outside into a sharp and steady wind. The rocker was there, turned on an angle, but she didn't sit. Around the corner of the cabin, the chickens were scratching in dirt. Rhonda the Rhode Island Red stood by the gate like she knew it was time for a hunt and peck, but Inez passed them too. Ash must have been up early and off somewhere. No sign of him this morning. Inez leaned over the narrow stump that anchored the garden fence and pulled off a leaf of lettuce, thumbed dirt from the stalk. It had rained again last night.

Standing by the garden, Inez found herself thinking again of David Milne and the day Kathleen Pavey had arrived at his cabin — painter and stranger meeting in the forest, falling in love, making a life together. This very thing was now happening

/ / / / /

to her, and yet some niggling doubt held her back, some worry she couldn't quite finger. Maybe that Ash was younger than she was? That she knew so little about him? That it was all so rushed? That they had no money? But if Pavey and Milne could do it, why couldn't she and Ash? There were fewer years between them than between Pavey and Milne. And after they met, Pavey had more or less just moved in. This despite the fact Milne was already married and despite the fact that all he had to offer was a shack in the woods. Meanwhile, he'd been living up there despite the fact it was miles from the nearest art gallery, miles further to the nearest art school.

Ash was handsome enough, youthful with a rugged air that attracted her. She liked his impulsiveness and he and Dennis were good together. Ash was more fatherly than Ray had ever been. These days since Ash's arrival had been her best in years — she'd laughed, she'd found herself smiling at passing thoughts. She'd been happy. Maybe her niggling doubt was just the scar Ray's departure had left.

Scout trotted over, tail batting air above her. She'd found an old tennis ball, and dropped it nearby. Inez gave the ball a throw and Scout dashed after it. The dog brought it back a moment later and Inez threw it again. This time it rolled into the woodpile and Scout lost track of it.

One way or another she needed money. And maybe Christian was right about the threat of a whiplash lawsuit. It was an injury doctors couldn't easily prove or disprove. She turned her head. Still stiff. There wasn't much to walking around with a neck brace for a few weeks. If she was willing to lie about things. Exaggerate at least.

Inez started into the woods, up towards the ridgetop trail. It didn't hurt to talk to a lawyer. She could at least give it a shot. Too often in life she'd let others take charge, abdicated responsibility. She'd left it to Ray to get her out here, stayed because leaving was too hard, left it to Christian to try to get them moving money. She could try a whiplash accusation, at least raise the threat and if that didn't help, so be it, they could leave with nothing. But at least she'd have tried.

Inez carried on until the clearing in front of what used to be Gunter and Maggie's cabin. Crows stood in the trees, calling to one another, a seesaw caw and response that carried through the forest. She peered through the window. Ash lay on the cot. His chest rose and fell, a faint movement under the blanket. Odd he'd wound up sleeping there but he looked peaceful and content so she kept walking.

Back at the cabin, Dennis was already dressed. "Go get the packs, plus we need to remember the library books."

"I didn't know we were going into town."

She didn't have a letter to mail to her sister, so she sat at the counter, pen in hand. Her mind was crowded now, a clutter of competing worries. So much news but also no news yet at all.

"Does maybe Ash want to come?" Dennis said.

"I was just there. He's snoozing. We'll bring him a chocolate bar."

"And one for me?"

"Sure."

"And a coke?"

"We'll see."

She dashed off a quick note, asked her sister if they came to stay, could she bring a friend. She promised they'd only stay long enough to get on their feet. She didn't mention that it was a male friend she had in mind.

If Ash wanted to haul across country to be with her, that was fine. A place together in Renfrew or Port Thorvald might also be fine. Small, easy steps.

Inez and Dennis struck out low across on the wet sand. Dennis had to stretch his legs to keep up. A hole showed in the canvas of his right sneaker. That would be an expense, new running shoes. "You should have worn your boots. The path will be muddy."

A rocky scramble to the lookout at the top of the ridge, and then they paused as they always did. A moment of rest, a moment to enjoy the view. Early morning mist had thinned to reveal the twin rocks that stood in the water two hundred yards from land.

Wind rippled the trees above, set the old wood creaking and released occasional drops — remnants of last night's rain. When Inez and Dennis reached the first fallen tree, Inez set her hands on the wet ground and crawled under it. She tried to keep her knees from touching so her pants didn't get dirty. Open meadow marked the halfway point and by the time they reached it, the sun stood high over the trees.

The cleft boulder was the last marker before the logging road: a giant rock that seemed to have split in two even though the halves held together. Beyond, the ground rose, a last short climb on uneven steps formed by tree roots laced through muddy soil.

Once at the logging road, Inez crossed into the woods on the other side and collected the bicycles. Six weeks since they'd used them and already new shoots looped the spokes — the forest quick to capture even that which had never belonged to it. She wheeled out Dennis's bike first and then hers, trailer rattling behind it. Maggie had built the trailer and Inez had inherited it. Goods up for trade were the one benefit of someone leaving. That's how she'd gotten her wheelbarrow and the canoe and the wetsuit as well as her weather radio.

Ten minutes on the hardpacked dirt of the logging road and they were at the highway: a quiet track that ended fifteen miles further north. Logging trucks travelled it, campers in the summer season. Port Thorvald lay in the other direction. Twenty minutes by bicycle. A straight line would be shorter still, but this road followed the contours of the land — all twists and rises, tight turns around rocks and hillocks.

They passed the gas station at Buckley's crossroads where a couple of cottages overlooked the bay and its pebble beach.

A car overtook them, small and black with mud streaked across its lower half, and then Port Thorvald appeared. A town too small to have outskirts, Port Thorvald started and it ended: over the bridge and there you are — a pair of houses, a fenced off row of trailers. There was a restaurant called Mary's Place, its open sign flickered in the window. Three trucks stood in the lot. Even this little town had a brightness to its colours that she never saw around Baker Beach — the high-toned sheen of hard body trucks, the manufactured red of a neon sign, house paints, store signs, even the whipped colours of the flag outside the community hall. The police station stood around back. If she was going to call what Teffy had done assault, she should start there, doctor after that, lawyer last. Do it the other way around and it would look like a set-up. Inez applied her brakes, and as she slowed, she turned to Dennis. "Will you wait a minute for me?"

"Aren't we going for groceries?"

"I need to talk to the police first. About yesterday."

"With the surveyor guys?"

"Exactly."

Dennis set his bike beside hers.

"Are you going to tell them about what Ash said? About what Christian's planning?"

"I don't know, Dennis. I just don't know what I'm going to do."

She wasn't sure of anything anymore, her own internal compass spinning free, but as Dennis turned and started across the street towards the park, she called, "What do you think of maybe having Ash come with us when we leave?"

"We're leaving for sure, then?"

"At some point, yes. Soon it looks like."

/ / / / /

A glass door with RCMP stencilled across it opened onto a cramped waiting room bound on one side by a short counter. Bucket seats lined the opposite wall. The office had only two desks and both stood empty. Which was fine, Inez still needed to get her story straight, needed to think everything through before she talked to anyone. She'd never been a good talker and despite having time on the way in, she hadn't rehearsed her account of the altercation on the beach. And she wasn't sure what to do about Christian's firebombs.

A bulletin board hung above the row of plastic seats, mostly public safety posters, a pair of notices about missing children. Just before she sat, Inez noticed a poster at the bottom corner with four black and white pictures and the words "Wanted. $20,000 reward." One of the faces caught her attention, and she leaned closer. The bottom left corner had a picture of Ash McCabe. The name under the picture was Peter Donald Osborne. Inez sank, her knees gave way and she had to reach out, take hold of the bucket seat to support herself. Three other pictures, three other names. Inez tugged on the poster's corners and the staples came free. "Wanted for Fatal Bombing at Esterway Ridge."

Beyond the counter, a door opened and a tall man in uniform stepped through. "Didn't realize we had a visitor. What can I do you for?"

Inez's legs still felt weak. They felt unreliable. Three steps to the counter, poster in hand, only she wasn't here to talk about that. At least she hadn't come in to talk about that. "My name is Inez Pierce. I live at the Point." Where was she supposed to begin? Her mind had gone blank.

"Righty right." The man sounded cheerful. It wasn't what she'd expected. Inez squeezed the poster. Ash McCabe wasn't going to move anywhere with her. Ash McCabe wasn't even Ash McCabe. He'd been lying. He'd been using her.

"How can I help you?" the officer said, and that brought her back to the moment.

"They sent people to survey and photograph and ask questions. We're being evicted."

The officer was nodding. A few short hairs grew from a mole on his cheek. She was supposed to tell him how she'd been assaulted, only she couldn't separate things in her mind. Ash McCabe. Moving money from Greer-Braden. Christian's firebombs. The threat of a lawsuit. Ash's scheme to leave together. Every thread connected to another, everything tangled.

"This man pushed me," she said at last. "I was just standing there. I think I've got whiplash or a concussion." Inez's hand rose as she touched the back of her head only that same hand held the poster. She put her hand down on the counter and there it was, face up. Her fingers rested on its edges. Peter Osborne. He hadn't even told her his true name. One lie after another the whole time he'd been there.

"Did this poster fall down?"

"No. Well, yes. I guess."

"These are the ones they're calling eco-terrorists."

"What's that supposed to mean?"

"The four wanted for the bombing that killed Owen Tuggs."

Her body went slack again. She knew Owen. And Linda too. Linda worked at Mary's Place, the restaurant in town that had hung three of Inez's paintings last summer. "Owen is dead? Linda's husband?"

The officer nodded at that, eyes cast down to the poster and the four faces on it.

Inez had shared her bed with a man wanted for killing Owen Tuggs.

"I know one of these people," she said at last.

"One of these four?" The officer touched the poster, turned it a little.

"In this he's called Peter Osborne only with us he goes by Ash McCabe."

"You're sure about this?"

Her lips pursed and her toes squeezed against the soles of her shoes. This was betrayal. Her breath cratered, a hard bite in her chest.

"This gentleman?" The officer's finger covered half of Ash's face and Inez's chin lowered in a brief nod.

"You want to sit down a second? Come around here and sit properly so we can talk."

"Listen, I actually came because I got pushed over. That's assault, isn't it?"

"I have to make a couple of phone calls. Just come on around, sit here and take a load off."

"My neck is sore."

"One minute while I call this in."

A fan started, a noisy grind in the duct work overhead. Inez watched the officer's lips move, but she couldn't make out his words.

They were kids, really. In the four arrest photos, they looked like kids — Derek Lyle Newfeld seemed about to smile, Arthur Kosky had a neatly trimmed goatee and bullet eyes, his lips pursed tight. It looked like he was holding his breath. Next to him Peter Donald Osborne stared out at her, bewildered. He looked wide-eyed, caught in the flare of a flashbulb. There was a woman too, and maybe that's what surprised Inez most: Fay Adele Anderson, her dark hair cut short to show a narrow, pretty face.

The buzzer sounded and Dennis stepped inside. "Are you still here because you're in trouble?" he said.

"No."

"Are you sure?"

"Absolutely."

"Did you tell them about the men yesterday?"

"I started with that, yeah." She tapped her fingers on the counter.

"What about Christian and his plan?"

"No. This may take a while. You want to wait here or go to the park?"

"You're not in trouble?"

"No. I'm definitely not in trouble, honey."

"Do you want me to tell him what I saw?" He glanced over towards the officer. "I did see the man knock you down."

"No. Don't worry about that."

The buzzer sounded again as Dennis opened the door and stepped outside. Cool air spread through the room.

A few yards away the officer set the phone down. "You know where this gentleman is right now? Peter Osborne."

"I do. I mean, I did as of a few hours ago."

The officer rolled his chair a few feet closer to Inez. "He's out at the Point?"

"Unless he's left."

"And you can take us?"

"I've got my bike and my trailer, plus my son has his bike. We're actually here to get groceries, drop off books, that kind of thing."

"We can haul all of that, you, your son, bikes and all. I've called for a second squad car." He offered his hand. "I'm Corporal Anderson."

"Inez Pierce."

"I've heard about your situation. For what it's worth, I'm a live and let live kind of guy. You know about the reward right? Greer-Braden offered it."

A twist of adrenaline dropped through Inez's chest. "Greer-Braden," she said. "They own the land. They're the ones evicting us."

"It's a sizable amount of money. Twenty thousand dollars."

"I'm not doing this for the money." But even as she said this, she understood all that this kind of money could do for her. She'd been scrambling to get five thousand dollars from them and now she was looking at enough money to cover a chunk of land somewhere, to set up a savings account for Dennis or a nest egg against future uncertainties.

"Sit there and try to relax. We've got about thirty minutes before backup gets here from Sooke."

"My son and I were going to get groceries, buy supplies, swap library books and check for mail."

"Can you be back in fifteen minutes?"

A chill to the air as Inez stepped outside, a stiff onshore wind. She found Dennis by the bikes. "What did you tell them?" he said.

"They're going to give us a lift home."

"Because you hurt your head?"

"We only have a few minutes. We have to be quick. Can you mail my letter and exchange our books while I get the groceries?"

Inez raised her bike, straddled it and began to pedal. When Dennis caught up, he said, "About Ash and maybe going —"

"Can we not talk about that right now? Fifteen minutes and we have to be back."

CHAPTER
43

Pete awoke scratching a pair of swollen mosquito bites near his elbow. On the other side of the grimy window, a pair of sycamore trees rose with gentle, mirrored bends. A fly hit the window, buzzed and banged against the glass.

He swung his feet off the bed and tucked them into his boots. Without a watch, he was unsure of the time, but it felt late. Too long spent bumbling around in the woods after the bear. That thought stopped him: the white bear. He'd seen it, he'd almost touched it.

Outside the wind was brisk — a curling onshore streak alive with salt air and the smell of the sea. The clouds were thin out over the water and the sun already stood high in the sky. Probably mid-morning by now. Noon at the latest.

Pete followed the track that led to the beach. A faint trickle of smoke rose from Inez's chimney. A hot breakfast would be just the thing. Up the makeshift path to Inez's front door and he knocked, peered in through the window. "Inez? Dennis?" No one home. He pushed the door open. The fire in the wood stove still smouldered, but Inez and Dennis were gone. The place stood empty and then he remembered how Inez had talked of going into town and laying some complaint against the man who'd knocked her down. He turned about, walked a circle on the wood floor of the cabin. They'd be in town, talking to a doctor or to a lawyer. Or to the police.

/ / / / /

A jar of oats stood on the shelf, and he ate a handful raw. He had to think this through, had to consider all the possibilities. Surely she could carry on a full conversation without anybody mentioning Esterway Ridge. It had been over a week, plus she had other things to cover, other things on her mind — eviction, moving money, this crazy lawsuit scheme. Inez might come home none the wiser.

Outside, Pete walked around to the side of the cabin and collected two eggs from the coop. Fry pan on the wood stove, he tipped in oil and scrambled the eggs. The beach lay under the shadow of clouds this morning, its long gentle band a dull tone in this light.

Last night he'd followed a spirit bear into the woods. That if anything was a sign. It had taken him to Christian's cabin. He'd disabled the firebombs. He'd given Christian a chance to back away from his plan.

Standing there Pete made a commitment to himself: if Inez came home without having heard of Esterway Ridge, he'd tell her himself. If what had started between the two of them was ever to grow into anything, he had to start being honest.

Once Pete had told her everything, if she wanted nothing to do with him, so be it, he could still find some corner of untouched land and live the life of a hermit. That road was still open. A new life in the wilderness. But if it was going to be with Inez, he was going to tell her who he was.

And so he stood in her cabin and waited.

CHAPTER 44

Dennis wanted to sit in the front of the cruiser so Inez squeezed into the back and turned her legs sideways — the cruiser had a wide vinyl seat that didn't offer much legroom. Outside, the world slid past. Inez stared out at the trees. Eventually they turned up the logging road, rose in low gear along the washboarded track. A few more minutes and they reached a tight curve. Inez leaned forward, pointed through the metal grill that separated her from Corporal Anderson and Dennis. "Park there in the turnout. If you don't get your car close against the edge, a logging truck might hit it."

The second squad car passed them and parked further on.

Outside it smelled like rain, the air heavy and damp. "We'd better get moving before the weather comes in."

Around the back of the car, the front forks and wheel of her bicycle protruded from the trunk. Anderson heaved the bike out while the driver from the second car wheeled the cart over. He was overweight, flesh pressed out against his uniform. Another officer brought over one of the backpacks filled with groceries. He had a barrel chest and a blunted nose. His name badge said Swartz. "You want me to carry one?"

Inez shook her head. She bent and reattached the cart to the bicycle so she wouldn't lose the bolt, nut and washer she'd been holding. "How about you stash the bikes behind the rock, Dennis?"

Once Anderson had the smaller bike out of his trunk, he lifted a duffel bag, unzipped it and produced a rifle.

/ / / / /

"Why do they have guns?" Dennis said.

"Stash the bikes away, Dennis."

"I think it's best your son hops in this cruiser and sits tight."

Inez waited until Dennis had wheeled his own bike into the woods then she stepped closer to Anderson. "He's not armed with anything. He walked into camp in a torn jacket and covered in mud. He'd been lost."

"Ms. Pierce." Anderson tilted the muzzle of his rifle towards the ground. "We don't expect to need any weapons. No one here has any plans to use them."

"Then why are you asking Dennis to stay here?"

"We're being careful. When we get there, you point to the cabin then back away. That's all you do."

Inez hoisted the canvas pack, rested it on her hip then slid her arms into the straps. She buckled the waist belt, and bent forward to take some weight off her shoulders. She thought she could still smell him, Peter Osborne, his scent still on her skin. Maybe this was a mistake. Maybe this was all a terrible mistake.

Dennis wheeled away the second bicycle and Inez struck out. She wanted to get moving. She wanted the distraction of activity. "The light pack is yours, Dennis."

The path fell away from the logging road in a switchback trail that hugged the hillside. The sun was already getting low. Closing in on four or maybe later. Passing into the open meadow, Inez extended her stride. The weight of the pack was a strain — ten pounds of flour, five of sugar, cans of stewed tomatoes, pasta, oats and kerosene.

"They're not here because of the fight, are they?" Dennis asked.

He was right behind her now and short of breath as he spoke. He must have wedged himself past Anderson, Swartz and the other one. Inez glanced over her shoulder. Behind Dennis, the officers were strung out single file, the heavyset one not even visible.

"Why are they here?"

"Ash is wanted for setting a bomb."

The canopy closed overhead. A pair of banana slugs lay on the shadowed path, and Inez sidestepped, pointed down at them as Dennis approached.

"You're making a mistake," he said.

"I wish I was. I really do." Those words came easily, but maybe she wished it was a mistake, and maybe she didn't. It all seemed so absurd now — starting again with the stranger. A man she hardly knew. On each stride, she could feel the pressure of the folded poster in her pocket.

Inez hoisted herself over the first fallen tree, pack and all. She stumbled while dismounting and the weight of the pack almost sent her sprawling.

They passed all their normal resting points, didn't pause at any of the landmarks, not the bearded tree nor the vampire-den stump. The canopy thinned. Open sky ahead, grey and cloudy, a heavy tinge to it. She could feel the coast's welcome, cool ocean air stretched its fingers up into the land. It felt like home.

At the lookout point, Inez wiped sweat from her forehead and ran a hand through her hair. She leaned against a tree, pressed her pack against it to take the weight from her shoulders. Her shirt was wet. Sweat trickled down past the waistband of her jeans. The sky looked dark on the horizon, rain on its way. Even then she might try to swim this evening. If there was enough light left, she'd draw as well.

"Does Ash know they're coming?"

"His name's not Ash, it's Peter Osborne."

She reached for the poster in her pocket, only the sound of the police officers stopped her, the three of them unnaturally loud in the forest. Better not to continue this conversation in front of them and she let her hand fall as Anderson emerged from the forest. He leaned against a tree trunk, rested the rifle against his leg. "Let's just take a break. After this we have to stay together." The man's chest heaved. Inez listened to him breathing.

"The moment you see him, give us the signal, or point to the cabin he's in. That's all you're to do. Dennis, it's best you just wait here, okay?"

"He can stay with me," Inez said. "You'll stay with me, right? Beside me all the time?"

Dennis nodded. Swartz arrived then and shortly after him, the heavyset one the other officers had been calling Bubba. He smiled in a pained way. Sweat rings already darkened the underarms of his shirt.

The descent to the beach was a slide and tumble path, steep with no steps. Carrying a heavy pack always made it a rush. Inez ran the last half of it. Once on the sand, her feet sank in and she came to a halt, momentum spent. Dennis also ran down and managed to stop behind her. Anderson followed. Halfway down, Bubba took hold of a sapling to steady himself. The tree bent. Swartz came last, took his time, stepped gingerly.

The three officers walked high across the sand, close to the treeline in order to stay out of sight, Anderson in the lead. He kept looking down to where Inez and Dennis walked — closer to the water, down where retreating waves had hardened the sand. He was checking in with them, keeping an eye out. Inez pointed. "It'll be a bit before we can see his cabin. It's high on the ridge."

"Don't point. Don't look at us or even talk to us. Don't do anything you wouldn't normally do."

A wave slid in and rose around Inez's boots, and for a while her feet kicked up little trails of water. Dennis stopped. He stood still and adjusted a strap on his pack while Inez carried on, sand soft and giving underfoot. The three officers cut stark figures against the trees. They were foreign, unnatural, too institutional for this place — peaked caps, pistols in holsters. A matter of time before men like these would be down here to enforce the eviction order. It might even be these men, Anderson, Swartz, Bubba.

Suddenly Dennis ran past. He had his pack off and he was sprinting. She called after him. She broke into a run and undid her waist belt as she went. The pack slid from her back. "Dennis," she called. "Wait." She saw it too now: a man beside their cabin with his back turned. It might have been Ash, it might have been Oscar. Up by the treeline, one of the officers shouted. She had a sense of them on her periphery, three men running high on the beach, kicking through loose sand, Anderson with the rifle tight across his chest.

"Stop," she yelled. "Dennis." And then the man beside the cabin turned. Oscar. Dennis slowed to a walk. He'd thought it was Ash. He stopped and stood still.

"Jesus," Inez said. "Jesus bloody Christ." She bent over, hands on her knees while her breathing settled. "You can't do that. You can't do anything even like that. You agreed to stay with me." A glance towards the ridge and she pointed at Gunter and Maggie's old cabin waving her other hand towards Oscar. "He's not the one." She jabbed a finger towards the ridge again. "Over there."

Swartz had his pistol drawn. His hat had fallen off. Bubba trailed. He'd stopped jogging altogether.

"I thought Oscar was him," Dennis said.

"You've got to stay out of this." She set a hand on his shoulder, raised her other arm and touched the top of his head, pressed down on his thick hair.

CHAPTER
45

Seated at Inez's counter, a movement at the other end of the beach caught Pete's attention. He leaned close to the pane of glass. Figures there, people, Inez and Dennis wearing backpacks, but more than just them. Further up on the sand walked three men in uniform.

Pete stepped away and a hollow centre formed in his chest. She'd reported him. She'd ratted. A quick turn around the little sofa, one tight circle of the room while he tried to think. No place to hide here, and even if there had been, Inez was there with the cops. She wouldn't hide him. All this time he'd been waiting for her she was busy talking to the cops.

He could step outside, try to talk his way out of it, but even while he was thinking this, he knew it wouldn't work. Running was his best hope. The panelled door at the back of the room led to the toilet. The space was cramped: toilet seat mounted to a narrow wooden bench, levered window above it.

Pete cranked the window. Still not enough space to slip out, but he banged on the glass, hit the edges until the pane came loose and then he hoisted himself and crawled down across an old wooden barrel.

A few steps from the cabin, Pete started through the long grass, body low until he was over the rise and into the woods. He broke into a run, an absolute sprint down the trail towards Seeley's. Within sight of the bay, he cut into the woods, a scramble at first — up a steady rise, a climb through loose dirt, across

/ / / / /

a bed of ferns. Low trees, blackthorn and salal gripped the flank of the hill. At the top he slowed and looked back. Blood hummed in his temples. Streaks of ocean showed through the trees, the dark water at the lip of Baker Beach.

Maybe it had been a fantasy from the start. Maybe he'd never have been able to set up a life with Inez and Dennis. There'd been something between them though — and more than just a spark. Even now, standing at the top of that ridge, part of him still wanted to believe she hadn't betrayed him and his mind played through possibilities — she could have stumbled upon the cops on the trail. Maybe the police had found out from someone else and simply bumped into Inez and Dennis.

Pete didn't stop though. He carried on walking and, in time, the sound of breaking waves receded, and his own ragged breathing swallowed the woodland noises. Keep a steady pace, walk a straight line, don't get lost. A single direct shot and he'd reach the highway: one foot in front of the other.

At the West Coast Road, he stopped and his gaze turned south to where the road curved and disappeared. A dragonfly buzzed past, wings close enough that Pete could hear them beat. There shouldn't be much traffic here, even now, late in the afternoon, but he couldn't walk on open road, not during daylight hours, not with the police down at Baker Beach.

Out here no one cleared the bush for fire starter. Jungle-thick salal grew head height, and he waded through it, hands raised to break a path. A chickadee called through the forest as he picked his way and tried to follow a path parallel to the road.

Inez watched Dennis. He'd turned his body from her and folded his arms defiantly across his chest. "It's going to be alright," she said. "In the end it's all going to work out fine."

The three officers had started up the ridge towards Gunter's cabin and soon she lost track of them — blue uniforms melted into the shadowed spaces between tree trunks.

"Run, Ash. It's the police."

Inez clapped her hands on Dennis, pulled him to her before he could say anything more. The boy fought though. He twisted, dropped low and stamped on her foot. That loosened her grip and he managed to pull away.

Inez lifted the poster from her pocket. "Come and look at this."

A quiet moment stretched then Dennis stepped forward and pushed her hand a little, moved her fingers so they weren't covering the reward.

"Twenty thousand dollars?" he said.

"My God, Dennis, they say he killed a man. Owen Tuggs in fact. Linda's husband."

"Money money money. Moving money, reward money. It's always money."

"You don't think we could use some money?"

"Money doesn't matter, remember? You tell me that all the time. Christian was going to set a firebomb, and you didn't care about that a bit."

/ / / / /

"I did care."

"But you didn't do anything. You didn't try to stop him."

"Do you know who Owen and Linda Tuggs are? They have a baby."

"You could have asked Ash about it. You could have talked to him first."

"Ash isn't even his real name. He's been lying to us, Dennis."

"He told me. He said he was in a protest group. That's how he knew what firebombs looked like." Dennis started across the sand then turned and faced her again. "You're the one who slept with him. You're the one who decided to move away with him."

"Dennis," she said, "please," but he'd turned to watch the officers return along the trail. Bubba was the first to emerge from the woods, face red from exertion. Anderson followed, rifle tucked under his arm. Scout barked and trotted out from behind the Painted Lady. Ash wasn't with them and some of what Inez felt was relief. There'd be no confrontation, no accusing finger aimed her way. There might be no reward, but at least she wouldn't have to face him. Arms open, she stepped across the sand, but Dennis was already walking from her, shoulders squared.

That was alright. That was fine. It was all going to be okay. Dennis was a wonderful kid, and he'd be fine, here or in town, city or suburbs. She'd be fine too, with or without a reward, with or without a man in her life. In the end, everything would be alright. As always, it was a matter of knowing when it was that you'd reached the end.

"What's going on?" Oscar called from the edge of the little orchard.

"Just give me a minute, Oskie."

"I only came down to ask, you know, about the assault charges."

"I said give me a minute."

"Then I saw the police."

Dennis stepped from behind the cabin with the kayak slung over his shoulder.

"That's not a good idea," Inez said.

Dennis was already in the shallows though. A spent wave lifted the kayak, and with both hands out, he balanced the boat and slid in. "Dennis." She jogged down to the water's edge. "Where are you going?" The boy didn't even have a proper paddle. The one in his hands was from the canoe. Two feet into the shallows, she grabbed hold of the stern. He slapped his paddle back though, splashed water in a fine spray across her face. Inez held on, both hands fixed on the kayak's very tip. "Don't do this."

The paddle swung again, hit her arm, and the shock rocketed into her shoulder. The kayak slipped from her grip. It slid out over the water while Inez staggered back, free hand cradling her forearm.

"Dennis." He was almost at the break now. Inez kept yelling his name until she sensed a presence nearby, a body leaning close. A glance back and Anderson raised a hand.

"When was the last time you saw Osborne?"

Inez looked out to sea. "My son's angry at me. He's upset, I told you."

A wave passed under the kayak.

"When did you last see him, Ms. Pierce?"

"This morning. He was here at the Point, up in that cabin."

"So he could have left?"

She looked about. "He wasn't chained here."

Bubba had placed himself by the chicken coop. Inez turned her attention down the beach. This whole stretch of land seemed slightly different now, off by a shade: the presence of the police, Dennis in his kayak, Ash's lies, her betrayal.

Christian stood at the northern end of the bay, a slight figure in the distance. He must have been tending his marijuana crop. He'd be upset to see the authorities poking about, upset about that like he was upset about so much else. Still, she couldn't quite believe Christian would set a firebomb. Although maybe this was just her response to Dennis's accusation that she'd treated Christian and Peter Osborne unevenly.

"You have a two-way radio here?" Anderson said.

"I do. I'm the only one though."

"You're familiar with the emergency band?"

"Never had to use it before."

"Channel nine." He raised his hand, touched his moustache a moment. "You got a way to lock your cabin against intruders?"

"For God's sakes, he's not dangerous. The dangers here are bears and bad weather."

"We're going to have a look around, talk to some of the other residents."

"That's Oscar over there by the wheelbarrow. Ernie's up by his cabin, but you won't get much from him. There's only a few of us left here."

Christian was headed their way with that lumbering walk. He was a bear himself.

Out on the water, a wave cut into the kayak and knocked it back, sprayed a plume of water over her son. He'd get out there then he'd turn in. He'd try kayak surfing. That's what he was always talking about. No harm done. As long as she could see him.

Swartz was on his way out towards the Point, a ginger step as he picked his way around the blackberry bushes. She was the one who'd set these three uniformed men loose on their land, in among their homes. Now he'd be nosing about in her studio, looking at the half finished painting on her easel.

"So it's happening," Christian said. "The fuckers."

"I brought them."

"You?" he said.

"He'll never make it past the break," Inez said.

"You going to tell me what the SWAT team is here for?"

"Peter Osborne. They say he blew up a Greer-Braden warehouse."

"Who?"

"Ash. Apparently his real name is Peter Osborne. They say he killed a man."

"By blowing up a warehouse?"

"Owen Tuggs."

"As in Owen and Linda? Well isn't this a soup of shit."

A wave broke over Dennis and he switched the paddle from one side to the other.

"Greer-Braden," Christian said. "The fuckers."

"Were you really going to set off a firebomb in retaliation?"

"Not anymore. Your man Ash went and cut holes in the bottom of the tubs. Ruined them."

That stilled her — another odd-shaped piece she'd have to fit into the puzzle of Ash McCabe.

"You know, he had a reward on his head?"

"What kind of reward?"

"Greer-Braden put it up. I think that's what they call irony."

Halfway down the beach, an incoming wave hit the bottom of Dennis's pack. The toilet paper was in there along with copies of the free paper she'd brought for fire starter. Inez started to run. Water soaking her food and supplies. That on top of everything else.

She carried both packs together and set them on the cabin porch. Christian was now talking to Corporal Anderson. Oscar walked around the garden, headed for his own cabin. Out on the water, Dennis had made it past the break and sat resting, kayak on open water. She waved and called to him. She yelled to come back. He'd tested the kayak, he'd proved himself, but Dennis gave one deliberate glance her way then turned and looked out to sea.

Better she didn't try to force the matter. Rain had already started, light drops turned inland by the wind. He'd paddle in soon enough. He'd get soaked and head home.

At the door, Inez slipped off her boots and hauled the packs inside. She switched on the weather radio. They'd left early and she hadn't listened to the marine forecast. The man reading it covered the north coast and then started reading the weather for the south coast. The signal was weak and the radio crackled with static. They had a heavy surf advisory in place. Storm winds were coming, only Inez didn't hear. She'd noticed the back door stood open and the little window above the toilet had been pushed out. She leaned into the attached outhouse and peered through the window. The pane of glass lay behind an old barrel.

By this time, the police were already on their way back across the beach, the three of them single file. Scout followed. The officers hadn't spent long looking around, hadn't spent long interviewing the other residents.

On the radio, the announcer had begun on the weather for the straits and then moved on to the lower mainland. Inez undid the clasps on her own pack and began to unload groceries. After she'd finished stocking the pantry, Inez leaned close against the kitchen window. A container ship hung hazy on the horizon. The clouds beyond looked low and dark. She hadn't properly listened to the weather forecast. The radio repeated the north coast weather then the north inland weather. Outside the rain fell harder, sheets of it angled by the wind and percussive against the roof. She opened the door and looked down the beach.

Dennis must have paddled over to Seeley's. Unless he'd gone the other way, up to Paulson Bay. A twist of worry tightened, a feeling low in her guts. Something wasn't right. At the head of the beach a path cut through the woods and out to Seeley's. Inez scrambled across the rocks. The woods were thin here but it was a good five hundred yards. Two minutes at a run and she could see into Seeley's — open water, dark, shifting ocean. Her heart squeezed and expanded, a thumping fist as she stepped down onto the rocks. They were slippery wet in the lashing rain.

A kayak. A goddamned homemade kayak. She shouldn't have let him go. She shouldn't have even let him build it. With her own stupid roll of canvas.

Paulson was another possibility. It seemed too much to imagine he'd crossed Seeley's and paddled all the way to Merchant Bay, not with evening settling, not against this kind of wind. She cut through the woods and ran across the beach, feet hammering the hard wet sand. Blood pulsed through her neck. Out on the water, waves rose and fell. The ocean looked ominous and vast, and nothing lay tucked in the folds of the swell, nothing but water itself.

She said the word Paulson. She said it to herself on the beat of each step, a chant, an incantation. Clouds dinted what was left of the evening sun. Shadows had begun to swallow the land, curtains slowly drawing. The rain grew heavy. Her clothes were already soaked.

Breathless, Inez reached the sharp slope that rose from the northern edge of Baker Beach. She pulled at branches, dug her toes in above roots and rocks, grunted as she climbed. No one walked down here to collect firewood, no goats grazed here and thinned the underbrush. She fought her way, waded step by step, the crash of waves muted by the woods around her until she emerged onto the pebble beach of Paulson Bay. The rain was heavy, the swell high, choppy and grey.

She screamed her son's name, yelled it into the driving rain. Nothing came back but the sound of the waves.

CHAPTER 47

Tab took an early-morning flight west. After landing she walked through the airport's glassed-in lobby to find the car rental company with the shortest line. At the counter a man photocopied her driver's licence and credit card then gave her keys to a Ford Escort. He explained the route north in a slip of a voice and marked it on a map as he talked.

Farmland surrounded the airport. Further down the highway, clusters of houses stood between fenced-off fields. Beyond them, subdivisions grew — knots of houses walled off from the road so that only peaked roofs and dormers stood visible. The highway widened, turned uphill. The car shifted into a lower gear. Woods rose on either side, tall dark evergreens — formidable, grand and dense enough that they gave a walled-in feeling.

Towns dotted the coast — one and two traffic-light towns, fast food restaurants, roadside motels, strip malls and sign boards: Welcome to Duncan, Welcome to Chemainus, Ladysmith, Coombs. She stopped for coffee once and further up the road refilled her tank. She arrived in Glendenning with an hour to spare. The first storefront was a bakery, then a hairdresser, a bank. A sign advertised tours of the old mill.

The Kettle Top turned out to be a wide building beside a video store. Tab parked in the gravel lot. Her legs ached and her back felt stiff. She climbed from the car and stretched, looked about, squared her shoulders and rolled her head. The town

/ / / / /

rose to the west on a low slope. In the distance, grey sheets of mountain hung ghost-like against the sky.

Somewhere nearby they were waiting for her: Art Kosky and Peter. Hopefully Peter. The others might be here too — Derek Newfeld and Fay Anderson. She'd seen their pictures in the paper. Peter had looked grim with shaggy hair, dark eyes, his mouth tight-set, but it was the picture of Fay Anderson that had arrested Tab. Bev had mentioned a woman involved, a woman she said Peter liked, and there she was looking into the camera, a pretty face, angular features, wide eyes, short cropped hair.

Tab peered through the Kettle Top's window: an open space with tables in neat rows. Two men sat at the counter drinking coffee. The chalkboard above them listed daily specials. A grey-haired lady with a carpet bag on her arm stood at the centre of the room. No sign of anyone that looked like Art Kosky.

More likely they'd be behind the café, somewhere just out of sight — in a car on the side of the road, waiting in a nearby barn or an abandoned house. Art had said he'd be watching her, and with that thought, Tab dipped her hand into her purse and felt for the envelope and the stack of bills.

Houses lined the low slope above the bakery, fenced off lots, a pair of yards backed up against the bakery's parking lot. Beyond them a gravel lane led uphill. Arthur Kosky might come down that gravel lane. Standing there in the parking lot she could picture it, and she tried to picture Peter with him.

The Kettle Top's door swung open and a man in an apron stepped out, threw a garbage bag into a dumpster then disappeared inside. A black and white cat rubbed itself against a fencepost. Footsteps on gravel startled Tab. She turned and spotted Art Kosky crossing the road.

He had his mother's wide lips, the same thick neck. He'd grown a full beard, and his clothes hung loose on him. He was alone. No sign of Peter.

"Is he here?" Her voice had gone dry. She gulped and said it again.

Kosky had a jitter to him, a hop and quickness as he closed the last few yards between them. "Where's your car?"

"Here. The red one."

"Give me the keys. I'm going to drive."

"And Peter?"

"Did you hear what I just said?"

"Okay. Alright." Tab was gulping air. She tried to calm herself as she opened her purse, both hands trembling. "Can you just tell me that he's here, that he's okay?"

"We're going to get in your car. Me in the driver's seat, you in the passenger seat."

"And we're going to see my son?"

"The keys."

She sifted through her purse — tissue, lipstick, a birthday card, her chequebook, silly to dump the car keys in with all this junk. Finally she found them, passed the keys over and walked around to the passenger side. She was close now. She just had to stay calm and hold herself together a little longer and she'd see Peter.

Art pulled so hard on the driver's side door it bounced on its hinges and came back against his hip. He started the engine, put the vehicle in gear and they lurched forward, a burst of speed.

"This isn't necessary," she said. "I mean, if you're worried that someone followed me."

"You're looking for Pete, right?"

"Of course. Yes. I mean —"

"And you brought the money?"

"Are you taking me to my son?"

"I need the money."

"It's in my purse, but I have to see my son first."

"The money," he said.

She reached in, dug around then raised the envelope. "Where is he?"

"I haven't seen him since Esterway Ridge, not since the action at the Greer-Braden warehouse."

For a moment, she was confused. The words came through, but her mind tangled with the meaning. "Wait. Where?"

"After Pete set off the bomb —"

"Peter set off the bomb?"

"We got separated. Fire trucks arrived. The timer was set short, just two minutes. The night watchman stepped around the corner. Pete turned to face him, and then the bomb went."

"I don't understand."

"We'd cut away a piece of fence but it fell back into place and after the blast it was electrified. Pete was still in there and we were on the other side trying to get him out. Emergency vehicles started lighting up the hill behind us. He needed to run through what was left of the gap in the fence, but he just sat there. The blast had dazed him, knocked him down."

"This doesn't make any sense."

They passed a fruit stand, an orchard, trees in neat rows, a kaleidoscopic blur on the other side of her window.

"He was trying to keep the night watchman alive. He was waiting for help, I think. So we went and hid the car."

She turned to him. "You left Peter there?"

"No, not like that, we just got the car out of sight. The police were coming up the logging road, fire trucks. I went back to find him."

She'd known Peter had been a part of this. She'd known he was at Esterway Ridge, but there'd been threads of hope, the possibility that he'd been only marginally involved. But now here was this man with his scrubby beard and his weighty body odour telling her that Peter had been the one to set the bomb, that they'd abandoned him afterwards.

"I did my best, Mrs. Harper. All we wanted to do was hide the car, but by the time I was back, he was gone. Fire trucks were there. We drove to the quarry, to our meeting point, and left one of our people there, left another at the nearest junction. I started driving around looking for him but when I finally found him, he didn't know who I was. He must have been confused. He ran from me. You have to believe I tried, but the blast had knocked him off his feet. He was probably disoriented. He panicked, he just ran into the woods."

The tarmac ended, tires noisy on gravel now.

"I wish I'd gone after him into the forest. I really do."

"You have to tell the authorities."

"I waited too long. I was distracted when I saw him, thinking of other things. I was upset. Stupid things. I sat in the car a few seconds too long."

"I want you to turn yourselves in."

"It's time for the money now, Mrs. Harper."

"Doesn't the fact a man is dead mean anything to you?"

"Someone had to take a stand."

"A stand? Because of some trees? Because of some loggers? You have to stop this."

"We're not the ones who have to stop."

"You killed a man. You broke the law."

"Sabotage was a last resort, and you have to believe me when I say that we didn't undertake it lightly. Greer-Braden is logging the last pristine old growth on the continent. And do you know who said they could? The government. Which actually owns millions in Greer-Braden stock."

"He had a family, a baby, a wife."

"I need that money now, Mrs. Harper. Two thousand dollars."

"If you don't have Peter, I'm not paying ransom."

"Ransom?" He put the brakes on, and Tab strained against the seat belt. The car swerved off to the side of the road. "I never said I had Pete. I sure as hell never said ransom."

"I just wanted to know where he is. I wanted to know that he's okay."

"That's right. Money for information. That was our exchange, and I've told you all I know."

"That he was the one who caused this man's death? This is the information I'm paying for?"

"It was an accident."

"How do I know you're telling the truth?"

"I wouldn't lie."

"Oh, I think you might. Blame Peter to try to get off."

"Put your purse in the back. Everything in it is a donation."

She clutched the purse, held it to her chest.

"Purse in the back and get out of the car."

Tab fumbled with the door handle. If she could get out she could run, but he grabbed hold of the purse strap, took her wrist and the purse slipped through her hands. She screamed. A car passed, and she kept screaming. She tried to wave. She needed someone's attention. Tears streaked her cheeks. "I'm going to call the police. I'm going to tell them."

"You think calling the cops helps anyone? Your donation helps. This money helps." Art's face was bright, his eyes lively. "I'll leave the car on the other side of town. I'm going to leave everything but the cash."

"I just want to know where he is." Her voice was almost a moan.

"I'd tell you if I knew." He undid her seat belt. "The car will be waiting for you on the south side of town."

She wiped at her cheeks. "Don't just leave me here."

"You've done a good thing. Now it's time to go home. Just walk straight down here, it'll lead to the main road. On the other side of Glendenning, I'll make sure the car's visible."

He gave a gentle push, but she didn't move. He pushed harder and this time she took hold of his arm, bent and sank her teeth in. Art howled and then he pushed her, shouldered her from the seat. Tab tumbled onto the gravel. The car tires spun and stirred up dirt. A U-turn and Art Kosky was on the road and headed south.

CHAPTER 48

The passenger door swung closed on its own, the momentum of the car brought it shut as Art turned south. Tab Harper came into view in the rear-view mirror, her body still on the gravel. Art's foot shifted to the brake and he waited. No traffic in either direction. He waited until Mrs. Harper pushed herself into a seated position and then stood. Art accelerated, felt about in the purse as he drove, pulled out a pad of paper, and then a few pages of a magazine folded in quarters. Deeper in he touched the spine of a paperback book, a tube of lipstick, a pouch made of soft leather. The purse was stuffed. He slowed as he reached Glendenning. He had to concentrate, had to make sure he attracted no attention. At a flashing red light, Art turned right to avoid passing the Kettle Top again, a brief detour. Once on open road, traffic picked up, Glendenning a blink of a town, there and then gone.

Art shook everything onto the passenger seat, spread the contents glancing down now and again. Finally the envelope caught his eye, red rubber band taut around it. He opened it and spotted pink bills inside: fifties. His body softened. He eased back into the fabric seat and released a fluttering whistle of relief.

Scrubby low trees lined both sides of the road now. They rose in front of him on a gentle uphill grade. The turnoff was coming. He signalled at the top of the rise, turned onto a track that led into shadowed woods then switched off the ignition.

/ / / / /

A bird called, a twitter and coo that sounded like a dove. Art considered wiping the wheel and cleaning the interior of fingerprints, but the thought was absurd. Tab Harper knew who he was. She'd sat two feet from him. His face had been on the front page. Art cracked the window, let in a little air and inhaled. He was deeper in shit now. If that were possible. Two thousand dollars richer but deeper in shit. A squeeze on the handle, and the door swung open. Art scooped up everything strewn across the passenger side, put the purse and its contents in the trunk, and left the keys on the seat. They'd parked the station wagon a few hundred yards ahead, out of sight around a bend in the track.

As Art approached the station wagon, Derek opened the driver's side door and leaned out. Art gave a thumbs up. "Done," he said.

"Two thousand dollars done?"

"Looks like it. I didn't count all the bills."

"Wow. That's generous." Fay had been lying across the back seat, but she sat up now. "That's really something."

Car in gear, Derek managed a turn and then drove around the bend. That's when they first saw the little red car. "I thought you were walking."

"I was."

Derek slowed. The track narrowed here and the two side mirrors almost touched. "Where did the car come from?"

"Let's just get on the road."

At the highway, Derek waited for traffic then turned south, down-island, away from Glendenning. They accelerated. Art opened his window. Minutes passed. "So?" Derek said.

"Tab Harper."

"Who?"

"Pete's mom."

"What? Jesus Christ."

"She was the donor?"

Art pressed his hand against the thick wad of cash in his pants pocket. "She gave me money, I gave her information."

"I thought it was a donation."

"She thought we had Pete. She thought I was bringing her to him. I think she's kind of going crazy."

The siren was faint at first — a distant sound carried by winds that grew into a loping drone. For a moment Art was unsure which direction the sound came from then a car appeared on the bend ahead, a cruiser travelling at high speed, lights flashing. Derek slowed the station wagon. Art pressed the sunglasses higher on his nose. The cruiser passed. Derek adjusted the rearview mirror and watched the cop car disappear. "That gave my heart a workout."

"She didn't want to give me the money after she found out I couldn't bring her to Pete. She seemed to think we were holding him ransom or something. Once I said I didn't know where he was, she wouldn't let me have it."

"So the cops just there," Fay said. "The car that passed us —"

"It might have been because of her. Yeah, maybe."

"There could be a roadblock ahead," Derek said.

"There's not going to be a roadblock. It's not far to the Duke Point ferry. We can just leave from this end of the island."

"Leave for where?" Fay said.

"The interior, Derek's cousin's cabin." He raised the wad of cash and held it for them to see. "Is everything set with your cousin?"

"Not yet."

"Derek, fuck. That was the one —"

"What about negotiations, publicize our demands, remember we talked about —"

"I just got us this fucking money, Derek. Why the hell did I do that if our master plan is to surrender? That was the one thing you were supposed to do, call your cousin."

"You don't need to tell me what I'm supposed to do."

"Will both of you please stop arguing," Fay said.

"We're going to the suite," Art said. "A couple of days and this will cool down. A quiet stretch and then we send that press release and head for the Slocan."

"Two days ago I told you we needed to present our demands —"

"It was a bad idea then and it's a bad idea now. Until we're in a position of strength."

"They know who we are now, Art. They know who you are."

"They already knew."

"What do you mean?"

"Our pictures were in the paper."

"What are you talking about?" Fay said.

"They know all four of us. Photos, full names, prime suspects."

The wheels hummed on the tarmac road. Sunlight bathed the car's dusty dashboard.

"Someone ratted." Derek banged on the steering wheel. Strands of his thin hair swung about. "Someone fucking told."

"We just need to stay calm and follow our plan. We have money, we have a place to stay."

"Our pictures are in the paper." Derek was almost shouting. "Do you know what that means?"

"We all knew this was going to happen. When was the only question." Art tried to keep his voice level and calm. "We lie low for two days, send the press release then head to the Slocan. Three quiet months while we plan our next action. Am I right, Fay?"

Derek cut in and Fay didn't have time to answer. "What if my cousin says no? With our pictures in the paper he might just say no."

"Jesus, Derek. We only started talking about him because you were sure he'd say yes."

"I'm freaking out here, Art."

"Just call your cousin and see what he says."

Art twisted around and looked towards Fay. He wanted her to say something, wanted her approval, her support. He reached out and touched her arm, but a moment later they hit a bump in the road and his hand fell away.

CHAPTER
49

Tab jogged back along the road. A cramp stitched her side, and her knees and her hip began to ache. After gravel gave way to sealed road, a small red barn appeared close up to the side of the highway. It turned out to be a fruit stand with two cars parked in the lot. By the time she reached the barn, Tab was walking. She leaned against the wood flank of the building and her body sagged.

Peter had been the one. A man had died because of him. It now felt like a great effort just to stand and it took everything she had to push off from the wall and walk inside. The air felt cool. Rhubarb, cherries and apricots filled the bins beside a bank of plums and cartons of berries. A young woman leaned against the counter near the cash register, her hair in a loose bun. A gold cross hung from a choker around her neck.

"Could I borrow your phone?" Tab sniffled and wiped her nose. Mucus had gathered in her throat, and she had to swallow before she could continue. "It's a collect call. For an emergency."

The woman reached for the phone. She had it on the counter before Tab had even finished her explanation.

"A man took my purse, my car, my overnight bag."

"Just dial 911."

"My husband's in Ontario. I'll reverse the charges. He'll be done work, he'll be at home."

The moment Frank answered, Tab began to cry again. Just the sound of his lilting voice released her. She turned away from

/ / / / /

the woman at the counter and tried to control her sobs as Frank asked, "What is it?" over and over. "What happened?"

Tab bowed her head. She'd told him she was going to meet Elwood Dewy, the lawyer Dick had recommended.

On the other end of the line, Frank said, "Take a deep breath and tell me."

Tab heard her own hoarse whisper, just a faint sound as she started into the middle of the story about the Kettle Top, Art Kosky's nervous jitters and the car he stole. Somehow in the middle of all of that she mentioned the two thousand dollars from their joint account and then at the end she managed to say that Peter had set the bomb. Her son. Murder.

The silence on the other end of the phone seemed enormous. Cars swooshed past a few yards from her. "Are you there?" she said.

"Come home. Nothing good can come of this. Just leave it and come home."

"He could be dead. He could be lost in the woods."

"Oh God, Tab. Please just come home."

"I need a favour. Can you get Inspector Burrell's number from my address book?"

"Tab, don't get any more involved in this."

"That man took my purse, my overnight bag. Everything."

"If I give you this number, you'll come home?"

"Burrell will want to hear this, and if it helps him catch them, it will be worth it, right?"

He set down the phone. In the background, a cabinet door creaked, a drawer slid open then Frank returned.

"They're kids, Frank, scared kids."

"It's time to let it go."

"I thought Art Kosky was the ringleader, but he's not that much older than Peter."

"Come on the overnight flight tonight. I'll drive out to the airport and meet you."

After Tab hung up, she did her best to smile at the woman then lifted the handset again. "One more call? It's to the police this time. In Vancouver."

Burrell answered the phone, his voice gravelly and sharp.

"I just saw Arthur Kosky," Tab said.

"What? Who is this?"

"Tab Harper."

"Mrs. Harper." His voice was warmer now, almost cheery. "I thought you'd gone home."

"Will this count? If you find Arthur Kosky, I want to know that it will help Peter."

"It will. Tell me where you saw him."

"In Glendenning. We met in front of a restaurant called the Kettle Top. He was wearing a leather jacket and a black turtleneck. He's grown a full beard, cut his hair short. He's driving around in my rental car right now. It's red, I think it's a Ford. And he just took two thousand dollars from me that was supposed to be to take me to Peter."

"Oh good Lord."

"I thought they'd take me to him. I thought if I could see him."

"He's on the coast, Mrs. Harper. You should have brought us in on this. We could have Kosky in custody by now."

"The coast?"

"Your son's been staying with some squatters out past Port Thorvald."

Tab let those words sink in. It meant he was alive. It meant he was alright.

"Where are you calling from?" Voices rose in the background. Burrell wasn't alone in his office. "Are you still in Glendenning? I'll dispatch a car for you."

"No. That's okay."

"We've just sent some officers to bring your son in, Mrs. Harper."

"Remember though, no shooting."

Tab walked out of the fruit barn and stood in the slanted afternoon sunlight. She could see the bridge from here. She was almost in town. The opposite side of the road had a sidewalk.

"Are you okay?"

Tab turned. The woman had followed her. She had a quart box in hand. "Would you like some blueberries?"

"Do you know a town called Port Thorvald?"

"Sure. Out along the coast."

"How far is it?"

"Five hours, more or less."

"Could I bother you again. I mean, is there any chance of a ride to the other side of town? This is a long story."

"What about the police?"

"I hate to impose." She paused there. The woman touched one hand against her fruit-stained apron. "The man who took my car said he'd leave it there. He'd park it and leave it and it'll have my purse and my bank card. I could get you some money then. I hope I could anyway."

"No need to pay but I should see if my husband can watch the store."

They drove together, past Glendenning's one traffic light and out to where the highway opened up on a newly sealed road. A police car passed them, lights flashing. Tab sensed the woman turning her way, but she was busy looking from one side of the highway to the other. The sound of the police car faded.

"Did he tell you where?" the woman said. "Any landmarks or anything?"

"Just that he would leave it on this road. The same road as your store only on the other side of town."

They were at the peak of a low ridge when Tab spotted it. "Hold on." The red rental car was on a narrow side track, parked under the boughs of evergreen trees. It meant the police hadn't caught him. Her phone call to Burrell hadn't helped.

"You think he could still be there?" the woman said. "You think this could be trouble?"

Tab opened the passenger door before the truck fully stopped. She strode over, almost ran. The car keys lay on the front seat. No sign of her purse though. She looked in the back then popped the trunk and walked around to check there. Her purse lay on its side. The envelope was gone. She'd expected that, but she found her wallet and held it up so the woman could see.

Settled in the rental car, Tab spotted a scrap of paper on the dash, a square torn from the bank envelope. It said, "I'm sorry," and on the other side it said, "About Pete."

CHAPTER
50

By the time Pete reached the gas station at Buckley Bay, the land stood on the cusp of darkness and the rains had grown heavy. In the cabin, the attendant had his feet up, his chair tilted. It looked like he was reading. Beyond the gas station, the three boxy cottages all looked deserted, the car he'd seen on his last visit nowhere in sight.

It was fully dark by the time the gas station attendant drove off. Pete stepped from the shelter of woods into the open. The wind had sharpened and drove the rain slanted across the land. A gust caught the screen door of the nearest cabin and banged it open with a sudden clatter. No lights in the cabins, no signs of life. At the pay phone, Pete dialled Jeremy's number and reversed the charges. Three rings until Jeremy answered.

"It's me. It's Pete."

The phone line crackled. Pete held the receiver in both hands.

"You can't call here." Jeremy spoke in a low voice. "I told you —"

"Did you do it?"

"Do what?"

"Did you find Art, did you tell them not —"

"Jesus, Pete, I don't know where they are and even if I did, I wouldn't —"

"They're holed up in the suburbs, you told me that. I just thought. I hoped. Things are going sideways here and I wanted to warn them."

/ / / / /

"I called the police," Jeremy said. "Anonymously. I told them about Thurlow Road."

"You what?"

"I told them about the dynamite."

"Oh God. Oh Jesus."

"You wanted to make sure no one else got hurt, and I wanted to make sure no one else got hurt."

"The cops, Jeremy? You called the cops?"

"I didn't tell them anything else."

"You could have just fucking looked for the others, you could have talked to them."

"You need to see a lawyer."

"I was the one who detonated it, Jeremy."

"Stop. Don't tell me these things."

"I'm stranded. I need help. Remember Mrs. Keener? She always leaves her keys in the glove compartment. You're two blocks away."

"I'm not going to steal you a car."

"The keys are right there. You could just borrow it."

"No."

Pete banged the handset down. He slammed it into the cradle and thumped his right hand into the side of the call box.

A step away and Pete turned to face the road. He knew what he had to do now, knew who he'd call next, the one person he could trust. He'd felt it looming, a physical presence travelling with him. Finding Fay and the others was a fantasy. The police knew who he was, and they knew where he'd been, and Jeremy was never going to help. Inez had betrayed him.

He lifted the handset, pressed zero and gave his name to the operator. It would be after one in the morning in Ontario. When Frank's voice came down the line, Pete almost hung up. "Who is it?" Gruff words, a bark. "It's the middle of the night."

He didn't want to talk to Frank, even if it was just to ask for his mother, but the operator gave Pete's name and the call went through.

"Peter?" he said. "Jesus Christ, Peter."

"Is my mother there?"

"No, she's not."

"Where's she going to be at one in the morning, Frank?"

"Hold on a second and tell me where you are."

"Can I just talk to her?"

"I said she's not here. She's bloody well looking for you."

"Oh," he said. And then, "How," but that was all that came out. The rest of his words were gone.

"Is that all you can say? Do you have any idea?"

"I don't need a lecture."

"You need to get your head examined. And you need to see a lawyer." He paused. "Your mother's arranged for one. I'm trying to remember his name."

"When will she be home?"

"Where are you?"

"On the coast. At a pay phone. It's not even at a town."

"She's back tomorrow. She said she was getting on the red eye last night."

"She came all this way to look for me?"

"Is all this stuff they're saying true?"

"That the world's a shit show? Yes. That we're raping and pillaging —"

"Cut the crap. Is it true you were there? That you were part of this? Do you have any idea what your mother's been going through?"

"The man walked in just before it went off. I was standing there. I was fifty feet away. It knocked me back. It flattened me. We posted a lookout just to make sure nothing like this happened. And then it did."

"I'm going to write down exactly where you are, then call me in the morning."

"I'm on the coast. On my own on the coast. I'll call you tomorrow."

"At the crack of dawn, Peter. Tab will be here by then. She should already be on a plane."

"Can you do me a favour, Frank? Between now and then, can you call someone for me?"

"Who?"

"Fay Anderson's parents. Her mother's name is Nancy."

"Is she one of the others?" Frank said.

"I'm not sure about her dad's name. They live in Kamloops. I don't know where Fay is, but maybe one of her parents could somehow get through and warn her."

"How do you mean, 'warn her'?"

"They need to tell her that the police know about Thurlow Road and they may also know about List Cove."

"I'm not sending some clandestine bloody message for you, Peter."

"I'm trying to stop anyone else from getting hurt. I just want someone to warn her."

"It's one in the morning here, Peter. Call back in six more hours. Your mother will be here. We'll get you in touch with that lawyer. Keep your head down and call us first thing. We're going to do everything we can here."

CHAPTER
51

Driving down-island, Tab retraced her morning route. After the mountain pass but before the tangle of suburbs, she veered off onto a minor road that led along the coast towards Port Thorvald. Dusk settled, and the rain began, a patter at first, but soon Tab had the wipers on high and after a time she had to lean over the wheel to see properly.

Some days ago he'd driven out here with a car full of explosives. This was her constant thought. She was tracing his steps: a pursuit ten days too late. He'd passed this way and he hadn't returned. Yet.

Two deer stood in the middle of the road, and Tab slammed on the brakes. The car skidded. It slid and Tab strained against the seat belt. A moment of stillness passed while her headlights lit the deer, tawny flanks, sharp ears.

She finally reached Port Thorvald just before midnight, pulled over when she saw a motel sign and opened her umbrella for the short walk to the shelter of the veranda. She rang the doorbell and the clerk came out in his bathrobe and held the door for her.

"Late night driving," he said.

"Late night and bad weather."

He wrote her name in a great broad ledger. "How many nights?"

"One, or maybe two. We'll see." Tab signed and the man lifted a key from the rack.

/ / / / /

"We'll put you in lucky twenty-seven."

"I could do with some luck."

"It's the Lucky West Motel. Every room is lucky."

She hadn't noticed the name when she'd pulled in. She'd just seen the words *motel* and *vacancy*.

"You can't get much further west and can't get any more lucky. You'll feel the same way once the rain stops. Or should I say, if the rain stops."

She knew this was meant as a joke, but she couldn't even raise a smile for him.

Outside Tab leaned into the wind as she followed the man across the porch and past the first few rooms. Beyond the curtain of shimmering rain lay open ocean, a great mass forked by occasional shadows. A strange thought took her: this is where the continent stopped.

"No one on either side of you," the clerk said. "You should sleep well tonight. Provided you don't mind a bit of a storm. It's been quite the shingle-shaker."

The man slid the key into the door marked twenty-seven. Tab glanced over her shoulder. A black and white police cruiser stood at the far end of the lot, and the sight of it stilled her. "Do policemen stay at your motel?"

The clerk turned, looked into the parking lot himself and followed the line of Tab's gaze. "Couple officers here on extended duty."

Once in the room, Tab leaned back against the door. All that driving with her eyes sandpaper dry and now she was wide awake.

She'd told Burrell that Arthur Kosky was driving around in her red rental car. Best to get it out of sight. At the very least she should park it down the road, and so Tab stepped back into the wind and rain, walked to the rental car and drove it around the corner, parked on a muddy side street. Engine still, she listened to the patter of rain drops on the car's hood.

If the police were still here, surely that meant they hadn't yet found Peter. It was a good sign.

CHAPTER
52

Three cottages stood in a single row just past the gas station: flat roofed buildings with squat, narrow porches. Up the footpath of the nearest cabin, Pete set his hand on the cold doorknob. Locked. He peered in through the window, cupped his hands there then stepped back into the wind and rain. A few steps around the side of the cottage and he was out of the wind. These cabins had no foundations, they were built on heavy posts set into the earth, a crawl space under each. A few more steps and Pete noticed an enclosed glass porch on the other side of the middle cabin. He climbed the rickety steps. The glass was thin and single-paned. A rock would break it, a decent-sized stone. He could curl up in there, a sheltered place to sleep. He backed down the steps. All these pebbles, and he needed a rock. Further down the beach, a bead of light hung in the darkness. Odd to see someone out in a storm like this. Whoever it was shouted something into the night. Pete stood still while the orb of lantern light neared. It cast up against a red raincoat, a stocky body. Christian. Pete waited until the man called again and then he was sure. The man was looking for Dennis.

"Christian?" Pete jogged a few steps down the beach. The lantern stopped. "It's me."

"Well, aren't you the man of the hour. Mighty fucking glad I bumped into you."

"I heard you calling for Dennis." Pete had to raise his voice to be heard over the wind and the rain.

/ / / / /

"He went out on the water, paddled out before the storm started."

"In this?"

"I've walked the whole way. Seeley's, Merchant, Bodega. Oscar and Andy went north."

"Did he take the canoe or the kayak?"

"Kayak. I wasn't even sure that thing would float."

"Fuck." And then a thought occurred to him: kayak surfing in the storm swell. "He's gone to Merchant Bay."

"I was just there."

"That could be where he is."

"I walked the whole frigging way."

"We should look in Merchant. That's where we need to go."

"Let me refocus this conversation on what the fuck you're doing here."

"Pass the lantern a second." Pete leaned forward and took hold of the handle.

"Fuck off with my lantern."

But he had a grip on it now. "Christian, he wanted to kayak surf there."

"Let go." A sharp tug at the lantern and the handle came free on one side. Christian stumbled and Pete had the lantern. The mantle still burned. He re-bent the handle, attached the end that had come free. "I'm just saying we should look."

"The cops are after you. They searched the place and when your real story came out, Dennis took off in that kayak."

"He's in Merchant, Christian." Pete strained his voice to be heard over the wind and rain. "I'm sure of it."

"If he's dead it's down to your sorry ass."

Pete began to jog. He ducked his head, ran alone along the pebble beach. This wasn't on him. This wouldn't be another death on his shoulders. Beyond the shelter of Buckley Bay, the water lay vast and dark save the lines of white churning for shore.

Along the flank of the bay, Pete had to pick his way past boulders, fallen trees and driftwood. Waves cut against the rocks and cast up plumes of water. Now and again, he had to crouch and scramble forward. He yelled only the wind took his words. He switched the lantern into his left hand. His right was numb, and he folded it into his pocket for warmth. Near the rounded hump of land that would take him down into Merchant Bay something rose in the water, a dense mass. It might have been the hull of a boat. Pete raised the lantern and squinted into the slanting rain. The light shimmered over the rocks and out onto surging water, but it was seaweed, nothing more — a dense mat rising with the waves.

Further down the rocky shore, breaking waves spat water right up into the trees, and he had to pull himself onto wet soil to continue. This put him on higher ground. He had a better view of the ocean, dark and frigid beyond the curl of breaking waves. Lantern held high, Pete screamed into the wind.

If Dennis was anywhere, he was here in Merchant Bay. If Pete was right and this was in fact Merchant Bay. Merchant should have been one from Bodega which was one from Seeley's. That should make Merchant the bay next to Buckley.

Pete paused at a driftwood stump upturned on the rocks. It would offer a view and so he pulled himself up, set his back to the wind and held the lantern at a distance. It lit the wet rocks with a glare but left the crevices between them shadowed and dark. He shifted his gaze along the shoreline and turned to look into the rain, but as he turned, his foot slipped. He threw out a hand, grasped at air as he fell. His right foot hit ground first, turned on its edge, lodged itself between rocks while his body weight carried him forward. A rocket of pain split his leg. He heaved in air and tried to extract his foot. Hand on the tree trunk, he pulled himself up. The lantern was shattered, bowl broken, glass strewn across the rocks. Rain fell anew against his neck and onto his exposed hands. He put a little weight on his right foot. Pain came, sharp and immediate — an electric current from shin to knee. He looked up and down the cove. No sign of Dennis. No sign of the kayak. A single step forward, a second, a third and he paused.

The wind had calmed and Pete was sure the world was lighter now. Maybe the clouds had thinned. The shrouded moon offered a faint glow. He raised his leg and sent his fingers down across his pants, along shin to ankle. He'd done it now. A game leg on top of everything else. For all he knew, Christian was at the pay phone reporting him to the police. Pete tried again to walk, braced himself, and limped along.

The moon passed between banks of clouds and in that moment of silvery light, something turned in the water. Pete leaned forward. A wave curled in. The water level rose and as it retreated, a tattered piece of white material showed among the rocks. Pete slid off the bank and limped down to the water, hands out to support himself. He kept his weight on one leg while the next wave rolled in and then he hobbled further, bent and gripped the canvas. A fragment of the kayak. "Dennis!" he shouted. The next wave was on him. Ocean water rolled over both feet, penetrated his boots with a cold shock that numbed his toes. He tossed aside the sticks and dripping canvas and yelled into the night. Another dozen yards and a second piece of shattered kayak turned on a wave, and that's when he spotted the mustard yellow jacket — a stain against the darkness of the rocks. The boy lay on his side just ten yards off. His legs were twisted, his body looked to be wedged between boulder and driftwood. Pete dropped to his knees and gripped Dennis's shoulder. Images of Owen Tuggs and his unnatural twisted limbs flooded in as Pete rolled the boy over. Dennis's head slipped back, a loose, muscleless movement.

"Say something. Please." Another moonless night, another body in his hands. This is how he'd knelt by the watchman, ears ringing, half blinded lifting the man's arm, the fist of it held tight, his skin blackened, soot marked or burnt. He'd pressed his fingers into the man's wrists for a pulse, and he did that now with Dennis, fingers at his wrist and then at his neck, between tendons. The boy's skin was cold, his face pale, his thin lips parted, hair matted and wet.

If there was retribution coming for Pete's wrongs it couldn't fall on Dennis. He couldn't let it fall on Dennis. He lowered himself, brought his cheek close, but he could feel no breath.

"Open an eye. Give me a sign." He pressed deeper into the flesh of Dennis's neck, and finally felt a faint heartbeat, the tick of life. "Dennis," he said. "We've got to go. We have to get you moving." Dennis mumbled something, words, a confused utterance.

"You're okay." Pete choked, his own voice stifled. "You're alive."

"Cold," Dennis said.

"I know, I know."

Pete peeled off his own jacket. The cloth was soaked, but he stripped down and fed Dennis's arms through the sleeves, zipped it up. One arm around Dennis's skinny waist and together they stood. Pete winced at those first hobbling steps as they began to move into the tangle of woods. It would be impossible to walk the contours of the shore: up the other side of Merchant, down into Bodega, then into Seeley's and finally across the Point. They had to cut overland. One step, two steps. Every shift and movement sent a grinding pain into Pete's leg.

"I want to lie down," Dennis said.

"Not yet. Not now."

A few more steps and Dennis stopped. He pulled away and leaned against a tree, sagged there. "She reported you. For the reward."

"Christian's probably reporting me as we speak."

"I need to rest."

"You can't. Not here. Time to move."

"They're saying you killed a man."

"It was an accident. It wasn't supposed to happen." He pulled Dennis from the tree and together they pushed through the underbrush. On such uneven land, a straight line was impossible, but Pete forced himself forward until Dennis again slipped from his grip. This time the boy fell to the forest floor. He curled there. "Up you get." Pete had to lower himself onto all fours. "You can't stop now."

Dennis's face was cold though. Even against Pete's numbed fingers, the boy's cheek felt chilled. "Time to get up now." He cradled Dennis's head in his hands. He spoke into the boy's ear. "Stay with me. Please." He shifted the boy's lanky body and managed to bend him over his own shoulder. He inhaled, filled his lungs, pulled on a low tree branch, and even then it took both legs to stand. A glassy shard of pain rocketed through his body. For a moment he went dizzy, a bright flash across his vision as his teeth ground down, pressed hard together. If he collapsed here, the boy would die of hypothermia. Simple as that. The police would find him lying here and Dennis would be dead. Pete willed himself steady then stepped forward. Carrying a hundred and twenty pounds, wet, cold and unconscious across his shoulders, he began to walk through the woods. One step and then the other. Pain reverberated through him. He tried to keep his weight on the heel of the right foot while he threw the left forward. Even then a fiery barb laced his leg. Half a dozen steps and he was in reach of a tree. Bad foot raised, he steadied himself against a low branch for a moment of relief. Another step forward and he set his sights on the next tree, walked to it. Three breaths and he pushed off again. Tears were on their way — a hot sting in his eyes.

Dennis's feet hit a tree trunk and the impact set Pete back. His right arm swung wildly to recover balance.

One footfall then another. Pete started to count each and in this he found a rhythm and a distraction. Twenty steps and he let himself pause. Another twenty. On and on. Looking into the sprawling darkness, a moment of doubt caught him. Had he been walking a straight line? He'd had his head down. He'd been dragging himself from resting point to resting point. Rain drummed the canopy above. Wind rippled trees. Dennis's hip bone dug into Pete's shoulder, and he tried to shift position, tried to resettle the boy. That's when he saw the bear. At least he thought he saw it — in the distance and off to his left, a luminescent white in the darkness. Pete took a few more steps. The bear seemed to be down on all fours, head turned back. Pete waved and the bear lumbered on. "Wait." Pete tried to quicken his pace. His ankle screamed pain, a bright angry burn all the way up his leg. Branches scratched at him. They tore at his clothes. His feet sank into the soft wet soil and he was panting, almost crying. The bear was still visible ahead, its haunches a faint white guide. Between the trees he caught only glimpses. "Wait. Please."

A few more hobbling steps, a shuffle and then Pete saw it: not the bear now but a light, the glint of human habitation. He called out. He yelled. Light ahead. No mistaking it. The bright white of a lantern. Inez's place. The Painted Lady.

"Dennis," he said. "Wake up."

Steps from the cabin, a cold fact hit Pete: the police could be in there. Inez at the very least. Step inside and it would all come crashing down. Inez, Andy and the others could take hold of him, radio for help. She could claim her reward. The moving money all these people wanted.

If he was going to keep running, he needed to leave the boy.

"Dennis?" Pete said. "Can you hear me?"

Ten steps from the cabin and Inez knew someone was in there. Through the window, she could see the door to the wood stove standing open with the bright glow of a stoked fire. Hope beat its wings heavy, a pressure in her chest and she broke into a run. Door open, a hot breath of air greeted her. Dennis's bed stood piled high with blankets, all the bed covers in the cabin, all the pillows, all the quilts and in among them Dennis's round face, his hair slick and wet from rain.

"Oh God," she said. "Oh thank you," and then Peter Osborne sat up. That stopped her. That wasn't what she'd expected — Peter Osborne lying in bed beside Dennis, the two of them under the tortoiseshell mound of blankets.

"He's still cold. Hypothermia. But he's alive."

Inez set the door closed behind her. A fire blazed in the wood stove. On top of it, a pot of water boiled. She stepped past the sofa and touched her son's head, his hair. She took in the smell of him — seaweed and salt water, the scent of open ocean and the smell of life itself. She wasn't sure if she was crying or laughing, but her chest heaved with quick tugging breaths. And here she was, her boots still on, tracking mud and sand about the place, a man wanted for murder staring at her from across the bed.

"You should get in and warm him," he said. "Better you take your clothes off first." He slipped from the bed and stood there, pasty white and bone-thin. Inez turned away as she began on

/ / / / /

the buttons of her own coat, fingers thick and slow as she undid her pants and piled what she was wearing on the cabin floor.

"I'm okay," Dennis said, but Inez pressed up against him, took his cold body in her arms and pulled him to her. Her chin nestled down against his matted hair. A deep breath and she closed her eyes. The smell of him was there still, hidden behind the thick tang of salt and sea. He was here, against her, and she could feel the very core of him.

"Where were you? What happened?"

"I didn't know. I didn't realize. It happened so fast." His voice creaked and the last of those words caught in his throat.

Inez wiped a tear from his cheek. Her grip on him loosened. The fire crackled and popped. She could wait for the rest of his answer. It didn't all need to come out right now.

On the other side of the room, Ash sat on a stool by the fire's open door. Peter Osborne. And he must know what she'd done. After all, the outhouse window had been knocked away. Surely that had been him — scrambling to escape when he'd seen the police on the beach.

"Would you close the curtains? It's better no one sees you in here. And if you could bring me the two-way radio, I have to let them know he's okay."

"Who is them?"

"The Coast Guard. Everyone's looking for him. I was supposed to wait for him here, but it occurred to me he might have been hiding, might have taken the kayak back to Phelps's old cabin."

Peter Osborne pulled the curtains above the sink and stove then crossed in front of her and closed the other set. "You're limping. Your leg looks bad."

He held out the radio, but he wouldn't look at her, wouldn't meet her gaze. Inez rolled onto her side, checked that the radio was on channel nine. A knock at the door and Inez raised a finger to her lips. She gestured for Peter to keep quiet. "Who is it?"

"Inez?" It sounded like Ernie.

"He's okay. I've got him. He's in here getting warm."

"I'm okay," Dennis called.

"Can I come in?"

"We're resting, Ernie. We'll see you in the morning. Thank you for your help. Would you tell the others? Tell them he's okay and we're resting. Tell them to let us sleep."

After the sound of Ernie's footsteps melted into the rain, Inez said, "You'd better set the latch on that door. Just as well no one knows you're here."

"Dennis told me. About the police."

"I see."

"I don't know what they said about me. I hadn't realized my name was out. I was going to tell you though, I'd planned to. This isn't how I wanted you to find out."

She flipped the switch on the radio and spoke into the receiver. She didn't say a word about Peter Osborne. She fixed her gaze on him as she spoke and once the radio was off, she said, "You wanted us to go off and start some crazy life together even though I didn't have a clue who you really were, didn't even know your real name."

"It wasn't crazy, Inez. I'd leave with you now if you'd go."

Crazy was the right word though. It was absolutely crazy.

"You wanted us for protection. You tried to get us to move somewhere up north without even telling us the risks." Just forming these words sparked resentment. He'd used her. He'd tried to, at least. He may have saved her son's life, but he'd also tried to use them both. "I've been through all this before, Peter, dragged out here and jilted."

Peter turned then. He looked at her a good long while. "Every word I said I meant."

"Stay the night. You should be safe here. I'm not going to tell anyone, but don't try to pretend you weren't using us."

They lay on their sleeping mats in the suite on Mulberry Crescent, all three of them awake. Art shifted onto his side and tried to get comfortable as he listened to the others breathing.

"I was just thinking," he said.

"About what?" Fay said.

"About the park ranger who cut down the oldest tree ever. You know that story? In the '70s when some scientist was taking core samples to learn about historical weather patterns, he got his coring tool stuck in one of the thickest trees he'd ever seen."

"You've already told this story," Derek said.

But Art was still talking. He was talking to himself as well as to the others, feeling his way through a story he still didn't fully understand. "It was in some windswept part of Nevada, somewhere remote. This park ranger came along and offered to help get the bit free."

"We've both heard the story, Art. They cut the tree down."

"There's a point here, Derek." The tree had turned out to be almost five thousand years old. This was the oldest being ever. Nothing even close had ever been recorded, not a tree, not a turtle, no ancient sea creatures. "It wasn't a logger or a developer that killed the oldest living being. It was a scientist and a park ranger."

"So what is the point? What are you trying to say?"

"It's called irony," Fay said.

/ / / / /

The stillness of the night settled. Art rolled onto his side and dug into his pocket for one of the sleeping pills he'd taken from his mother's medicine cabinet. He wanted to say something about taking that two thousand dollars today, something about pulling the purse from Tab Harper's hands, hauling it from her, scraping and scrabbling, something about facing the mother of the man he'd watched run off into the woods on Esterway Ridge.

"I've just always been so convinced we're right," he said at last. "We were justified, we were on the side of history and science."

"We agree," Fay said. "We all agree."

"About what?"

"I don't know. Whatever you're talking about, Art."

"We've got over two thousand dollars. You know what I did for that money?"

His fingers had scraped along her arm. There'd be flakes of her under his fingernails, traces of DNA, the tiniest parts of her against his own skin. He touched the spot where her teeth had clamped down on his forearm.

"I could have gone after Pete," Art said.

"What?"

This was it: his own guilt an agitation at the edge of his thoughts ever since he'd met Mrs. Harper.

"Today I told Mrs. Harper that I probably could have stopped Pete if I'd run after him into the woods, and it's true."

Fay turned towards him. "What are you talking about?"

"I drove back. The car scared him and he bolted for the woods."

"You told us you hadn't even seen him." The sleeping bag fell from her as she sat up. "Not even a sign of him is what you said."

"I was within sight of the emergency lights. It was chaos."

Across the room, Derek rustled in his sleeping bag. "You saw Pete?"

"I didn't think there was much I could do," Art said.

"And then you lied."

"Fay, I'm trying to tell you what actually happened."

"You son of a bitch."

"I wasn't thinking straight. I was upset, alright? It all happened so quickly it wasn't even a conscious decision. Emergency vehicles just a few hundred yards away, him gone, me still sitting there."

Fay stepped across the suite's floor and turned. "I'll tell you what was a conscious decision: lying about it afterwards."

"Because I knew you'd react like this."

"Keep your voices down," Derek said.

"I trusted you. We all trusted you," Fay said. "Days now I've stayed on, endured because I was in up to my neck and didn't know how to leave." She pulled the door open. "Well fuck it."

"Don't storm off," Art called. "Wait a second."

The door slammed shut.

"You're letting everything go to shit, Art."

"They fucked in the car at Thurlow Road after we left. Pete and Fay. Nothing's gone right ever since."

Art lay down, turned and tucked his hands under his head to act as pillow. Fay would be back. She just had to walk it off. Come morning she'd return.

CHAPTER
55

Inez slept restless and jittery. Twice she awoke and reached out to be sure Dennis was there and still breathing. She'd done this when he was a baby: a nighttime panic would carry her over to his crib where she'd lean her cheek close to be sure she could feel his breath.

The third time Inez awoke, the fire had burned down to a red heart of glowing coals, and she slipped from Dennis's bed and added more wood, refilled the pot of water on top. The cabin was dark, but she didn't go back to bed. She dressed and once the water had boiled, she made a cup of tea and drank it listening to Dennis and Peter breathing — the two of them on either side of the room, a soft and steady chorus, the sound of life.

Light cracked the morning sky, and Inez parted the curtains above the sink. Shadows retreated and revealed the room. Inez stepped outside. The wind was a soft lick and the blue of morning looked forgiving, remorseful. Marks from the rain still showed on the sand, an imprint dimpled across it. Waves rose and turned with a crack. Seagulls cawed. These were the noises of a peaceful land.

The chickens clucked and scratched about as Inez walked around to the coop. She bent the wire gate and one by one they slipped out to graze. Rhonda led as she always did. Inez dug a hand into the straw, felt around, pulled out a pair of brown eggs and then a third one, speckled white.

/ / / / /

This was one of morning's rituals, the marker of a normal day. Coffee was next, but before she made it back into the cabin, Inez spotted two figures striding down the beach, dark uniforms, flat topped hats. They had the steady determination of men with a destination in mind.

She could let the cops walk on in. Some part of her knew that. In fact, she didn't even need to go that far. She could simply walk away and allow them to knock. They'd look inside and find him themselves.

Inez's grip tightened on the eggs, the three of them warm in her hands as she walked out to meet the officers.

Swartz was there, but Inez didn't recognize the other officer. He was a short man with a wiry frame, and he looked down as Swartz spoke.

"Christian Davies live around here? Got a call last night. He said he'd seen Osborne."

Inez shook her head. She had to be careful here. She had to control herself. "He's just trying to get the reward money."

"How is Dennis?"

"Fine. Recovering. Just came home on his own. His handmade kayak broke apart. Miracle he's alive I guess."

"I'll make a note of it."

"Make a note of what?"

"In the report. That he walked back on his own. You say his handmade kayak broke apart?"

"What report is this?"

"Missing minor report. Social services and all. You want us to take a look at him? Happy to run him in to a doctor."

"He doesn't need a doctor. He's sleeping. He needs rest."

"Osborne hasn't been back, has he?"

"No, I haven't seen him."

"We're going to talk to Mr. Davies then take another look around."

The officers started towards the apple trees and the wood

carvings. Inez looked down at the eggs cradled in her hands. Was she an accomplice now? She'd lied. She'd misdirected them. Deliberately.

CHAPTER
56

Pete awoke to the sound of voices outside. He cocked his head and held still. Inez and someone else. Propped on his elbows, Pete tried to look out the window. A scrape and a thump from out on the porch and whoever had been with Inez was gone. The door opened and closed. Inez crossed the room, stood above Dennis's bed a moment before she noticed Pete watching. "You're up," she said. "You're awake."

"Who was that?"

"Doesn't matter. They're gone now."

"The police?"

She stepped a little closer, stood arm's reach from the dresser that blocked off part of the room.

"I suppose I should go and see them."

"They left. I saw them off."

"What about the reward?"

She took his hand and applied a gentle pressure. "Sit down and rest. We've got to get you better."

"I saw a white bear," he said. "You're going to think I'm crazy, but it guided me here. We were trying to cut across the peninsula from Merchant Bay."

"Spirit bears would be pretty unlikely here. On the island, I mean."

Two nights in a row he'd seen that bear. This couldn't be coincidence. He couldn't have imagined it two nights running. "What do you think that means? If I did see one?"

/ / / / /

"I'm not one for meanings," Inez said. "Maybe it doesn't mean anything."

"Last night I almost left Dennis on your porch, almost walked away thinking I needed to keep running, and then I thought of the white bear, and how it led me here. It sounds crazy, but I'm sure it means something. The night before that same bear took me up by Christian's cabin. Afterwards I put a chisel through those two firebombs so he couldn't use them."

"And you attribute these things to the spirit bear?"

"I didn't know he was there, Inez. Owen Tuggs, I mean. It was an accident."

"You know his name?"

"I tried to stop him. Crazy thing was we put so much effort into not hurting anyone, did it all in the middle of the night, waited there so we could watch it go off instead of leaving two hours on the timer. We were trying to do something good, something important, something no one else seemed willing to stand up and do. And then it all went wrong. The blast knocked me down. A few steps closer and I might be dead too."

"It sounds awful."

"I was the one who set it. The detonator didn't work so we had to set a timer, and we drew straws. A woman named Fay Anderson got the short straw, but she said she didn't know how, couldn't work the timer so I took it."

"You were doing her a favour."

"I could have backed out, could have said I didn't know how the timer worked either, and maybe that would have been the end of things. I didn't though. At Christian's cabin the other night, I cut open those two incendiary devices so that Christian could back out if he wanted to. Same chance I got only I figured maybe he'd take it."

"Rest a few days. No one knows you're here and the police aren't likely to barge into my cabin looking for you."

"And then what?"

"That's your choice."

"If you turn me in, at least something good will have come of all this. Twenty thousand dollars is a lot of money."

"Apparently you're not worth that much. Five thousand for you, twenty for the whole group."

"Oh."

"That was a joke. A moment ago I told the police I didn't know where you were."

"You shouldn't have done that. You're what, an accomplice now?"

"Ash," she said. "Peter."

"You need to go tell the cops you've found me. I'll sneak over to Gunter and Maggie's cabin. No one needs to know I spent the night here."

"Now you're telling me to turn you in?"

"If you don't, Christian will."

"He doesn't even know you're here. Take some time to think this over. I lied to the police to give you the chance to make your own choice."

"I'm done running, done hiding and lying. Living that way poisons everything. Isn't that what you said last night? It ruined what might have been between you and me, came close to killing Dennis. That spirit bear led me here. It didn't take me out to the road to keep running."

In the morning, Tab stood on the footpath in front of room twenty-seven. The view across the road tumbled down to the harbour where the water looked calm. Light waves lapped the rocky shore. In the wake of last night's storm, all held quiet. No sign of the police cruiser that had been in the lot.

At the front desk, the clerk who'd checked Tab in last night leaned on the counter, newspaper spread in front of him. A coffee urn stood nearby along with a stack of Styrofoam cups.

The clerk looked up, folded the newspaper back on itself. "Help yourself," he said.

Tab lifted a Styrofoam cup. "Do you know why the police left?"

"I didn't see either one this morning. Perhaps they didn't care for our complimentary coffee."

"They're not done their work then? I mean, they haven't checked out, haven't finished their extended duty?"

"Are you in some kind of trouble?"

"I'm looking for a squatters' camp."

"Baker Beach isn't a stop on your average sightseeing trip."

"Do you know where it is?"

"Not exactly sign-posted. What takes you there, if you don't mind me asking?"

Tab sipped her coffee. The heat of it travelled down her throat and into her chest. "I think it's where my son is."

The clerk began a sketch of the coast — humps and bays on a swollen body of land. His tongue poked out as he concentrated.

/////

"They're being evicted, you know. One of the big logging companies owns that whole peninsula. Ten or fifteen years some of those folks have been there, draft dodgers, hippies, all of that, except no one in head office seemed to know."

The clerk turned the map around to face her. "You'll pass a gas station with a rocky beach and a few cabins. That's the start of the peninsula. Next left is a logging road. Stick to it a couple kilometres. There's a turnout. From there you have to walk in. You can't miss the trail."

Tab glanced at her shoes. "All I've got is these flats. I hadn't expected to be trekking through the woods."

One step back and that seemed to end the conversation. Tab raised the hand-drawn map in a gesture of thanks. She knew where he was now, or at least where he had been as of yesterday.

Around the corner from the motel, Tab sidestepped a string of muddy puddles to find the rental car exactly where she'd parked it, half hidden by a forlorn-looking woodshed.

CHAPTER
58

Sunlight streaked through the room when Art awoke. The suite door stood ajar and a stripe of light spread across the floor. After a brief moment sitting up, Art's head sank back and he closed his eyes. That sleeping pill had done him in, its metallic taste still coated his mouth.

Derek's sleeping mat was empty and his bag lay tangled beside the narrow foam mattress. A dent still marked the bundle of clothes where his head had lain; a few feet further on, Fay's sleeping bag formed a downy puddle on the concrete floor.

Art stepped across the room and shouldered the door closed. It was odd the door stood open, odd Derek wasn't in the suite. And Fay hadn't returned yet. Art crossed to the washroom, relieved himself, turned and sat on the toilet seat. His body wasn't awake yet, his mind wasn't either, not by a long shot. Derek could have gone to call his cousin, or he could have gone to look for Fay, lots of perfectly simple explanations.

Art leaned against the toilet's tank and checked his watch. Eight-thirty. He'd slept until eight-thirty. One deep breath then he shook his head as though to reset his senses. There had to be a note somewhere. He walked through the suite, overturned some of the newspapers then stopped and drank from the tap to clear his mouth. They'd always said to come and go while it's dark, minimize the risk of being seen. And they'd always said to leave a note, let everyone know what you're doing.

/ / / / /

Art dug into his pocket where he had five more sleeping pills. He'd have to cut them in half in the future. "There's possibilities," he said out loud. And there were possibilities: Derek had been the one advocating negotiations and even a plea bargain. But more than likely he was at a pay phone trying to call his cousin and it was Fay he should be worried about — dragging her anger through the woods on the back side of Mount Warrington. And he deserved it, some of it at least. It would have been a lot easier to tell the truth from the start.

Art pressed his right hand against the bulge in his pocket. He still had the money. That was a relief. And then a sound outside attracted his attention, a human sound. Some kind of grunt just beyond the walls of the house.

CHAPTER
59

Inez fried eggs on the pot-bellied stove. Pete lay on the bed listening as the oil hissed and bubbled in the pan. "What will they do with these places? Once they evict you."

She turned, metal spatula in her right hand. "Tear them down."

"Even your place? This one is almost a real house." The ceiling was drywall. The three lantern hooks planted in it formed a perfectly even triangle.

Inez flipped the eggs and a moment later she said, "There's someone out there."

Pete shifted, raised himself onto his elbows only Inez was blocking the window. "The police?" he said.

Surely they'd be back, just a matter of time until their return — if not today then tomorrow, soon. The important thing was not to be caught here. Not under Inez's roof.

"A woman," Inez said. "But she isn't dressed like a police officer."

The middle pane of glass now framed the woman on the beach perfectly — long black coat, red umbrella open even though it wasn't really raining, just a faint coastal mist. A few more steps and she paused, turned to face the woods.

The oil on the stove popped. Inez stepped back and pulled the pan from the stovetop. Dennis had his face up close to the glass. "Looks like Deborah, the home school support lady, except she'd never carry an umbrella."

/ / / / /

"I think it's my mother." Pete spoke these words the moment the thought occurred to him and even then it seemed absurd. His mother wandering the beach. This beach. Baker Beach. She was on a flight. She'd have landed by now. And he was supposed to have called her, but he hobbled across the room and opened the door all the same. Outside Pete raised an arm and waved. A few more steps and he called out. He was sure of it now and he watched as recognition settled in. Her body went stiff a moment, then she raised a hand, covered her chin and mouth as she started to run.

She was talking even before she was within earshot, but all she said was "Peter." She said it over and over then she took him into a fierce grip, seized his body and it almost tipped both of them over. Hand out, Pete braced against the cedar shingle wall. His mother's breath trembled in his ear, gasps, a low tremor.

"You'd better come inside." Inez stood in the doorway behind them.

A little pressure and Pete pulled away from his mother's grip. Big silent tears rolled down both her cheeks — wet streaks on skin that looked drawn and worn. She wiped her eyes. She wiped her nose, and Pete led the way into the cabin. He set the door closed as she folded her umbrella. "This is Inez," he said. "This is Dennis. This is my mother. Tabitha Harper."

She was doing her best to compose herself, he could see that. She wiped her eyes again then ran a finger along the front of her coat. "We've got the fire on," Pete said. "Why don't you sit in here and warm up."

"I need . . ." she said. "A minute."

She took three or four short, hesitant steps then sat on one side of the sofa. He'd never seen her looking so worn. "Looks like you managed to find me," he said.

That must have struck her as funny. Her eyes widened. "I don't know where to start. I mean." She choked out a short, convulsed laugh. "It's been so long."

"Perhaps it's time for a cup of tea?" Inez said, but his mother waved it off. She was warming up to important words. She gestured him closer, raised herself a little. "We need to talk. The police know you're here. They'll be coming soon, I expect." Pete leaned back. "They've been by. Twice, at least."

"And they know? These two?"

"You mean Inez and Dennis?"

"Peter saved my boy's life."

Dennis raised a hand and his fingers wobbled in the air.

"I've talked to the police," Tab said.

"So has Inez. So has everyone. Except me, I suppose." An inexplicable lightness buoyed him now, an ease he'd discovered in his surrender to the inevitable. Whatever he did next, it didn't involve running or hiding.

"I've asked Inez to turn me in." Pete touched the edge of the sofa. He was still standing, and his sore ankle had started to ache.

"For the reward?"

"Not the reward. The police came by and she said I wasn't here. She lied to them. She harboured me. She's got a son. It's just the two of them."

"Peter, listen, you're the one who needs to turn yourself in."

"No, Inez has to. Otherwise they might charge her. She can't risk jail, she can't risk losing Dennis."

"I've got you a lawyer. I've got someone to negotiate for you. Can you tell them where to find the others? Art Kosky? Fay Anderson?"

"You want me to rat on them?"

"Peter, just tell me if you know where they are."

"I called your house. I talked to Frank." That seemed an age ago. "He said you were on the way home."

"Peter, honey, you need to do everything right from now on. If you're not careful, this will all land on you."

"Why do you say that?"

"Art Kosky told me you set the bomb."

"You talked to Art?"

"Is it true?"

"The man just walked in," Pete said. "He'd been sitting in his truck, maybe sleeping there then a moment later he was at the corner of the building. I was looking right at him when the bomb went off. And he was looking at me."

"Will you tell the police where the others are? If you can do that, we can set the terms."

"Turn rat?"

"You don't need to see it like that," Inez said.

"That's what it is. Turning on my own people."

"Is it the woman?" his mother said. "You don't want to report on Fay Anderson."

"That's not it."

"It's okay. I understand. I know about the two of you, I mean, I've pieced it together."

"Mom," he said, but it was Inez he turned to. "It's not what it sounds like. Fay and Art are a couple. She and I, we never were."

"I get it," Inez said. "They're your friends."

They were his friends, and yet all that seemed distant now — just days ago and yet an age had passed.

"If you can say where the others are then we should be able to make sure nothing happens to Inez."

"I think they're in the Western Additions. That would be my best guess. I don't know the exact house."

"That's a start."

It just occurred to him now: one of the houses Nathan's dad had been building would be a good spot to hide. He'd gone into bankruptcy with three or four houses half finished.

"Inez, you should still turn me in. It'll ensure you and Dennis are safe and you'll get some money as well. Something good will have come of this. It'll be like your aunt said, everything will have worked out in the end."

"Ash," she said. "Peter. There's a difference between some good coming out of this and everything working out. Those two are not the same."

"Listen to us, Peter. You can keep her name out of it or ask for some kind of immunity."

Pete turned to Inez. "This is your chance."

Eyes fixed on his, her chin dropped to her chest and he let that sink in a while. "We'll be fine," she said at last.

"There's one thing I have to do then, an errand to run. Give me a minute."

Outside the wind had a refreshing bite. A moment in the misty rain and he began walking. He still had to limp, he took his time.

The skid trail led up through blackberry bushes. A few berries had already darkened and he picked one as he limped past. At the door to Inez's studio, he didn't bother removing his boots. Across the paint-speckled floor, he unfurled a pair of paintings. One after another, he lay them in front of the banked windows, a still life, two abstracts and a landscape that caught his eye, trees above a pale, turning sea. Back at the bench, he removed still more. The light was thin and it was hard to make out the colours clearly unless he took them right over to the window. Colour was so much of what she did, so much of what he liked about these paintings, the world as witnessed by Inez Pierce. His favourite among them had a luminescent sky, rippled grey with a splintered forest below. He rolled two other paintings with it and put the rest away.

CHAPTER
60

The moment Art heard the noise, he knew. A grunt just beyond the front wall of the house set off a depth charge within him. Up against the Gyproc wall, he edged back the sheet of cardboard and looked out through scratch marks in the film that coated the glass. Police cruisers lined the cul-de-sac. A uniformed officer aimed a rifle at the house.

Art sprinted across the room, eased the door open. No cops in the yard. Sixty feet to the fence and the shelter of forest.

Into the small stairwell then four steps to level ground and he ran flat out for the woods. Blood hummed in his ears, his heart punched his ribs. Someone shouted. A sharp voice, an urgent call. Ten yards more. Fence and then forest. A thunderclap echoed among the houses and Art's heart stood still as his hands took hold of the fence's crowning lattice work. Two cops stood at the side of the house, pistols drawn, one with his gun pointed skyward.

"Down. Now."

Ancient forest loomed beyond the fence, a dark sprawl up the mountainside. Hands on the fence's top rail, Art's fingers blanched white. He could risk it, hoist himself over and sprint into the woods.

Another look back. The nearer officer had settled onto one knee, arms straight, pistol held in both hands. "On the ground." The hammer cocked, and the sound was enormous.

"Face down. Hands spread."

/ / / / /

Art stepped across the grass. Hands raised, his body sank earthward, his cheek pressed into grass still moist from the morning dew. An officer called out and fainter voices rose behind him.

A weight hit hard and sharp against Art's back — a foot or a knee, the pressure of a body on him. His spine arched and for a moment he couldn't take in air. He tried to push up, tried to raise his body, but now someone had his hands — one then the other and the cold metal of handcuffs. The weight was gone from his back. He inhaled a long desperate breath. An officer squatted beside him. "Is Fay Anderson on the property?"

"Fuck you."

"If she's here with you, we're going to find her, and it's a whole lot easier if we get some cooperation."

"Too late. She's long gone."

A sharp tug brought Art to his feet. Men on either side of him now, tall figures, one shouldered Art forward.

Lights flashed on the nearest of the cruisers, bulbs rotating bright inside the siren deck. The car behind looked empty, and both passenger-side doors stood open. A two-way radio crackled. Someone shifted about in the front seat of the third cruiser. Art caught a glimpse of Derek Newfeld's face and pulled free with a sudden bolt. Both car doors were closed, but he spat on the windshield just as heavy hands yanked him back. A tug on his collar and Art sagged. The ground gave him a jolt, and the cuffs that held his wrists dug into his spine, a sudden shock of pain.

"You ready to cooperate?" The officer bent over him. "Because I want you to let me know when you are."

"Fuck you, and fuck Derek Newfeld. You can burn in hell you rat son of a bitch."

CHAPTER 61

The four of them crossed the beach together, Pete's mother and Inez on either side of him, Dennis a few paces ahead, bundled against the morning drizzle — layers of shirts and sweaters with the hood of his raincoat pulled up.

Once across the delta of stream water, they paused. From here the trail was steep, an uphill scramble, and Pete wasn't sure how his ankle would fare. He pulled himself first onto a piece of driftwood then took hold of a sapling. Inez set a hand on his back and supported his first uphill steps.

At the lookout point, the path widened, and with room to walk side by side, Inez carried the rolled paintings in one hand and put her other arm around Pete's shoulder.

Mud sucked at their boots and as time wore on, Pete's right foot dragged. The pain was there, alive and bright in his ankle as the trail rose on a steady slope. He had to haul his body the last few steps. Labouring on the edge of exhaustion, he followed the switchback path up to the logging road. His mother had rented a two-door sedan and he could see it through the trees now, red car streaked with mud. When they reached it, Dennis laid a finger on the rear windscreen and marked a single straight line down the mud-splattered glass. His mother opened the passenger side, laid the rolled paintings on the seat, then flipped it forward to allow access to the back. "You'd better lie down. At least until we get on a ways."

/ / / /

Pete raised his chin. Tears stung his eyes, but by looking up it felt as though gravity might keep them at bay.

Inez took hold of him, turned his body into hers. "You're going to be alright." Her grip tightened. "Remember: once you reach the end, you'll see that everything turned out alright."

"Not for everyone, not always." Tears blurred his vision. One rolled down his cheek. "Not for Owen Tuggs." Pete could barely get the name out. He turned his face into the crook of her neck, but eventually she shifted. Dennis stood an arm's length away, twisting his right foot, working his toe at a divot in the ground.

"I'm going to send off these paintings. Or my mother will. Between the two of us, we'll try and get you a show."

"Those paintings are yours. Keep them or send them off, it's your choice."

Dennis hugged Pete briefly, head turned to the side, arms loose — a moment of contact, no more. Pete drew a hand across his face, wiped at his damp cheeks. "I'm sorry. For everything I did. Sorry that I caused all of you this trouble and pain."

Inside the car smelled of vinyl. It smelled of newness and of lemon cleanser, and as Pete settled into the back seat, he could see how dirty he was, pants streaked with mud from where he'd crawled under the fallen tree. His last shower had been before Esterway Ridge. He shifted sideways to protect his injured leg. Dennis pushed the door shut.

For a moment, Inez and his mother talked outside, their voices low until Inez tapped on the dirty window and peered in, smiling, pale lips drawn thin. His mother opened the driver's door and settled. The little car shifted under her weight and a moment later the motor turned. Inez stepped away and raised her hand in a wave.

The car started forward with a quick heave. Pete looked back through the narrow line Dennis had cleared on the windscreen. Inez stood waving, and then she was gone, obscured by a bend in the road.

Once they reached the highway, Pete edged lower in the car. Through the window, he watched the tops of trees, an ancient green set against soft grey skies. These were the colours of Inez's land, the colours of his land: deep green, dusty blue, trees and sky in shades that cradled the whole of the world.

They hit paved road and the world seemed quieter. The car hummed along. They passed into Port Thorvald and his mother turned. "Maybe you should flatten a little more."

Pete turned his attention to the ceiling and the tan fabric that hung there. Through the window, the tops of occasional buildings flashed by, shingles on low pitched roofs, now and then the roof of a trailer, a glass window. They passed a flagpole, its halyard rope swinging loose.

The grade rose. The car settled into a lower gear. Pete's mother adjusted the rear-view mirror for a look at him. "Inspector Burrell from the RCMP is in charge of all this. He's a good man. He's going to be pleased you can help locate the others."

She switched the radio on after a while, rolled the dial across bands of static until a faint voice came in. The news, or maybe the weather. The reception came and went as the car followed the coast's twists and turns. At some point they passed the logging road that would have led to Esterway Ridge, but Pete missed it. He'd closed his eyes. He needed to rest.

Voices rose and fell on the radio. They wove in and out of Pete's thoughts, talk radio chatter while he tried to form some kind of pillow with his hands. He wanted to sleep. He wanted to keep his eyes closed until all this was over. His right leg stiffened, a brief, involuntary convulsion. The back seat didn't have space to fully straighten his leg, but he tried to arrange himself so his injured ankle rested against the side of the car.

"That woman said you saved her son's life."

"Inez and Dennis."

"I know."

"Those are their names. That woman. Her son."

"Hopefully the prosecutors will take that into consideration."

Outside the earth looked scorched, a war-torn stretch — land blackened and trees broken. A fire had run through and levelled all they could see. A couple more minutes of driving and the woods returned, a dark blanket on either side of the car, broad branches nestled cozy and tight.

His mother said something he couldn't hear, then she turned up the radio. The speakers rattled, the sound tinny. "Brought into custody after an early morning raid." A woman's voice cut across the radio. "The RCMP have set a news conference for 1:00 p.m."

"They've got them."

"What do you mean?"

The news announcer was still speaking in the background.

"No," she said and the word was long and drawn out.

"It's okay, Mom."

"The police. The others. Those people."

"It doesn't matter. It's fine." He shifted forward and reached out his hand.

"It's not fine. Nothing's fine. Nothing at all."

"Listen." He touched her shoulder. "Can you turn the radio off a second?"

Into the silence, Pete said, "I understand, Mom."

"You don't. You don't have a clue. I spent days. I spent thousands of dollars and I finally found you."

"Thousands of dollars?"

"I found you so you could plea bargain. The lawyer was going to arrange everything." She cried as she spoke, choked on her own words. "So you could have a life," she said.

"You should pull over."

"Some kind of life. At the end of all this. Get married. Kids. I wanted —"

"Mom," he said.

"And now." She shifted around and looked back at him. They were on a downhill stretch, the road a gentle, curving grade.

"Mom, the road."

"I'm watching the damn road, Peter."

He could see part of his mother's face in the rear-view mirror. She looked old. She looked drawn and worn. Both hands gripped the steering wheel but she kept flexing her wrists, turning her hands in and out.

"When I was in the woods, I carried Dennis unconscious on my back. I'd hurt my leg. He was on my shoulders and for a while I wasn't sure whether we'd make it. We were lost. I thought he might die. I didn't even know if he was alive up there on my back. Then I saw this white light and it turned out to be a bear. A white bear. It led me all the way home."

"A bear, Peter? A polar bear? We're talking about the police. We're talking about murder charges."

"A spirit bear guided me. Twice I saw it, and I wasn't afraid. The bear wasn't afraid. The night before it led me to one of the cabins where they had —"

"They've got them, Peter. The RCMP have those people. That's what matters. Didn't you listen?"

"I did listen. I was just trying to tell you about something important. Some kind of, I don't know, some kind of miracle."

"So what do we do now?"

Pete shifted onto his side and reached down to touch his swollen ankle. "Whether I rat on them or they rat on me, does it really make that much of a difference?"

"They'll blame all this on you. They'll say you set it. They'll say it was your fault."

"I did set it. We drew straws and Fay got short straw, but she didn't want to, so I set it."

"But then it's a fluke that you set it. It's only by chance it was you."

"I could have said I didn't want to. We all could have. But

I just wanted it done and over." He stopped there and looked out the window.

"What if I took you across the border? I could drive you twelve hours south and still make it in time for my flight."

"Inez knows the family, the Tuggs family. They had a baby girl, a nine-month-old."

His mother adjusted the rear-view mirror again and looked at him. "No one would know. I could drop you off somewhere in Washington State or in Oregon."

"To spend my life running, hiding, lying to everyone I meet, abusing the trust of others?"

"I could get some money at a bank. You could stay with your father a bit if you think he'd keep quiet."

They were reaching the outskirts, urban sprawl, rolling developments and cookie-cutter houses. The ferry terminal stood beyond those blocks of homes, water just out of sight.

"You need to stop this, okay, Mom."

"You could have a life there. You could start again, with at least some kind of a life."

"That's not what happens though. The lies you tell, they distort everything. You can't have a relationship in a life like that, not a real one. I'm not even sure you can have a friendship."

"You know what will happen, right? You'll be the scapegoat, the last one to get his side of the story on record."

"If I do this now, maybe one day I can have a real life. I might never be able to say everything turned out alright, but maybe I can still have a life."

Outside, the houses were a blur, neat frame structures, one after another, house and garage close up to the road, freshly shingled roofs, mown lawns. Car, garden, house, garage. Pete kept his gaze steady and let them pass in a blur. He could see himself. From a great distance, from miles and years away he could see himself, in that little rental car, speeding east with his mother at the wheel.

/////

Acknowledgements

Some people call Vancouver Island's 1993 logging protests "the war in the woods." This is a misnomer. The protests were peaceful. This book is fiction.

For those interested in learning more about activists in Canada who turned to violence, *Direct Action: Memoirs of an Urban Guerrilla* by Ann Hansen is a fascinating read. Also of potential interest are two documentaries: *If a Tree Falls*, which follows a group of Earth Firsters in the western US deemed "eco-terrorists" and pursued by the FBI, and *Sombrio*, about the lives of squatters on the coast of Vancouver Island.

Inez's aunt's advice on page 156 comes from Jeannette Walls's memoir *The Glass Castle*.

I have a long list of people to thank for their support and help in the years it took to write this book. Many people read versions of the manuscript and gave vital feedback and advice along the way: Gail Anderson-Dargatz, Nerys Perry, Craig Boyko, Jack Kirchhoff, Marni Jackson, John Balogh, Sharon Thompson, Malcolm Griffin, Kim Longenecker. I also want to thank all the friends and family who have put up with me moaning and groaning about this project for so many years, including

Ed@261, Matt, Tim, Chris, Jeff and particularly John and my parents, Sharon and Malcolm.

I had the great good fortune to work with Barb Howard and Kelsey Attard and want to thank them for their wonderful work along with everyone else at Freehand. Sam Haywood did far more for this book than just find it a home. She read numerous rewrites and stuck with it through thick and thin and I want to thank her and the rest of the team at Transatlantic. Thanks also to the Canada Council for financial support and to the various coffee shops that have allowed me to sit in a corner, earplugs in, hoodie up, scribbling away — Bean Around the World, Union Pacific and Cafe Coffee Day to name a few.

Finally, and most importantly, I want to thank my wife, Kim, and three daughters, Evelyn, Tessa and Vivian, who did without me for hours a day as I worked on this novel and who put up with all the trials and tribulations that came with that work. I love you all.

Daniel Griffin was born in Kingston, Ontario, and has lived in Canada, the United States, Guatemala, the UK, Germany, France, New Zealand, Mexico and India. His short story collection *Stopping for Strangers* was a finalist for the Danuta Gleed Award, and he holds an MFA from UBC. He currently lives in Victoria, BC, with his wife and three children, where he is at work on another novel.